"Sections are brilliant and wicked and they show how much of a stern dazzler Sorrentino can be."–*Kirkus*

"Sorrentino is a bright, educated man–balancing difficult dialects against obscure notations, addressing readers and reviewers, boldly playing with form. At times his language approaches a Finnegans' wakefulness."–*Los Angeles Times*

"A wild and crazy book, lavishly inventive, full of surprises, sometimes exasperating, often exhilarating."–*New York Times Book Review*

"A lively, outrageous, funny and comedically inventive story."–*Publishers Weekly*

"In *Blue Pastoral* Gilbert Sorrentino has done what artists always try to do: he has made and shaped a work whose brilliance–in this case comic brilliance–is awesome, pure, and perfectly executed."–*Washington Post*

"*Blue Pastoral* is bedazzling. Its language–and what else is literature but language–dips and dances. Read it."–*New Statesman*

"A brutally hilarious literary explosion in which a world of pop-cultural clichés gets a freewheeling linguistic drubbing."–*Library Journal*

Books by Gilbert Sorrentino

POETRY

Black and White
Corrosive Sublimate
The Darkness Surrounds Us
A Dozen Oranges
The Orangery
The Perfect Fiction
Selected Poems: 1958-1980
Sulpiciae Elegidia/Elegiacs of Sulpicia
White Sail

FICTION

Aberration of Starlight
Blue Pastoral
Crystal Vision
Flawless Play Restored: The Masque of Fungo
Imaginative Qualities of Actual Things
Misterioso
Mulligan Stew
Odd Number
Pack of Lies
Red the Fiend
Rose Theatre
The Sky Changes
Splendide-Hôtel
Steelwork
Under the Shadow

CRITICISM

Something Said: Essays

Blue
Pastoral

Gilbert Sorrentino

Dalkey Archive Press

Library of Congress Cataloging-in-Publication Data:

Sorrentino, Gilbert.
        Blue pastoral / by Gilbert Sorrentino.– 1st Dalkey Archive ed.
            p.   cm.
        ISBN 1-56478-251-4 (alk. paper)
            1. Musicians–Fiction. 2. Travel–Fiction. I. Title.

        PS3569.O7 B64 2000
        813'.54–dc21   00-058955

Partially funded by grants from the Lannan Foundation and the Illinois Arts Council, a state agency.

Dalkey Archive Press
www.dalkeyarchive.com

Printed on permanent/durable acid-free paper and bound in the United States of America.

Contents

1. Dr. Vince Dubuque Is Called Upon to
   Introduce Our "Subject" 1
2. In Which Dr. Ciccarelli Points the Way 6
3. Blue and Helene Have a Good Long Talk and
   Make Plans 12
4. A Domestick Quarrel 15
5. Blue Improves Helene's Coiffure 19
6. Blue Finds and Takes the Pushcart 23
7. A Brief Note on a Traveling Library 29
8. The Homely Carte, or, Blues Ecclogue Joyned
   with Helenes 32
9. Interlude: On Blue's Bicycle Clips. 34
10. A "Column" in a "Newspaper" Gives Blue an
    "Idea," Soon to Be Revealed 38
11. Blue Begins Reading "La Musique et les
    mauvaises herbes" 45
12. Blue's Grant Proposal: Experimental Piano 49
13. Speech by Rep. Harold "Hal" Glubit 53
14. Puissance Art Disdayneth (A Dramatic
    Eclogue) 60
15. In Which Blue Discovers Marys-londe and Is
    Given Advice 64
16. The Gavottes Read a Country Drama to Lift
    Their Spirits 69
17. Blue Receives a Sign 76
18. Eros Briefly Grins upon Our Dusty Caravan 82
19. The Sheep Interlude 85
20. "La Musique et les mauvaises herbes,"
    Continued 89

21. The Cart-Repairer............................... 95
22. Around the Campfire............................ 99
23. The Cart Repaired, the College Discovered........ 104
24. Dr. Bone Shows the Lab to the Gavottes; With
      Learned Commentary 108
25. The Gala Cocktail Party 113
26. In Which Dr. Poncho Meets the Avid Blue......... 118
27. Elegy for Jacques-Paul Surreale 123
28. Pastourelle: Dr. Poncho Tells of His Afternoon
      of Ecstasy..................................... 128
29. In Which Poncho Takes a Poudre and Bone
      Playes Dumbe 131
30. The Gavottes Come at Last to The University 134
31. Dr Dubuques Eglogue Joyned with Miss
      Clarke Grables: An Erotickal Interlude 138
32. Doc Dubuque's Idyll, or, Ah, Nature!.............. 143
33. The Doc Makes Blue What Men Yclep a
      "Deal" (Or So It Seems) 147
34. "Blarney Spalpeen" Gives a Speech on St.
      Patrick's Day 149
35. Miz Gavotte Tells Her Mate a Little White Lie...... 158
36. Father Donald Debris, S.J., Gives a Talk on Sex 162
37. In Which Dr. Dubuque's Insincerity Is
      Revealed 175
38. "La Musique et les mauvaises herbes,"
      Continued..................................... 179
39. The Couple Somewhat Cheered 187
40. Wonderland of Opportunity, Where the Apple
      Mocks and Blossoms 192
41. The Graffiti Set Up a Wild Twangling 195
42. Blue's Reflections on Time 198
43. Land Where Guitars Softly Creep 202
44. A Southern Idyll................................. 208
45. A Transition, from A to Z 213
46. Big Black's Lecture: Elegy on the Theft of
      Black Flowers 216
47. Dazed, Our Friends Reach Nawlins, Looziana 222
48. To Expand upon the Subject....................... 225
49. Slightly Crestfallen, They Leave Nawlins,
      Slightly Crushed.............................. 230

50. Blue Writes a Mysterious and Haunting Song....... 231
51. Secrets of Tej-Mej 233
52. A New Lease, or Is It Leash, on Life for the
       Gavottes 239
53. The Panegyric on the Faithful Cart 242
54. Captain Basura Appears, Makes a Curious
       Offer, Is Rejected, and Threatens. 245
55. "La Musique et les mauvaises herbes,"
       Continued.................................... 250
56. The Land of Enchantment 257
57. Le Blason Médaillon 273
58. In Which the Desert Sands Become a Colorful
       Riot.. 274
59. "La Musique et les mauvaises herbes,"
       Concluded 281
60. The Gavottes Are Petrified by Awe 290
61. The Great Ditch of the Great Southwest
       Greatly and Grandly Appears to Blue as
       the Grand Symbol of the Profundity,
       Nobility, and Gravity of His Hopes, Now
       Almost Realized 294
62. Perhaps It May Happen by Chance................. 296
63. California! The End of the Quest 301

The subject of Pastorals, as the language of it ought to be poor, silly, and of the coursest Woofe in appearance. Nevertheless, the most High, and most Noble Matters of the World may bee shadowed in them, and for certaine sometimes are: but he who hath almost nothing Pastorall in his Pastorals, but the name (which is my Case) deales more plainly. . . .

My Pastorals bold upon a new straine, must speake for themselves, and the Taber striking up, if thou hast in thee any Country-Quicksilver, thou hadst rather be at the sport, then heare thereof. Farewell.

Michael Drayton, 1619

Blue Pastoral

« 1 »
Dr. Vince
Dubuque Is Called
Upon to Introduce Our "Subject"

And now, ladies and gentlemen, honored guests, hangers-on, vagrants, idlers, and good-for-nothings, a brief talk by Dr. Vince Dubuque of The University on the hero of this tale, the tale itself, and sundry matters.

("Scattered" and diffident applause.)

Thank you, honored folks.

I see him now! Somewhere out there in that gloaming that we call the Past that Time forgot—his ratty beard and frizzy hair, his hearty grease sandwiches, his rusted bicycle clips. An unlikely hero, your good faces seem to say, not all of them so good, but. May I present him? It is a hot afternoon, these attendant scholars are a roiling sea of sweat beneath their pretentious robes, and even my Private Assistant, Miss Clarke Grable, seated here demurely at my left, seems adrift in a coma of the old ennui, as the beloved song has it. I will make my remarks brief, here under the saw-leaf coryza and the dwarf axilla and the unbearably lovely buckeye gastrula, nodding and bending as is their ancient wont. So.

Serge Gavotte is the man's true name, and I will outline, so to speak, his adventurous beginning; the ensuing parts and parcels of which shall unfold if you will but continue to turn the pages of the "book" that we are all pretending to want to read, or something. Literature works in mysterious ways, it is metaphor raised to the heights of shattering simile! Serge Gavotte, yes. And on a typical morn. His ratty beard, his frizzy hair, God bless the mark, his rusted bicycle clips, his sweat-stained paper bag within which nestle and crowd his two grease sandwiches. He leaves the house, thus. An ordinary morning, and Gavotte wends his trail toward his lonely job as plastic-lens tester or something equally gauche. His shirt is nondescript, his trousers, shiny now from years of labor, direct from Mays, onerously bear that description called "irregular." And as sure as I am Dean of Funds and Meetings, they were! Or are! Clasped, however, smartly and alertly around each slim ankle by a bicycle clip, a reminder of Ga-

1

votte's checkered past, although here at The University, we prefer to pronounce it "chequered."

Who was this Serge Gavotte? And why was he chosen to set out on his Great Quest? Not so fast! I'll answer your importunate queries as best I can, but first things must come first, as the patient grizzled farmer knows, the bent agricola, hunched over his zucchini bush. Who? His past is a mist, a kind of dim haze of nagging memory, a zephyr of odd scents, the shining bridge that spans—Oh Where?—the lost river of childhood. We know however that he was shipped from pillar to post as a youth, from school to school. He was a rip! And his student exploits, gems, even, yes, opals and garnets of good clean fun, earned him a reputation far beyond its cost in human error and occasional heartbreak. Pouring glue in the coffee. Placing chewing gum on his teachers' chair. Who can forget the time he put salt in the sugar bowl? Marks of comic genius, my friends, yes, Comic Genius, so that all who came in contact with him cannot be faulted for thinking that he would grow up to be a Larry or a Curly or perhaps even a Moe! Some few went so far as to say he had the makings of a Shecky Green, but plodding hyperbole was as rampant then as it is today. However! His legend was such that it forced him to assume nom de plumes. Or is that noms de plume? My Gallic is a trifle dim, and those of you who have come to be my friends since I assumed my duties here at The University, know how this grieves me—nothing on earth I like better than to coil up with *Le Match* or *Oui, Oui, Paris* of a winter eve. But let me not recount to eager ears the sacrifices I daily make! He had to assume these aliases, these false monickers. My notes here, prepared in part by Miss Grable, give a few of them, which, if I may be forgiven, as it were, I shall rehearse. Rehearse? That's what it says here, and who am I to doubt the written word, the bold letters here indited by my Private Assistant, slightly heavy in the glorious beam but who's counting? Aha, ha, ha.

Boris the Bum, The Piano Killer, Stompo, Hair Freak, Wrong-Way Russian, The Soviet Schmuck, Brooklyn's Curse, The Duke of Schnorrer, Left-Hand Louis, Chopsticks, Wack-Off, Peach Sucker, O'Malley's Mouth, Lazarillo de Knishes, Garbage Face, Peyote Sipper, and Foodpicker. Not a pretty picture, is it? And yet, it was his croass, I mean, his cross. But wherever he went, to whatever distant seat and far-off chair of learning and knowledge, he was soon found out. Hence, his education was, as it is phrased in places like Sal's Billiard Academy, a bust. Yet he met a lovely girl, well, lovely, O.K., a girl, one with full lips, flashing eyes, impeccable linen, and softly drifting dandruff, her name itself a kind of poem, Helene Lundi. And what else would you believe but that they were soon married! For every Serge, my friends, there is a Helene, and the conversed opposite is also true, else why would the world, especially odd places like Jimbo, Utah, and Gonif, New Jersey, not to mention those countries jampacked cheek and jowl with foreign types, e.g., Sahib, Rhodesia, be filled to the creaking gunwales and mizzenreefs with astonishingly homely, not to say really ugly couples? And their kids, so to speak? Jesus Christ Almighty! I opine. But enough, I ween, though not without some minor regrets.

They married, which takes us right up, by a twist of Fate and linguistic wizardry, to the present, that is, right here and now, with the fruity odors of giant ankylosis and blue angina sporting in our collective nostrils. But his job, his honest job, I hasten to submit, as Miss Grable, who is perspiring slightly at the moment, albeit with a lot of class, will corroborate as being not too bad a position, lovely word, glutted Serge Gavotte with boredom and horrid malaise, another word from the snowy peaks of Old Provence. Yet it was a malaise that dared not breathe its name! Yes, my drowsy friends, that great soul kept it all bottled up inside him like a big jug of seltzer keeps its bubbles all enchained. His spouse, the oddly off-center and unusually strident Helene, now big with child, and suddenly! a little mother, just like that, of a fine boy whom they called Zimmerman, knew, by consulting her deep feminine feelings, that all was not cheer and skittles at the Gavotte house, no, nor at the V. N. Rose Lens Co. either. Call it a lucky shot.

For Gavotte père, whatever that may convey, had a secret. Yes, a rather dark secret, crepuscular and somber, shady and umber in hue. In his depths, those depths that still harbored the pain and fear of being dubbed, for instance, Shit Pickle—and there's a handle that will follow you down the windy Halls of Time if I ever heard one!—he had the powerful and almost unbearable urge to be a musician! We professors here on the dais, we laugh, yes, melting, as we are, in the sunshine, like Sambo Tiger in the nursery rhyme, or like Ruth, we laugh! Ensconced as we are here at The University, most of us, with that sweet, oh God *how* sweet! tenure, cannot imagine what it must be like to want anything beyond our positions of responsibility in this great University, *The University*—and it *is* a great university, you can tell by the low moans of the cicadas as they gorge on the cucumbers that crawl the walls of Lamont Hall. Is it for nothing that the motto or whatever it is called, on the sinister bend of the shield of this place is *De Mortuis Nil Nisi Bonum*? I don't think so, but could give you a better opinion if I had a touch of Greek, the which tongue I do not cleave to since my studies were all in the field, and it is still a growing one, of Sales Techniques of Surplus Goods, and the only Greek I ever learned was *caveat emptor*, which, roughly translated, as the good members of the Classics Department here behind me will attest, with all the varied strengths of their pounding and Helen-leaning minds, means "Bleed Them Dry," or, to be a millimeter more elegant, if not exactly precise, "Suck Them Empty."

In any event, we cannot, and by the dull, if not quite complacent, visages that you, my sedulous listeners, present to me, out there in that sun that could split rocks, you neither, can—I have misplaced my unerring thoughts for a moment, so if you will please . . . oh, yes, none of us can understand exactly why Serge Gavotte had this hidden dream, a dream that drove him to the misty window-pane of an eerie midnight to look out upon the brooding fields and strangely silent streets, while Helene slept on in peace, her breath raising and falling down with that curious phenomenon that a man—I think his name was Galen—called breathing. That old Roman was a crackerjack! No! We laugh! it says here, but by Christ Almighty, I can't imagine exactly why it . . . oh, I have allowed my sun-blasted orb to wander, as an orb may when given but half a chance, back up the paper upon which Miss Grable, whose bosom is heaving patiently, penned these notes. We have, if you will pardon a small splinter of light wit, *already* laughed! Ho ho. O.K.!

We cannot understand this thudding and overwhelming urge, but it was *there*, it was there in such a stern guise that Gavotte finally succumbed to it and availed himself of such *instrumenti* as could relieve him of his red-hot desire to play, play! Of such courageous flesh is Freedom made, as well as Art! But we know all these stirring banalities exactly like a book, do we not? To be sure. And these oddball cheapo things he bought—a tinwhistle, a Jew's harp, called nowadays, I under-stand, because of the protests of Banzai Brit, or some other esteemed rabbi, a juice harp, though whatever that may suggest swims out there in the vasty deeps of blue far beyond my poor ken, yes, and also a ocarina, a real deadbeat harmon-ica, like, you know, a Crackerjack-box type, and the Lord only knows what all else.

He played, oh sweet Mother of God, how he played! Against time, against the inundating and proscribed thought that he might well have talent—how to phrase it?—zero, against the wails and colicky pissing and moaning of little Zimmy, he played on and on, *possessed* by this instrument, or, shall I hint, instru-ments? just like Kirk Douglas, whatever he's doing in this speech, and I will speak to Miss Grable about it. And it was not long before he got a real bad mouth infection, some type of infarction on the gums or an impacted dentine, some-thing that made it necessary for him to tell Helene . . . the Truth! The lovely lady, as smart as an old whip, was not surprised, nor even struck into a state of sheer amaze, since she had long suspected that the obsessive and not exactly, uh, how shall I phrase it? *lovely* sounds that drifted up from the basement, or from the bathroom, or from the hall closet at any moment of the night or day when Serge was at home, were not, as her droll husband had informed her when she first got on a wonder about them, "the death cries of expiring cockroaches." He could, when the need arosed, turn a mean phrase.

But this painful swelling of the gumbones, yes, this sudden miasma cast upon our budding Freddy Martin or Johnny Long, was a blessing in disguise, for it sent Serge to see the famous mouth seer, Dr. Ciccarelli. Of which the next, or really the *first* chapter, will treat of. Chapter? Oh yes, we are all agreeing to pretend that this is a "book." Thank you for your attention, but, hold it, hold it!

Before you go, I want to introduce you formally to my Private Assistant, Miss Clarke Grable. She is *not* my secretary, no. She is *not* my filer, no no. She is *not* a female person employed to answer phones and letters and generally stand around and pick up her salary, n, period, o, period. Then, what is she? As Dean of Funds and Meetings, you must all be as aware as I am, and by God, *I* am aware, that I am always being bothered by many of you wrong-o professors, you shiftless "students," some term, eh? and whatever shabby citizens wander in out of the heat or rain or whatever weather is tending to occur around here. I have here then Miss Grable, who has a long history of blocking doors, getting messages wrong, compounding problems, and the ilks and like. She will be, as it were and so to speak, my trouble-shooter, and will see to it, with all the expertise in her remarkably solid frame, and I seem to be seeing her now as if for the first time!— my goodness, she does cross her legs nice—uhm, ah, will see to it that you don't bust my hump, as the phrase is rendered in the patois of the demotic vulgate.

("*Scattered*" *and feeble applause plus a vulgar sound from the* "*crowd*.")

Thanks for your undivided attention, given without quotient, to say the least. And now, if you will good-naturedly go along with the whole "book" dodge that has been foisted on us—and with a great deal of unseemly eagerness, I might add—you will "set off" with Serge Gavotte on his adventures if you will but turn the "page." I'm sorry; if you will but "turn the page."

« 2 »

In Which Dr.
Ciccarelli Points the Way

Dr. Ciccarelli, of Italy, has, for some years now, made his home in the United States, where his oral expertise may be employed to its fullest.

I no like-a dis phrase, Doc Ciccarelli says.

Doctor Ciccarelli, as buccal fans know, has, for some years now, made the oral cavity his area of expertise, practicing his arcane systems upon more mouths—and in them—than it purposes here to reveal.

Ats-a nize! "Purposes to reveal." Class!

Hmm. Oral expertise: *has been* employed, uh, optimally? To best effect? Does nice work? Tops in the growing field?

"Purposes to reveal," dammit. Also, call me joost-a Doc Chick, O.K.?

It was through the avuncular Doc Chick that we heard the long tale that follows, not *so* long. Heard part of it anyway, *parts*. The parts that Doc Chick is involved in. Not too many, now that I thumb through the pages.

Now that *we* thumb through the pages.

I purpose to reveal, kid, whatever goddam tings you wanna hear an' also pay me for, like you got here in this goddam country with the soggy pasta, what you call the consultation fee?

We will be perfectly delighted to meet your financial requirements, Doctor. Within reason, ha ha ha.

You talk what I wanna hear. My mamma was wrong when-a she say all Americans are stupid. They got no culture, they don't know nothing, they think-a the governmenta's real, they don't know how to talk to women, they can't dress or eat nothing good, but goddam they know how to buy tings!

We are often termed "A Nation of Consumers." Here is your retainer.

What?

Your retainer, your retainer! Money!

O.K., O.K., take it ease! You got a face on you like a dead clam.

6

There's really no need, Doc, to . . .

O.K.! I, Doc Chick, known hither and wide to all-a the poor marks with the mouth problems as Dr. Ciccarelli, a name that calls up to mind-a the Isle of Capri and red wine to you ignorant Yankee slobs, and I gotta the place in a mural right up on the wall behind my Carrara marble table like you see in the *Times*, I have treated the hero of dis story, Serge Gavotte, and may God help him with a handle like that! This was before he took on what has come to be known as his Ur-name, Blue Serge, though he has many other, evocative, and, one might even venture to say, poetic names. Mr. Gavotte came to my office one day, unheralded and unannounced, unknown and unsure, unshaven and unequal, undone and unhappy, unquoted and unbraced . . .

Wait! We are in a slight dilemma, good Doc. Somehow, that, uh, how shall we say, stage "greaseball" accent, direct from the beloved Hollywood "films" of the 30s and 40s, has disappeared from your speech. It makes one . . . think.

Ha ha! How delightful that you've noticed. That is my—I like to call it *my*— "golden-earring-and-drooping mustachio" accent. It works wonders with idiot WASPs from the clamorous plains and environs, especially when employed at sidewalk feasts like those of St. Anthony, San Gennaro, and Santa Rosalia, by Italo-Americans, all of whom are Ph.D.s. With the accent, a few shrugs and hand-talk, and that white smile preceding the well-known and beloved infectious laugh, my countrymen get rid of mountains of eighth-rate "food" that would ordinarily be used to bait rat traps. Also useful in shilling "games" of— ho ho—"chance." It is my warm accent, my winning accent, my I-am-so-grateful accent, my great-big-family accent. It is the accent used when some poor contadino is queried by the police as to the source of a few hundred grand in cash found in an old AWOL bag. You get the idea, right? Works something like that other famous speech tic, the brogue. But enough ethnicity! I have said that Mr. Gavotte, an ambulatory fen, appeared one day at lunchtime, crestfallen and aspout with tears.

We remember, Doc.

Doctor! you Methodist churl. Why is it that there is not a religious booster around with a spot of class? Always droning on about Jesus as if he is down at the candy store behind the soda cooler just waiting for you to walk up to him and babble sodden trivia about the accursed Yankees—a strictly Protestant team, by the by—while he figures out how to save you. And incidentally, make you rich. I have an interesting theory got me chucked out of the National Conference of Christians and Jews: All Protestants are really Catharists who couldn't make their ice-cream parlors go and so invented Joy. Sound good? Joy as in Bum Car;

as in Dull Job; as in Big Color TV; as in Friday Night Hump. Also as in that latest plastic kitchen trash from Bloomingdale's in tacky tan, vulgar vanilla, rosy rose, and cantaloupe splendor. Stop me if I'm off base, flashing blue eyes.

It is not only the WASP who frequents that great emporium of savoir-faire and laughable prices, Doctor, as you must know.

My Christ! You give somebody a monicker like Clark or Mercer or Shuttle-worth and he takes to wearing reticent navy-blue ties and talking about economics. That's a joke, solemn one. Can't you stop thinking about your bible-black Mercedes even for a minute? Ever notice how the WASP face gets like old leather? Sort of like the visage of a debauched Tom Sawyer carved in a white prune?

This is, we insist, Doctor, a narrow and bigoted viewpoint of one of the great, how shall we phrase it? *segments* of mankind—a segment from which has come almost all your presidents, senators, congresspersons, your oceans of thieves, murderers, and, if you will forgive the expression, leaders. It is also noted for its magnificent and successful campaign that has managed to propose, as incontrovertible fact, the notion that *it* does not own the world, but that the Jews do. That con is, as they say, a wowie!

Shut uppa you mout! See? You see how you've driven me into my warm and gregarious role again? The man with the loud tie and the chalk-stripe suit who has never been unhappy one day in his whole life? Except maybe once, just once, when he was small, and a fleeting illness of a Sunday made him miss his beloved mamma's—his fat and ruddy and hardworking mamma, she of the black dress and hair in a bun—spaghetti. The man who thrives on violence, cheap wine, and checkerboard tablecloths? The man who lives in the kitchen? The man who invented the pencil moustache? But what has all this to do with Serge Gavotte, the subject of today's talk? And also, as if you didn't know, *tuttipazze*, the subject of this whole "book"—just under way, I admit, but getting there, whatever that means. And may your creeping Methodist Jesus with a lamb under one arm and his other raised to the starry skies have mercy on the unfortunate bastard who's writing it!

Enough, Doctor, of parry and riposte! Too many pages, too many words, too much paper! Do you expect a publisher to actually *pay for* printing a book like this? A book that will not be carried to the beach, smarmed over on in-depth talk shows, made into idiot motion pictures, major all? Tell us about the damaged and/or diseased *bouche* of Bleu! Tell us of the cures miraculous, the advice good, the ambience hearty of the consultation room. Tell, so that it may at least seem as if we are carrying the narrative forward, ever forward, to what stirring climax, who can tell?

O.K., sports. The young chap, hairy and hulking, his symbol, panache, gui-don, coat-of-arms the bicycle clip couchant, entered my office. I reconstruct, for your files, the conversation, give or take a few hundred adjectives.

Dear God!

It will take but a moment for those who like to check and ascertain, look up and verify, to check and ascertain, look up and verify this portentous scenario, a bottom-line word if I ever heard one, close-shaven exec. As I have said, Gavotte enters:

Gavotte: You dig on my mouth all swolled up, Doc?

Doc Chick: Sí. But who the hell are you to come in here, all akimbo? How you find me?

Gavotte: Have a heart, Doc! Looka this mouth. You ever see anything like this goddam piece o' meat? How the hell I'm gonna play with a mouth looks like an old seabag?

Doc Chick: Is disgusting. (Here a retch was heard as far as Queens.)

Gavotte: So? What's the verdict? Is there hope?

Doc Chick: Here, you lilting little cadenza, let's stuff it with these various dried *fruttos* and wrinkled leaves, an old necromancer's remedy that, in my ca-pacity as mouth-croaker to the Stars, I have committed to memory.

Gavotte: Veelzh bedda alreadda, Boc.

Doc Chick: And furthermore, I don't want to know *how* you got this fat thing under the nose here, but I'll tell you one thing.

Gavotte: Mm.

Doc Chick: Just a glance askance out of these wise old owllike eyes of mine informs me that you have a Great Musical Soul bursting and glowing within and dying there in solitary splendor from frustration. You are, I can tell from your gnarled hands and blank stare, a lens grinder of some sort, n'est-ce pas? Don't! Don't try to talk—I don't want to know how your mouth metamorphosed itself from the sweet little thing its basic configuration tells me it is in its natural state, to the Big Mac that now distorts your visage. Dare *I* whisper it? The cheapo har-monica from a sundries shop? The loathsomely shellacked recorder from some dump on the corner, where that six-bit "instrument" nestled amid dusty fire-crackers and rotting Trojans? And you have been, I know, blowing your great red heart out! Yes? The labors of a fool! Herakles himself was no dopier when he contracted to scrub and wax the Cretan maze! You must—you *must*—study the PIANO! It is that oddly shaped and hard-to-carry instrument that calls you; your gnarled hands, your sweaty callouses do cry out in accents stentorian for its tinkly pinging! Study! Study! And as you study, and you need, I can tell from your glazed expression, no teacher, travel the length and width and heighth of this great land, learning as you go, meeting the people who will be your inspira-tion, the simple folk of Terre Plaines and Nebraska City out there in the great states of Omaha and Tucson where the sunset collapses in its panoply of horribly depressing colors! Until, *until* you come to that secret place wherein you will find the Perfect Musical Phrase. It is there that you must build your church, my rude sonata.

Gavotte: Umphh!

That is it, bosom cheeches. The nutshell, glaring WASPs. He left, and we may now pursue him for page after page, "chapter" after "chapter"—him and his balding spouse, Helene, and their wonderful son, Zimmerman, pursue him un-der all his mystic names, now become fabulous song and the stuffing of story.

You really expect us, Doc, to believe that it was you who sent Blue Serge on his vaunting quest?

Aye, 'twas. I may not have said *exactly* that . . .

Aha!

I said but, go home! Slap some carbolated vaseline on your nauseating mouth and lay off the old lady for a while.

You mean that the condition was caused by . . .?

No, no. I joosta no wanna to aggravate the condish. The mouth malady was, and it was as clear as the space in a congressman's head, from vast bowlfuls of tuna helper, a common malady among you folk.

That's better—but you are once again slipping in and out of the comic grease-ball accent, Doc.

Mind-a you bizziness.

Doc? Say, Doc? If my mouth swells up again like it did, I mean, when I'm "on the road," what do I do? Where do I get the fruits and leaves and such? The greasy shlock you recommended?

What the hell are you doing back in this chapter? Get out! Out!

Yeah. What you want, caro mio?

Out!

Fruits and leaves? A bundle, a poultice, a grab-bag of daffodils and straw-berry roots, rutabago blooms and crawling treponema, lavender peony stems and shady fusillade?

You betcha you life! The busting muscat, the dozing corn shock in season, and shuck when out, the pink-walled violet, even an algolagnia or so, to taste.

Thanks, Doc.

I've never seen anything—

The way she go, wailing Baptist! You do someting nize, hey! They wanna do it all themselves, at-home remedies, like that, you know?

But how will Blue . . .? I mean, how will he manage to . . .?

Get a curious peach in his mouth? Ha ha ha! I'd like to be a little maggot on the wall *that* day!

Odd how, despite our enormous superiority in all things—the criminal and ignorant histories of our forebears, for instance—we find you oddly amusing.

Facciabruto!

« 3 »

Blue and
Helene Have a Good
Long Talk and Make Plans

His great muscled teeth flashed for an instant, but whether in a smile of gladness or a grimace of pain, none can tell, least of all I. Flashed, then flickered and died.

My great gnarled hands lie lifeless on the piano keys, Blue said. It must be a sign.

Apple, Serge? his wife Helene said from the crepuscular corner of their comfortable, yet unimportant living room. It was her habit to sit there of an evening so that Blue could not discern her hair falling out.

His teeth glittered for just a moment.

My great gnarled hands, I said, Blue said, lie lifeless on the piano keys—only the white ones, by the by. And you offer me an apple? Although I can't see your hair I can imagine it, falling, falling, falling with the ineluctable movement of Fate. Don't you have any peaches?

But you can't play the piano, Serge, Helene whined reasonably.

Just so, Blue said. Yet Doctor Ciccarelli has advised me to stuff my mouth, swoll up like it gets, with fruits and leaves, sloes black as jet, and so on, and get cracking on my piano studies. I am not, in my heart of hearts, a lens grinder, as well you know.

Doctor Ciccarelli, the Mouth King?

And he also said that I must travel, travel, travel all through this great country, searching for the Perfect Musical Phrase. There I shall settle. Will you . . . come . . . with me?

Oh, Serge! And she rose from the shadows in a cloud of finespun hair and dandruff that caught the light somewhat like an aureole or halo; that looked, in the light, sort of like those two things, or one or the other of those things; and tripped across the room in this golden nimbus and/or aura, which latter enveloped her.

12

He's having trouble getting out of this sentence, Blue said.

Of course I'll come, Helene said. And are these some of the leaves and fruits that the doctor advised you stuff in your mouth? Here, let me. A sloe, a lemon, a tomatl, a quizzical pear and a magical plum, plus God knows how many blowing elm leaves and proud staghorn sumac fronds and Christ knows what else!

Mmphh.

I'll pack! Of course you'll be taking the piano?

Mmphh.

And his great gnarled hands were still at last, still and calm for the first time in what seemed months but was in actuality but a week or a week and a half at most!

After our really good and long talk, Helene, Blue said, of just a few hours ago— or was it days? God, it seems like days, since time fleets by so madly when one is in the throes of fantasy turning to reality, I know you'll agree, all pink and white as you are in your heart of hearts and soul of souls, that I have reached that moment in life when it is time for me to leave this dead-end job of grinding lenses. Is it not so, my bun?

I *have* agreed, Blue, Helene simpered. Perhaps you've forgotten . . . ?

She was ravishing in an old, yet richly embroidered *schmatte*, set off beautifully by the snug-fitting *shapiro* left her by her old grandmother, the one who had the wise and beautiful things to say about life from the depths of her rocking chair on Essex Street.

You have so much to offer, Serge, your eyes, your glittering beard, your great hands chockablock with latent power . . . Will you be taking the piano? When I last quizzed you on that point, you said but "mmphh."

Take the piano? Ha ha ha! His hirsute laugh rang out upon the very stones! My necco, somehow I feel that I am, in some odd and mysterious way, a piano myself! And if not, then, by God!—and here he declaimed a thunderous oath— I plan to *become* all piano.

And . . . and . . . I'll still be your helpmeet?

In bosk and dell, in lea and glade, in glen and holt, in orchard, how, hew, and vale, in the hundreds, give or take a few score, of extempore eclogues with which we shall stun the yokels flung out like so many miggies and peewees across this windy land, you shall come! And be! And he laughed his great gnarled laugh!

And Zimmerman, our darling chee-ild?

By God, Zim! I'd almost forgotten the little F-clef, or however they term it. Of course! Although I dig on your mother heavy, I don't appreciate her making *him* wear a *shapiro*! What exactly is a *shapiro*?

Oh, Blue, Helene laughed relievedly, how should I know? Granny Rocco tells how the *shapiro* has been in our family ever since the old days, when the family ran the egg-cream dodge in Bialystock. But even *she* has no idea what it is.

Well, let the little tick wear it anyway then! I am nothing if not great of heart and anyway, why should I give a fuck if the kid looks like a gawm wimp-liver? Do you get me, sweetie seltzer?

Your voice, as you said "tick," had the timbre and quality of a small yet exquisite spinet. Oh Blue! We are going to make a success of it after all.

You can bet your run-down mocs on it, sport! And now, let's roll up a couple cocaine-peyote bombers and get *down*!

My great heart! Here are a few handfuls of honey locust leaves and nodding sprays of linden and magnolia ferns to "bind" the pow'ful whacker. Also very big in terms vitamins and enzyme juice.

And you ask if I'll take you! My black-fly!

« 4 »
A Domestick Quarrel

... never did that, never! Never *never* treated you the way you treat me all the time, Serge. Oh God! You can be as cruel as a sharpened tooth!

Don't call me Serge, weed-hair.

Oh God, so cruel! Like that just now! I speak to you so nice, so reasonable, ask you a question or something and what am I supposed to think when you emote such like: "Go shove your hair!" Hah? Or "Fuck off with your balding noggin!" Hah? When you walked out this evening, proud Serge, you know of which I wanted to do? First, I wanted to get my mitts upon that cheap knife with the plastic handle that your tightwad of a mother gave us for our *anniversary*—sweet Jesu!—outen the kitchen draw, or drawers, and just *stick* it, like, dig, puncture it right in my *neck*. Don't laugh, cruel flinty skin, I have a college education, yes, make a yawning incision in my own neck! And then I thought that mayhap I'd get a pair of shears or even scissors and cut my hair off down to the throbbing roots! I'm a person, Serge! I have inalienated rights just like any other human-being person, distaff though I own up to be! And you know how I am about my mother, all chock-a-bock with weeping tears, and yet you walked *out* on me to-night, walked out and left me all alone waiting for the phone to go "brr-ing-brr-ing" like it often does in novels with my mother on the other end making me crazed. I'm thirty-six years old, you know I can't cope with being thirty-six years old without some warm, supportive words and things and such, a hug, a kind remark, a fleeting moment of French-kissing, maybe a little shtup without you humming "The Trolley Song." I don't *need* a present, a little bibblo of a gift or whatever, but you dint get me a thing, not even a little remembrance, no, you spent your money on piano records and things très musicale, and I, I am thirty-six years old today with my still-young hair falling out in chaff-like handfuls so that I have to wear a babushka every day so that the fascist chauvinist spicks of the teeming stews of the brawling avenues don't call on me names like I have to hear at home, belike: "Cueball" and "Flesh-Head" and "Sconce-Shine." Things like unto the asperities what you cast toward me! Them spicks learned their deep unnatural rottenness from folks like you! No small wonder that they are always

15

schlocking up their rice with bean juice! Are you asleep under that colorful blanket, Serge? I want you to listen to me, Serge, I am a person with legitimate person-needs, something like a book reviewer who would rather be in Maine writing his or her "novel" with his or her large comfortable feet in the fire. And what narrow-hearted wight can blame him or her? None! yelps the chuffing gale! My thirty-sixth birthday, and I've been a good wife, interested and boned-upon in everything you do, asking intelligent questions about your lens career and whatever. And don't you think that I'd like to walk out anytime I want, le-da-de, like you take such hasty powders when you wish to? But I can't! I can't walk out, Serge, because even though I am a human person with needs and wants like any other person in the world, and also with a teacher's license so that although I may have somewhat lost or carelessly misplaced my figure . . .

Har har har! Serge muttered.

. . . I am still a human *woman*, cut into the same moldiness and stamps as Elsa Koch and Madame Nhu and other great leaders of their yearning people. Yet I feel . . . trapped . . . just like some kinda animal, a kind of semblable to a wolf or a bear or sumpn.

Like unto a yak or duck-billed platterpuss?

I can't cope as a female-being person with feeling like a yak or something and being a little on the plump side in the rear area there, even with a casually loose schmatte on, and with my hair thinning a little bit, don't laugh, and also being thirty-six! You wish to know what my mother what bore me said when I reminded her that I'm thirty-six? Who cares? she bit off. *Who cares?* We all got to grow up sometimes, she said. Even Golda Meir was thirty-six once, she tittered. Don't you think, feeling, as I do, like a fox or a caged bird which wants to flap and sing his little wings off, that I'd just like to walk out and spend the house money for some things like piano accouchements and booklets of grinding-tool techniques or something, but you know I can't. Because, you know why? You know wherefore it is as impossible for me to do as it was for Caesar to avoid the raging dirk that shoveled out his quick? Because, Serge, I am the mother of a chee-ild! You have your piano and that quasi-Indian blanket what I give you when we used to sit up on the roof and drink peyote together and talk about how one day we would lick the world! But I don't have anything but a coupla cheap wigs from Fourteenth Street whom make me look like a Negro whore especially when my eyes are all red like theirs are often—I don't say all the time, but often—from thinking and crying myself to a restless sleep in my humiliation of not receiving a little thought on my birthday when I had to face Elatia Farn and Sarah Slatz and their questions as to what you gave me and I had to lie and lie about the "something special" you'd ordered from across the troubled seas what had not arrived yet. Cruel deception which turns its bucked teeth backward and snaps them quick into the fibber's writhing fletch! Are you *asleep?*

Avast and eke belay, you febrile wench, else I'll take the cat t' ye! (The cat runs with all celerity from out the chamber, or "room.")

Cruel! Now that you work parts-time it's worser with you around the house all the time reading *Popular Mechanix* and *Check My Beaver* and in front of somebody like I, with a degree in Education, what has substituted in some of the finest schools in the flung-out boroughs, and with my hands all red from Spic and Span cleaning your harmonica and pipe thing with the little holes every day. When I think of how it used to be, it was like a trip, maybe even a jaunt, to Venus or Mars, for you were on the jaunt with me. The way we et Noodle-Roni right out of the piping pot in front of the TV without clothes on, we were so proud and free in our human-person naked fletch, and the big bottles of cream soda—we used to call it just "cream," remember?—that we guzzled down with the salads I'd create from sorrel leaves and licorice roots with dainty chunks of Kraft American and wine mixed up with cream cheese, with the big lumps and fardels catching the mellow sunlight as it peeped at us through the grimy windows that looked out over the park where all those wonderful ethnic hunkies would be under the banyan and Dutch elm trees, beating each other to pieces and all laughing their great workers' laughs through their good-natured black-and-blue teeth, and jabbering in Polish or Yucratian or whatever wonderful warm language they spoke, just drenched in vodka and warm beer and stuffed with kielogi and pirbasa and cabbage shards, and the grass all tromped down for yards and yards around. And the petunias and phlox and hematomas and little curs cavorting and poo-pooing all over the brown strong limbs of the young people—the wonderful wonderful young people!—stretched out under and also on top of the broken benches and the vast acres of smashed bottles and used needles and dried cundrums that set off the old rust color of the rotting seedless grapes spilling from quaint and curious paper bags, all so simple and true and honest that I thought such a world could never end! Especially when we really embroiled ourselves into it with some oregano spice cakes dotted all over with teensy bits of chemicalized stuff like unto bacon that was then only nine dollars a pound, those were the days, and the rubber plants would shake in the stifling breeze blowing in the window carrying the pure sound of the Con Ed plant hysterically blowing off steam in yet another emergency that we were not to fret or worry about and the dust would just fly off of the plantain leaves that we insouciously draped about the rubber plants, and later, later, mix in with our raw-bean salad with sesame croutons and rice delight which we learned about from that funny cock-eyed man in the park used to stand under the old rotting sycamore and expose his private. Remember we called him, dubbed him, really, "Old Uncle Pee-Pee"? He was one of the last of the truly yawningly deep and four-squared souls left in that little idolic world, oh, how I remember how you said you'd give a million, yes, that was the phrase, you'd give a million bucks—it's all coming back to me!—you said, to be like him with no thought of anything but the way the sun dappled the area of his trouser fly and the odd feeling the deep rich feeling of accomplishment it gave him so that he thought nothing of making his simple repast out of a few old Good Humor sticks and the wrappers that held spicy cuchifritos, something that I always wanted to learn how to create, cuchifritos with marianari sauce served on those big radish leaves with handfuls of timothy and fugwort gone to seed to mop up the tangy gravy, and after that snow peas in orange rinds with chilies and lemon pop all over and once, *you* probably don't remember, we had a small simple picnic under that noddingly diseased horse-chestnut tree that made you fall in love with me all over again so that you stuck your wad of Bazooka into my yearning lip! Avocado peels and okra shoots in a mold made from raspberry Jell-O with peanuts and cherry tomatoes and all surrounded by delicately flavored coconut shells and halavah bits on a bed of soft and slightly browning escarole or some kinda ginzo bush along with Crisco on bialys and plenty of piña jugo with sprigs of nettleweed and sawgrass to give it that certain je ne sais quoi. I can't believe we lived such a life, Serge. And now . . .

Forgive me, my dolling snap bean! I've been blind wit staring at my rippling dukes! *Can* you . . . forgive me?

Oh Blue! My love! Of course—and e'er I breathe a syllable o' censure vile and eke coterminous I'd as lief implode my face unto the haunt o' fishes an' the snarling barracuda who savages the floors o' Neptune's condominium!

Then come here, my quiv'ring kohlrabi, and I'll suck your coif like I used to in those days of old delights, and perhaps some of that am'rous magic will retoin! We can but hope, and yet: My wires, such as they are, do thrill and thrum!

≪ 5 ≫

Blue Improves
Helene's Coiffure

Helene, my shock, I'm going to repair and renovate—not to mention slick up cold and grooved—your coiffure, with some debonair twists and flourishes and turns, bights, and sheepshanks so it will come out all resplendently dapper. You'll look like a bride again! How long ago it endless seems!

I'm in your powerful and surgically perfect hands, Blue dumpling, whatsoever you want to do with me, I say aye! and aye! again, and yet again, letting my voice ring and clatter in the welkin high above, the one now creamily bespattered with extra-thick clouds.

No need to wax so fulsome, fond asparagus. Ready? Rivet your gaze on the mirror before you so that you can see what I'm doing and I'll supplement this visual aid by also tipping you off vocally as I go.

Solid!

First, I grasp hanks and locks of crudded, feltered, and bejungled hair in both hamlike fists and mess it around improvisationally to give myself an idea of how you look *au naturel*, without the aid of that vast battery of creamy pastes and gelatinous dandruff-fighting lotions that clutter and jam what we laughingly refer to as your dressing-table. Then, when your crowning glory is a fetching mass of tangles and snarls that perfectly complement the bloodshot eyes that stare in pop-eyed abandon back at you from yonder looking-glass, I step back to see where and how I shall attack the very problem that my artistry has created! *Bon.* Satisfied, as I hope you are, my precious nit, I slather your sconce with many many ounces—how many what man can tell?—of Wesson oil, or some other oil, low in cholesterol nuggets and supremely heavy on poly-unsaturated greaseballs. You'll note how it bubbles and oozes and slides down these crafty cowlicks and knots unto the very scalp and its ancillary roots, dig? Now, we give it a minute or two to seep into the follicular capillary system that ceaselessly and loyally carries vitamins and minerals and proteins and Jesus knows what else type of nutritional elements to your noisomely gleaming hair, but which has been

19

clearly goldbricking and fucking up royally, so to speak, of late—else why would you be sorely vexed by this touch of baldness that threatens your Venusian aspect—all chick and a mile wide, babe. *Voilà!* Now, while we allow this stuff of dreams, this stuff that has the uncanny consistency of schmaltz from the finest of pedigreed hens and blue-blooded capons and roostercocks, to elbow its way down into the deepest subcutaneous micromolecular zones of your oddly squared-off skull, I plunge a veritable squadron of combs and brushes into this special turquoise-tinted solution simmering away at my calloused albeit purely formed and dashingly proportioned elbow, now unfortunately racked with various aches and pains, suffering as it is from pianitis. But why do you leap and jump about, my pip?

Oh Blue! I just saw a strange and hairy, an *animal* face glancing in the window with a steely, spooky eye, or, to be precise, a veritable *pair* of eyes!

Let me check this bestial creature out, my goose, lest it be a mangy lycanthrope, intent on feral chomp and rend. In the meantime, I'll let my tonsorial equipment simmer gently, while you, and I so implore it, must close your vapid eyes so that this slimy potion, now dragging along every fucking vitamin yet known to great and irrepressible mankind, does not steal into those, your sparkling eyes, and render you unsighted. Aha! I see the dangerous creature, standing there and gazing at me all nonchalant and unconcerned, and with, as the vulgar patois has it, some pair of balls! Begone, you twerpish rogue and gross degenerate morphodite!

Oh Blue, my heliotrope bouquet! What manner of cruel slinking creature can it be who would so blatantly direct his sadomasochistic stare upon a lady all slopped and iced and gilded with unspeakable and loutish goo?

Only the remarkable Savior can say, and that's my deep opinion . . . and yet, now that I scan him close, especially noting well his walk, or amble, and now that I see him leap belike unto a carnal pogo stick into the perfumed air of spring or whatever goddam season holds us in its thrall, I wot that he gambols and bleats just like a very lamb. By all that's musical, it is a lamb!

A lamb? Oh Blue, my straining pectoral, does this portend portentous evil tidings, ever close to us and ever slouching nearer, like that tough beast in the famous Pennsylvania poem?

That, I cannot ken, nor search out in the soft grey crap that humankind hilariously cleps the cerebellum, if I got the right word for the pulsing organ. But what I do know is that the little bastard has been joined by sundry buddies, all lambs such as he, and all matted and begunked with Nature's kindest remedy for dry and itchy hides—I speak, of course, of wondrous lanolin!

So you feel it's stupid bullshit to be nervous as a coot? Whatever that last-named thing may be?

Of course, my ruby *bouche*! These foolish little schmucks, clumped and mobbed up as you now can see as you open wide your peepers, are standing in moronic innocence just outside the window, gazing at you and at this hotsy-totsy operation, like unto wooly statues which know not what they see but ogle anyway, dumb sons of bitches which they are.

And so I *do* see as I ope my blinks. They kind of get upon my nerves, frail broad that I am. I do not cotton to the idea that they watch me, all unkempt and dopey, with my coif a sight!

Fear nothing, sweetest scallopine, I'll make short work of this, your witching curls, and be all done before these idiotic infant sheeps have a chance to shake their horrid tails. They make me slightly nervous too, with their imbecilic gaze, but a man who has his spouse's hair in such a state learns how to press on and ne'er say hold!—until her coiffure is such that it beats that of fairest Helen all to shit.

You are an *artiste* right down to your black and splintery fingernails, my ragged gladiolus.

Allons! I now run this gigantic comb all through this healthy and yet horrifying schlock with which I have enlacquered the few poor hairs that still you sport, dragging and savaging its sturdy, stout, and steaming teeth through each unruly clustered tangle so thick and matted that your gleaming *capo* looks as if the rats have been a-sucking on it all betimes.

The shooting agonies reach down unto my very armpits, yet I command you to press on!

Command me nothing, gentle twit, but rather beg me to continue in my task—a task for which I have all greatly volunteered. And now, see? The comb, clutched famously within my expert duke, has done its magic work and your hair is slicked back and molded to your freakish head belike unto that curious cap that milliners have dubbed a yarmulke. The vile and noxious grease that finds itself clotted 'pon your rather dirty nape is that surplus devoutly to be wished, for in its bowels is the dandruff and the filth and scale and lice that once held sway within the stuff your bean produced, the stuff that I have always called your glist'ring hair, may God forgive my small prevarication, and if He gets one glimpse of you, my cookie, He'll shrive me of each sin I have committed—aye, in word *and* deed!

I feel so . . . so . . . good, in the entire ballyard that nestles just above my forehead, my blazing maple leaf. And how wonderful my poor hair looks as you go into yet another awesome shtick with your zipping fingers. Wow!

Well may you say "wow," humble sausage of my heart. Now dig on the ambidextrous way in which I whip these once-lank tresses into glamour! Now a curl, now a wave, now a sweep over each ear and a bob and fall and brave upsweep *chingado*, topped off with a restive bouffant beehive, the envy of every simple broad who ever whiled her nights away in the dazzling bowling alleys of sunny Jackson Heights!

Oh Blue, my blowing maize, I hardly know myself, I'm almost young and beautiful again!

I don't quite follow you in re your term "again," but anyway, you are at least half-ass presentable, despite your vastly imbecilic clothes and that hilarious nose of yours, so peculiarly itself that Joe Miller could get by with only it as lonely subject of his crapola corn.

I stand and flush agape. All words fail and falter and I sigh.

And while you sigh your buttocks off, pimiento spread, I'll take this excess and devastating muck I've combed out of your slathered hair and chuck it full velocity upon those leering sheeps! Aha! *That* made the little faggots bound away! And good riddance to you, you bucolic creeps! Don't let me catch you all aslouch again, your glazy eyes pressed nakedly to other people's windows! Get your own transparent windows if you like the life of Tom the Peep, you hairy schlepps!

Your powerful and aggressive words zing all up and down my spine like in the lyrics to that old and moth-chewed song the public loved adoringly unto a man. You are every item I desire, prodigious Blue.

≪ 6 ≫

Blue Finds
and Takes the Pushcart

And so, O Muse, with fair Helene's hair all frizzed and ratted into gouts of pulchritude, the family Gavotte was ready to "hit the trail." And yet, no means of transportation was there for the intrepid three, though Great Destiny hawked and choughed in the keening wind!

We peep down (or up) upon the sinewy Blue, his hair all feltred in anxiety, churning and thudding his way beneath the *arboris urbis*, the ashy hobblebush, thug squashberry, swamp loosestrife, jimbo pachistima, pimpface polyester, and all the other clumps that shoot and yearn throughout the streets and byways of vast Gotham—not to forget the loathsome ginkgo!

Arghh, shot Blue the Serge. The time is ripe and mellow for to split and take ourselves away! My spouse's hair is bossed and slathered, my mouth is clearing up, the magical piano trembles in anticipation, and, the veriest acme of the whole routine is the not-lightly-given imprimatur of profound Doc Chick. But how to cram and pack the crap we'll need and hurl it all, ourselves included, West?

Sing, Muse, of the Port Authority! Sing of the Ninth Avenue upon which its ass-end abuts and jowls all cheeklike! Sing too of the strange vehicle that nestled by the curb, abandoned all alone by mortal men, as 'twere no more than a rotted limb of cockwood, the noisome crud of which the awesome Bion speaks, or sometimes croons. Something like a pushcart and yet not a pushcart. A-decorate with arcane symbols unlike anything the humble ragman or the swarthy apple-vendor would give a twiggish fugg about. The Serge did halt, his muscled toes digging furiously at the pavement, his eyes all bright as with the agued kinch.

Is this a cart? huffed Blue. The genre of which the cant and mores and gross platitudos of the day call pushcart? It is belike and sort of like the pushcarts that collective memory hath implanted in my brain, all awash in sickening nostalgia, sort of akin to the oddball vehicle my old Uncle Max once schlepped with keening tzuris through the pungent, manly streets of the Old and Lower East Side of bygone yore, those streets all shaded with the dread ailanthus, o' which the *New York Times* writes each two or three year or so, no doubt laboring beneath some fatal curse. And yet its weirdo shape, its amateurish pictures and designs, its funny little "roofs," and the bald and gross-visagèd fact that it has four round wheels instead of two, take it far, far from the league in which grizzled Uncle Max did play, a phrase I like to use to make the stranger think my uncle's putrid life was but a lark.

Sing, Muse! Jump with fairy feet upon my cheap and mass-producèd ball-point pen, taken from a Sheraton Hotel, and guide its smeary "nib" so that it writes with accents grave and somberous of the lonely cart that Serge's banjaxed eyes did light upon.

Its tentlike roof or hood glittered in the hazy sunshine, all vertically stripèd black and white, like unto a stick of licorice candy, sort of, but not quite exactly, since the stripes were not curling around or whatever they are prone to cogitate therein, and so on. And yet! 'twas not "all" stripèd, for the front part of this canopy was of a solid color, grey in hue (or tone), yes, grey as the bleary eye of ancient ram when he doth sport upon St. Michaelmas!

Upon this ventral bombast, all dazzling as the famed Lorenzo's treasured marmalade, two curious and crabbed figures were indited by a hand with all the skills of Pegleg Vulcan, a old eyetalian doomed to whang and smudge his days away in the foundries of Olympus hight. The topmost symbol showed what seemed for all the world to be a star, or else a bitter asterisk, which in the Greek of Homer and that whole demented crew of yodeling troubadors, means little star, and thus betimes, what boots the fucking difference? Yet but a moment's pause may give us thought. It could as well have been a flower, or the blossom nodding sweet and swell of same. O Muse, help me to scrawl down the names of various flowers that this asteriskish thing might sort have looked a little like, I do implore you as a faun begs for his blushing nymph's be-pansied crotch atremble in the bosk! Or purlieus thence!

It resembled but a puling tittle the majestic whang pylorus, insofar as its pistils crinched a bit of dusty albumen; or the cowpoke adenoma, that luscious succulent that catches lemonpeels soft flying in the Bexar County twilight; yet there was about its glizzy purplish aura a hint that grunted speckled adenitis, the hardy cactus that attacks the hikers' Pepsi-Cola; but one would not go far astray to think it krishna foramen, in that it had the odd aroma of your basic vegetable blue plate; a close-inspection peer, however, at its wicked stamens might urge the dimwit botanist to think he'd come across the whiplash fovea, that amoral plant long suspected of ripping the modest skirts from Girl Scout leaders in the nooky glades; Dr. Harry Hare, however, of the Wildlife for Jesus Federation, showed a bloom much like it on his mammoth Terre Haute Telethon last year, and described said bloom as the hump synovia, an obnoxious weed that grows in a mucky compost made of tuna mulch; still, a layman's guess would come down

24

on the side of the jazzbo ganglia, since the woody stem was all encrusted with identically oozing acne-blots; yet and yet, the whole had all the crud and infestation of the rainbow hallux, that monstrous hollyhock that men, in trembling dread, have dubbed "Wayne Newton Plant"; but all in all, if one were to picture forth this boutonniere so as to make all people see it instantly, it was a twin unto the wimpy hematuria, a type of slogbed phlox that has its kinky way with Rosedale housewives while their husbands chuck their bowling balls akimbo and abaft.

Just beneath this pimpled asterisk, or little star, or else a flower, as we have bravely hopped out on a limb to name a few, please see above, whizzed forth to Blue's slow-plodding eye another crazèd figure. Lo! a shallow basin in which was stuck a kind of upright stick, or maybe sturdy plank or log or faggot of what seemed to be a type of item called by men, yea, e'er since the time that brawling Hector scared the shite out of his little son with wearing of some dumbbell hat, wood! And all atop this wooden plankish thing blared forth upon the day another kind of goddam star! This one five-pointed, or, as the sweating masses call it, your ordinary common star, known to symbolic logic as a stellar presentation, belike at times to shitfaced drumbling knaves the stars that they remember with a shudder of recall from grammar school. But Blue, though wacked out by the sun that scrabbled at his corneas, saw at once that this chintzy figuration might well have been, or meant to be, or yet, it wert! a palm tree all free of the encumbrances of coconuts. Or tiny stinking monkeys!

A palm tree! But by the Great Jesu, O what a palm! A growth the likes of which one might imagine shading Mickey Mouse or some other cutesy vermin, or maybe even the grotesquely weird animals of cartoon farm and field who ceaselessly gabble and palaver to keep their minds off the stunning fact that they whank about the glades and heaths sans genitals! It was, in some disturbing way, not so much a palm tree as it was something else. But what, O Muse? Fill me with the unmixed wine of art and letters, or even, yes! of post cards, that I may scratch and scribble on this lonely sheet its akiltered image, lambent in the haze of muscled midtown! Canta!

It had the gimpy silhouette of the puffy decumaria (mordecai), that sweaty grass that humps in secret innocent electric typewriters; yet there was about its pullulating shape somewhat of the calm St. Johnswort, that virago of a limp legume which smiles eternally in elevators; yet what sunburned camper, complete with fruit bar, would not quake in thinking of it as a runaway example of the dour jive-ass silverbell, that traipsing fungus that in dead of night devours "chuck" and empties stout canteens; a minority of foundation scientists swear that it was not unlike the silky-camellia all-in-one, beige, black, and white, that hankers to wrap itself around the staidest matron in the sanctity of her boudoir;

25

bigmouth pepperbush? but yes! in that its simpy gnurled appendages did clinch whatever steak au poivre did happen by within the shady glen; yet, cloved and hugged it not to its bamboozled self a soupçon of the penetrating character of the clubfoot sandmyrtle, that queer and beetly creeper that flourishes within the very core of Southron novels?; however, in a certain light, the rank growth, like the flushing minniebush, seemed to sport a bevy of iridescent spangs, like the ladies of dainty thighs much loved by Doctor Tom; though those who holler that the simpering shrub featured forth itself belike your roaring stumping Western soapberry, that spends its bloated youth amid depraved daguerrotypes, are not far off the mark; the consensus but of disheveled lab assistants appears to be that this "palm tree" was neither more nor less than a freakish outgrowth of fat-ass redroot, famed for fakery, terrific transvestite, bald of bean and astonishingly dim behind its domino.

Below and just a chitch in front of this glistering roofish item, was a smaller roof in shape somewhat like a parallelogram, or rhombus, or whatever Euclid in his crazed meanderings yclept such curio. And there, dead center on its spanking blank, what ho! an urn, and not unlike that urn so loved by each and every Greek, even their unravished brides! On either side of this two-handled jug, able in its girthish vastness to hold up to eighteen gallons of that nectar called by sage Euripides pure Yankee Bean, Blue's eyes did pop to see the virtuosic forms divine of eke these wacky characters: a coupla fishes, coupla bedbugs, and a coupla pelicans. Sing, Muse, what this did all portend if it portendeth anything! Or sing of mighty Serge's words, or croaked facsimiles thereof, and such betimes!

What doth this all portend if it portendeth anything? mused Blue upon the azure air of that alabaster avenue so far from the scroungy lights of Broadway and its crappish plays. These things must stand as "symbols"—wot a woid! The tunnish oin bespeaks, it actually shouts and hollers, of a fullness, thick and curdled like your frozen custard, that will be my Life when I depart this fabled island, than whom, Satan except, no one can live in peace, or send his childers to a decent school achock with WASPs, but must, bedad, watch the kiddies sport with peers whose skins are of Cimmerian hue and who speak that argot rude known as the "motherfucker" dialect. So much for this fatted vat. But what can mean these crippled hilarities, these tandems rude bedaubed of fishies, bugs, and birds of big fat mouths?

So did Blue breathe his dumb interrogations to the unhearing air, awash, as is its wont, with klaxons and the brutish stinks of "produce." Then, as esoteric reams of numbers plotz upon the brain of idiot savant, the true and hidden meanings all collapsed upon him, falling in a dusty rush as doth a drunk pitch forward on the sloppy table in his favorite neighborhood saloon.

Great Zeus and Such! shrieked Blue. It comes to me in a rush as swift and beeline as the freakish Mercury, that distorted lad with feathers all asprout upon his twinkly feets! It all portendeth Great Success! Of that there is no gasp of doubt. My arcane and eruditical researches whiz into the front porch of my cerebellum and I recall the truths of stern biology, but oui! The fishies, in their drive to larder up their tummies, scoff up legions of the humble bedbug; and in turn are wolfed by ox-eyed pelicans; and every man will tie the feedbag on in snappy trice when pelican is set before him on the groaning board, howsomever, it will be admitted that this oily bird is best served roasted in a baste of pine nuts, okra fronds, and childermass; or else prepared marengo-style, glopped o'er with twitchy crayfish and a dozen sunny sides. Thus steps out smartly straight before my wised-up eyes the March of Life! Yes, the Great Law of the Jungle and the Christian Way, i.e., compete your weaker neighbor into tattered scraps of junk and blame it all on God! Is it any wonder then that this more-or-less united oligarchy's potent banks all gleam in reverential hush akin to choiches?

Yea, these portentous symbols glitter forth the silent memorandum that I, Blue Serge, am meant for Greatness! And that all who stand in front of my success express are to be raveled, chonkered, wrenched, and blastered in thrilling sympathy with the somber Laws of Nature. As the fishies eat the bedbugs and the pelicans the fish, and as divinely shapèd man sops up the corses of the pelicans, so will I take my place in this wise scheme and devour each and all opponents to my raging wants! Great Jove thus speaks to me in subtle signs that translate straight to pure unfettered gringo-ese!

Then tell, O Muse, how the beams of that conflagrating star that men in their cowering mode have dubbed Big Solly, did shine upon that spackled vehicle, making it lo! to appear as puissant and as terrible as a newly laved and idiotically pricèd auto, of the kind your mogulish tycoon and swiftly famed celebrity doth buy a grossish passel of! Tell how King Jupiter, with a flick of filthy finger on which bloomed an ebon nail, did make this bourgeois wagon seem to the loutish Blue as slick and glossy as the evening news! Tell how the cart did reach its twinkly "arms" out, so to speak, to coin a buboed solecism, so that the dim-bulb Blue was all a-fascinate with thinking that this noble gig was parked upon the clappy street for only him!

Great Pushcart, then descanted Blue, O chancred brougham of majestickal waukegan! It zips into my thoughts as quick as cockroach into kitchen crack, that you, O sacred chariot, wert meant for me, and only me, to aid my holy quest! O wert it thus?

And then the cart, in oddly weak and piping voice, did actually speak! But just to Blue, whose "face" proclaimed him as a type of personage known to the

men of ancient time, as a cony, now called variously sucker, sap, and mark. Blue
Serge Gavotte, it ponderously squeaked, in true tradition of Great Leadership,
you see the dopy little head, 'pon which is daubed a spindly smile, that head, I
strong attest and threaten, just below the overarching canopy with all the bugs
and fishies and all the other odds and ends of bullshit fair indited thence and
such? This leer is meant for you! Yea, as sure and splendid as the sawfang pink
doth grin upon the careless fly it thinks to pinch and collar, thus to bash and fry
up with its morning eggs!

I see, O handsome hansom, harangued Blue, his pimply eyes fair starting from
that head in which lurked all the arcane secrets of the growing lens trade.

Well, boy, this loopy smirk doth mean that "I" doth wast but meant for you to
take unto your very own, to clip and close unto your chicken breast!

To take? To clip? To have and hold as men do clutch on burning sands an icy
cola drink or other effervescent poppy potable?

Yea, even so! I am the doughty vehicle 'twert meant for you, the engine of your
fate and Karmic destiny. That's why I sit here in the glop and dogshit of this
clinkered avenue. I wait for that sure hand that is attachèd to your arm to seize
upon my very quick and such and schlepp me all away.

My twinkly coupe! Is it but so and thus?

Indeed, O raunchish paladin of swell romance! It boots but naught a flash of
time—Great Plodding Time!—to lay your calloused yet artistic mitts upon me
and swift break into a lopish gallop. Else a steady jog!

It is but so and true and well I mean to cotton to whatever thus!

Then did the knobkneed Blue embrace the magic wagon in full view of all the
human offal and the riffs and raffs of hoi polloi who'd gathered moblike at the
wondrous spectacle of Blue, in all his quivering delight, speaking wingèd words
straight at an old abandoned wagon, left as jetsam by whatever cult of bimboed
scalawags. Then did he hump and heave and roll away the talking cart!

His equipage korreck! His mode of travel bunked and battened down as is the
squatting nuthatch in the misty fall! Thus did they rattle on toward home and
sweaty packing up and fevered fond farewells! The road! The road! The road
screamed temptingly as thus it doth and always will! So must it ceaseless wast!

« 7 »

A Brief Note
on a Traveling Library

But holt! and soft! Lest it be said, and, if all things go as they have always gone, it *will* be said, whatever that portentous "it" may signify, and significance, by Great Jesu's broken sconce, is all the current rage! That is, lest it be murmured that this meticulous joinal dared to withhold information from its reader, there shall be set down here a catalogue of the books that the Gavottes packed snugly away in the Cart before they rolled quietly onto the pine-besmirched macadam.

Picture then, if you will, a quiet evening. The sun, a pale magenta-yellow glob of crud upon the ancient sky. The leaves whispering and groaning under the assault of countless millions of gypsy moth caterpillars, known to etymologists as "hairy worms." The zephyrs tiptoeing 'round the eaves of the stunned houses in Vast Suburbia, there to fall down belching chimneys, and collapse into rugged septic tanks. The shy rodents savaging their lice and fleas. Yes! Picture Nature in her ordinary, everyday make-up! Nature, dozing and dreaming up perhaps an earthquake, or a small typhoon, a tidal wave or shy tornado, or maybe a spanking-new disease!

Serge is packing up the Cart, while Helene assists, resplendent in a burlap dress the color of what an impartial observer might dub "ooze." They are about to speak actual dialogue, the kind one reads in novels rugged as a septic tank or tanks, as see above.

I'm packing up some books, my palpitant flamingo root, Blue smiled tenderly, some warm and wonderful old friends that we can curl up with on the old trail when hailstorms bust and zap with wild abandon the roof of this our cart; or when twisters loom upon the far horizon. Thank gosh I fucking thought of it!

You think of everything, you swatch, the lady gleamed. What would the, as you call it, "old trail" be, without some well-thumbed, dog-eared volumes to delight the senses and fertilize the mind with their renewing horseshit? What volumes from our beloved stacks are you so carefully lading there, as lade you must?

29

I'll apprise you of these dear old pals, Serge said. And then there issued from his throat, by way of his mouth, of course, the hearty bellow that made his bride's vitals quicken and, at times, actually sprint! I have here *Pushcart Maintenance in the Field* by Anton Harley, a spiffy how-to book that will prove invaluable, chock, as it is, full, of easy-to-understand diagrams and tips, along with a breezy biography of a big wheel; *Supper at the Kind Brown Mill and Other Rustickal Pieces* by Joanne Bungalow, a small garland of inspirational poems that are guaranteed ne'er to bring a blush to hidden cheeks of mother, sister, sweetheart, or wife, so filled are they with icy chastity; *Stolen Fruit* by Jymes Vulgario, a little gem that can only be described, according to the *Pfarmville Pfrig*, as "shemmering"; *The Truth About Vegetables* by Harry Krishna-Rama, a prose work that evokes a world of variously factual sentences; *Your Ass Is Itchy: Mange in Pack Animals* by Trinidad Burros, V.M.D., the snappy little number that might best be summed up as a treatise that is almost like a momentary painting that quickly disappears; *Eating Your Honey* by "Beeline" Lingus, all about a gent who fell into a bare den but was saved by his fanlike ears—a passel of woodsy boffs; *Sexual Fulfillment in the Woods* by Birch Humpper, a thinly disguised *roman à clef* about Emerson's two-week stay with Henry Ford at the fabled spa, Walden-Saffron; and a "companion volume," Henry's own privately published *Repairing Your Tree's Crotch*, the classic study of what the *Adlerian Review* called "barking in the act"; then there's *Wild Fruits of the Lower Hudson* by Stonewall Cerrado, the latest in the "Perry Agony" series, a tightly constructed gem that deals with sex as a manifestation of the food-gathering process; *Country Album* by Nicholas DeSelby, a *nouveau roman* in which the West Wind tells a Blue Story; *Staring at Salad*, the blockbuster by Jayzee "Fleur" Belle, the big, inside novel about the lettuce industry that Tony Brouillard called "the most important novel of the last two weeks"; *American Lake Poetry* by George Stardust, a big, bold, brawny anthology of, as Mr. Stardust notes in his Introduction, "the seamy, yet tender poems of that group of majestic, half-forgotten American bards who live on the shores of our majestic, half-forgotten American lakes"; *Rich Hours Amid the Mint* by Colonel Bela Brilliant, Miz Belle's husband, a "weekend" counterfeiter and the outgoing president of the Lettuce Combine; *A Doom of Daffodils* by Armand Bientôt, a sex-mystery set in the glittering frenzy of the New York magazine world's "fiction" departments; *Lick Up a June Beet* by Derace Kingsley, a new paperback on food that James Gotee called "a rebellious book to 'turn on' the quirkiest palate"; an unpublished novel, in actual xerox copy of the original translation, by Jorge Cabrón, called *Gypsy Midnight*, which, although I have not read it, has a history of death, sex, black magic, and bewilderment behind it; and for dollink Zimmerman, a favorite of his, *The Daddy and the Drake*—little Zim is, as you know, driven to the alps of rapture by the meticulous descriptions of the garbage that the heroes of the book discover on divers nature trails. I must also mention *The Red Swan* by Dermot Trellis, a book that, I suspect, might serve to—heh heh—help us get it on sex-wise, could I but unearth the pornography from the murk of its text. Do you think we are, how you say, set, my tit-nosed craneswallow?

Is a wondrous bunch of tomes, Helene blushed. But there's a small and peppery little novel that I have just begun to peruse upon the last few evenings that I'd love to read aloud to you, or you could like maybe read to me, after really hard days on the old trail, hump-busting days, as they say in the streetlike purlieus. It is a cute and perversely risqué little book, translated from the Frog by Harold Roseate or Horace Rosebush or Harry Ross or something, called *A Weedy Music*. The original is titled *La Musique et les mauvaises herbes* by Anon. Can we take it with us?

Of course, my biblemane, Blue chuckled around the kazoo that had started suddenly from his rugged lips. In the fucker goes!

Thus did they prepare for the life of the mind on the trail in the sun and the rain and other nudges of Fond Nature! So 'twill ever be!

And with that, the sun fell heavily into the scrolls of silver snowy sentences, and the water also.

≪ 8 ≫

The Homely
Carte, or, Blues
Ecclogue Joyned with Helenes

O climbe *Helene* climbe on this lustie Carte,
All raynbowed lyke the rotting Sloe or Plum,
Its whyte lyke Snow, its black jette as your Fart:
Climbe on *Helene* and rest thy stynkynge bum.

HELENE:
Ah *Blue*, musician faire, thy words are white,
As putride Egg-plante in foul galauntyne:
O look, the Cartes wide canopie so bright
Doth make the slow wormes arse count not a bene.

BLUE:
And see *Helene*, the wheels lyke Pepper-ringes,
That in a Salad drown in stynkynge Oil.
The spokes resemble Cowcumbers and things
That nameless multiplie in charnel soyle.

HELENE:
My female parts rest on this Cushion faire,
Like doth the scum on steeming cabbage Pie:
'Tis yellow browne as dung-encrusted Pear,
And firm yet softe as muck in noysome Stie.

BLUE:
And jumbled therewithall the antick daubs,
(A Blobb, a Palme-tree, and a greesie Pott),
Do decorate the canopie lyke Slobs
Whose Mouthes are filled with Tuskes all green with rot.

⟨ *Blue Pastoral* ⟩

Heigh hoe *Helene* thy Toes are thick with Mud,
Lyke Holly-hocks all pelted down with Rain,
They twitch as with an Ague of bad blood,
Or lyke a bird-beshitten Wether-vane.

HELENE:
Ah *Blue*, my heart, thy wordes as brightly shine,
As do the jaundiced Days-eyes on these Rails,
As tainted Herring, flaskes of Rhenish wine:
Thine Eyes flashe blacker than my dirtie Nails.

And as the Smegma voydes its loathsome Seed,
So doth my heart shoot out its ball of Love.
I shake and tremble and my Pants Ive peed:
How grynnynge Cupids darte speedes from above.

BLUE:
Those sweet soyled Pants shall be our ensign brave,
T'announce our motley Waggon to the World:
The knighte, the heretick, the caitiff Knave,
Shall gape to see thee blush, thy Drawers unfurled.

HELENE:
Thy speach is lyke the Thunder in the aire,
Or lyke the creeking of these snot-green Wheels.

BLUE:
Thy nether parts so ravyshyngly bare,
Do glister lyke a Barrel-full of Eels.

And so my damp *Helene* the tyme has come,
To push this multi-colored Waggon West,
Euterpe tootes her Pipe and beates her Drumme:
The twanglynge dinn infectes my leaping Breast.

HELENE:
Sweete *Blue*, my roguish Turnip, my old Hatt,
I see the sweate upon thy Face like fat,
And now the rusted Push-carte sighs and heaves,
As rolling, smash we Fruites and Flow'rs and Leaves.

≪ 9 ≫

Interlude: On
Blue's Bicycle Clips

Blue had many different reasons, philosophical and otherwise, for collecting and wearing his bicycle clips, and many different styles of clip, and many different modes of wearing his clips, very few of which had anything to do with the current fashion, the *dernier cri*, if you will. His clips came in identical pairs, and it was Blue's penchant to wear them, always, *as* identical pairs, never splitting a set; it was also his penchant (some say it was his obsession) to wear one clip on either ankle, and to wear the pair in identical style on either ankle, never mixing pairs or modes of wearing same.

This "philosophy of style" probably had its roots in the many reasons that Blue had for collecting and wearing bicycle clips. He had no bicycle, indeed, he had not possessed a bicycle since his childhood (and even in those zesty days his possession of a bicycle in no way assisted him in learning to ride one). What were his odd, his checkered reasons, then? For collecting? For wearing? For wearing in so many diverse ways? We do not pretend to know, nor do we flatter ourselves that we can understand the "ideas" and "theories" hereafter noted. We hardly understand our own. With this caveat to the reader we venture forth and suggest that he collected and wore his quirky clips because of odd and even weird "needs" (as they say), most of which were, even to Blue, hazily mysterious as well as rather egregiously childish, if not infantile.

There is a possibility that he wanted to look like a rotten potato, since few doubt that the middle of his head, head, head was lead, lead, lead; yet he rarely dressed all in green, even when endeavoring to approach the chic splendor of Tommy Snooks and Bessy Brooks (two friends of his adolescence who had the perverse impression that it was always eight o'clock). Even though he swore that he believed in nothing more than ally-ally blaster, he was wont to assert, when quizzed on his sartorial preferences, "Love me, and I'll love you," or, and perhaps more disconcertingly, "Lullaby, Baby Bow Wow." As has been observed, although his brains were stuffed with corn and hay, he was a proud beggar—a

34

sop-sick bold-faced jig who cried for pie and who, when all alone, sometimes thought he was Jumping Joan, famed "unmentionables" model (though in June he changed his tune).

Though little Sergey wanted to play, his wife and helpmeet, the constant Helene, was not of silver: for instance, the north wind did blow on the poor poor thing, she was the best little donkey that ever was born, and her eye was too sore. Blue yearned to kiss a maiden all forlorn or, failing that, to attract a dirty slut and lie in the dirt. In truth he was a crass, dull jack-a-dandy and pondered such absurdities as: *How best to roast a snowball?* and *How many strawberries grow in the sea?* Certain authorities, in retrospect, have taken his erratic and eccentric behavior to be a manifestation of the sublimation of his desire for a gown of silk and a silver tee, while other, equally eminent researchers considered such behavior natural to a crooked man reared in a crooked house.

Blue himself usually maintained, sometimes belligerently, that his interest in the bicycle clip stemmed simply from the love he bore for Rosy and Colin and Dun, three childhood friends who, so Blue insisted, were sweeter than cakes and custard, and sharper than crying mustard. On other occasions, his answer to all questions as to his odd penchant was that his clips were substitutes for feather beds and wooden legs, neither of which, he laughed, would march him to the top of the "hill" and march him down again. Yet knowing, as we now know, that he was full of woe and had far to go, it may be the case that he simply felt the need to have more than just a bare cupboard to ease his misery on those days when he could not "blow his horn" (read: "play his piano") and was sure to cry.

Who can tell? The patient Helene once blurted that it was all but a frantic attempt to emulate the legendary Plum Duff, a childhood idol and raving simpleton who thought himself to be, in Helene's words, "a twinkle-diamond in a high sky," and who often claimed that he "liked to sally 'round the sun and moon" in order to "wash the spider out." But if the existence of a "Plum Duff" is to be given credence, why should we not be equally credulous anent the rumor that a pig without a wig suggested the bicycle-clip affectation to Serge? In all events, his wearing of the clips—his very possession of the clips—allowed him to run fourteen miles in fifteen days, certainly not a notable feat (no pun intended), yet, to put a good face on his slow, sleepyhead, greedy-gut ways, he couldn't work any faster.

It must be borne in mind that Blue thought himself wondrous wise behind his eyes, and since it is common knowledge that his father had stepped, *sans* bicycle clips, right in a puddle up to his middle in order to extend a pathetic fantasy as "King of the Castle," his son, Blue, often pecked off his nose to spite his case; i.e., he "marked his mood with a T," as it were. For what it may be worth, genetically

35

speaking, his father could eat no fat, he could eat no lean, he once, in amorous mood, got into bed and bumped his head, and he swore, to the end of his long and vacillating career (he couldn't decide on plum or plain), that each Arbor Day was the occasion on which he saw a balloon go up to the moon.

None of these speculations by us and statements by and about our subject can help us to get at the root of Blue's delight in the homely bicycle clip, and one may find more profit in sniping at the belief, which is nothing but a monstrous fiction, that proclaims the novel but absurd dictum: "All the world is paper and all the sea is ink." Finally, the simplistic remark made by an anonymous wag, to wit, that Serge employed his bicycle clips to warm his pretty little toes, may hold an Absolute Truth. On the other hand, there is a large minority that dismisses Blue and all his works and ways, with the ungenerous and even cruel judgment that he was nothing more than a dingty diddlety, an assessment that cannot be satisfactorily disproved.

The styles and fashions of his collection are, perhaps, more easily apprehended as to their intelligibility; that is, that since Blue was a firm devotee of the *lex campionis*, whose most salient tenet is "Nature art disdaineth," his taste in bicycle clips ran to the bucolic. He possessed clips in the fashion of the little marvel peapicker, big Mister Radish nose, favorite Whitney crab louse, quick-baring Haralson, pink-clump cameo, Anthony waterer (dwarf), penngift choke-out crownvetch, double pink starlike fairy, early mottled contender, Commodore Bush Kentucky wonder, old home pencil pod, vigorous class butterwax, compact fresh moongold, relish tendersweet tidbit, smooth royal Chantenay, Detroit dark red, King Mono explorer, firm flesh ruby queen, glowing gold nugget ball, tremendous Downing creamy yellow, gross fuchsia malleolus, Illini cob xtra, candystick cobby freeze, black swag Mexican, green-skin smoothie (dark), wonder-white amaze, tolerant Spartan dawn, triple scab mech, solid early belle cherry, French white bottom, rose China brittle, yielding baked blackini, semi-open Bennings green, squash oblong delicata, popular warted (Hubbard-type), pink jumbo Hungarian, Des Moines table ace, Laxton big Dakota progress, hot weather wando (summer), exciting Minnesota orange honey, tough Congo rind, rocky sugar rock (green-fleshed), gray Charleston iopride, triple streaker delight, big prize Max (custard-thin), fiery Jim Numex, Roma royal meaty chico, zippy verde tomatillo, small-juice bellarina (cold-set), fantastic early-girl cascade, self-blanche green wave, and ice-crisp reliable header.

It was in his styles of wearing his varied clips that Blue's invention showed itself most fecund, most impertinent, most playful. He wore his clips with a flair that *made* fashion, rather than followed its dictates. He adjusted said clips on his person in the single-ankle clutch, meat squeeze, slide-knuckle gripper, red-dog bite, chic scrimmage foot-pincher, birdie swathe, big-toe chukker, bunion scrum, cancha arch-cross, two-ankle jab, double-play caress, blitz nipper, eagle muffler, cesta enfolder, double wrap, left-handed slider, conversion sticker, driver scarf, four-thong frontis, skin-grab hat trick, triple long hug, basic-T gnaw, two-knot brassie, metatarsal dunk clasper, dermis-love scraper, high inside change, down swaddle, comfy spoon, shuttlecock sheepshank seize, dashing flare basket, bone force, single-wing prodder, flat-palm mashie, half-around wicket hold, full fly-front nelson, calf force-out, instep jigger, tri-laced bunt, baffy stroker, clip *au na-turel*, jug-handle grasp, double-wing probe, four-toe cleek, lapped-seam half-nelson, bails corn-encloser, flat-footed niblick, open-heel century, rosy-fingered homer claw, sammy intertwine, front-opening slide, scroogie wrench, and blind side-clipper.

« 10 »

A "Column"
in a "Newspaper" Gives
Blue an "Idea," Soon to Be Revealed

Tall, stately, flashing-eyed Lesbia Glubit leans back into the pillows of the choc-
olate-brown, crushed-velour couch in her studio ("It's really just an old *sewing*
room," she smiles), and laughs easily at something a visitor has just said. In her
openwork crocheted jeans, matching halter, and transparent plexiglass high-
heeled mules, she looks more like a statuesque Las Vegas showgirl than the influ-
ential, perky wife of the powerful Chairman of the Congressional Liaison Committee on the Arts, Harold "Hal" Glubit. Always overflowing with optimism
and energy, she seems even more animated today, bursting with ideas and opinions. She has just returned from addressing a group of high school art teachers in
the Oklahoma public-school system, and is still delighted over the surprise and
shock that her characteristically blunt comments aroused in those rather con-
servative educators.

"They were really tickled," she says, sipping at her fresh mint iced tea ("Gosh,
I *love* mint, don't you?"), "when I said that as far as I was concerned they were
right to think that their children—their *doggies*, for gosh sakes—could paint just
as well as Polack or Rossko or Frank Klein, or *any* of those other foreign so-called
modern masters." She grimaces pertly at the last word. "But they were *completely*
bowled over when I told them that the wallets and lamp-bases and pot-holders
their pupils made in arts and crafts class were Art just like Rembrandt Van Gogh
was, and all those other old-timers in the Dark Ages. I think I could have been
elected Governor then and there—but one politician is enough in a family, don't
you think?" She throws her patrician, yet strongly earthy head back and laughs
delightedly, her soft fall of ash-blond hair shining in the sunlight that cheerily
floods the spacious and immaculate studio. "But you know," she says, suddenly
serious and biting her lips together, "I really *do* believe that all art, *great* art, that
is, and not this stuff made for the so-called intelligentsias, comes directly from
the foolish hopes and the shattered dreams and the stupid aspirations, and, yes,

the small disappointments of the common folk. Look at the Indians, for gosh sake! Nobody ever gave them any lessons and look at those gutsy blankets and jugs and things. The vitality and strength of them! The alive vibrancy of buffalo robes and bows and arrows and canoes made of old pelts and such!" She sighs, moistening her full bitten lips, her perfectly manicured nails nervously darting in and out of the holes in her jeans.

Lesbia, or "Lez" as her friends on the Washington art circuit call her, with no small touch of envy and admiration, has always been known to hold unorthodox and rather gaily risqué outré opinions "about *everything*," she roars, happily, even, she confides, as a cheerleader and carhop in her native Ohio, where she was born and spent the first nineteen years of her life. "Oh heck, sure," she twangs, her eyes far away now, "I shocked my teachers *and* my customers back there in Plumber's Friend. Gosh sakes, all the time! I used to wear a rubber Dylan Thomas mask once in a while and those really *great* checkerboard pants he liked. Gosh, how I loved, adored, I guess, that wonderful, mad, raving man's work. 'When the October wind pushes up my hair with fourteen fingers,' " she quotes from memory, and for one split second seems on the verge of leaping from the couch. "Wow!"

It is no secret that her Senior Essay, "The Squalor of Andrew Wyeth," is still spoken of with hushed awe among the members of the Arts Club at Dead Creek Central High School, but Mrs. Glubit refuses to take credit for what has been termed its "iconoclastic brilliance." "Just really an adolescent attempt to, what do you call it? bust their lumps," she chuckles deeply, lighting her fortieth cigarette of the day. Her cigarettes are made of wheat bran, and to her exact formula, by a small, exclusive Georgetown tobacconist whose name she refuses to disclose. "He's a super-wonderful gay ecologist, really into whale songs, the Hemorrhoids Foundation, and solar-powered Judy Garland dolls, and I wouldn't *dream* of embarrassing him." Her eyes are far away again. "I practically *lived* with Dylan's poetry for three years,"she goes on, folding her long dancer's legs under her vibrant lissomeness. "He's so vital and strong, so vibrant and, I don't know, *alive*. Is there another modern poem that can compare with 'Do Not Blow Gently in That Good Wind' "?

But if her problems as an "art-rebel" (her own wry term) were pronounced at home, they were relatively mild compared with the difficulties her unique and cannily individualistic ideas have plunged her into here in old-line and innovation-suspicious Washington, where, she cheerfully and mischievously admits, she is known as "Boat Rocker," and where she had society abuzz last year when she arrived at a White House dinner, in honor of President Bruto Larsen Depravado of the Anti-Communist League of Central America, clad in a brown-paper tuxedo. And as the Chairperson of the Washington Women for Artistic Expression Club (WAX), and the first delegate to the "Art Is Life" symposium held last summer in the rubble of a Palestinian village, she has frequently become embroiled in disputes over funding for the arts. Some say that her high profile has been damaging to her husband's career, and that her activities in the art world have been partially responsible for the Ethics Committee hearings that Rep. Glubit faces next week. Lesbia Glubit colors at this, her emotions flickering across her face like red storm clouds, and jeers, "It's all just nonsense, for gosh sakes! They're trying to say that Hal was involved in some sort of 'impropriety' concerning some old *sheep* when he toured New Mexico last fall. Hal? We have our *own* herd of sheep out on the lawn behind the Jacuzzi shack and Hal hardly even *looks* at them! As his wife of twenty-four years," she says evenly, snapping off her words, gesturing crisply with her cigarette as her eyes spark and smolder, "I know that Hal is partial to Directoire lingerie. *Period*." She insists that her spouse welcomes the hearing and prays every evening for it to begin in the little chapel that he built with his own hands in a small glade near the sprightly rill that the Glubits have enthusiastically named "Our Rill." "Gosh, yes, he's so *anxious* to clear the air, to get all these charges out in the open so that he can defend himself and exonerate his good name in public, before his constituents and his family and the great American people."

Lesbia Glubit worries, however, that the long siege that her husband has undergone has interfered with his work as Chairman of the Anti-Christian Subversion in Education Panel, and that it has forced him to set aside initial plans for expanding the Art for All Fellowships for which he acts as Congressional liaison. "It's just the most *perfect* sort of job for Hal," she whispers. "He's so vital, so strong . . . there's something so vibrantly . . . alive about the darling. Like a gutsy work of art by someone like Tom Wolfen all by himself." She lights another cigarette and her eyes focus dreamily on the enameled ears of corn that hang, in daring asymmetry, from the ceiling, admiring their hard, clean lines, and, with characteristic modesty, neglecting to claim them as a unique creation. She "potters" like this, she will say, when pressed, "in my few moments of spare time," and declares that such work relaxes her and clears her mind of all ideas and thought. "Art is really better than Valium," she smiles distantly. "You can feel the hard knot in your stomach just melting, you feel yourself *tingling* with vibrancy and a kind of inner, almost a . . . religious strength." She quickly, and brusquely, gestures toward the ceiling, and confides that the ears of corn may symbolize rustic peace and innocence partially masked by acquired sophistication.

"But why talk about *my* daubs?" she whoops, looking admiringly at a tiny Krabo "Crayola" collage that subtly dominates a corner of her writing desk. "I suppose you've really come to hear about WAX and the work that we've been doing. I'm really *insanely* proud of it all—the way we've *slaved* to bring into prominence all the marvelous artists who are not part of the established art world." At the word "established," Lesbia Glubit's almost harshly strong and aristocratically bulbous nose wrinkles, and she stubs out her cigarette almost viciously. "I'm—we're—so bored, so tired of the usual work-of-art theories about style and things like that propounded by foreigners and big-city types, people that are really totally unrepresentative of the true artistic impulse of this great, vibrant, strong, *alive* land that God gave to our ancestors. The President himself, for gosh sakes, just the other day, was telling me how much he admires, for instance, the Aunt Jemima pancake-mix box ... what did he say? 'Makes us all proud of the America that once was, and, God willing, will be again.' Now, I don't know about anybody else, but I feel that that wonderful, *wonderful* man is a symbol of the hopes and dreams and yearnings of the American people—of their doubts, their inabilities, their ineptness, their human mistakes and greed and ignorance. I feel," and she looks out the window at the lonely sheep cropping steadily at the lawn, "that all these are mirrored in our President. Why not, then, their artistic tastes?" She leans back on the couch, exhausted, but her eyes are snapping and crackling with the unquenchable spirit that has made her legend. She does not call the visitor's attention to the framed photograph of the President that hangs above the couch, and that depicts a relaxed leader in a pair of shearling earmuffs, and, in his strong hand, the message: "To Hal and Lez and their wonderful sheep."

"WAX has begun, as you know, to turn its attention to the 'small' artist, the arts-craftsperson, the person in the small town or on the farm who makes rug hooks and model missiles, the isolated yet talented person who makes his own thongs and corks, the person who sews his name on his hat or shirt or somewhere. The *real* artists of America, beyond"—she sweeps her long and perfectly tapered, yet oddly gnarled and powerful fingers through the air—"the effeteness and downright *fruitiness* of Fifth Avenue and Hollywood Boulevard and their snobs." Suddenly, her athletically willowy body uncoils and she is off the couch that she has had, she has proudly made public, ever since her husband was a major in Headquarters Company of the Fighting Blue Star Devils during the police action in Korea, during which he was decorated for rescuing the company clipboard from a dayroom that was being repainted. (Hal, Lesbia noted in a recent interview, "doesn't like to talk much about it.") "Hal wanted me to buy something really marvelous for him to come home to," she blurts, when her visitor mentions the elegant couch, "and I don't think there's *anything* more *real* than crushed velour, do you? It has such a wonderful vitality and strength, such a

41

sense of alive, vibrant power!" She is talking as she bounds across the room with all the agility of her close ballerina friend, Debbie Sucoff, in "Cafard," and skips back, beaming like a child. "Look," she glows, and the visitor stares in silent awe at what seems to be a miniature reproduction of the famed Golden Arches of McDonald's, made from hundreds, perhaps thousands, of french fries, each casually, perhaps even insouciantly, yet meticulously, painted a bright yellow.

"You see?" Mrs. Glubit breathes, smiling with the beguiling and girlish innocence that even her foes on Capitol Hill acknowledge literally explodes with an indefinable charm. "This is the work of the most remarkable artist I've encountered in years and years! An old retired sheep shearer from Dubuque or Terre Haute or some wonderful, *real* state like that where people are still kneedeep in the earth . . . very, very few dark, foreign people in those great wildernesses, although," she quickly and graciously adds, "I've done many benefit things and auctions for Jew persons in Israel and places like that, Lebanon, Jordania, with Shucky Blitz and Jerry Duke. But do you *see*? Do you see the *space* in this piece? The mystery? The mystery of the *space* of all America? The vitality and strength and vibrant aliveness of America in this wonderful sculpt object?" It is, indeed, even to the visitor's untrained eye, wonderful, and she is as enthusiastic as she dares in the company of her brilliant critic-patron hostess. "Of course," Lesbia Glubit pipes, "of course you're right! It does have that aura of the strange, almost uncanny livingness of space! And this man—Bill Socks is his wonderfully curt American name—this man," and her voice drops almost to an awed whisper, "never has had an art lesson in his life, never has gone to a museum or a gallery, never has seen an art book or a post card or a reproduction of *anything*. Yet, you see how purely and powerfully he has captured the raw strength and throbbing vitality of this powerful image of the vast *space* of America?" She holds the sculpt object out so that the late afternoon sun glances off it with a kind of strange joy. "This uncanny artist has just been given a WAX grant to continue his work." Lesbia Glubit throws back her powerful, amazingly alive, chiseled face and her graceful neck trembles as she laughs delightedly. "I spoke to Mr. Socks on the phone last week to congratulate him and to ask him why he used french fries as his medium and he said—oh, this is so marvelously artistic—he said that he had run out of pickles! Isn't that wonderful? Isn't that so genuinely, so scrupulously representative of the true craft-sense? So utterly unaffected, so sweet, so *dumb*, like a Buddy Hackett or somebody talking about *their* artcrafts." She curls up on the couch and lights yet another cigarette, glancing now at the brilliant watercolor series done for her by Bart Kahane and inspired by the great French surrealist, Paul Valayne's, major novel, *Gallant Fates*. It comes as a shock to the visitor that Mrs. Glubit looks exactly like the lovely shepherdesses

42

in the rough-hewn yet accessible Kahanian world. As if reading the visitor's mind, Mrs. Glubit turns and says, with a hard and precise urgency, "Bart has had *some* formal training, yes, but there is a great raw primitive strength there too, a marvelous quality of innocence, a supreme lack of knowledge about painting that gives his work a kind of—what shall I say?—*vibrancy*. An . . . aliveness, a gut power and vitality!"

Turning to the compelling Socks from the haunting Kahanes, with the briefest of stops to caress adoringly with her eyes the strangely vibrant "totem piece" by Etta Peeche that sits on her coffee table, Lesbia Glubit, her features almost violently intellectual in the sunlight, says, "It's the utter, the unabashed simplicity of the Socks thing that I love, the extraordinary, almost predictable *banality* of the piece, so much like a marriage of, say, one of the President's speeches, a union leader's demands, and a Warhol film—that incredible sense that one has that the creator doesn't really *know* anything at all! That he is all . . . reaction and greed and thrumming—is that a word?—*flesh*. Gosh, the vibrant power of it, the *thereness*-wise quality of it!" To break the rapt silence that has intruded suddenly, the visitor asks if she would care to comment on the dozens of art-works and craftpieces that thrillingly, almost feverishly, clutter the Glubit home, this old munitions plant that Lesbia Glubit has redecorated, "with, I must admit, the loving and expert assistance of Bruce Prong of Bold Opinions, Inc., the eco-designers." She has completely changed the mood of the home as well as that of another building in back of the fallout shelter, a building, now a studio, that was once a barn, used by Mrs. Glubit for potting and weaving and knitting, and where, she maintains, she can almost hear the lowing of the cows that once inhabited the roomy space. "They almost—I know you'll think I'm silly—*talk* to me of what this earth once was, before the anachists and swarthy people started screaming about their rights."

"They're all on loan, of course," she assures her visitor, indicating the art that holds the warm old house in thrall, her voice slightly blurred with emotion. "But one begins, gosh, one begins to think of them all as old, old friends." Her deep womanly bosom, a constant reminder that she spent her early years picking cabbages in the windswept and locust-choked fields of southern Ohio, heaves, as she glances, soft-eyed, about the room. "Something like Jesus," she says, almost to herself. "Even Hal has grown to appreciate many of them, although his taste, before he met *me*," she barks appealingly, "ran to the garbage-dump neo-realist school—Vladimir Snatch, Leonard Brouillard, Garp Gardner—those people." Her face is a perfect, noncommittal mask as she carefully pronounces the famous names. "He had a very difficult time accepting and understanding the sur-abstract and proto-neo-surreal pieces, especially that series there on the sideboard,

the gesso-cellophane group of "turd structures" by Jigoku Zoshi. He said—
oh gosh, Hal is so real and unaffected—that they looked to him like a bunch of
s——." Her laugh is so sudden and piercing that the birds out on the lawn rise in
a frightened, twittering swarm. "He's come, however, to see that the commonest
images can be, in themselves, art, true art, an expression of total disgust and an
invitation to nausea, a cleansing nausea, a way of burning evil impurities away,
like we did when we dropped the A-bombs on the Japs."

The setting sun is throwing long spears of golden light on Moss Kuth's "Ero-
torug Number Three: Blind Ravish, With Heels," that develops its powerful
sexual motifs across every inch of the gigantic tapestry that hangs over the bar,
and that darkly dominates the space of the entire room. Lesbia Glubit moans
softly as she looks at it. "Now, that wall-object . . . Mouse—that's our pet name
for Mr. Kuth," she says mischievously, "told me at the opening of the Greater
Texas Art and Rodeo Fete last year in Killeen—and what incredible art-persons
are emerging from *that* area of the country!—that every one of the sado-eroto
images in that piece is reconstructed from his memory of all the pornographic
films he watched in all the motels he stayed in during his lecture tour through
the Sun Belt last year—when he was giving all those wonderful talks and semi-
nars as part of the Reverend Tyrell Bloat's Art Is God Crusade." Her visitor remembers and Mrs. Glubit is extraordinarily pleased.

Now she glances at her watch and stands up, apologetically explaining that
she has to get dinner ready for Hal, "and get into my Eva Perón apron . . . I think
that true camp has a real place in life, don't you? It's so . . . powerfully gay!" She
will be making, she confides, a variant of the classic Provençal dish, *coq au vin*,
substituting tuna for the chicken and "just dabbling around with different wines
and herb things." She adjusts the chic little apron around her trim figure and
laughs self-deprecatingly. "I was going to make lamb chops with cheese, but Hal
. . . well, his troubles with . . ." The visitor understands and walks slowly toward
the great, six-inch-thick steel door that the Glubits have preserved from the original plant, to "keep the nasty people away . . . I don't have to spell it out, I'm sure,"
Lesbia Glubit snaps heartily.

Her visitor shakes her hostess's enormous hands, hands that hold her for a
moment in a powerful and tingling grip. "Just tell them," she says, slowly, "that
it is our ultimate task to build, as John Wadsworth Whittier said in his magnificent 'Snowblind,' 'large audiences.' " The great door swings open noiselessly to
reveal the rolling emerald lawn adazzle in the golden light, and the visitor remarks on the sudden, breathtaking beauty of the bird-droppings on Mrs. Glubit's white Jaguar sedan—the unexpected loveliness of the free-form, greenish-
white smears against the pristine white of the vehicle. "Now," Lesbia Glubit
smiles, "*now* you've got the idea." And the great steel door crashes shut.

« 11 »

Blue Begins
Reading "La Musique
et les mauvaises herbes"

I SCHOOL AGAIN!

The broccoli garden of the University. It is the first day of class. The students are seated about tables. Marie Mamelle and André Lubrique are standing at the window. Mr. Aine, Professor of Music, enters into the broccoli garden.

MR. AINE: Hello, Miss! Hello, Mister! How do you go?

MARIE: Hello, Mr. the Professor! At the beginning of school we are always of the good humor.

MR. AINE: In effect. Who is the jolly young woman over there at the table in front of the window?

ANDRÉ: It is Sophie Jupon. That is a student of Gardening.

MR. AINE: Ah, Sophie. What a charm! And who is the boy?

ANDRÉ: It is Gaston Gaine, the brother of Monique.

MR. AINE: Oh yes. Monique Gaine is in the Class of Bassoon of Mrs. Chaud.

ANDRÉ: Sophie is very nice built, is she not?

MARIE: Yes, and she is always of good humor, even when rain falls in a large sheet upon her life. But let us go to class. It is the hour, is it not?

ANDRÉ: Yes, it is the hour. Good-by, Mr. Aine!

MR. AINE: Good-by, Mister! Good-by, Miss! Good-by, my dear Sophie! See you in a comics paper, switty!

II WHAT LESSON!

The students are in the classroom. It is almost nine hours. Robert Caleçons is at the window. He regards the young women who pass. Suzanne Jarretière is at the blackboard. She makes a giggle as she draws the idiot portrait of the professor. The bell tinkles. Mr. Aine enters into the classroom. He closes the door and says a good day to the students, which to him say a good day. He regards for a small moment the idiot portrait of him but seizes no notice of this. Then the professor speaks.

MR. AINE: It is nine hours. We are going to commence right away. Robert, count up the students of the class, if you please.

ROBERT: One student, two student, three student, four student, five student . . .

MR. AINE: Very good, mister! Continue, Suzanne, if you please.

SUZANNE: Six student, seven student, eight student . . . oh, Mister the Professor, I have a great ennui of this.

MR. AINE: All right, then. How many students are in the classroom?

SUZANNE: We are ten. Six boys and three young ladies.

MR. AINE: Good, Miss Jarretière! André, count the windowsill plants of the room, if you please.

ANDRÉ: One windowsill plants, two windowsill plants . . . five windowsill plants?

MR. AINE: Ha! Ha! Well, it is nearly that, but a miss is as good as walking for a mile, it is not so? Hm. Is it that you love much the music?

ANDRÉ: Yes, Mister Aine. I love much the music.

MR. AINE: You love not too much then the . . . gardening?

ANDRÉ: Yes, Mister Aine. I do not love *too* much the gardening.

MR. AINE (*enchanted*): Is it that the music is easy? Ha! Ha!

ANDRÉ: No, mister! The music is enough difficult!

MR. AINE: But you play well for a youth who regards without cessation always the young women who pass.

ANDRÉ: That is Jacques who regards them even more!

MR. AINE: Ah? Pardon me, if you please. Do you play the music at the house of you?

ANDRÉ: No, mister. We dig always the turnips at the house of me. But I play music with my comrades of the class.

The class continues thus until ten hours. The students make a number of the snores. The bell tinkles and the students quit the classroom in a large bustle. "Until tomorrow, misses and misters!" screams Mr. Aine. "And, Suzanne? Don't be a naughty young lady any more, or it might be that I will make the discipline on you!"

III THE OLD BOARDING HOUSE

It is ten hours of the evening. Charles Ordurien and Émile Fesses are in their chamber, at the old boarding house. Charles is seated at his desk of work and is preparing his lesson of the history of the accordion. His comrade of the chamber, Émile, is standing near to the window, his ocarina in the hand. Their neighbors, Robert and André, are at the cinema.

CHARLES: Émile, why are you not studying?

ÉMILE: I have not the inclination to study, my comrade. I have the blue. And you, my old man, you are not studying either?

CHARLES: No, I have the bad in the head. I love better to chat.

ÉMILE: But we have three lessons to prepare, is it not so?

CHARLES: Yes, if you count the exercise of tree surgery. And then, we have twenty pages to study of the history of the accordion and a composition to prepare for the carrot class.

ÉMILE: Oh truly, I have not the inclination to study today. Or tonight. À propos, where are our neighbors?

CHARLES: They are at the cinema. They don't work too much.

ÉMILE: In effect. When they are not at the cinema, they are playing at the bridge.

CHARLES: Yes. And also, sometimes under the bridge.

ÉMILE: Ha. Ha. In effect!

CHARLES: And you, you love better your ocarina than your studies, is it not so, my old man?

ÉMILE: Yes, *my* old man. I do not like of much my studies. They are of a type of work like the planting of the cabbage. Foh!

CHARLES: Play me, do, some thing. You play very good the jive.

ÉMILE: I do not demand more! Everything has made through hazard, and I have here my instrument. I love always to play of the ocarina and I love more to play the jive. I will play some tunes of the "Paul Whiteman."

Émile plays some hot bits. Then they prepare their tree surgery, their history of the accordion and their carrot lessons. They are working until eleven hours. Phew!

IV AT THE CONSERVATORY

Suzanne and André are nearly always an ensemble. André is not very serious; he blithers constantly and he loves always to play with the young ladies. At the end of the month he is always without a nickel. Suzanne, on the contrary, loves to work. She aids André to prepare his lessons and she often lends him two of the bits for to finish the month. She is not always of an accord with André but she likes him well. In the evening, Suzanne and André work often in ensemble at the conservatory.

ANDRÉ: Suzanne! I blither at you. You don't hear me?

SUZANNE: Yes, my dear. I hear your words.

ANDRÉ: Why you no respond to me then, my baby?

SUZANNE: I am not responding because I am finishing your paper on the autumn crocus.

ANDRÉ: Finish it quick and make me a "French" lesson, what?

SUZANNE: The lesson in "French" is not hard. Make it to yourself, my old man. Ha. Ha. Ha.

ANDRÉ: It is not possible. You are too much of an idiot! À propos, I am warm. Let's a little bit go out in the bushes?

SUZANNE: No, my old goat. Me, I am cold.

ANDRÉ: Oh well. Let us rest here then. Give me your skirt?

SUZANNE: Here it is. And now let me be tranquil.

ANDRÉ (*ravished*): Do not have a fear. I work *now*. This jolly item makes an aroma of the roses. Much good!

SUZANNE: It is not too much late that you work! But, take a guard of the old piano tuner down there. He is lancing us with furious regard.

ANDRÉ: He irritates me with the furious regard. Down the tuner! But is it that I irritate *you*, Suzanne, my chicken?

SUZANNE: Oh, be reasonable, my old shrub! You don't *irritate* me, but . . .

ANDRÉ: I don't irritate you, but I blither much, is it not so?

SUZANNE: Yes, it is that. But after all, I like you well, my old sugar beet. Though you are not to rend off my lingerie!

ANDRÉ: Pardon. I lost the control on oneself.

The discussions between André and Suzanne are finishing always like this. Sometimes, Suzanne makes André a "French" lesson. She is a good professor.

« 12 »
Blue's Grant
Proposal: Experimental Piano

My Dear and Esteemed and Honorary Congressman Glubit:

I am a young person of thirty years of age or so, *Gavotte*, *Serge* is my name; some call me Blue, as you will see if you think about it, this makes my pen name, Blue Serge. It is like a kind of a joke. Because I am deeply interested and in love with music of the expermentil type, and other types of music as well; so you will probably "get" the joke, BLUE SERGE, since Blue comes from the idea of a type of music, "the" Blues, of which, I have a feeling that you have heard, Honorable Representative Glubit, or "Hal" as they are want to dub you in the paper whenever you are in the news in a snapshot with your colleegs, or your charming and attractive wife; who, by the way, I am certainly praying and hoping is now over the unfortunate bout she had with cough-syrup addiction, and, has also set to rest the seemy scandal that dragged her name in the mud concerning some activities in a drive-in movie. I am so delighted that she has found Jesus and now cooks and sews while she listens to classical music in your wonderful home. It is wonderful that she has found Peace, as I saw in a paper the other day while at the campfire with my lovely and understanding spouse, Helene, and my strapping little fellow, Zimmerman, who we named after a folk-singer that you will soon guess, if I am any judger of men, of course I mean the famous Zimmerman Blanque, the young fellow who fell to his knees with Our President and prayed that God would strengthen the dollar; it is hard to imagine that he is the same rebbel who used to advocate drinking peyote and allowing Black people to attend the Yale Club.

You are probably saying, What in the heck is this young fellow speaking about by saying, around the campfire? And this gives me an oportunity to come directly to my point in terms of my passing remark about my life's great Passion, expermentil music, both playing it and the composition of the latter as well. For I am "on the road" so to speak. And why? I can imagine you asking quizically as you relax at poolside. Permit me, respected Representative Glubit, to pen a little of my History concerning my request for an Art for All Grant.

Ever since I was a small child I have been deeply moved by musical expression of all varieties. As a boy, my loving parent's gave me toy pianos and harmonicas and ocarinas, that the young boys at the time called sweet potatoes, but I don't know why. Anyway as you see, my whole life has been devoted to music. For a couple of years now I have owned a real piano, plus other instruments, to whit: juice (Jews' harp), harmonica, sweet potato (?) and such things. But my true love is, the piano!

I have suggested that I am "On the road." That is because a very wise, and wonderful doctor in New York City, the great metropolis where I reside and work as a lens grinder, told me because of some medical problems I was having with my oral interior cavity that I would always have these problems unless I satisfied my basic human needs. You can imagine how amazed I was when, the doctor told me I should set out on a search for the *perfect musical phraise*. That is why, I am "on the Road." I am traveling across the country with my lovely family in a pushcart I found outside the Port Authority Bus Station in Gotham town, and, my old and faithful piano. It is tough going especially, and you can picture this, up hills! And down is no bargain either, if you know what I mean. Also, I am not too well off in a financial sense.

It is a terrible thing to be a broke artist in this rich country, especially an artist like myself, who is seeking to expand and improve the Art of Music. That is why I am requesting this Grant from the Art for All Foundation. I will add to finalize this letter to you, my Proposal in the discipline of "Expermentil Piano" and what I plan to do in this field with any money that I might be so fortunate as to get.

I should tell you, before you start to peruse over my Grant Proposal, that, strange as it may seem, I have *never had a music lesson in my life!* Yes it is absolutely true. In the time that I have had possession of my wonderful old piano I have discovered for myself, practicing at least a half an hour a day whenever I could snatch a moment out of my busy life, how to play most of the wonderful old song from Porgie and Bessie, All the Things That You Were, and, some of that other old favorite, Green Old Dolphin. What is amazing about my learning so much of these two great Show-Stoppers is, that a friend of mine, who is, a very old friend that was in the Buddy Hackett J. H. S. orchestra, when we were boys growing up on the teaming streets of New York City, he told me one night after I had performed my repertoiry for some close acquaintances that my wife Helene had over for a seder which, as I do not think that you are a Jewish person you should know is a dinner that Jewish persons have on their special Religious hol-

50

idays, although I am not a Religious person; I mean, that I am not one of those Jewish persons with black hats and beards and white socks and such, or like in Israel a Jewish person who looks like an Arab and rides a camel but, I am a normal American-looking Jewish person; and my wife, for instance, does not have her head shaved off although, my wife Helene has had some trouble with her hair that seems to be falling out sadly, without any assistance from her Religion whatsoever. It is just Nature's great way.

But to go on. This old friend of my youth from Buddy Hackett Junior High, after I had played my selections for the assembled guests of which, he was of course one, his name is Sheldon; he told me that it was amazing to him, since it seems that I had played these two old nostaljic pieces, actually about one and a quarter pieces since, as I have hinted I am still learning Green Old Dolphin; without, this was the amazing part, Sheldon said, playing any of the black keys! It was really very funny and exciting that he said that as you will see, and perhaps be surprised at my early artistic ignorance, because I had no idea that you could actually play anything on those little skinny black keys! I thought that they were a sort of a decoration to make the piano look nice. I was really excited by this because after thinking deeply about it and tossing and turning all night after the seder, I suddenly realized that I could learn thousands of more notes and cords; I mean that I saw that a person could play all that he can on the white keys and then sort of start another artistic career based on songs of the black keys. I understood all this just before the doctor mentioned told me about my needs.

I now end with my Proposal that is submitted with great respect.

GRANT PROPOSAL, EXPERMENTIL PIANO   *SERGE GAVOTTE*

1. Take my piano in an as-is condition as of now, or, as-is when the terms of the Grant begin, and walk along the top of it in a pair of sturdy hiking boots, and to enhance the visual impact of this sight, wearing a pair of bicycle clips from my collection, nice and firm around both ankles.

2. As I stroll back and forth on my piano, I will smack and bash the keys with a branch torn from a tree that happens nearby. This whole performance will be performed in the woods, or, in some meadow or glades or someplace like that.

3. As accompanyment to smacking and bashing the piano keys I will sing and hum pieces of tunes about Nature of a folk-song and hottenany type, such as, the Weemoweigh, Wabash Cannonball, K-K-K-Katy, Lost My Mojo on the Brazos; and such like renditions. This is in order to blend a.) expermentil music com-

posed by purely sheer chance. b.) the Heritage of our great national music. c.) the wonder and glory of Natural Ecology. d.) the symbolical image of the Artist as a wanderer in the forests of the middle-class bourjose.

4. To add the undisputable elements of the Artistic life that are extremely important, I will occasionally suggestively touch myself in the pelvic, groinal area; Showing how thus errotic feelings are changed to Artistic one's by the well known fact of subliming them all into other things.

5. My wife, Helene, will take films of this Performance and this film will be shown at expermentil film festivals all throughout the nation. This way the great Art form of the cinema will be welded to the Art form of Expermentil music.

6. I will perform this Musical Happening in different locations throughout the country as I wander about, depending on how much money I get.

7. All this will be done together with my relentless search for the perfect musical phraise.

I hope, my Esteemed and Honorable Representative "Hal" Glubit that, you will carefully consider my Proposal and that you might even consult with your delightful and attractive wife who is, I know deeply involved in the Washington Women for Artistic Expression organization; as I saw in the paper recently and also a few months ago as she was observing senile and blind mentally retarded Vietnamese refugees finger-painting coasters for the USO. A wonderful woman!

With respect, I remain, as always,

"Blue" Serge Gavotte

« 13 »

Speech by
Rep. Harold "Hal" Glubit

Good evening, ladies and gentlemen. I come into your snug and wonderful homes tonight in the fervent hope that you will let me say just a few words in order to prove that when the going gets tough, the tough get rough, as a great American, and great man, once said, I believe at a country fair, surrounded by pies and pickles and great bushels of wheat and chaff and other such proofs of American folk-wisdom, and at a time when great effort and sacrifice were demanded of him. Yes, Abraham Lincoln! The very name gives us pause.

As most of you know, I have, because of the irresponsibility of the reactive agents of the media, which seems to believe that causing disruption and heartache in the lives of innocent people is a sign of "freedom," I have, I repeat, been cruelly and unjustly charged with moral turpitude, that is, doing bad deeds. Further, I am also aware that most of you, my fellow Americans, brave in the face of tornadoes and droughts and financial sacrifices, are aware that I must answer these charges next week before a Congressional Ethics Committee, a group of my distinguished peers who have never been caught, ha, ha, as the warm old joke goes in the halls of Congress. Of course, I jest. I hasten to affirm that I welcome with open arms this wonderful, God-given opportunity to face my distinguished accusers and clear my name, attacked as it is by these baseless allegations.

My family, even now gathered around the homely hearth and the Christmas tree, has suffered enormous mental anguish and emotional strain, not to mention nervous stomach and general irritability, because of this time of tragedy and crisis in all our lives. I would *like* to spend the long and lazy days, that are the heritage of all Americans, napping under a tree in the countryside, or lolling by a peaceful stream with an old fishing pole, my thoughts far from the hurly-burly and hustle and bustle of public life, warmly and wonderingly smiling at the bees that hum and buzz amid the honeycombs. But I cannot! In the tradition of George Washington at Valley Forge, I will stick it out if it takes all summer! The life of an elected representative offers no easy victories or simple solutions. I have, as most of you know, been presented with cruel choices: I can ignore my detractors and inquisitioners and permit my good reputation to be ruined, or I can face them and stand beneath the pitiless glare of their questions and the harsh light of their innuendoes.

I have chosen the latter course, having come to my decision after long and serious discussion with my beloved and recently hospitalized wife, far into the small hours with the midnight oil burning—ever burning. This decision was based on hard realities, since *you*, my fellow Americans, with your sense of justice and fair play, the great heritage brought to these indomitable shores by the teeming Pilgrims, *you* know that there are no simple solutions when it comes to slander and gossip, no magic wand by which they may be waved away. The battle will be, I know, long and hard, but I pledge to you that my head, though bloody, shall remain unbowed. Yes, I welcome the fray as I welcomed it when I served alongside General "Milky" Kidwell as a proud officer in the Fighting Blue Star Devils, *humbly* welcome it as I so humbly and gratefully welcomed each one of my twelve Bronze Stars.

This evening, I want to take a moment to probe the quality of the ridiculous charges that have been brought against me, charges that not only fill me and all fair-minded citizens with justifiable indignation, but that cut me to the quick because of their unspoken intimation that I am not a friend of Nature, that oldest and most fundamental of concepts, as the American people know and believe, and as I too know and believe in my heart of hearts. Nature! As a boy in my small home town of Griteye, Kansas, I recall, as if it were only yesterday, slicing up frogs and worms in the high school biology lab, compelled by these urgent tasks to a sensitivity to human needs in human terms. Later, in college, where I first discovered my love for the arts, I restated my deepest convictions by making excellent grades in life sciences the bottom line of my education; and as a major in the "Devils," as we boys so fondly called our proud unit, I found that, basic to the very fabric of the military, was a deep and loving understanding of the woods and fields and rocks and mud of the great gift of the vast outdoors. One of the most powerful weapons in the great arsenal of democracy is the love of the common soldier, the frank and open-faced GI, the boy from your home town or great metropolis, or a home town or great metropolis much like your home town or great metropolis, a simple, softspoken boy, yet with the heart of a bull and the courage of a lion, the love of that boy, my dear friends, for the simple grass, the ear of wheat, the ant and bird and lowly toad! Basic research has shown that the value placed upon human life by the American fighting man, far from home, yet happy and accepted with doughnuts and Coke in the USO clubs that I, as you all know, have fought long and hard for, that value rests squarely upon the deep moral obligation that he feels, that boy, for the idea of Nature turning the corner into a happier, freer world, a world set free from the shackles of totalitarianism and anarchism by our nuclear arsenal! It is ingrained in his simple, yet great, fiber. It requires sacrifice, but what worthwhile thing does not? And yet, without further delay, we must never, *never* forget! And while the Almighty God shields our peaceful land from tyranny, *may* we never forget! In such a way, do they carry their share of the burdens of freedom, these pink-cheeked boys, and also those brown-cheeked boys who also serve, as Rudyard Kipling, in his wisdom, said so long, long ago. If his words have any meaning at all, my dear friends—do *we*?

Contrary to every principle of international law and even human decency, I have been accused of—in the exact words of my cowardly tormentors—"suspect activities with sheep." I have had to make many painful adjustments in my life because of these vicious slanders; I have been shouted down by disruptive bands of radical ecologists and vilified in the media in editorials and cartoons, some of which have done a great disservice to the American people, and prevented me, because of the mental anguish caused by them to me and to my recently crippled wife, from carrying out my duties in the difficult area of the arts, areas in which my expertise and hard-earned compassion as a conscientious legislator with years of experience on the Hill, is often taxed to the utmost of the bottom line of excellence, as most of you know, I'm sure. I may add that I look forward to making this defense, and to stand in the hard light of cruel choices, since I know in my heart, and feel compelled to repeat, that I have done nothing for which I need be ashamed, nothing for which I need reproach myself. I am only saddened that the time that all this has taken has acted to impede the development of honing in on the worldwide problem of education and the arts and other major priorities that I know the pain and disruption and heartache of, like famine and earthquakes and human rights for all the people of the world.

Even my enemies in the liberal media concede that I have been doing an excellent job and that my years in the Congress have seen a healthy growth in certain sectors of American life that have been particularly hard hit. But my availability is running out as I go through these difficult times, working patiently, as I have been, to resolve this crisis and meet these challenges. I have no reason to fear or to despair, even though there are no quick and easy answers, and certainly no magic wands to maintain self-discipline. "Suspect activities with sheep," they charge. Yet I answer that I have always acted responsibly and as a proud American and good Christian when near our gentle, woolly friends. Some of them, I concede, and will be the first to admit, are very pretty, and display, as a constructive response to the pitiless light of insistent inquiries, an extraordinary charm. I have, and it is no secret to those who have known me over the years, often found myself on the verge of petting and caressing them—as I did when on my last fact-finding trip to the heartland of my constituency on the solemn and yet bravely brooding plains. This I gladly admit with open hands that are basic to the fabric of the law. I maintain that it was a constructive response and that I shall always be prepared to initiate it as well as other and perhaps more demanding constructive responses when the issues warrant them. But this humble act of solemn homage was the bottom line of my investigations, and I submit to you, my friends, that I did not exceed my authority as a public servant in any way. At no time did a sheep farmer perform an act of extricating his presence from my presence, nor was I ever in a solitude mode with one or more of these sheep. Top authorities have stated in committee that petting and caressing sheep helps build a more productive America, and those who bear the burden of public office know that a happy and more productive nation cannot be abolished by decree, the decree of a few radical-minded tyrants of the media. Yes, I have had to make hard choices, even cruel choices; yet I know that I must fight for the right to tell the truth as I see it, the truth that stands forever courageously as the spot where the buck stops for all responsible leaders of this once-great, and soon-to-be-great-again nation, that has been moving forward ever since our hard-won victory over international communism and atheistic anarchy in Vietnam, ever since the day that we grasped to our bosoms that shining light at the end of the long tunnel of war and sacrifice!

Bogged down in bickering and delay, a panel of eminent medical authorities has not been able to achieve consensus as to the condition of certain of these sheep, either at the present point in time, or at a past point in time, that is, the day after I returned to my office in Washington to assume my duties to provide some relief and take all available steps in this difficult transition period that we are now entering. And this delay *in spite of* the fact that the entire nation feels a sense of urgency about these painful adjustments and the cold statistics. This panel, drowning in bureaucratic red tape, seems united and determined in one thing—*not* to exonerate me, despite the overwhelming evidence that those few sheep are in excellent condition, and far from showing any signs of having been the innocent victims of "activities." I feel certain that the traditional sense of fair play that exists among the American people will compel the Ethics Committee to awaken to their solemn responsibility, a responsibility, I am compelled to reiterate, that I too know the awe and unpopular heartache of. It is far beyond the time for mere empty gestures, especially in this era of the worldwide skyrocketing of a sensitivity to human needs, and an almost desperate sense of urgency that cries out to be heard! It is certainly not the time for narrow partisan politics, but a time when all the members of both great parties should rally to bind up old wounds.

Added to these fundamental causes in every area of challenge, most of you have been made aware, in the last few days, of a further slanderous attack upon my reputation and my devotion to integrity. The moguls of the media, the nabobs of negativism, the sultans of suspicion, have seen to it that I have been accused, tried, and convicted in the media of another charge of which I am wholly blameless. I have received information and I have received irreproachable signals that these unspeakable allegations have been designed to bring about the cancellation of my announced plans to run for another term in the House. But, my friends, I shall not cancel my plans! No! Now that we are about to turn the corner and leave the long and sad road of broken promises, the people will, I know, rise as one glorious body that will not be stayed. These additional smears, the cowardice of which I shall address in a moment, must be stopped in their tracks! I have never been one to refuse to face cold facts and despite cruel choices, to set tough measures.

These slanders, as you know from the stories that are spilling over in the media, are centered in the false allegations, and how I welcome them so that I may show them up for what they are, of a Miss Martha Clifford. This unfortunately disturbed young woman, of whom I seem to have but a vague memory as one of my many campaign workers, claims, in her sad delusion, that I wrote her certain letters signed with the ridiculous name "Henry Flower." She further claims, and how my heart fills with compassion for her troubled, even retarded state, that these letters are immorally suggestive in nature, and that they include quotations from the outspoken poetry-writing of the poetess Lorna Flambeaux, with whose works I am totally unfamiliar. I have decided to defer comment on these preposterous allegations, except to say that Miss Clifford, who is not prepared at this time to enter into serious discussions concerning these fantastic charges, is an unwitting dupe of greater and more sinister forces. I am willing, I indeed feel a deep moral obligation, setting aside for the moment the cruel burdens of office, to meet with her in a calm and rational manner, in human terms, and with our attorneys present. I feel that no man in public life should be immune from the cold clear light and raw statistics of minute examination. But should a private citizen, a deeply and pathetically confused young woman, who, at this sad rate, will in the near future be the number-one enemy of sensitivity to human needs and dignity, *also* be immune? I don't think that justice permits such flagrant lack of sacrifice.

Miss Clifford has suggested, on a network-television news program, that I, as this fantastic fabrication "Henry Flower," mention, in her words, "weird things with soap"; that the letters speak of "adventures in the bushes"; that they quote "at great length" from Miss Flambeaux's "really raw and obscene" poetry-writing works. These saddening hallucinations are transparently designed to impose upon me the role of the hapless defendant, shackled by the heavy burdens of office and the role that I play in the legislative processes of this great nation. This emotionally crippled young woman, whose very name awakens only the vaguest spark of recollection, clearly feels no twinge of justice and fair play and no deep moral obligation to the universal reality of standards. She surely must know that this pathetic invention of hers will be picked to pieces in the cold and cruel beams of inquiry and shown to be a way of reaching her great goal of short-term fame. That is why she has refused to release to a clamoring media anything but so-called photostatic copies of these so-called letters. Letters that I—taking precious moments from the cruel choices and moral burdens of my sense of urgency and the duty of my responsibilities—supposedly wrote to her. How sadly absurd! Her act, though the act of an emotionally unstable fellow human being desperately in need of expert psychiatric help, must be viewed much the same as an act of international terrorism. And so I am prepared to invoke the principle of self-defense because of this assault upon certain sectors of my character. That is, I charge Miss Clifford with vile self-promotion! Yes, my friends, this charge is basic to the fabric of a free society, a nation about to enter on the road to a moving-forward process into a world that guarantees a fair share to all its citizens. Yes, even the most humble! I charge her with, I am compelled to repeat, self-promotion and the publicizing of her name and person, at *my* expense, a process entered upon in order to accelerate her fame, a fame that is still in the pipeline but that has not yet been reflected in the notoriety that, I charge, she fervently desires to be showered upon her by the public that has always been available to take all necessary steps toward a winner.

I should and I will now proceed with other verbal-type measures in order to make clear certain proofs to resolve this crisis. At the exact same point in time at which this pathetically misguided young woman was taking steps to attack my name and sacred trust, she was appearing in the current issue of a degraded publication that panders to the basest and lowest sector and area of human nature. I refer to the monthly magazine, *Hump!,* in which Miss Clifford, Miss Martha Clifford, called, in these pages that insult and debase the American woman, Mariette Cliffe, appears in a four-page color-picture story as this disgusting magazine's "Miss Garter Belt of the Month." How sickeningly vile! Are not this young woman's charges against me startlingly transparent? Isn't it clear to all thoughtful and morally straight Americans, poised as they are on the verge and the sheer brink of hard questions and profound moral choices, that Miss Clifford saw her chance to capitalize on the upcoming Ethics Committee hearings by further blackening my reputation by a manipulation of factually false data? And all for the sake of short-term fame!

As I have suggested, and repeat in the strongest possible terms, I welcome these allegations. They will enable me to protect the quality of my moral burden and my hard and cruel choices; that is my solemn responsibility, and I shall not shirk it. They will permit me to embrace anew the integrity of often restated convictions. They will, and are, even now, compelling me by the effort and sacrifice they demand, to the sense of the universal reality of painful adjustments. Effort and sacrifice! Terms, my friends, that cannot be vanquished! Terms that must have passed through the somber thoughts of Douglas MacArthur, that saint of the battlefield, when he first heard the dark news that a few of his troops on the Yalu River were being forced to retreat a little . . . yet he persevered in his effort! And his sacrifice! Effort and sacrifice! And even more importantly, rather than abolishing these panic-stricken slanders, these neurotically self-seeking slanders, by decree, I am now more determined than ever to place no trust in magic wands in the most fundamental defense of my solemn and deeply understood moral, yet *human*, obligations to the simplest and deepest terms of my vows of office.

In conclusion, dear friends from the blizzards of Maine and the swamps of Florida, to the mud of the Midwest and the smog of California, all of you, let me say that there have been, there are, and there will be no broken promises softening the harsh burdens of my sacred trust. This I vow to you! A more productive and decent America expects no less, and deserves much more. We are standing at the crossroads of a strong and progressive destiny, and as we take the path into a common humanity of a world of prosperity and stern moral imperatives, we may say, as did Franklin Pierce so many years ago: "Most fundamental! Most wonderful! The extraordinary array of deep moral pain and joyous unbearable burdens that we choose to embrace with a glance toward our harsh but blessèd duty. We are on the verge!"

I thank you all, and may God bless you. Good night.

« 14 »

Puissance Art
Disdayneth (A Dramatic Eclogue)

SCENE: The leaf-strewn and tyrooned esplanade, alleyed in the zangent sun, the odor of cherry blossoms affonted all in the air, and borne by wifts, just after the planging, toporite speech by REP. GLUBIT. In the far vast, the slow blurm of anxious winbows, slarm, yet hoark as blumbering tomatoes in the slow ballooming of September.

Enter BLUE, HELENE, REP. GLUBIT, and his aide, LUNK.

BLUE: A-say! A-say, powerdong and efficacious Leader! Oh, as the common lilac brents in hanged aslaver, enfundus of the wapping sun, so do I gronch and toad beneath the glasp of your so blastred wankèd eye, a loosome maggot nannyberry, poosant Dux, my muskled Congressman! I base, I base, and cronk the knee in volitude.

GLUBIT: Zounds! Ofeely burk this jesting lamster who doth quilp and quark my chesterfield? Ha! I do not reck his garf nor yet his nausee ambro, swink as bristly sarsaparilla, and blue as dido cucumber. Lunk, to it, blankèd ordinary!

LUNK: Har! Har! I'll cratch and smither all his scotch-broom blancophiz! Away, you snowbell scurd! Clear fast!

BLUE: Oh, por favor in your voozing play, most formidous and towered devil's-club! I call myself "Blue" Serge Gavotte, the creepy thing what penned and zipped to you, a-gulping clefstone of a mens, a sweetie billet, whingeing for some crankly lettuce to expround my teeny art.

LUNK: Scumball staggerbush! Begone! (He makes to cratch Blue's blancophiz.)

HELENE: Squeek! Squeek! Was it for such horrendo that I scramped up coppers for to save the whales and porpoisins? Carried testamentoes wheedling libertad for folk who dug on mooning, sackrinn Jesu? Oh woesome plote! For this I delved with nit-sprown hippies to seed the krishna's lucred acres with wholesome whin and pondspice?

60

BLUE: My tweet-voiced hammock-mate!

LUNK: Greeling twat! I'll scunge your osseous corse as well to boot, and pound you in the soured mulch as cully as a cissus—or a venomed hoptree! (Threatens HELENE with his larrup.)

BLUE: Don't lonk her nates, I wheengle you! (Aside:) O sobrous time!

GLUBIT: Hold, Lunk, my coeurish ancient! You have infinous time to brench this pair o' floots who shake like sweetgales in the vaxed and woorèd hurrinado. Let me but rap and parlant with 'em for a nonce, as fits a rexy integer like me am.

LUNK (groaning): It shall stook as your empyrean-ness wishes. (To BLUE and HELENE:) Scrullish blobs of grossed pipsissewa!

GLUBIT (to BLUE): Blatted carl, you enounce a billet penned and zipped abaft some lettuce?

BLUE: You convose all dexter, high-life Representative, I ween a lot.

GLUBIT: And this was shekels to emproud a art?

BLUE: Again, you've whomped the brassy tacks, my Chef.

GLUBIT: And, dumbo farkleberry, what art do you enclip?

BLUE: Weird experimenting cum a zonced piano, Eminous.

GLUBIT: Aha! A choose that shows your moronicity all candored as the woolly pipe-vine on the cat-house wall. And yet, although my earish organs are slapped together of a tinnish stuff, that svelty chunk, my spouse, the cosmetickal and aromatikous Lesbia, a spicebush meleed with a supplejack, yaks on mightily anent the faggish art.

BLUE: I raunch and scar all sanguinary these my knee-bones in dumbstruck adoramation of your swanky hump-mate.

LUNK: Up! Up! You bolus of a spittled, stinksome leatherwood!

GLUBIT: Soft, Lunk. Let the lumpen speck to drool and quinge. It sends feral zingoes all up and down my spine-cord. (To BLUE:) I hold a bedlamitic notion to embrave your bolsa with the moolah you empant for.

BLUE: O potentous Dooch!

HELENE: May granolas and vimmy herbs plonk and platch upon you!

GLUBIT: Conserve your toading drecky lingua, what hath as small spot here as doth a titi on a ice-rink! For you must blurt and burble to my harshoed satisfaction the answer to a quiz and all with narrow-perfect punctilissimo, youse toords!

LUNK (threateningly): And if you fok up, or even frigg the veraciousness of your replize—Ahar! I'd amour nothing morest than to blash and crinch you into talc, you wormy chinquapins!

BLUE (cringling): But foost away, O masted Imperato, and I'll scrample up my cerebellata for the reponders oll korreck.

HELENE (a-pinkie): As will I, Your Furor.

GLUBIT: Then, my dulloed tamarisk and ake my willied cinquefoil, a-futter me but this: Foist, did your nobilitous and glittray Congressman—thass me—beyant the urbish clammer, and amid the toothleaf dryas, tulip trees, sourwood, and drapping bladdernuts, in veracity improng some stupo sheeps? And, segundo, did this identico polysageous Rep—again, I mean moymem—sloom cartas troo the post, cartas chokked with erotickal and pornamorous sluck, to one Miz Martha Clifford, a tittied, beamish princesstree, if ever one was vued?

LUNK (stronking his leadish bully): Parlee right, my grimbling yellowroots, or Lunk'll bansch you into mucksh!

COP (entering hoddily): Whut dis? Do I bespoy me eedolato, Humpy Hal? My chappoo is dopped to yer, My Gosh! But whom be dem scumbrous wankos dere? Dey besprake a tandemite of heebie hipperoonies.

LUNK: A brace of anti-kristarchites, goddish copper. Asince Sir Glubit sprecken, they been beggaring, the wumps!

COP: Beggaring the sageous Hal? I'll jungeon dem belike two dangèd fetterbushes! (He crimples BLUE and HELENE with bangling steely changs.)

GLUBIT: My fundo thankees, zealot coppo. Yet holt a jott, for I am plingling for these nadired chinaberries to give reck and replondito. Tawk, caytiffous muttballs!

LUNK (swatching BLUE and prinking HELENE): Hablo, lespedezas!

COP: Scurfled hip-heads! Kikey fongs! (He twists the bangling changs.)

BLUE (bubbering): Though deeped in basèd awedor of you, my Czarish Sconce, I am poshed to spik the truth. I assump that you, indade, beneath the nopping bilberry, did enhump a couple sheeps; and, two, that boining smuts, by you inscribed, were zapped to Martha, the clitorical Miz Clifford.

GLUBIT: Fowlish scrud!

HELENE (a-blench): I do bleeve so also, Crood Potentor.

GLUBIT: Chunkassed nannypoop!

LUNK: Har! Har! Hoor! I'll bronk your crockles unto morte!

COP: Though me tudding heart embangles wit you, Lunk, morte is eighty-six! Is not too koolish, dig?

GLUBIT: Unlease them! Vaunt! Abaft and wongo! I can ill a-clasp another scandalment.

LUNK: But, Ominence . . .

GLUBIT: Avaunt, I say! Unlease, bullicious fuzz!

COP: Oy kin slup 'em in the slamgow, Roaring Rajah.

GLUBIT: Nopo. I wish the shitefaced duo domped like drooped cassiopes beforch the District Line. Out! Out! My stomach gorgeons.

LUNK (thunking their arsesfat): What fortunatic bomble-crapps you are. *My* wish is to enflagellate you both unto the oozy bloshes of your quicks.
COP (herding BLUE and HELENE off): Pee-peed snottochunks! Git!
BLUE: Awow, awoe. Thus great art is oft enfathomed.
HELENE: Screek, scrake. So arty martyrs grow like groundsel-trees.

Blackout

« 15 »

*In Which
Blue Discovers Marys-
londe and Is Given Advice*

The which Serge Gavotte, being before mentioned, and having departed the glistring Capitol, is here set forth more largely, complayning him of his great misadventure in his Quest, whereby his mynd was alienate and with drawen not onely from Helene and Zim, who moste loved him, but also from all former delightes and studies, as well in pleasaunt pianno-poundynge, as singing, catterwauling, and other his laudable exercises. Like April shour, so streme the trikling teares adowne his cheeke. Forswonck and forswatt below the broade beames of *Phoebus* golden hedde, the sayd Serge, plongd in payn, his tressed lockes ytorne, creepes beneath the pushcarte. The soote shade there somewhat cooles his madding mynd. There hobbles up the road a rustick shephearde all mottlie tatters, and of idiotick phiz, and thorough his oaten reede he blowes his wonted songe:

Tell me good pilgrim, what garres thee greete? What? Huh? Hath some badd wolfe thy tendre lambes ytorne and scoffed? Or is thy bagpipe broke? Thine oaten reede? Thy sweete potatoe or thy hellish concertina? Thine eyen, lyke jesting Aprille, quench the gasping furrows thirst with rayne! Or so to speke. Thy cheke appears a swymmyng-hole or else a catarack of splashes made of many catts and dogs, a curious quibble that, all trimly dight with rustickal insanitie. So, pouring traveler, the while I plange and bimp upon this reedy tooter given man by Romish *Tityrus*, pry ope thy rosie coarsened lipps and yawp thy loud lament.

What doeth make me mourne, moronickal churl, is that my holie Quest for the perfect phrase of musick is brasted up before it fayre commences. I whom sullein care does afflict my brayne, did leave the city of vain idle hopes, departing but a fourteen-night ago, or as thy dimly spluttering toong might blurte, but half a

moon apace. The crampe my joynts benomb with ache from humpyng all these
fardels in the pushcarte here which serves now as a cubb that does delay hott *Ti-*
tans beames, and humpyng too the swollen instrument the swarthy Moor yclep-
eth a pianno.

A pianno! By *Syrinx* daughter without spott whom whilome lickerous *Pan* did
cover in a fielde of Cowslips so that the redde rose of her cheke depeincten cre-
mosin, such the powre of his thrustyng arse, I never yette did heere a gigantickal
accordyon yclepped and nombred swich a thing. A pianno! How do you clip it
to thy breste to tear from out its gutts the frightfull noyse sike unpleasaunt thing
has dwelling in its bowels?

Siker old turde, thy mynde is decked with trash and swacked with fond mongolity! You are yblent and wood as *Ajax* bashyng in the milk-white lambes in windie
Troye. A pianno is a boxx unto itself and on its ivorie keyes I mene to plink a
sunshyny phrase all perfect as the musick from a besotted paddy's jank. But
whither fynd? O woe is me! The road has raft me of my merriment!

Ivorie keyes? Beyant the ground all strowed with Daffadowndillies, Cowslips,
King-cups, the prettie Pawnce, the Torticollis and the wall-eyed Variola, there
cowres a towne hight Marys-londe, of lustie shepheardes and their mangowe-
brested doxies, wherein the pipe the tabor and the tymbrels do be blaste and
smited from rosie *Iris* time till *Selenes* silver rayes turn all to moon men. Your
whingeing pilgrim tells of leas and meddowes not of corn or rye but of a weede
that drops all lewdly in the mudde its seedes of fayrest ivorie. In swich a londe the
rude and raunchy folke sicker know of musick, golden daughter of *Apollo* and a
knott-hole all ablush within the shady bosk, certes?

God forke the lightening on your honest sconce, encrusted buddie! I jump up
lyk a tygre or a bere whom fiers bees stynge to wildish vex! My pushcarte, my
pianno and my good wyf and son who sleping lye below this mound of crappe I
clep my gere, will renneth to this ivorie londe, and quick as black men in queint
canvass shoos. And to you, pyping rubeish imbecile, much thanks and thon-
drous graciados!

Then as the sunnye beame glaunceth from *Phoebus* face in swich manere as the
thonder cleaves the clouds, so that its christall rayes emboppe the seely Serge
upon his jollie sconce and his poor braynes gin to boyle lyke mutton gloppes all
medled up with greese in a huswyfes pott, this Serge gins to renneth adoune the

road untill the londe of Ivorie and thumppynge songe. Then loe, perdie, and well-awaye, among the wyld vine and the ivie there he spyes, lyke a lambe ysquawk-king in the wolves jaws, the walled towne yclept Marys-londe. He flyes as if on fluttryng wing and stretcheth hymself at large from East to West, doune hill and up dale, into bogg and brambel yplonges, the blazyng pushcarte and swoln pianno, and eke fayre Helene and snottie Zimmerman, gastfull of their lyves as they spede thorough the Holly-hokkes and Days-eyes in a chokyng clowd of dust and corses of insectes foul and lothsome. Anon they passe into the towne to car-rols lowde and Serge lookes round, his woe lyk smoke that sheddeth in the skye. Soon spying out a neatsherds boye, a lustie carle whose phiz was lyk unto a crynched potatoe, Serge rove these jollie words unto his colieflorie ear.

O pierless boye, I ken the nombres here do flow as fast as springe doth ryse: and so my brayne gins swette and glister lyke bright *Argus* blazing eyen. I see thine honest folke do lead the Millers rownde, the rustick galliard, the corantoe brave, and eke the goodlie turkies trotte, while with voyces loude as *Stentors* they doe sing and set forth delectable controversie so that all the woods them answer and their eccho ringe. Men clepen me Blewe Serge, and no man can my musick match, the which I tare forth from this dapper box, the queint pianno, a-bash-tynge of its ivorie keyes as thick as spottes in the proud Peacoks broomish trayne. Yet have I basht erst so long with payn, that all mine fingres do ben rent and wore, I hardlie oke hold up my heavy head, and I am all forlorne. For, jollie stew-faced frenne, I seke the very parfit phrase of musick, yes, a phrase to pitch great *Jove* upon his potent hammes! Now list: Upon the road that leads thorough mucke and noysome schmattes but lesse than a howre since, I did bonke into a drum-blyng imbecilick knave who, all decked in spittle and a gowne of falding grey and gruesome, told me that here in clamrous Marys-londe thy resounding folke my cornie feet might sett upon the path to *Olympian* felicitie and stopp these stremes of tricklinge teares that endorp my once brighte and twingling visage. For this old caytiff puttanato, though slackt the tenor of his stryng, into the porches of mine ear did pour a tale of fantastickal matter, ytouching on a mightie weede that droppeth seeds of pryceless ivorie. Soon as I gynst cipher two plus two I lifted up myselfe out of the lowlie duste: your celestiall musick and sweete ivorie seeds, the brothers of the keyes on my pianno, augment the thought that here in banjaxed Marys-londe, a weird folke dwelleth whose thought is all of carolling and dauncing and of whanging oaten redes and pipes and swich untill they brast. Where better place to find the parfit phrase I wayle for all the dayes till blakke nyght cleaves my helmlesse and nitt-packed sconce? Reward me then my pokky starker, do.

Har har, hoo hoo, and well-away! Thou art a babe as simple as a cackarooch. Tom Piper, for swich be the name of that patch-arse flieblowne turd upon the filthie path, has his braynes yrooted in his fondament. And thou, Master Blewe, where is then thine ear? It muste be fashioned out of tynne. This fowle, rumbaging, rownch, horraude, and clanching noyse is no thing lyke musick, but the tempestuous shriechs and clatter of sencelesse wormes. A parfit phrayse? Ho ho! And ivorie seeds? Hok hok! Heere groweth Rose and Bryer, false Labia, Juniper, poxy Kinesia, Eglantyne, Firbloome, the purple Aphasia, Cypresse, bastard Moly, the stynkynge Ailanthus, and the cock-leaf Ginkgo. But we have nor ivorie seedes nor weeds to droppe them, bumblynge clodd.

By *Christes* blood and His precious bones, I mourn, lament, and holler ruthfull to the louring skie! O woe! O lackaday! O balls and shite and onyons! The shitte of bulls and ybroken glasse!

Soft you my plaintive clowne. Sette your shoos that wexen dayly browne with crudde once more upon the road that ledeth to the place where *Phoebus* cooles his fyrye face ech night. For on that dooleful road towers the Universitie. There, certes, schollars yslonking thorough their bokes will halte their pedantrie and raunch thy woe from out thy pitteous brayne.

Then faire well honest lumppe, I gin to schleppe towardes brighte *Phoebus* tubb or sinke! The nyght nigheth fast, yts time to be gone.

Blewes Embleme.

Vinto non vitto.

GLOSSE

Plange) play an oaten reed off keye.

Bimp) spitte moste foule into an oaten reed.

Nombred) naymed foolishlie.

Swacked) fylled to brasting.

Mongolity) fiers stupiditie.

Plink) play, as a pianno, in ignorance of the blakke keyes.

Jank) emptie Guinness bottel in wiche Irish-men whose temples are distayned with wine do blowe.

Graciados) according to Chingado. Graciados por las señoritas tronadoras.

Emboppe) smashe wyth foul disdein.

Gloppes) chonkes of meat spoyled with barbarous magotts.

Crynched) fryed untill a blakke cole.

A-bashtynge) thumpynge with fistes and elbowes.

Oke) yea, indede, yopp.

Schmattes) glewie claye and not, as some fondly guesse, a shaypless gowne.

Bonke) bumpp into, encountre.

Endorp) make uglie as synne.

Twingling) such pretie word denoteth both twinkling as the sterres and
twangling as soote carrolls.

Puttanato) a baud, pandar, whore-mongre.

Banjaxed) astonied intoe jollie imbecilitie.

Starker) a knave be-lyke the slobbring ape.

Rumbaging, Rownch, Horraudde, Clanching) descrybing clamorous dinne as
of divils and deemons in Hell.

Crudde) mixture of dung, mud, claie, pyss, mucke, myre, swylle, and namelesse
fylthie elements.

Yslonking) poring, reading, scanning withouten joie or pleasauntrie.

Schleppe) hurle the bodie forward though slayn by blynde ennui.

Embleme.

The meaning hereof is darke: for Blewe by his pressynge forward to the West is
certes not subdued and so sayth the embleme. But he is vanquisht with ruthfull
dismay at the wordes of the stew-faced frenne in Marys-londe. The ambiguitie
ariseth from this, that a man who is vanquisht must needes be subdued, as has
always beene rehersed. Yet Blewe confoundeth thys understanding by his actions.

≪ 16 ≫

The Gavottes
Read a Country
Drama to Lift Their Spirits

Supper at the Kind Brown Mill by Joanne Bungalow

MOTHER: Well, Rita.
RITA: Well, good Mama, how you been?
MOTHER: I'm hearty, lass, but warm; the weather's warm;
         I think 'tis mostly warm on Bingo days.
         I met with Butch behind the shed: said he,
         "Mama, go in and cool your fiery heels."
RITA: Yes, do;
         And stay to supper; put your briefcase down.
MOTHER: How come, you painted punk? It's purest calf!
RITA: Cockeye, boy, get up and kiss sweet granny.
         Leather! Ha! But hold! Who cares?
         Some call good churning luck; but, luck or skill,
         Your butter mostly comes as cold and golden
         As if 'twere Christmas! I speak all arsewise, see?
MOTHER: Oho! All but this oozing slab that I
         Put here for Butch, the cunning morphodite;
         He always loved my butter.
RITA: That he did, God bless the hearty imbecile.
MOTHER: Has your speckled hen laid any eggs today?
RITA: Not yet; but that fat duck that I told you of,
         She hatched eleven out of twelve but yesterweek, bedad.
MOTHER: I mean to say, has she brought off her brood?
         I speak still of the old and crippled hen.
RITA: But I speak of the fat and faithful duck,
         Old crone.

COCKEYE: And Gammer, they're so tarnation yellow!

MOTHER: Aye, my lad; yellow as this butter here,
           Or as the gold that Gammer cleps her teeth;
           Or as my sweetie Cockeye's nit-packed hair.

COCKEYE: They're my ducks, Gammer; Daddums says so, reck?

MOTHER: You selfish little pig!

RITA: Yes, Gammer, he is a little pig; why,
           Butchie means to sell the duckies when they're fat,
           And put the money in this mattress here;
           And all to send his little Cockeye off to school;
           So Cockeye would not touch the duckies, no,
           Not he. He knows that Daddums would be angry else,
           And bust his arse.

COCKEYE: But, oh, I want to play with one; I want
           A little yellow ducky-wuck to take to bed!

MOTHER: A chill of fear bedims me that this Cockeye
           Here is like unto his pa; a morphodite!

RITA: I beg you close your mush, old wizened dam,
           And hold sweet Cockeye while I take him off to bed. (*Exit.*)

MOTHER: Hold sweet Cockeye while she takes him off to bed?
           It's plain as cowflop that poor Rita's mad!

Enter RITA

RITA: I must be going bonkers, ha, ha, ha.
           I think I asked you to grab holt of Cockeye
           There, while I would take him off to bed.
           Imagine my amaze and my red face,
           Aye, red and warm as Bingo days, when I
           Saw I held within my stringy arms
           Nowt but a pile of air! Oh, ha, ha, ha.

MOTHER: I kenned that you were acting mighty weird.

Exit RITA *with* COCKEYE
Enter BUTCH

BUTCH: Well, Mummy, 'tis a fortnight now, or more,
           Since I set eyes on you; by God above,
           And sure as it's October with its rotting gourds,
           I do believe, and so, I must insist,
           It's more like eighteen days!

MOTHER: Aye, Butch, my dear; but
             I reck that you been busy: so have we.

BUTCH: We? Oh, you do speak of father.
             I'm all agog and plumb wore out
             With fattening my tiny ducks. How does
             The good and inarticulate old man?

MOTHER: The geezer creaks about and does his work;
             But he grows stiff, a little stiff, my queen,
             Aye, in all those joints save the big one I love.
             Well-a-day! He's not so young, you know,
             By twenty year as I am, no, not twenty year;
             And I'm past sixty 'spite this ton of rouge.

BUTCH: Great Jesu's bones! That means he's, holy cow!
             Past eighty! No wonder I'm a morphodite!
             Still, he's hale and stout belike unto Cortez
             Silent in his pique in old Connecticut;
             And seems, the knave, to take some pleasure
             In his pipe; and seems to take some pleasure
             In his cows; and lambs, and gooses, and his
             Faithful duck. Aye, and a pride therein as well.

MOTHER: And well he may, bemuscled twisted boy.

BUTCH: Give me the little one; he's giving you
             A charley-horse, the kicking, wakeful rogue;
             He drives us batty with his loathsome squawls
             Just at daybreak when blushing Reet and I
             Are trying to tear off a quiet piece.
             What? You little oaf! Would you make a fist
             In da-da's curls? A filthy father, certes,
             And you as clean as spick; but ho! you haven't spent
             The blazing noon a-crawling after ducks!
             Aha, you laugh, you toothless putz?
             But if you live but seven year or so,
             These mitts of yours will be all grimy too,
             Aye; covered with a layer of crud and poo-poo
             From scrabbling 'round in swamps and rat-holes
             As are on the mere; whatever that may be;
             And you'll love mud, all manner of mud and dirt,
             As your father did afore you; and his father too,
             Aye, the same old duffer who's now all stiff

In every joint but one, if Gammer speaks the truth.
Yes, tot, you'll wade after young crows and stuff,
And spoil your clothes, and come home cold and torn
And wet; then, you know, you'll feel the cane;
Aye, I'll bash you in your arse, my lad!

Enter RITA

RITA: Don't spew such bombast to the blessèd babe!
How can you, Butch? Why, he may be in Heaven
Before the time it takes to tell of it;
I mean, I reck, the time you tell of here;
To him and Gammer sitting on the hob.

MOTHER: Look at the tyke. So earnest, such wild eyes,
Though crossed, just like his idiotic brother's;
He thrives, my dear.

RITA: That he does, thank Jesu on his Rood.
My children all are strong.

MOTHER: 'Tis good to know and well I wot of it!
But what mean you when you do utter "all"
Your children? I reck but three unless my eyes
Are blind with gummy rheum and crazed as is my brain.

RITA: 'Tis neither business it of yours; or Butch's.

MOTHER: Ah, well. Sick children fret their mother's hearts
To shreds and tatters and to orts and sherds;
And do no thing to help around the house;
A plague of buzzing, stinging bees on them!
But how now? Where's your little lass? I know
That you and Butch do keep her here, though well wot I
The blooming harlot bears no monicker;
Tell me I err; and faith, blow up the blaze.

RITA: Your daughter, my dear sister in the law,
And Butch's sis; she from whom he borrows
Frocks and high heels on St. Crispin's Day,
Came and begged her of us for a month or twain.

MOTHER: Well, well, she might be 'cuter than the rest
Of us, aye, that she might, the painted tart;
For she sits on her fat arse all the day;
Yet pays her way. A sober husband, too:
A stupid man; yet honest as ever fell

72

Into the sump, and withal fond of her.
But lack-a-day! She is missing summat
In the way of brats; aye, she recks it well!
Beshrew my zounds! If she but knew, as well she might,
How her poor ma did bust her hump! What ado!
And what a moil with my eight or nine or so!
Brats, aye, forsooth; they bring us lots of love,
But what a peace and quiet when they go far hence
To gaol or to the army or to marriage bed;
As you did, Butch, my strange and vap'rous fruit.
Aye; children are not rare.

RITA: How well I wot you speak, I reck, unto the point,
Old wrinkled Gammer in your dirndl rags;
No, not rare; no more so than the newtish eft.
But Hannah; is that her whorish handle?
Hannah must not keep our nameless tot too long;
She spoils her putrid as a dozen eggs forgot.

MOTHER: Aha! Folks be spoiling all the kiddies now;
When I was getting regularly shtupped
'Twas not the case indeed I ken and wot;
We made our childers cower in blind fear;
We made them slave, kept them in order,
Was this not so, my tousle-headed queer?

BUTCH: You were not proud of them a lick, old dame;
I know it well, as salt does sting a gash,
But busted each and ev'ry chop of ours,
Aye, once a day, and twice or thrice o' Sabbath,
You palsied, lunatic, and blear-eyed hag.

MOTHER: Yet you weren't bad by half, you bunch
Of sluts and bums; I sometimes felt a twinge
Of care, and once, some score of years ago,
I ween, I gave you each a gen'rous gob
Of peanut butter that I'd made one day
When I was whipping buttermilk and whey
'Gainst the encroaching freeze of January.

BUTCH: Aye! And sick as spavined gooses did we moan.
I remember clearly 'twas that day my sister,
Sandi, my dear sister who had the scarlet gown
I joyed to frolic in at football games, did die:

That peanut butter, Mum, was made of lard,
All rotting with bacteria and such.

MOTHER: That was, you wot well, you foul-spoken fairy,
Many a long-gone age ago; besides,
Your precious Sandi was a slut, in spades,
Who'd rather tumble than eat honest curds.
And now that you have made my trembling head
All achy, thinking on those tear-dimmed days,
I seem to have a recollection, son,
That you, yes, you, strange Mistress Butchie Boy,
Did a voice clear as a morning starling have,
Aye, like Fanny Brice or Babs Gonzales.
Do I invent of holy cloth, or wot correct?

BUTCH: I could a sweet lay belt out on occasion.

MOTHER: Of course you could, you shambles of a twit!
And now I recollect your dim old Da;
How he did love to hear you honey croon!
Though he, poor slob, had what the doctor termed
A tinhorn ear, or something such as that,
And could not recognize one tune from another,
The poor work-broken, sweaty lummox.
Do sing, my strapping fag; clap up the skies!

RITA: Yes, husband, sing. Oh, Mum, 'tis sure as rye
He got his brassy throat from you, aged clot,
And not from your arthritic spouse, Old Leech.
Yes, sing, so that this pewling brat will sleep.
I implore and beg you of it, for and sooth.

BUTCH: What number would you like to hear me hit?

RITA: That swell song of the blushing gentleman
Who is so shy he won't remove his pants,
And dies of inanition of the crotch.

BUTCH: Aye; of the purple grapes and crimson leaves;
But, Mum, put your shawl and bonnet off;
And Rita, lass, I hauled some cresses in,
Whatever weed that that may signify.
Just wash them up, toast the fatty bacon,
And scramble up a bowl of eggs or so;
For let's to supper shortly, ere we pine. (*Sings.*)
What? You little punk! Who would think it now?

74

No sooner do I cease my chant, than you look up.
What, by God's wounds, would you have your daddums do?
Sing from now till crack of doom, you dribbling snot?

MOTHER: The glutton heard the bacon on the fork,
And aye, the fork too, sputter in the flame;
He also heard his mama's heavy step,
And the quacking of your duckies at the door.
Where did you get that song? 'Tis new to me.

BUTCH: I bought it of a roaming peddler, Mum.

MOTHER: Did you so? A peddler, eh? Oh, ha ha ha.
Well, you always were a mark for love songs, Butch,
And the odd and lisping men that huckster 'em.

RITA: Cute Butchie, lay the kid's head on your arm;
And if you'll schlepp him but a minute more,
Or the nonce or two, and sing another verse,
He needs must sleep t' escape the dreadful noise.

BUTCH: Do you sing, Mummy, do.

RITA: Aye, crazed old hunkie, do; 'tis a long, dry moon
Since we have heard you sing your innards out.

MOTHER: Like enough; I'm old now, 'spite my bouffant wig;
And the girls and lads I once did lullaby,
Can now eat plates of soup right off my sconce.
Why in Heaven's name should I sing some old crap?

BUTCH: Why, to pleasure us; just sit there in the ashes
Where you are, all snug and warm and smold'ring,
While I pace gently with this yowling brat.

MOTHER *sings*

RITA: Asleep at last; and, bedad, 'tis time he was,
Or the sweet hay was not once the green, green grass.
Turn back that homely sacking, Butch, my hub,
And lay him down; and, Momsy, will you please
To draw your chair up to what we call the board?
The bacon's burned unto a crispy toast,
And the eggs glow yellow as the duckies
Which crash betimes right through the window pane.

They eat, ringed by adoring ducks.

75

« 17 »

Blue
Receives a Sign

Down this westering road, said Blue, we must hump our weary frames, my juicy bamboo seed. For it is somewhere past the glimmering horizon that we shall find The University and, perhaps, the answer to our quest, if gallant quests may be said to have an answer—or maybe not!

Hump on, brave Blue! My wrinkled soles ever faithfully do plod in your booming wake! Or e'en that which the spavined world doth laugh like craven flies to wild apostrophize! Or is that wildly?

Huh? A radio? harked Blue. And like chucked away by someone into the noisome vetch! Probly don't work worth a roily fuck, but let us see . . . hmmm. Static, crackly sounds of faint electrical impingements . . . and, what? A human voice!

Let us, my lumbering bear, dig on the quaint sounds of this woodsy environ.

Shh. The voice grows clear as mountain stream achock with salutary pesticides . . .

". . . yessir! Ole station WASP right here in Hamhock, West Virginia, WASP, the howl of the Alleghanies, the home of the hoedown hits, the rendezvous of the rubes, the crux of country, the pinnacle of plastic, the house of hype! And who'm I? Yore favorite DJ, Big Boog Vinch, playin' only the tunes that you like! This portion of our million-dollar show is brought to you by the Reverend Dr. Piscardi's old favorite, Gel-O-Mowth—for breath like a lamb—and Dr. Piscardi's *great* new product, Oro-Sux, for great gums and a gorgeous gob for guys and gals on the go! I'm onna turn yall over now to the Reverend Dr. P, for his daily message of Hope and Peace, a break in the middle of the hectic day, yessir, that fabulous moment that we all know as the Piscardi Pause. And after the good Reverend talks to yall, ole Boog'll be back with some more fabulous country socko and rocko!"

"Good day, ladies and gentlemen. This is the Reverend Dr. Piscardi, humbly wheedling his way into your cowering Christian hearts, and a-hoping that your sweet smiles, given you by the grace of JE-sus, have been made just a little more dazzling through the use of one of the plain country products that JE-sus hisself asked me—many years ago, while I was sunk in sinful fleshy lust and lechery and vile alcoholic stupor, silent upon a mountaintop like Sergeant York—yes, asked me to make for his greater glory and his . . . LOVE! So whenever yall put a big ole spoonful of Gel-O-Mowth well down in there among your gnashing molars . . . whenever yall roll an Oro-Sux lozenge—and they're now available in two new flavors, pecan and persimmon, as well as in the regular standard delicious flavor, witch hazel—yes, whenever yall roll one around in your mouth, sweetening your breath and strengthening your teeth and a-making your gums pink while yall get through your busy modern lives, I beg you, I BEG you, down on my KNEES, to think on JE-sus, and remember that my little company is dedicated to HIM! Yes, my clean-living friends, every time you buy one of these humanitarian products, you are siding with JE-sus!"

It sounds, my foursquare weasel, like the hearty baritone of that urbane swell, Doc Chick! Can it be a sign? Blue quizzed.

"Last night I was sitting out in the weeds behind my old red barn, picturing my beloved maw rock and creak on the wooden porch of agonized memory, yes, and a-thinking on how my wild and depraved youth cut short her clean Christian life, cut it too short, and a-wishing that JE-sus had found his way into my stony heart with his little tender feet afore that dear ole woman passed on. I am not ashamed to admit that I sat there in the tall Missouri razorgrass and the squinchback clover . . . weeping! Yes, weeping like a gentle gal who's lost her drawers and's feared to come home and face her paw. I KNEW that I had done gone and dedicated my life to JE-sus and his grace! I KNEW that my good country products were a-helping, in their humble country way, to make life cleaner and sweeter for the good folks—and their mouths—of this mountain country! I KNEW that I had put fornicating and blaspheming and drinking behind me, like unto JE-sus's command to Satan when he done ordered him to get in line behind him! But! It didn't seem, there in the peaceful twilight a-falling on the tumbledown hencoop and corncrib, to be . . . ENOUGH! And then JE-sus, a-knowing that I needed help and support in this crisis, stepped into my heart with a thud! He didn't say nary a word to me, but suddenly I remembered something that had done happened to me years ago, just after I had been RE-born! And I knew that JE-sus, yes, JE-sus Christ, wanted me to tell you a story, that JE-sus, hunkered down among the sheep, wanted me to express his wishes.

"This was something that happened many years ago, my good Christian friends. Just about the time that Abnerville got throwed up on top of the Wheeling High School Official Fallout Shelter during a fearsome thunderstorm. Many of you kind hearts have wrote to me out of the goodness of your trembling spirits, telling me of your opinion that this catastrophe was JE-sus's manly judgment on

Abnerville because the Jee-yew drugstore there on Main Street did not choose to carry the Piscardi line of pure Christian products, but carried, instead, some Godless Jee-yew products from Nee-yew York. Be that as it may—it is not my purpose to speak of what JE-sus has in mind as far as them Jee-yews are concerned, but it surely was a judgment on them when a couple hundred of them, mostly Commonists, was a-killed by the Nazis, who, when all is said and done, were good, hardworking Christian people! Some folks think that they done paid the price, these dozen or so Jee-yew criminals, for the crucifixion of Our Savior on a cross shaped like—and it is a historical fact that scholars don't want yall to know—a Hebrew dollar sign!

"Anyways, about the time of JE-sus's vy-rile manifestation in the streets of Abnerville—and who all can forget how the great whirlwind of his righteous wrath whipped that Jee-yew druggist's Commonist beanie-hat spang off his head and cast it upon a heap of offal over to the town dump?—about this time, a group of dark-skinned, bleeding-heart anti-Christs in the legislature, that corrupt Sodom and foul shame of this fair State, got themselves into a foreign-inspired, evil, Commonist cay-bal, and tried to sneak through some anti-GUN legislation! Yes! They were a-fixing to take our GUNS away from us, a-knowing full well that the country is ridden with anackists and do-gooders and fellow-travelers who all want to tear the pure little Christian babies outen their mothers' wombs and then make them all read schoolbooks that are corrupt with stories about swell-headed niggros and sodomite fornication and atheist-Jee-yew ideas! And even stories that tell our innocent children that there is something wrong with defending Christian freedom by a-blowing up a passel of Commonists!

"And at that time, filled as I was to the brim with the FIRE of JE-sus Christ's power and LOVE, I knew what my duty as a hard-working Christian businessman was, a businessman who had done spent long hours in the lab under the guidance of JE-sus to bring the first batch of Gel-O-Mowth to perfection, I KNEW what that duty WAS! I set out on a holy journey all through this hallowed land so as to bring to dust this unholy Commonist legislation. I asked only one question of the good country people who send these Judases to the State Capitol, where most of them spend all their time in lustful drunkenness with Jezebel secretaries and other impure young women who show off their bodies without no modesty atall! I asked these honest folks who tremble afore the grinning face of JE-sus one question: If these hook-nosed Commonists take away our GUNS, how are we all going to kill varmints? I did not even have to speak on the anackists and such! JE-sus done inspired me to mention only varmints! And it was enough!"

That *is* the voice of the fabled Chick, Blue muttered breathily. Something about the way he weaves magically the most boring anecdote. But what is he

78

doing out here in the leaf-strewn boonies? Is it an . . . accident . . . that we "found" this radio in yonder blasted foliage? Or else . . . ?

Let's listen hard, my powerfully muscled spouse! This might be what they call, in distant and star-spackled Hollywood, "Kismet."

"As all you good ole country people know, we are hemmed in on all sides by . . . LIVING THINGS! Knothead polecats, wartface spudchompers, fanged blue ducks, eyeball turkeycocks, the dreaded singing raccoon, and a hundred other vermin and varmints, living and scuffling around in the leaves and mud, eating anything they all can, and breeding in sinful sweaty pleasure like a covey of ignorant niggros. If we let these beasts alone, what do you all think would happen? Yes! Yes, my craven Christians! They would soon outnumber us all, eat all our vittles, ravish our daughters down to the creeks at night, take our jobs—and soon there would not be a Christian left in all of West Virginia! And the infection would spread and spread until every Christian *everywhere* would disappear, or else shut his mouth about JE-sus for good, a-feared that he'd be et up by a horde of pusfaced hawgs! And if there were nary a Christian, it figures that there wouldn't be no Christ! Yes, they were a-trying to destroy JE-sus!

"When the courageous folks of the muddy peaks and scorching valleys thought on this for a while, thought of a life without JE-sus to fill them with fear and terror and those healthful night sweats, they riz up with a roar of righteous savagery and threw that Jee-yew law in the sump! Where it belongs, the darkest sump, where the bright light of JE-sus's grin will never be seen. I am humbly proud of my small role in defeating these Christ-killers, as well I might be. And though the varmints continue to breed like the sex-crazed and lecherous animals that they are, the good folks are a-keeping their numbers down with the avenging fire and hot lead blessed by JE-sus hisself!

"A final word, my dazed-in-Christ brethren and sisters. While I was a-bringing the word of JE-sus to the towns and villages and shopping centers round about this holy land, I was often asked to address large groups of God-fearing people: the Daughters of the Sacred Fetus, the Brotherhood of Christ the Sharpshooter, the New Baptist Bund, Inc., the Taxpayers' Rifle Squadron, the Pro-Jesus Mountain Pogroms, Inc., the Poll-Tax Party, and many another. I took care not to offend . . . and how? By holding in my mouth at all times an Oro-Sux lozenge, secure in the knowledge that my breath was as sweet as the breath of a baby lamb, and knowing too that the healthful juices a-sloshing around in my mouth were a-purifying my breath at the same time that they were a-making my teeth as strong as steel and my gums as hard as mountain shale! And if Oro-Sux stood up under this kind of a test, imagine what it will do for you, as you go about your daily business!

"I thank you. This is the Reverend Dr. Piscardi, the Mogul of the Mouth, blessing yall in the name of JE-sus Christ, and reminding you that sweet JE-sus hisself, was he among us today in his glorious million-dollar flesh, would, I have no doubt, use these Christian products, these Christian products inspired by his LOVE! God bless yall till tomorrow, and sweet breaths to yall too!"

"Thank yew, Dr. Piscardi! That was a message to inspire us all, and it kind of makes yall think about what life is all about, don't it? Big Boog Vinch here, of course! And here to round out this Piscardi Pause with a song for all you folks who are a-shuffling down the ole highway of life—Yessir! It's the dynamic country hit of the year, Blackie Bob Hunko's 'Diamond on the Blacktop.' Sing it, Blackie Bob!"

Don't be blue in the black rain
Oh the Lord's a mighty good cop,
Ask him a couple things about pain,
Dark night and a diamond on the blacktop.

Once worked in the field
Sweat like a man
Married the girl of my dreams,
Alone now in dark and storm
Lord, what do it mean?

Recall a soft kiss,
Bitter tears but I left,
Hot, mean honky-tonk queens,
Alone now in dark and storm
Lord, what do it mean?

What do it mean? What do it mean?
What do a honky-tonk queen mean,
Lord?

Drinking rye whiskey and beer,
Gambling all my pay,
My wife was so clean, so clean,
Alone now in dark and storm
Lord, what do it mean?

What do it mean? What do it mean?
How come my wife was more clean
Than a queen, Lord?

My farm's gone and my bride,
Some boys and girls too,
That must be Abilene.
Oh, alone in the dark storm,
Jesus, what's it all mean?

Jesus, Jesus, Jesus,
That's small for Abilene,
My Lord?

Don't be blue in the black rain
Oh the Lord's a mighty good cop,
He'll ease up your pain in the rain
In the night, he's a diamond on the blacktop.

If that *was* the legendary Doc Chick, Blue confided—and I will swear on my lens-polishing contraption, e'en all o'ergrown with scabrous ivy as it is, that it is—that fact, gently intertwined with the earthy lyrics of this twangy canto, makes for a true and boldly portentous sign, indeed! The diamond on the blacktop must be a simaphor for the brooding University—somewhere yonder far! We are on the right road, my sweltering dogie!

Oh, Blue. Nor did I ever doubt your righteous brilliance else! Let's push!

The phrase is "let's push on," my rough-cut marmalade. What a card you art, and always wert, to boots! Ho-ho-ha!

Then they got crackling once again!

Or "cracking," as the modern phrase would have it.

But have it . . . *where?*

« 18 »

Eros Briefly Grins
upon Our Dusty Caravan

As we chunk forward through the blowing tares, my fairest box, I feel in the deep marrow of my throbbing bones that we are fair and truly on our way. Peruse said road, my faintly coloring wife!

Just so, be-biceped hunk. And what blessed relief. Yet, I feel but a jottish faint from all the sun my urban frame is not yet used to. The lucky Zim, like pike besplashed in icy pool, sleeps 'neath the schlock we call our "stuff." But this teeny canopy is no defense 'gainst vicious Sol's bright darts a-torrid, hein?

I'll haul our lowly coach beneath the blue inviting shade of nodding wombat here. I too feel hotly sweatish.

Aces, champ! And thus bedimmed climb up here thus to stretch and rest the sinews taut that you've long wrenched and vilified. Oh do!

I'll hence anon upspring, and putz to him who says a thing!

How trembling all my girlish nates do quake.

Take off your hat, my aloe. It's so hot!

That's not a hat, you tender squit. Hmm, it *is* still hot betimes.

It's *not* a hat? But then . . . ? Oh whew. I ooze and drip.

No, my craggy churl. It's what the rigors of the road and pond'rous slog have metamorphosed my coiffeur into. 'Tis not the dainty whiz of locks you spun, dear sweet galoot.

Sparkling and curvaceous thunder! It has the eerie shape of your fedora hight, and summat of its color too, like catfish stunned beneath an avalanche of humble pone. And yet, despite my crass mistake, flop on your back and tear my breeches ope!

My rambling blot! I thought you'd never hint your manly needs. But what think you of this other posture? 'Tis loved by those who favor knocking off a quick one in the kitchen while the tuna glops and nicely browns. Besides, it's so much cooler on my kneebones.

All reet with me. However steaming wench doth spread, I'm honored in the breach!

I'm honored by your sturdy poke, my hearty bungle.

Aha! How wild the warp and woof of wifely weft and wedge!

Thus doth a breeze spring crazy from the lolling meadows brast!

Oof oof oof, oof oof.

Whoopee! Whee! I reck not if my coif falls out, so let me buck!

Speak things that have a shade of subtle dirty filth to them, my peewee. It assists to help keep staunch and true a certain part of my anatomy. So lisp all softly through your fillings vast the porny stuff that true Christians evangelical do wallow in when they're in solitude.

Eee. Eee. I know your corkscrew human needs, voluptuous peach.

Then utter, wife, ere I slip out and, slipping, bash my elbows something fierce!

Sheer-black dwarf mistletoe! Hairy-crack catawba-tree!

Ohhh. Ooofff. Wow. And et al.

Big-tit common buckthorn! Butternuts in froth of lace!

Oh ump and huff! Oh Sacred Billy Graham! Whompp!

Lithe autumn-olives in transparent panties!

Whooff!

Sans crotch!

Fooff!

A Merry Widow clasping bouncy big-hipped and false jessamine!

I think that I . . .

Silk-buttocked garter-strapped and red-lipped tupelo!

. . . may void what great Erasmus dubbed the vital "seed." Wahoo!

Priapic imbecile! Heaving womanly embonpoint nestled in frail cups of stretchy rhododendron satin!

I do! I will! I spill and cascade thus my manly juice! And holler forth all stentorous as is my ennui'd wont, e.g., eeeeeeek-oh-ho!

And thus all fluttering I join thee in a wifely shriek, i.e., aieeeeee!

'Twas marvelous heavy and exceeding boss, my perch.

I felt like frail Justine who never failed to bump into a freak.

And now, since we are wild for health and strength and thus do straight eschew tobacco, let's have a snacko. What sort of victuals crouch in silent putrefaction 'neath these mounds of "stuff"?

Oh, Blue, my shining crow. You know I never feed betwixt what I am pleased to call my meals. Nay! Not if dread trumpet creeper nods in battle-fury vaunt!

You do not *what*? Then who are you indeed? You cannot be the sylph Helene, a broad whose noshing never ceaseth but in slumber!

Your heartless cruelness will out, as awesome Nature makes the caterpillar tear and rend the baobab. What? Not Helene?

I say not, no, or gumdrop-eating trees do not exist in hot Arabia! Why look, you seedy dandelion, this *is* a fantastickal fedora clenched upon your sconce.

Oh Blue, my rain-bespattered rusty lawn chair! I do admit my folly, yes, it is an old fedora on my bean. I wear it out of love for you, since yesterday the gritty wind blew out such massive quantities of my mousy locks I went in dread lest you should look on me as the stewed Comanche gazes on a ginger ale! But I am your Helene, 'spite this grim fedora. Can't you see?

I see, I see, amazing eft! But never lie to me again, for I despise and shrinketh from a broad which fibs to me, especially upon a day when I have shined my cache of bike clips!

My potent juniper! How I love it when you call me "broad." I feel like someone in a racy read, or showgirl deshabille in festering Las Vegas.

You'll always be a broad to me, my cheap romaine. And now, the fact you shelter underneath the brim of said fedora somehow fills my veins and arteries and such with steamy blood. Once more, my tender toad, up with your skirts, I do beseech you in a whispery mood of burgeoning amour.

Probe, oh probe again, my weird hyena! Plumb and dip unto my womby deeps, O hairy hawk! Pop me square right in the middle of what high-school boys yclep the nookie! I yearn and drop an Amazon of sweat! Pulsating ox!

Whammo, thus! Bull's fucking jaundiced eye !

Oh, oh. Oh, oh. And so on, honeyed aphid! Whoops!

« 19 »
The Sheep Interlude

Hard following upon that exceeding peachy shtup, my aromatic hubby, I am refreshed and crackling all a-zip with vim! My eyes peer down the lonesome trail with rejuvenated strength. 'Tis as if I spent a lustrum in an orgone box, thus doth my sated aura dominate this earthly frame.

I can get behind it, hon! I too am full to strange repletion with a pulsing throb of vigor! And so, let me haul and heave us forward toward the Goal! (He hauls and heaves apace.)

But stay! Hello! I hear a bleat upon the wind! Can it be so?

It is a bleat as of some tragic lambkin caught up in the briers!

It rents my heart. Oh, rescue him, or it.

I'll plunge into the tares and haul the wooly bastard out! (He plunges. Noise of ripping tares and cracking glades. After a time, Blue reappears.)

Although I ripped a throng of tares and cracked a brace of glades, I could not find the animal. And yet . . .

'Tis not the will of Jupiter or either Jumping Jesus. But what portends "and yet"?

This occasion shuttles to my brain, as ripe bananas enter vast metropoli on chugging freight trains, much sheep lore. Which, if you will settle back upon our worldly goods, I'll retail unto you. I made, while in my beardless youth, a study of the sheep, and I would like to share this store of useless knowledge with you, my iridescent starling. Sharing, as you know, my tongue, is the greasy cogwheel that keeps a marriage ever fresh, yes, that plus a decent salary and an occasional boff. Those of us dedicated to the higher things do not like to speak of "boffs," but there, as they say, they are.

Oh, share and retail ever fresh, my fond musician!

To save us time, I'll lug while I retail, if that is jake with you.

I dig the whole idea profoundly, sweets.

The sheep, as oft you know, or mayhap you have guessed, is a mere ruminant mammal of the genus *Ovis* and the family *Bovidae*; great Ovid was named after them, which is why he slapped together what we call the "Pastoral," a form that for some hidden reason has appealed to wild-eyed poets down through all the ages. There are lots of types of domesticated sheeps, the first ones being house-broke, as they say, on the scaly heights of Pelion some seven thousand years ago by the humble Jimmy Arvenites, the youth who first concocted Yankee pot roast. Although, to the unpracticed orb, they look alike, they are different in many a way, and each has a personality that glitters in the deep heart's core! Let me run it down for you in terms of nomenclature stern.

Run, oh run, my rough-hewn Sousa!

First, who can forget or long impugn the *Cotswold*? Ah, the gross and sooty-tufted Cotswold, who warms the heart because, despite his loathsome teeth, for-ever bucked, his disposition is as sweet as Father Flanagan's. In some quarters of this reeling globe the slob is dubbed "the fuzzy freak," yet his heart thuds on, exuding sunlight.

And what of the *Dorset*? That ringing name that conjures up hamstrung vi-sions of the crass unspeakable? Its only penchant, scholars know, is to gobble up, assault, and glut each scone and crumpet that grows wild in England's green land. Its minuscule hoofs are all misshaped, thus to assist him in digging the little rascals from their loamy oith.

And the *Hampshire*! Let us shout its homely name with heads on high and throats all swolled with bursting pride! The honest folk that infest the Blue Ridge Mountains have dubbed this smiling chuck the "Miss Congeniality" of the sheepy world, since every individual of this happy race, ram, wether, and ewe, will clip and tumble with any member of the kingdom mammalian on God's old earth and at a moment's notice! Also a coupla snakes and newts.

Then there is that guy the very thought of which and whom does make our eyes bulge with alacrity, yes! the *Karakul*. Its nigra wool so prized by bombar-diers and congressmen! Its voice so grating and its eyes so sloe! This shuffling dude is thought to be descended from that legendary sheep Ulysses ate on his first date with fair Penelope. Thus History doth make morons of us all!

Long ignored by the vulgar madding crowd, yet ever living at the deep heart's wide-flung door, we have your crouching *Leicester*, pronounced "Licorice." Called by wags "the cockeyed wonder," this brave and bloated fellow won his spurs in Cromwell's time by jumping off the high board at summer fetes, and, to the delight of the assembled Roundheads, landing on his back. Andrew Marvell notes his clumsy oddity in the lines he gives to say a contemporary member of the breed:

> Stumbling on Melons, as I pass,
> Insnar'd with Flow'rs, I fall on Grass.

⟨ *Blue Pastoral* ⟩

And do I hear you think aloud the magic word? I mean, the *Lincoln*! Though afflicted by the Irish curse, a need to laugh at davenports, its cream is prized by knowledgeable tribesmen. Named for our dear President, Old Abe, 'twas he that giant must have seen while lying wounded on the Bijou's stage in Little Old New York. His last words were: "I see some sheeps upon my own dear property, the Plains of Abraham."

Also but, we deny and give the shoulder cold, to our everlasting peril, to the scourge of the jonquil, yet with a heart of purest platinum, the swart *Merino*, who being Eyetalian, is a little black-eyed number, dedicated to leaching forth throughout his long and happy life, tons of that wondrous mozzorone cheese, thus making this his adopted land the foremost exponential of exotic foods.

May I include the *Oxford*? Ever mounting, though awash in sweaty perspiration, toward the ineffable "Yea!" this hard-pressed breed, pigeon-toned and dulcet-toed, is alack fast dying out, since two of three lambs born to the startled ewes is but a morphodite.

And so petite that he can hide beneath a sprig of violets, there can be no aspersions cast upon the dandy *Rambouillet*. A saucy Frenchman, he, who loves nothing better than to stand agog among the creaking oaks, his wickedly incisive frog-talk zonks out the soul of this openhanded nation. Enchanté!

Demure, yet bold as brass in every faucet of the gantlet of cruel existence, we now turn to the *Shropshire*, "sissy of the moors." No bigger than a man's hand, this lightfoot lad hides in weeds all day and by night slinks forth to crop and nibble the shoots most tender of the gorse-blooms that suffocate the heaths and meadows of all Wales!

Then looms the burly *Southdown*, brusque and buxom! The heart pounds wild and free to look upon this hombre who repays stern discipline and who requites the cruel yet kind lash by stealing apples for the lissome shepherd.

And last, though the mind doth goggle to report it, there lurches wild the *Suffolk*, a crazèd beast more horse than sheep, whose solitary hobby is to jump through hoops of burning gasoline upon the glade!

These then, my locust, are the sheeps that men have tamed. But there are also feral types, belike the *Asian argoli*, who sacks the baloney of the lone explorer in the Gobi; the *Barbary sheep* or *Aoudad*, whose dread castles made of sand dot the wilderness of windy ergs; and finally, the stalwart *Bighorn*, the mocking symbol to untold generations of weary hubbies of their wives' intrepid indiscretions.

Thus, my chooch, this interlude of curious odd learnings. Do you feel the intellectual fire in your frame?

I boin all up with education deep, delightful Serge.

Yet what's that creak? That sickening crunch?

87

The cart sways and doth . . . Oh! It's broken down!

Avaunt! 'Twill teach us not to hump and tumble on it! God grant that we may find a cart-repairer!

I'm sure we shall, dear weasel, for a sign we passed while you were in your teaching bag proclaimed that we are now in great Ohio.

Ohio! If we can't holler up a cart-repairer here I'll eat your so-called coif! (They settle underneath a muskelonge while Zim eats ravenously some hapless nearby ants.)

« 20 »
"La Musique et les mauvaises herbes," Continued

V THE PICNIC OUTING

Today is Saturday! It makes so nice, that Suzanne and André don't envy to pass the afternoon at the conservatory or the greenhouse.

ANDRÉ: Let's make up a picnic outing.

SUZANNE: Good idea. Let us pass to the store of foodstuffs and then go on the edge of the lake.

ANDRÉ: I am of accord. But I have not too much of the mazuma. Have you any mazuma?

SUZANNE: I have a little piece of the mazuma. Let us go there, no?

SUZANNE (*at the store of foodstuffs*): There you are then! I have some bread, some mustard gobs, some weenies, some pickle chow, some honey dollops. What makes it to buy still, my old weed?

ANDRÉ: Here are some potatoes fried in the cans. I love them well. Yom-yom.

SUZANNE: Me also, I love them. But we have not enough of the mazuma to buy any.

ANDRÉ: Oh craps. Well, and what is it that we drink, along with the foodstuffs over here?

SUZANNE: Some whisky for you and some gin for me. Does that go A-One with you? These beverages untie the moral knots, so it is said.

ANDRÉ: Very *well*! And buy me some cakes, if you please. I have a hunger like a tapeworm today.

SUZANNE: Ha. Ha. What a crazy young person you are! But yes, I buy some cakes. Do you much love the ones with a form of phallic symbols, the "Twinkies"? I love them very much.

ANDRÉ: I have much heat when I regard you them regarding.

89

SUZANNE: O.K., my old kink. I am truly enchanted by the idea of making a picnic outing. At home, the dinner is always so ceremonial. For the commencing, there perhaps is some kohlrabi stems in ketchup boats or pig-hock soup. Then there is the meat of the lamb or the goose with the greens and the fat of the backs and the white beans and finally the pudding of the chocolate with Graham's biscuits and the synthetic cream. I then am so filled up to the neck that I must make the excuse to depart away from the table and loosen up my unmentionable raiments.

ANDRÉ: Enough! I am of a complete folly with the famish and the heated lust also.

SUZANNE: The eyes on your visage pop from the head in regard of my body structure. And my sack of foodstuffs. Ha! Ha!

André and Suzanne pay the sweaty owner and with a large sack quit the store of foodstuffs. They mount each others in the auto of André and arrive some few hours later on the edge of the lake. Alas! The sack of foodstuffs falls into the current and sadly they live some moments of small agreeableness. They have much gloom to regard the foodstuffs cruising to the far side. Oh well, they mutter, and again mount each others in the auto to pass away the afternoon.

VI A FAILURE TO RELATE

Alice Cuisse, who is the comrade of the chamber of Suzanne, is ugly as a sin; however, she is a charming young woman that all the world loves. When Suzanne and André have a failure to relate, it is always Alice who arranges the things.

ALICE: What is it with you, my dear Suzanne? You have much of lessons to prepare on sycamore scrofula in the gentle ewes, yet you do not work.

SUZANNE: Oh Alice! I am very vexed up with André. If he telephones to me tell him that I am not here.

ALICE: O.K., my little girlie. And I find that you have reason.

SUZANNE: He is a brutal chap! He is lazy, egotistical, impolite, and a gluttony pig.

ALICE: I am completely of your opinion! Your young friend is of a great slobbishness.

SUZANNE: You have reason, ugly chum. But let us be just, if it attempts to kill us, even. He has some qualities also.

ALICE: Maybe so. But he is a sloth, egotistical, crude, and a grand swine.

SUZANNE: Softly, my charming homely pal! He has a good heart, a fine finger with the concertina, and a formidable thing. And when I have the blue, he finds always the way to make me titter or else, guffaw. Just last day I chuckled fit to crack a guts, as the Yankees speak, down on the edge of the lake.

ALICE: Oh yes? What did he make to achieve your cracked guts?

SUZANNE: Oh, he made the risky blague about a "Twinkie." But yes, he always can make me achieve to smile.

ALICE: And when you are of good humor, my little jolly tart, he finds always the ways to make you sob.

SUZANNE: Alice, why are you so mean? Is it for that you have the face to halt a clock of eight days?

ALICE: Better such a face like this than to have the feet with the round heels!

(*The telephone sounds. It is Alice who responds.*)

ALICE: Hello! Is it you, André, you pig? Eh? I am preparing the lessons on the fly of Spain. Suzanne is no place to be discovered . . .

SUZANNE: Alice! Give me the phone, you jealous flea! André? Don't quit the phone! It is Suzanne. Alice was but making the attempt to smash up my hump. You know what an envy she makes about our "French" lessons . . . yes, she is a disgusting phlegm.

ALICE: What a beauty of a slut you are! I have a great hope that you flunk out the bee-pollen examination.

SUZANNE: Eh? But yes, André, I of course pardon. No. No. It is me who is a beast of a chick. In front of the conservatory in ten minutes? Pack up the over-night baggage? Oh, my dear buddy, *o.k.*

ALICE: I pray to my God that you terminate up with the bun in an oven. You hobo!

SUZANNE: You have a jealousy for that André conserves his grand thing for me and not for you—you mouse-face dowdy!

Alice and Suzanne enter upon to slap and scratch each the other faces. They soon make however a stop since they are old comrades after all. Alice lends even to Suzanne a black lace négligée she received as a funny joke. Suzanne packs it in the baggage right up with her other intimate costumes.

VII A GOOD RENDEZVOUS

Yesterday morning, André took the coffee with Jacques Derrière, a student of musical spoons. The two young folks are of good friends since a long time. As they are serious students, the tone of the conversation was enough elevated. They are commencing to discuss a subject that interests sharply both the two of them.

JACQUES: My friend, felicitate me. I have made the acquaintance of a jolly young lady of the School of Fertilizer Arts. I had a good rendezvous with her yesterday evening.

ANDRÉ: Bravo, my old man! And how have you found the jolly young lady? They are charming of a habit, the lady students of the School of Fertilizer Arts.

JACQUES: That jolly student is no large intellectual, but she has many qualities. For one example, she has a formidable brace of the long legs . . . or should I tell, for two examples? Ha. Ha. Also, the large crocks upon the chest.

ANDRÉ: In effect, my old man! And is it that she gave to you some interesting "formulas"? Heh. Heh.

JACQUES: We had not to speak of the artificial dung, my dear old cabbage. We passed the evening at the erotic cinema. They exhibited the American film, "Hellions in Hosiery." I had great heat. Wow! And she paid for her seat.

ANDRÉ: Naturally. A poor student has not enough spondulicks to pay two seats of the dirty cinema. As Mademoiselle "Gams" is a jolly lady student, she comprehends well the situation. What did you do after the base film?

JACQUES: We took one cup of coffee near the cinema. We spoke of the filthy film, of our dull comrades, and of the situation of the garlic fields of Provence. As I have told, the jolly miss has few brains. Thus, when I made the small blague that I might pay for *her* seat, I have a fear that it passed away above her skull.

ANDRÉ: Thrilling, you old crazy face! Then, how did you terminate the evening?

JACQUES: To make some economies, we took the omnibus to return home. We did much beastly things therein. Then, in the vestibule of the house of this jolly miss, she made me a very interesting demonstration. She declared that the young lady students of the School of Fertilizer Arts learn much of the acrobatics. My God! Enchanting. Yet this morning I felt myself to be much like the little twisted cookie our old German friends have the inclination for.

ANDRÉ: The "pretzel"?

JACQUES: But yes! The "pretzel." This jolly young posy can of truth sock it quite of an abandon!

ANDRÉ: You had some good chance, you roguish mongrel!

JACQUES: In effect! I can hardly straighten up the back even now.

André and Jacques continue to chatter of interesting vile subjects. For example, André says Jacques of the "French" lessons that Suzanne makes on occasion with him.

Jacques has much irritation since Suzanne with him makes nothing but the ridiculous farces or speaks of her Fern Seminar whenever he pleads to disrobe of her the garments.

VIII THE SEASONS

Since three days it is raining without arrest almost. All the students put on of the waterproofs or carry the umbrellas. At the moment where our story commences, André has lost his waterproof in a turnip acre, and as the umbrella of Suzanne is not big enough for to protect all two of them, the young friends await the finish of a torrent in the entranceway of the library, where they have been to read upon some shameful, however exciting, narratives.

SUZANNE: Truly, I do not love this beast of an autumn! All that rain over there annoys me in the end. I love more the spring when it makes the sunshine, and I can stroll about the street or boulevard with the short skirts to reveal the legs, so as to give to the men the flushing face.

ANDRÉ: I believe perhaps that I am like the rain, since too, I annoy you in the "end," when I make the chance. Ha. Ha. This is but the joke, my broccoli. Yes, the springtime is a pretty season, of course. But I love also well the autumn. It is nothing of more amusement than a good match of football, even same when it rains. Except perhaps the naughty and risky spirited behavior of two young friends in the front of the fire that is ablaze!

SUZANNE: I like the football, me too, my old rutabaga! And as for the fire that is ablaze, well, is a location of good aspect for a careless "French" lesson, eh? But I don't like the rain, no, I regret the beautiful days of summer when I voyage to the beach.

ANDRÉ: You regret the days of summer because you know to stand up in the front of people and look jolly in a small bathing costume that reveals the long legs of you and a pretty backside. You naughty little sheep!

SUZANNE: Jacques Derrière finds that my large jugs are pretty too in the bathing costume. He should have been confiding to me that a brief peer at my flesh gave him to desire to bite quietly my thighs.

ANDRÉ: Jacques Derrière is a bag of the scum! I will hit his face off him for an insult of this order. I make insistence that I only can find you jolly with your clothing removed, or pieces of it!

SUZANNE: I love it when you are crazy of jealousy, my old big-nose person.

ANDRÉ: Me, I find that you are jolly also in a briefly made costume of skating when one goes to skate on the ice in winter.

SUZANNE: You sweet some thing!

ANDRÉ: Yes, I do! In effect, you are how the English men and women call "ripping" in the costume of skating. I shall have been always dreaming of your pretty gams in tights with the very, very small skirt that conceals not well the brief panties beneath. I often must take a seat at the rink of skating to make an avoidance of self-embarrassment at gazing at your flesh.

SUZANNE: Do you mean that the "poker" of yours gets very firm? Ha! Ha!

ANDRÉ: In effect, my fantasy! There is no young woman so jolly as are you, Suzanne. Even at this moment I feel a strange itch of my loins.

SUZANNE: How gallant you are this morning! It makes me feel as if the rain and cold that give me the blue are far from here. And a slow stare at the bump in your trousers makes a special tonic for me.

ANDRÉ: Let us voyage back into the privacy of the library, good?

SUZANNE: I have a great hot for you, my charming roughneck! Let us go back again.

Suzanne and André find themselves beneath a table of the reading room. It is dark and warm, and they cast off some raiments. Then the two young friends attempt of some interesting perversions. It continues to rain without arrest, but they are absent of cares.

« 21 »
The Cart-Repairer

As the sun busted down on beautiful Ohio, and they lounged in the shade of the friendly muskelonge bush, wee Zimmerman asleep, his little tummy bulging to satiety with his hearty meal of friendly ants, ho! an ancient rube appeared, his back all bent with cares, yet with a gleam and sparkle in his wise old eye. 'Twas the cart-repairer come, attracted by the odor of disaster, to that humming glade, or whatever.

Heh, heh, the ancient churl emoted, in the manner of the well-loved Dr. Whore, fabled wight! I've come to fix yon busted cart, my bearded husk!

I am be-zonked in wild amaze, quoth Blue. I was about to holler for a cart-repairer, seeing that we sojourn in the purple haze of quaint Ohio. And here you stand, begrimed with gluey soil, old cornstalks, and withal ungartered and un-braced, honest wrinkled hind.

We cart-repairers know, aye, as if a bird did cheep and squawk to us, when e'er a cart collapses, cracks, shudders, sighs, and busts all down. It is a gift given to a very few, for which I give the beamish Jesu thanks.

And thanks again and yet again. I fear this cart, whose prime is past, is all we own—my svelteish helpmeet here, my snoozing son, and I—and all we have to get us down the road where we do point our faces. It is, like poets chant, our proper steed, or, t'amend that, *I'm* the proper steed, you dig?

Such ween the breaks, croaked the elder dope. A thousand accidents the trav'ler's hopes subvert or checque. Now let me fix my watery orbs upon the damage, if I may. This pulpous mass, I take it, is the "cart."

'Tis, wheezed Blue, or what might, with greater 'cuteness, be called the husky terrene dregs of same.

Becalm thy mind, perplexed with irksome thoughts, my Jewish pal, and let me checque this damage out. And you, dear Madame, my pomaceous chunk, let waft your rich embosomed odors over me while I inspect this sober vehicle. 'Tis years since I've been so close to flexile wench!

I blush and quail that thou shouldst think me swell as apple-cheese, deterio-rating gaffer. But here! Take my embosomed odors, and eke my ambrosial streams of sweat that perfume the air with musk, so as you fix our humble waggon.

Aha! spumed forth the honest dumbo. Certes, as mattin song doth send the horny priest aflying from the nunnery, I glaum the trouble and, heh-heh, decipher plain its cause as if 'twere writ as large as turgid fruits in brisk October!

The cause, old hoary schmuck? evinced our Blue, the while the spindly Helene stood all contiguous to the ancient handyman.

Though worn with work and years, honked he, I can still espy a busted axle caused by a hump tossed off in wild abandon. Sir, I say that this simp'ring lady here, your spouse, by utmost vigour screwed, and not too may days ago if that, did exert such pressure on this oldish vehicle with the violent socking of her excited arse 'gainst same, that it did crack the axle here.

'Tis a shrewd guess, nosy dodderer, smiled Blue.

I redden all like juicy plums 'fore frosty blasts deface 'em, sighed Helene.

Nor fear that I impugn you twain gimpolas, the geezer quipped. In scorching youth a hubby's blood doth turn to mellow liquor when he glances 'pon the plump Ausonian hills his wife doth sit upon, aye! Then his post cylindric oft doth swell with weight excessive and Great Nature maddens him so that he must again employ the pondrous engine in what great Ecclesiastes dubs a shtup. Is it not so, my efficacious cluck?

You've whacked the nail upon its steely head, old bawd, cracked Blue.

I needs must hide my boining "face" in my voluminous snood, said queer Helene.

But enough of this enflaming talk, the artisan suggested. Disburthen thou thy luckless cart of its rich provender, supplies, comestibles, and all the other crap that flesh is heir to. E'er hasty suns forbid to work, whatever that may mean, I'll set about my task.

O lucky day that found us just outside perfumed Ohio when we made the two-backed beast! screamed the dainty wife.

Yet hold! the crookback sniffed. Short are our joys. Mine eyes, now that I don my cheaters, dig that the axle-winch that helps support the ring-job here, is smashed beyond repair. Ugh!

Are we then doomed to halt our holy quest? sobbed Blue. Oh shitty vanity! Oh how mortal saps of their shriveled hopes are widowed!

I'm quelled with intenerating woe! said wifely Miz Gavotte, and fell all down in quick collapse.

Nay, nay, quoth the faithful old mechanic. Let me now walk among the well-ranged axle-trees and sprockets, let me size right up the drive-shafts and the odd hydraulics. Aha! 'Tis as I thought. I can complete repairs effect, but I must craft with careworn hands another axle-winch. Let me ope my kit and now prepare materials for thy succor.

O brave magician! Blue enthused.

Delightful clot! Helene admitted from her bed of bramble-vetch.

The job's not hard, but it should take all nigh upon two days, during which time may I suggest that you camp out in the woods a league away? There you shall find some rude and rugged folk who've come to gather footballs late discarded by the crack-brained natives.

Gossip whispers that these pigskin spheres do make a tasty stew, drooled our protagonist.

I reck it so or else let welkin froth upon the violent insensates! grinned the wheezing lumpen.

I sure could scoff all up unto my rough chapped elbows such a steaming bowl of mulligan, gasped the prone Helene, her mouth all filled with od'rous goldenrod.

Then go! the churl declared. But first I'll tick off as it were with stylus hight and also eke, how I will go about this task. I've made admission that the axle-winch that helps support the ring-job, the main one that employs the king-post and the rake, is busted quite. To fashion clean and spiffy one that will outlast the very cart 'pon which I'll stick it, why, 'tis a job capacious of the juicy hord, or withal summat! First, the cornice bracketing and naked flooring must be lathed into splint'ry yet puissant sills and two, or maybe three, odd scarfings. At the moment that perfection seems a-gallop as the mighty steeds in windy Troy did chomp and whinny, just then, and fine as maiden's-hair, a trussing beam must be devilishly mortised, and rudely forced into a tenon, all despite its wheezes. Then, with a massy brad-awl and a gimlet-peenball, purlins must be chunked into the collar-beam, the queen-post, and the struts, already clipped and jazz-boed with rough strings, apron piece, and beading-keys. At this point, honest carpenter doth, if he be wise as slipp'ry publisher, shoot a orison or trice to Jesu, nodding off in Paradise. For now, with his purlins hot to snap as wench's garter, a miter-butt and tie-couple must be winched and rip-sawed into groove and that oddball slab of weighty iron men have given name of tongue, though Christ knows why. If this maneuver spangs, as well it might, then one is past the, you should pardon gross substántive, hump. 'Tis then but a task, familiar to the hand of any klutz, of some quarters, carriages, a rafter-roof, a fishing, coupla joints, zinging out a frame by lengthening beams, a touch with the cross-cut differential, plus a dab of mold in the transmission, simply done with the homely gouge, the jack-plane, and the joiner's-gauge. A final boring of the pitching-piece, and a chinch of wedge-cutting, all in easy strokes, and then a flourish with the smoothing-plane to bring the entire motherfucker to sublimity. Then, zut! We takes the spanking axle-winch, slather it with grease, and whang it quite into its

97

wonted spot, there next the faithful ring-job. And thus, rapacious fugs, you may hump again o'er hill and dale where e'er the wild goose honketh!

O geezer pure, whinged sweet Helene, thou, more wise than fair Caligula, shalt steep thy grisly sconce in beer ere thou do 'gin.

Thankee, titless one. 'Tis my vast pleasure thus to pleasure thee. Yea! Nature rejoiceth, smiling on her works lovely, to full perfection wrought!

Vigour gives equal title, stated Blue. A wondrous phrase, yet all methinks devoid of meaning.

We blush with the pomaceous harvests of thy craft, old sock, chirped up Helene, while the rude mechanic doused his sweaty scalp in lager cool.

Such profit springs from tools discreetly used, the old one wheezed from out the foam. And now, take you to the woods to join the football folk, whilst I attend my labors here. After two suns have plonked into the ocean, then return and thou shalt find thy cart champing at the well-known bite.

Thus, the happy pilgrims wended toward the nearby grove, while the windy glades did ring with the keening screams of steely peen!

« 22 »

Around the Campfire

When one lives, I mean to say, homely brothers, *lives* in the country, Blue said one chill evening with a twang of fall in the air as he sat in front of the blazing campfire somewhere in Ohio, one is compelled to do things, to become one with the slow and even heartbeat of the land and its mysterious gizzard and liver and other deepset organs, do you get me? One learns to—how shall I phrase it?—shift. Make do. Slap together. Patch up. Be handy. You've all read or heard tell of *Martin Chucklehead*? Like that, babes. I've learned, learned through bitter experience, through my own mistakes and I've made plenty, puh-lenty, a myriad or trice. Ha ha ha!

His great blocklike teeth rippled and flexed, then flashed for an instant in the sudden flaring of a knotty balsa log, whipped into frenzy by a blast of frigid air—from Canada! Flashed, yes, and as suddenly flashed out!

His great deerhide shirt swelled with Manhood!

There was a sharp, one might say an acute intake of breath among his auditors, honest ragamuffins all, huddled close to the crackling blaze, vacuous faces held suspended, like so many steaming beefsteak pies, in the air that strangely swirled about their plaid shirts and rough denim trousers, not to mention their stout corduroy shoes.

Or . . . boots.

The dark forest seemed to press closer.

Betimes, Helene huddled deeper into her homemade sleeping bag, the Lord knows what dreams etching a thin yet fetching smile on her thin, gnashing lips, as well as her wide and voluptuous mouth.

The mouth of Woman!

Zimmerman, at the edge of the huddling bresh, ankle deep in a stray puddle that bore mute testimony to the typhoon of the day before, crushed frogs with single-minded purpose.

Yep, Blue continued, if it may be said that this vast heart ever continued anything, Yep, he said, looking long into the smoldering bowl of his corncob with a silent wish that it were tobacco that smoldered there instead, Yep, he said, look-

99

ing up oddly, 'bout that time, up in Maine it was, I took the monicker of Bucol Suck. 'Lowed as how I could blend into the background, be taken for a reg'lar salt-lickin' clamsucker, your everyday down-east crackerbarrel. Took to fellin' trees and tearin' stone fences up by the roots. Fished many a cold deep stream for bignose crackies an' muskiejugs, an' dropped splintery lobster traps into tarnation knows how many sumpholes where the big 'uns loll. The stars, well, my gum! the stars looked so close to a feller's face that you 'lowed as how you might reach up and touch 'em, specially if you was a-swingin' and a-hollerin' and a-screamin' with fear through the crystally rhinestone air on a blue-ring birch limb, shootin', just shootin' up to the sky while a riled-up grizzly down below chomped away at the trunk o' the tree, his snoot all smeared up with honey like Willie-the-Jew and a big bullass pike in each hand. Feller learns to . . . live . . . with the slow movement of a land like that.

His interlocutors, silent up to this point, remained so, their eyes shifting embarrassedly from the lost dreams that burned rather steadily in the flames before them and the creaking and sighing limbs of the great Japanese maples that grew so thick and close that they made the day of the forest into night, although now, it being night, they didn't know that and so were content. And not a man jack of them could deny, no, not one of the rough and ruddy hobos could deny that old Osiris and the Pig, Syrian and Cassavetes, Vishnu and the Four Brothers winked down upon them fixedly from above in their mad wanderings. But where? And, for the love of God, how? There was a dearth of dry eyes as the grisly flapjacks addressed themselves to this silent yet awesomely persistent query.

And then the snows, Blue continued, those great white howlin' blizzes that blowed down from the Yukon and the Klondike, and the bone-snappin' nanooks that would sweep in in their tracks, cold snaps so devilish fierce your bones would crack like crabshells and possum teeth as you fell to your knees on the slag ice that covered the whole world. An' on what was, just a flash o' time ago—and here he allowed his greasy nose to reflect the prancing light of the fire to illustrate his metaphor—a drowsy pond up to its ass in honeysucker weeds an' mornin' priscillas, you'd be starin' into a hole you'd gouged outen the ice to find yourself eye to eye with a canny old specked koala or a sawbuck chopperlip, at home in his vast watery tundra and, I swear, boys, smilin', yep, smilin' at your presumption! The winter skeeters 'd worry and tear at a man too, by dad, right through his great thick layers o' bengalee fur and turkey grease that covered him from head to toe. Till all was a nightmare o' howlin' sastrugis, velocitous gale-rime, and black sassenachs, and the buzzards! Ah, bless me, fellers, the glacier buzzards, hungry as starved coots, gawkin' and preenin' and crowin' on the branches of the hangdog birch and the Dutch elm in which the hurricane blast soughed and chuffed! Yessir! give a man days and weeks and months o' that type o' life, and he comes to know he ain't no more'n a pork rind or a rabbit ass in the great scheme o' things. I vowed, in the long nights o' just such a winter as that, never to hurt or betray in any way atall a bit o' snow again! Not even a solitary cutesy flake! Nowhere on the face o' the earth! My wife over there, whose thin smile, as you can see, threatens to beat, or at least tie, the brightness o' the fire itself, even when I heap a renfrew twig, all full o' sappy juice, on its blazing face, can bear witness to it. She was there with me, hunkered down in a fondue hut, cookin' and meltin' snow and chompin' moose fur into tasty stew, barely alive in front of her little greaseball fire, her eyes far away, far far away, and in them a feller could see little tiny pictures o' home, if he looked close. Home!

At this homely epithet, each rude visage brightened for a moment and then drifted far away, as if each had set out on its long weary journey through the dense cystitis vines and towering salvia trees, to find it.

Or . . . them!

And yet, with the very next flog of the boreal winds from the gelid tundrae just beyond the hill that the cantaloupe of a moon had thrown into odd silhouette just beyond the wooded ridge, now lost in shadows, the visages returned to their mocking and grim possessors, each settling heavily and with a groan on the un-shaven column of a vast neck that called it slave.

That one word that rang so horribly. Slave!

Yet which it, the visage, in acrid vengeance, mocked in turn, and viciously, ah God, *heartlessly*, grimmed as well!

But a man learns from these adventures, Blue cheeped on, almost with the very cheep of the glacier buzzards that he had so darkly called up.

His chapped lips cruelly savaged his corncob.

His dark eyes were lost in the star-spattered skies that formed the ceiling of autumnal Ohio, its sleeping towns, its body shops.

Its Indian mounds!

But when winter comes, as it always does in this neck of the woods at least, Blue continued, knocking the faithful corncob wildly against a faggot who wordlessly hissed, yet still, still in time to the dying croaks and whimpers of the frogs that young Zim was sedulously putting out of their slimy misery, till, fi-nally, the bowl of the pipe he called chum arced through the air in a lazy parabola into the very bowels of the jolly blaze, at which a jump and toss of flames yet threw the sodden faces of the rapt apple-knockers into strange relief, Spring, Blue laughed, great, roarin', mucky, swell, and juicy spring! is a-steppin' right on its heels, dig?

The rubes grunted as one, their lips trembling.

Eyetalian poets know this, Blue blurted at last. And the good Lord knows they make the best creelwinnies and crabflickers on the New England coast, rough, cold, and rocky as it owns or something. And, by gumbo, a far holler from the stinkin' melodious country the greaser runts hail from!

At this jaunty reference to the feared and hated dago, the spiky heads and quivering mouths of the woodland band nodded and gaped, in that order, gaped until the spittle and drool from their broken, stained tusks sizzled and buzzed in the demented flames like so many charred and split mickeys.

Yep! And spring did come! Blue guffawed. The rivers and cricks thawed, the yeller-nosed butchies spawned and spawned, hurlin' their shinin' bodies as God intended, out o' the streams and flatbeds, the sinkholes and stalagmites, over the fields and cornbrakes and roofs and chimbleys, the bresh, the shrebs, even over the rotting rock fences a-jammed and a-cluttered with the bodies o' neighbors and wimpies. Yessir! The buds rioted in busts and detonations o' color, the green-gage phloxes stood up high as old oaks, the blue-bottles churned and drowned in the new butter that covered the earth! Helene took to kneadin' the dough that she'd planted before the first hurricane fell, and she baked and broiled many a toothsome delight, let me tell you, all to the wild yelpin' o' crickets. She was a woman, fellers, a woman, workin' around the house all buck naked, as human a female person as God intended Eve to be.

At this intelligence, his yokel audience gulped back . . . tears. Tears of Manhood, tears of Pride . . .

Tears of rampant Envy!

Their dazed miens had the appearance of men, strong men, rough and un-polished men, borne backward in time's violent career to a lost moment of un-leashed lust and its unsatisfactory consummation. Yet they were silent but for a scattered whinge or two.

Men!

And the scream o' the red magool, Blue mused on, the great rivulets gushin' Life! The rocky soil turnin' and turnin', the chink-eye toad, the shitface beetle, the swoop swaller, the barndoor ratfucker, the bare-tail snake-eater, the whoop-ing picayune . . . Life! And the eye gets clear! And the skin gets hard! And the hands get tarry and so almighty powerful that they bust through barn walls and threshers on their own account. Lord! And Zim a-growin' and Helene . . .

She stirred. From somewhere in the depths of her nokomis sack a soft femi-nine yawn vied with the odd chirring sound of the earthworms. Great Nature had seen to it that they had blundered their blind and simple way into the blaze! Blue looked away into the dark that had settled about the top of the shadowy muskwillow that served as their roof, his heavy face as one of granite.

A tear hung at the edge of a stray lash!

Zimmerman was almost a man!

Each dirty flint of a face seemed to agree with this unspoken sentiment. Each grizzled jaw nodded in unison and together, smiles fleeting.

Yet . . . was it really a yawn that had broken the stillness of the campsite?

They settled down for the long arctic night, sheltering as best they could from the eerie bights and worringers that swept and reswept the little clearing, their woodswise bodies deep beneath heaps of dried poppy limbs. Even Zim, little, sad, lonely Zim, finally came crawling out of his ice-glazed puddle into the circle of flickering light, his shoes torn savagely by the feral death throes of the frogs he'd butchered for morning chuck!

«23»

The Cart Repaired,
the College Discovered

Lo! then the sun, swimming like a crazy person underneath the earth from the vasty West to the timbered East, broke, splashing, the waves of the grey Atlantic, whew! in the nick of time for dawn to "break," as such it often will, or hold enough!

And at its first faint rays of wishy-washy light, the gnarled and pasty-visaged cart-repairer smashed through the brambles, briers, and other loathsome plants to waken Blue and his beloved family. The kindly popular mechanik found them there, deep in sleep by the cold grey ashes of the evening's fire. With his gap-toothed smile, spake he thus, to wit:

Bestir your snoozy limbs, all needles and pins-a as they needs must be, stretched as thou art on this cold toif. Oh waxen man, oh boon companion of the terra gross! Your snazzy vehicle is all repaired, and, belike, as good as new! Fleet and falcon-like, and pining to be crammed with all your crap unto its very gunwales, if such a maritimic term may be applied to such a thing as is your antic cart! Up! Up! and wake! For the sun has scattered into flight the shades Cimmerian and eke the hick-faced football-eaters who did here last night make glut and scoff with thee and thine!

Then did Blue rise and wake his fambly. Then did they make a frugal repast on the shattered frogs that Zimmerman had snuffed. Then did they wade and labor back into the ferny dell in which the cart reposed, awaiting yet again their pleasure, and, by Jesu's Rood, the humble brougham did shine almost as bright as did the crass piano, all acrouch beneath a banyan! The thinning-haired Helene fell to her knees, busting yet again her busted nylons. Shambling Zim drooled gouts of spittle on his dicky. And Blue, his eyes fair starting from his cranium, did thus apostrophize:

O Cart! My pal, thou art now as eminent as bitched ascites, firk as sunspot-blue clostridium, sheeny as a swift colitis, and rampant as the omnipresent fascia; have I pricked down your semblance to the cherry-pink fistula? the nodding abasia? the confused edema? If not, then let me prick! And you do look like those great weeds that grow in mummia, the myalgia and the myasthenia as well! And too, the mist that hugs thee close is cousin to the onychia of changeable pale. Thou art sprue and stroma! Swart as Hermes' ebon urticaria, that he doth wear in's buttonhole on Sundays! And over all, the odd perfume of the Hackensack stenosis wafts. My puissant Cart! My clawed xanthoma! My adored old waggon, true as spreading-leaved tinea, from whose boughs the sweet xerosis all depends, though splayed with your Italian roseola!

Thus did he speak in tones at once stentorian and dumb. Then did the three, with the querulous aid of the old rube, who, e'en at this early hour, was half in the faithful bag, load up the patient cart with all their "goods." The piano was quick-roped with hawsers to the cart, Zim chucked aboard, and Blue then turned with rolling eye unto the wasted hooligan, while Helene stood all insouciant nearby.

With what, old bruto, can I make recompense? he said. I have no wealth, but I can rip you off a bar or twain of "Green Old Dolphin." You look as if you'd like a ripple of the rhythm, nu?

Belike, pardy, and grovel, croaked the swaying oaf. I'd more enjoy, and e'en delight in sharing, but the space of but a fleeting moment with your lissome lady in the scrub.

With this, the honest lecher leered and fell to unbuckling his codpiece as Helene trekked with immodest speed into the nearby hedge, her homely skirts a-flutter as was her girlish heart, her thighs akimbo.

Well, mused Blue, I'll have to think on it, and as he thought, the sound of gaiety venereal issued from the blushing leaves. Five minutes passed, then ten, while the doughty Serge did wonder on the duffer's odd request. Then, I'll do it! shouted he, until the welkin rang, or maybe jingled just a bit. And as he gave his husbandly O.K. to our mechano's plea, what? the old bum ambled forth into the clearing, with Miz Gavotte apace behind.

I thank you, gen'rous dick, the old rogue winked. 'Tis been ten year or since that I did gambol thus. And was it then a titter that flew like a chicken hawk from the delicious lady's lips?

Not quite aware of what adventure had befallen these two folks, our Blue thus deft removed it from his mind, aswim as was its wont, in deeper thoughts.

Then did Helene mount up upon the cart. Then did Blue shackle to the traces and the bights and bits and harnesses and all kindsa stuff. Then did they creak out onto the road, the Western wind carrying their scent behind them as they headed toward brooding Indiana, where other high adventures did await them maybe.

The Savior knows how long they schlepped and slogged abeam and truly well a-lubber throughout festering Ohio, but it was at least a sennight. They camped by rills and trestles, the wondrous sounds of chickasaws and weevils all their lullabies. They savaged the modest pickerel, the pendant apricot, the greenish gage. And of the snappy water all pellucid of the great Ohio and the Sasquatch they partook to slake their quench. Then, one day, just as Rosy Dawn did lift her pinky in the East, our three adventurers espied, beyond the wildly heaving canopy of ginkgos mixed with hazelnuts, the shining towers of—could it be—The University?! Serge swift heaved against the traces and the caravan rolled on in clouds of aromatic dust, crossing into Indiana at exactly 10 A.M. by Helene's heirloom Ingersoll, left her, in sly Gallic fun, by her Uncle Proust. But that's another story, and, belay, a good one that'll keep the hob a-bubbling on the spit while old Boreas whacks the picture windows as we slosh our toddies by the friendly firelight! Aye! up to our elbows in the roasted crabs and rocked in great hilarity with descant profound of the latest "books."

In a kind of trice, the Family Gavotte was on the campus and a hurried word with a student of Courd Science cast Blue down for a nonce or two, as he learned that this was not The University, but Annex College, affiliated with the potent U, but not, as they say, "It." In funk peculiar, they stood and stared agape, bereft with soil and laden down with burrs and throstles.

A man all nondescript, yet tweedish, pipe-y, all baggy flannels and with wrinkled face and smile to match, his wise old eyes a-pop behind his rimless specs, approached in a swirl of falling ivy.

May I assist you kindly folks in kindly ways? My name is Bone, Dr. Weede Bone, Rector of the College, and laden to the brim with good intentions. Why not come to my office, slip out of those vetch-bespattered clothes, and have a small, yet satisfying lunch with me? Our motto here is "From Egg to Apple," which, while quaint, is quite impenetrable, no? And then he laughed his great warm laugh, his meerschaum dancing gaily in his mouth.

I seek The University, Dr. Bone, Blue commenced, and ran down his tale of quest and art, whanging his piano now and then, and helped along by his nattering wife. Weede hearkened to their tale, and puffed reflectively.

While I, my boy, the doughty academic said, cannot for a moment lift your crest, fallen as it is in the recent knowledge that the U lies further West, I may lighten up the fardels and valises of regret that settle down upon your hairy clavicle. That is, our Assistant Adjunct Temporary Chairman, Dr. Ryan Poncho, who is the right-hand man of Dr. Vince Dubuque, and placed in his position by that gimlet-brained Administrative Dean of The University, also chairs the Musical Department, and will, I feel certain as did Spencer Tracy of his God in that old flicker, *San Francisco*, furnish forth some phrases music-wise that will whet and tang your appetite for the "Real Thing" that may await you, even now, at our feared, adorèd U.

Oh Dr. Bone! My heart is rollicking as purple gentian when a tortilla unawares comes near its maw! Can I ever thank you?

Tut, tut, the white-haired sage implied. Come, let's to lunch. Leave the kid. I'll see to it that a grad assistant, deep in food lore, chunks him some gruesome chili from the student lunchroom, or mayhap a "sandwich" from the odd machines that dot and vend about the campus. And they scuffled through the glory of the fallen leaves and rotten melons toward the Rector's office, the while that gent nodded greetings to the ruby cheeks and huge incisors of the students has tening to class.

<< 24 >>

Dr. Bone

Shows the Lab to the
Gavottes; With Learned Commentary

As the sun glanced through the legendary ivy-throttled windows of Dr. Bone's austere but comfortable office, that hoary academic, Blue, and his helpmeet, leaned back on the venerable leather-like furniture that was strewn about the room. To a man, so to speak, as oft one must, they picked their teeth and sipped their cherry Kool-Aid.

Before I trot you out and introduce you to our reigning musicologist, Doc Poncho, Dr. Bone declaimed, his voice the burnished tool he used when handing college presidents yet another imbecilic plaque, perhaps you would be interested in lending me an ear or two.

I lean forward in my chair all breathless, Blue gulped.

My body also points its flesh toward you, good Dr. B, Helene blurted in addendum, as was her well-known wont, as those of you who've followed this hegira surely know. As for the rest, have with you to Coney Island!

The true work of this college, boon delightful chums, the Doc began, outside of course the teaching of the young—marble-eyed and badly dressed—since this is first and foremost, not to say primarily, a teaching college, not a center for research, and you may add that fustian to your list of cherished platitudes, the true work, I say, of Annex College is the work done in our laboratories. We have been, for some years now, and under many a juicy luscious grant, engaged in finding cures for and preventive measures against the age-old oral afflictions that have beset mankind since the sad day in 4000 B.C. or thereabouts when our horny mother, Eve, got her a bad case of the sponge-gum from the apple that she wolfed.

What? said Blue. You mean . . . ?

I mean mouth grief, I mean buccal mis'ry, I mean your basic loathsome ills that pitch disease into the old food-hole, dusty traveler, Doc Bone chuckled.

Blue glanced in wordless amaze at Helene, whose mouth had flown open like unto the fly of a soldier in a whorehouse. Together and as one flesh they thought (since "I" know everything about them, ideal reader, sitting there and waiting for the story to "pick up a little"): DOC CHICK! But they held their breaths, and 'Slid! a good thing too, else the ivy that was climbing up the drapes had been blasted to a mess of home-fried pottage.

Perhaps, my pals, you'd feature ambling slowly with me to our modern labs, while I show you some of the things we're squandering our kopeks on? Thus Bone, peering out from clouds of noxious Rum and Maple.

Reet! said Blue and saccharine Helene, two minds that beat as one.

And there they were at last!

The lab! How abustle it shone and jigged! How the white coats and thick lenses of bespectacled technicians glimmered 'mid the smoke of endless stultifying pipes! How different from the sloven shop where Serge was wont to spit and polish lenses! So this was College!

Let me explain, sedulous gleets, Dr. Bone rapped on, some of the simpler processes we waltz about with here in our immaculate laboratories, simpler, I say, since such will not too onerously tax your lowly brows. And even though I'll strain to set and jellify the stuff as best I can in layman's terms, I fear you'll merely stand and gawp, such is the esoteric bullshit that I'll spout. Think of me, sweaty pilgrims, as a doctor or a lawyer, cant and argot washing o'er my tongue as does the great Niagara inundate poor Canada!

We'll strain our best, an' we gawp at last, Blue quipped, the stunned Helene already frozed with wonder.

Check! Weede said, tamping or whatever in or down his fragrant calabash. You may know, he said, sucking flame, etc., puffing smoke, etc., cradling the handsome bowl 'pon which was carved by stupid craftsmen all kindsa ugly shit, that in the past—and right up to the present!—such coises of the mouth as gingivitis, pyorrheal slime, trenchmouth, foot and mouth disease, galloping caries, abscessed lower lip, fistula of the soft palate, desiccated root canal, foetor gummae, carpet-tongue, morning breath, logorrhic pip, Cosell's disease, harmonica irritans, and such-like horrible afflictions, were and are treated with such homely medicines as busting muscat, dried fruttos, wrinkled leaves, dozing corn shock steeped in algolagnia, daffodils and strawberry roots, rutabago blooms, crawling treponema, sloes black as jett, lavender peony stems, the shady fusillade, and, not to forget, the curious peach. You may know this.

I hadda idear, murmured Blue. Helene gooped away in eerie silence, her "thoughts" on Zim, who even now was rending mercilessly what the quaint inhabitants did call a "hoagie," a kind of sangwich that the great Caligula invented in a throe of lust.

Excellent good, old Bone rejoined. Now then, obsessive sloggers, follow close my cogent lecture as I commence. Starting in that corner of the pristine lab and moving clockwise, let me expound upon some of the all-important break-throughs while you silently or otherwise applaud all-potent science, endlessly questing for the light and truth and the really heavy bread, as has been its wont since that rainy morn that General Westinghouse, known as the mutter of invention, was whelped in a humble filthy hogan on the smelted plains of legendary Boise!

Expound abaft! Blue murmured. There's nothing like an education to make one plumb the deeps of ignorance.

Well put, old pip! Over there you can see a vectographologist plunged into some arcane metamorphoses. At the moment, she is macerating the crooked poplar in a double-bottomed cucurbite until it citronizes; then she will endeavor to sublime the residue till the green lion appears *in fumo*. When a dollop of luke-warm menstrue is added to the resultant chang, putrefaction will ensue and zut! with luck, a dandy salve to rid the teeth of citronella stains. Our next technician, the lass whose lab smock hardly can disguise her lusty charms, is at the moment placing a tutie in a crystal phlox, a kind of lembek made expressly for us by Burris Bags of Brooklyn. The *sanguis agni*—issuing from the pelican—that your astonished eyes now light upon is very close to the fabulous guelder-rose of Nature, but without that shrub's destructive stink. I am drowned in hope that this swell gunk, something like the lost pink brilliantine that blooms aberrantly in starlight, will prove a boon to those afflicted with the fever blisters of fellatio. Moving right along: do you see that four-eyed wimp a-tingle with the thrill of high research? The redberry moonseeds that he's chopping into the liquor of Mars in his simmering alembic will soon give forth your *materia liquida*, and one that dances with the colors of the peacock's tail. Yowzah! This juice, wisely blended with a pinch of red man and a handful of white woman, can be used, if God is good, as the rinse to thoroughly dissolve the venom in the mouth of one of those unfortunates who has, by design or accident, ingested tuna helper. This may be the greatest boon to dumb mankind since Dr. Robinson slapped together what he chose to call—and what a choice!—his magic bullet! Shall I continue? Or is your simplike brain piled to the attic with info that you can't digest?

Go on, Dr. Bone. I feel an almost physical delight, akin to meeting someone who's never heard of Woody Allen.

What a wondrous simile! Something like an anapestic diorama! Well then, I'll venture on, as Columbus said, to sail, to scuttle, and to sink, yet not to quake or reef a single boom-yard!

Columbus! the cuddly Helene declared, starting for a fleet out of her gawklike trance. I weep still when I think upon him all bedecked with plastic Xmas icicles adrift on Hudson Bay! Thus always those who strive and tack about!

Easy to see why such a wifely person was the toothsome cause of your banjaxed cart! Dr. Bone leered tutorially. But andiamo! as our ceaselessly laughing friends, the hard-working ginzolas say. At our next "bench" you may descry a feverish team clustered all about an aludel cheerily bubbling on the hob. The *equi clibanum* is causing a perfect inceration in the common catalpa and it turns, even as we stare, into the plumèd swan! A dash of lato and azalea in an hour will produce an ointment that, swilled around with zernich, may prevent God only knows how many poetry readings at the Y, its powers being such that, when ingested, it produces aggravated laryngitis. Another curse lifted from the soul of suffering humankind! We work here, cutey, we don't play, though often we are held in greater scorn than weird Capaneus's Sears and Roebuck stepladder. At the next table, aha! we see The College's most gifted scientist, his apron heavy with foundation loot, and in the fourteenth year of his heartbreaking quest for the elixir that will make all men sing with the voice of the gringo nightingale, Pat Boone. A lonely search that has broken many men and that contributed to the death of Albert Einstein—but let that story rest in peaceful darkness. You see him, pockets jingling, up to his worn-out elbows in *aqua fortis*, chibrit, sericon, his nose jammed in a bolt's head, a red-hot gripes egg twixt his agued knees, shredding devilwood and merds in furious abandon into boiling azoch, clouds of crow and mists of pale citron swirling round his sconce, waiting for the chrysosperm to come forth in the projection. This is his three hundred and twelfth attempt, yet he does not flag, remembering that the great Thomas Albert Edison hit on the waffle iron on his nine-hundredth shot at it—along the way discovering the heating pad and baseball! Thus serendipity blunders into glory!

I understand the drive and potent power of his quest, Blue swallowed. Yes, down to my bone-like marrow!

I had a hunch, old cokes, that you would especially "dig on" his crazed and magnificent obsession, the tweedy prof mused fetchingly, deep-sucking on his toasty cherrywood, his wise face atwinkle in the aromatic fumes.

I admire the cut of his jib, Helene added, lost in a sigh as she thought on her farflung youth, now plunged into the oblivion of grimacing age, wrapped, as it sometimes is, in the toga of responsibility. How swiftly, she sobbed, we are wrapped in the toga of responsibility!

Cedant arma togae, Weede chuckled.

I love the sound of that wop-talk, Blue admired. Soft and mellifluous it is as a weeping willow crashing slowly into the roaring flood. But, Dr. Bone, is that, as they say, it, as far as the lab obtains?

All but one table has been checked out and explainized, the kindly time-server nodded. There are some . . . other . . . "things" going on in our top-secret prioritized labs in the sub-sub-basement, but they are not for the prying eyes of laypersons, if you follow me? I can only hint that they touch upon a reduction of the vocabulary of world leaders to a clutch, a teeny pile of words, mostly of your nounal type, to spare them jabs and uppercuts of foul embarrassment when dealing with the great unwashed, who, as you know, ask a question on your rare occasion. These words would cover *all* contingencies!

Perish forfend that I should gaze upon such deepish stuff, blenched Blue.

That is jake with me, old socks. And now, our last project, taking place before your wildeyed gaze. Here you see an athanor, in which a graduate assistant and what seems to be a "friend" of his, judging by her popeyed glance of young desirous lust, are dulcifying dental floss donated by the leper colony just down the road, oh, 'bout as far as you can throw an ax-handle, a invaluable community in that your basic monk, your priest, your down-at-heels missionary, go there for their graduate work in Humility and Compassion, plus a short course in Self-Abnegation. Well, that is neither here nor far. This dental floss, steeped and wallowed in the juice and slime and spittle of the basic leprous type, is run through your putrefaction, your cibation, your projection, burned and incinerated and scorched up real good along with pieris, sweetbells, smoketree, other herbs, and a cross-let of jamoke. The result? If Our Powerful Creator smiles, and the Federal lettuce keeps on drifting in, this young rake and his sweating punk will some day educe from out this small inferno a salve so potent that a person, in the comfort and the privacy of his own home or apartment—even his furnished room!—can smear it on a rotten tooth and, by God! the fucker will dissolve and vaporize, all in a trice, and without a ort of pain!

'Tis hard to credence, Blue said, amazed by this latter phrase.

Yes! But true, however strange! I don't have to tell you, Weede said in an elaborate aside, that extremist dentists have vowed to destroy our work! Yet we press!

Is that the "works," Professor Bone? Blue said, perhaps a little sadly.

That is the shebang, dear friends. And now, let us wend to my apartments. We'll have a bit or bite of supper later, and I'll take you around to meet Dr. Poncho. Surely you can stay a day or so? The College would be honored. To chat, to guff, to rap and shoot the shit—how savory the thought! And, too, Miz Gavotte, to have the delightful prospect of your company brings out the latent gent in me—and I'm sure Doc Poncho will feel à la ditto, Bone leched, his impeccable grey flannels all abulge.

Of course we'll sojourn for a sun or trey, Blue grinned, while the fair Helene blushed wildly, a strange heat powerful as flaming Sterno sloshing through her loins, or whatever women have down there.

« 25 »
The Gala
Cocktail Party

Pain, the sagacious Dr. Bone was saying, flits through my sensibilities, accompanied by no small modicum of embarrassment, since it is my tortured yet stern duty to inform you, my dear Gavottes, that Dr. Poncho, embroiled as he needs must be in administrative tasks, will not be able to greet you tonight. He will, however, see you tomorrow, and lay, as the hep phrase runs, some heavy sounds on you. In the meantime, I have, with Dr. Poncho's blessing, arranged a small yet gay, if not gala, cocktail party for you, at which you may meet some of our most distinguished administrators and faculty. Shall we repair to the Dan'l Boone Room?

Thus saying, they . . . and so forth.

And there they were! What cascades of academic glitter! What a fine madness of the intelligentsia! What milling and wheedling! The wonderful persons circulated and chatted, drank and staggered, consumed "dip" (whatever that may be), and the like festive routine. Sing, Muse, of this catalogue of shits!

There came Brenda Fatigué, Regius Professor of Office Fashion; Ed Flue, Associate Professor of Logging; Burnside Marconi, Instructor in Televiewing; Syrup Concoct, Poet-in-Residence; Benjamin Manila, Chairman of the Stationery Department; G. Root Garbáge, Counselor in Venereal Diseases; Jedediah Mange, Vice-President for Member Development; Winifred Zinnia, Corsetiere for Rector of the College; Socks O'Reilly, Chief of Tension Calisthenics; Marcus Podium, Ellsworth Harelip Professor of Speech and Drama; Heinz Pogrom, Horst Wessel Professor of German Philology; Gladys Bung, Dietary Tactician; Fifi Galleon, instructor in French Jobs; Catherine Thigh, Director of Sexual Services; Nicholas Syph, Bureaucracy Professor Emeritus; Yvette Risqué, Associate Professor of Auto-Erotism; Francis-Xavier Silhouette, S.J., Chaplain; Pedro Manteca, Professor of Fast Food Studies; Chastity Peep, Instructor in Vaginal History; Angelo Bordello, Disciplinary Dean of Women; Manatee Brouillard,

113

Connecticut Professor of Fertilizer Studies; Idyott Dymwytte-Pyth, Instructor in Ur-Critique; Rastus X. Feets, Professor of Black English.

And circulating, smiling, chatting, laughing, the Gavottes moved as if . . . as if . . . in a dream!

"Alas! One acknowledges, sadly, sadly, that ladies' intimate garments are unattractive in direct proportion to their comfort."

"The sturdy old oak, falling heavily, crashed spang through the dorm windows, whereupon a cloud of flies rose up, buzzing in terror and chagrin."

"The first television 'sighting' took place in Dublin in 1904, when one Francis Aloysius McGlynn dropped his transistor radio and a little man, holding a bar of lemony soap, crawled painfully from the wreckage."

"Night is/and life is/what means/means be life."

"After being dated and stamped, then stamped and dated, the incoming mail is sent to the Dating-Stamping clerk."

"You've got your basic buboes, your running chancre, your clapperoo sacred and profane, your gleet malaise, your Spanish pox."

"Caught the lad in the act of self-gratification, so the benighted Scoutmaster stripped him of his Personal Health Merit Badge."

"I'm most proud, I think, of the fact that General Champagne, while dictating the peace terms, was marvelously trig in my featherweight foundation in ecru with black nylon-lace panels."

"The old Army dozen cures your basic born-again Christian in about three or four weeks."

"Duh perfeck eckshershize izh: 'Hash dow sheen budda bride lilygrow?' "

"Some uff mein goot Chewish frents from zuh fordies seem to haff . . . disappeared!"

"The fatback is then gently sautéed in two ounces of King Kong and a quarter-cup of oleo."

"It is permissible, even salutary, for the modern woman to fantasize a touch of sodomy with the office boy while in lawful embrace with her spouse."

"When the boys returned, simply *mad* for some clean, blond, smiling American poon, what was this once-great nation's inadequate response?"

"The truly efficient office should be able to complicate *everything* in just under six months, taking into account, of course, the zeal of the staff."

"With the skirt discreetly lifted to the upper portion of the lower limbs, and the underpants crisply rolled to that point at which said lower limbs are jointed, the clitoris may be surreptitiously massaged while dining, at the theater, or even in the office."

"I also serve who only blandly prate."

"We have almost achieved a breakthrough in the instant wiener."

"The vagina, long since accepted as reality in Mesopotamia, was first observed beyond that state's borders in the fourth millennium."

"I take absolutely no pleasure in chastising these remarkably lovely, luscious, desirable, nubile, and altogether terrific young women."

"We actually had to turn a thousand people away the evening Shecky Green gave a dramatic reading from *October Light*."

"The progression is crystal clear: Joyce, Beckett, Costain, Jong."

"When ah be's gwine, ah be's gwine to Jericho!"

". . . invented by a gay Presbyterian minister—pantyhose, I mean."

"No tenure *yet*, though I am known everywhere as Johnny Acorn!"

"I entered and saw Mrs. Marconi in the most *extraordinary* position."

"They/whimper."

"I don't exactly know what an 'envelope' *is*."

"The affected member is plunged into warm Pepsi."

"Putting it into a honeydew is also recommended."

"The new gym shorts offer just a wisp of gentle control."

"Leaping high into the air, you intertwine the index fingers."

"Yethhir! That'th mah baby!"

"So ve burned der files."

"Yes, radishes! Skewered along with soybean balls and okra."

"The beautiful poems of Miss Flambeaux have saved many marriages."

"Yes, my famous 'Tuesdays' *are* booked months in advance."

"If it calls for eight copies, make twelve."

"The woman then places her ankles alongside her ears."

"In Indianapolis, God's hand is everywhere seen."

"What precisely is 'bread'?"

"Recent studies suggest that men who wear athletic supporters suffer from vagina envy."

"After four in the afternoon, the supple birch switch is best."

"Who dreamt that the dead salmon would grow into a lusty azalea?"

"The walking-stick is always a symbol for a specific Western angst."

"The baddest dude be's Gentian Washington."

". . . the *cruel* corset? Cruel? . . ."

". . . lifts his meaty hands to prey . . ."

". . . during the commercial break, large amphibians . . ."

". . . cer/tain/ly . . ."

". . . the tongue, now crisscrossed by small paper cuts . . ."

". . . the vast warehouse, filled with impounded toilet seats . . ."

"...*bursting* through his BVD's, it..."

"...her lacings, whipping through the air, caught the Monsignor..."

"...now, the full bosom, during the eight-count push-up..."

"...wit duh lipz inna shmirk..."

"...undt vhen der rosy dawn lighted up Auschwitz..."

"...the hamburger, partially rotted in the soil..."

"...Havelock Ellis, delirious in the ladies' room..."

"...even the most modest will lift her skirts if..."

"...having typed it on green tissue instead of light blue..."

"...the role of the pleated skirt in spontaneous orgasm implies..."

"...in baseball cap and cassock, I often wander through..."

"...the tuna is tossed with tiny marshmallows..."

"...imagine Danaë's surprise when all this gold..."

"...while one young lady is spanked, another sometimes..."

"...the piccadills and stoccadoes, well irrigated..."

"...herring-motif in Malamud's juvenilia..."

"...Dean Bordello an' me, man, we be's whoppin' an' whompin' on..."

"...curious linguistic apparatus that often in disciplines that favor a particular array of the marvelous stretchiness of that post-war if you do understand a latex well can it be a swell campus support for what? is that the various social services or can it be a kind of utter lovely parameter when just a tiny bit of although they are a kind of "fingers" if that's the specific kind of pastrami did you ever understand for instance what array of the most dedicated Doctorow? Gardner? Styron? often at mass it is in my mind that this campus this hallowed ground this garter belt flushed but it's most tough when in the very middle of the squash surprise a gentle zephyr at the egress of the people from Washington are there skirts just quietly lifting and the marvelous slice of Bermuda that decorates but also wraps the old ribbon in the same cellophane that the unfettered thigh decides to plant itself alongside the beloved peonies that have oft buried a mackerel like the Indians? sure enough into the gym fell a large bag in which the ivy mixed with an odd how shall I say "novel" that makes one almost dense with flannel and yet not quite tweed although it is in a sense marinated in a cheaper wine your zinfandel your kosinski your screamingly boring onslaughts of what in Algiers? but of course not something for every day they dub it "dub" is a bitch "dub" it anyway the maniacal Jung deep in Mein Kampf and dosed up good with what? with what? oh dear sweet Jesus the tailored suit the bull clap because it can give you the tenure that you would suck spit for and knock a bull down on his knees if they have such articles of apparel unknown and not given the respect that ensues in Scranton that city of lost marines and the dry rot in the great nodding elms and if tenure is the guerdon of those who lift skirts and bull trousers and spaghetti soft and mushy the way it be's when they's be's got the lesson plan and the rosy reddened and tingling how shall I say in Tunis in the darkened office around five or so of a winter evening the sound of Marrakech and the soft sobbing as we watch the snap beans and the impeccable white of the knee hose and down there around the ankles is the mimeo machine andhg therzwx wehytu eogghji wh tuouh to thyrhtyyehyheuuhr jo joyk blamdurf oi gurdhujhut uh uh uhh uhhhh uh uh uh uh oooooooohhhh . . ."

Supper, with Dr. Bone, was, the doctor being the soul of genial warmth, a small yet festive occasion of genial warmth. They looked forward to the morrow with benign alacrity. Things were certainly looking "up."

Well, sweat-face, Blue said to Helene. Things are "looking" up! He seemed almost . . . *happy*!

117

« 26 »

In Which Dr.
Poncho Meets the Avid Blue

The dawning hence and thus the flaming sun, pinkish-gold as weird Miami bungalow, did clamber up the sky! Yes, it was the following day, and Blue, an ornament unto his time, waited in the little room without the puissant Ryan Poncho's inner sanctum, a-jiggle all with noives. Then the door swung open slowly to reveal the Doc, his face, as novels love to say, wreathed in smiles. Or so to speak in elegiac spondees.

A kindly face, alarmingly like Dr. Bone's, topped this hearty scholar's frame, and as Blue followed him into his cabinet, he noted well the crisp insouciance of Indiana couture, thus: He wore a dark-blue wash and wear, carelessly baggy, the cuffs of the trousers to the brim with lint; his lumpy feet were shod in highly polished, down-at-heels wing-tip brogans; to guard him from the Hoosier blasts, a hand-knit bulky cardigan of oatmeal wool clung close to his "body"; his pockets bulged with a myriad reports; his socks, of thinnest whitest lisle nestled at his shoetops; his vest, bereft of two buttons as was Apollinaire's in rosy Texas, sagged quite fetchingly, shining with tobacco stains; on his watch chain hung the noble emblem of the Rotary Club; his white starched shirt, with collar slightly frayed, served as background for his polyester cravat, brilliant red with a motif of tiny yellow palm trees, this latter item anchored with a tie-clasp which commanded "THINK."

Come in, my son, the doughty educator laughed. Weede—Dr. Bone to you—has said that you are laden to the brim with good intentions, though you schlep the fardels and valises of regret that you have not found the perfect and ineffable phrase of, how do you call it? music. I am afraid that here, where the sunset collapses in its panoply of horribly depressing colors, you will not find it either, my rude sonata. Yet, embroiled as I needs must be in administrative tasks, sit, my innocent cluck, though crestfallen and aspout with tears, and we will chat, guff, rap and shoot the shit betimes, though I am tortured with compassion seeing that you have been blowing your great red heart out on the piano that you cleave unto.

118

My heart leaps up when I behold the pain glow in your eye! Serge whined.

Although I no like-a dis phrase, ats-a nize, Poncho countered. You talk what I wanna hear, here at old AC, far, far from the smelted plains of legendary Boise, where they know how to buy things!

Many thanks, good Doctor, it is my pleasure entirely to meet the man who is not only the Assistant Adjunct Temporary Chairman of this whole shebang, but who is also Chairman of the . . . Musical Department! Uh, Blue limped bravely on, Doctor Bone implied that . . . that . . . you might . . .

Ha, ha, ha! Calm your fears, inept crusader! Weede—and by the by, did you know that he is the man who invented the pencil moustache? No matter. Weede, I said, I say, honcho of All-Important Breakthroughs in the chemical something or other, has told me of your rather impertinent desire to hear a few musical phrases which, while not in your ineffable class, will give you a jagged ort of a idea of the type of thing you will dig on when you get to The University! The gimlet-brained Dr. Dubuque will knock you off your lilting little cadenza, chief! And you may lay to that! These wise old owl-like eyes portend same. In the meantime, though I ask myself, Who is this chooch to come in here, all akimbo? I will help you with a clutch of belle musique, knocked out on an platinum kazoo, given me by a confidante of the great Blue Barron.

I gripe and writhe in fiery expectation, gasped our pilgrim, eyes a-pop.

Thus thou ever must! And with this, the repository of ancient Midwestern wisdom amblingly shambled to his massive oaken desk at which, 'tis rumored, Robert Bly once popped some actual corn, wild husks and all!

The odd machines that dot and vend about the campus, the stalwart mentor quipped, can offer nothing like . . . this! And thus saying, whipped from a drawer the instrument elite.

Blue, his face the memorable one of a dead clam, blanched at the sight of the relic.

Good monsieur, Poncho smiled, settling his cardigan, you got on you a face like a dead clam, which, though you are marble-eyed and badly dressed, sets you off in dazzling chiaroscuro, or summat like.

Blue sprawled dumbstruck in amaze, his shining orbs fixed piercingly upon the ancient African pipe that somehow glittered in the Doctor's duke. It was as if, to Blue, great Pan hisself had crashed, hooves first, into the still retreat, and stood before him, shooting off auras scintillant to beat the band.

Now, this snatch of sweet melodious glop has made men's eyes look, as our friends, the Frogs, say, one at the other, such is its wheedling force. And with that he raised the pipe unto his lips and blew:

O Lady of the Tattered Slip! quoth Blue, his tongue starting from his mouth in ecstasy, and, yea! finishing as well. Can this be music? It seems more like unto the distillation of a pizza with garlic and *alice*!

Har, har! Ryan Poncho whooped. Though ofttimes cant and argot wash o'er my tongue, when I set this priceless kazoo unto my lip, I am fain to set the table on the floor! And, with this, the elegant hayseed let forth another blast which may be thus notated:

With this vast melodious canto ringing in his vexed cerebrum, Serge fell upon the Persian lying vaingloriously on the floor, and, at this moment, sound asleep. But these are more than decibels! our pilgrim quavered. These are fairy sounds urged from the airy syrinx and the timbrel, not to say the caduceus of pie-eyed Dionysos! At this great name, the Persian stirred in joy.

Pay no heed to that Arab pinned twixt you and the parquet, brave voyager, good Poncho spoke, but bend your ear-shells to this wild-soaring chord, a veritable mélange of the diatonic mayhem of the staunch Crusades! And whistling a blast of carbon dioxide through his metal reed, he played:

A kind of carnal joy spread over Serge's countenance, the while he rolled and gyved within his friendly jeans. By the lascivious Jupiter's great straining codpiece, thus he wove his song, this is more pungent and spectacular than a politician's rhetoric! And with this he rolled his eyes along the snoozing Persian, begging for, yet afraid of more, as a damsel roiled in the sin of Manichee.

Just one more, the sage leader smiled all crinkly like Edmund Gwenn. And this, I warn you, is as close as I can come to The Ineffable; hip to this, dear wanderer, imagine then what the Primal Phrase must be like, why man, 'tis the musical equivalent of the philosopher's stone, changing the dumb yawps of the sublunary world into aural ambrosia; and without a moment's stay, the Doc bent to his dazzling task and let loose upon the office air this bar:

By Xanthippe's favorite clout, gasped Blue, I shudder in a throe or two of wild abandon, and feel my manly juices gushing gaily from my loins as if I had beneath me Miss America, rather than this Arab in his noisome toga! And all a-grit, he let the act of shame sweep him to the bright empyrean, wherein the seraphim and cherubim fell into clouds, bought trumps, and otherwise got through their endless days. And yet, he said, when Nature hight allowed him speech, you say that this is not the Great Phrase that I seek? 'Slid! I hunch and blench in thinking of the vigor and the beauty of that Sound!

And you shall hear it, valiant stooge, carped Poncho, or these old eyes have never feasted on a co-ed's thighs!

Blue had staggered to his feet, weak as Agamemnon after being banjaxed by Aegisthus in the shower. I fear that I must rest a day or two, he wheezed, here at The College, if I may. These notes, this music of the spheres, has enervated all my vim. I must recoup my strength before facing . . . The Ineffable in leafy Illinois!

An excellent idea, my gallant! And tomorrow, may I suggest that you stroll into town to witness a memorial for Jacques-Paul Surreale, the late Chairman of our Gardening Department, dead one year now of a surfeit of fringe-tree root in coralberry sauce. The latter is a speciality of the famed Indiana Club, WASPs only, no jigs, tie and jacket at all times, ladies' grill, supper dance Friday night. No matter. But it might be just the thing to calm your nerves and prepare you for the road.

It sounds indeed unto and all belike same tonic-like.

But certainly, the Chairman twinkled. And while you dig and get behind this blubbering memorial, perhaps your wife—whom, I understand, is charming as a new-sprung beautyberry bush—might like to shop away an hour's span or so in our Mighty Mall, as chicks adore to do.

It sounds like just the ticket, Blue mused, although I have little or no hunch whatsoever what that weird idiom portends. I'll impart this idear to Helene, who, even now, is ironing her old fedora somewhere on vast campus.

How I love a woman in a hat! crooned Poncho. Madonn'! It makes-a me craze! And with that, he ushered Serge out into the blasts of vicious sunlight that whacked the land. Tell your faithful spouse, he said, to take the lonely, quiet road that runs behind the Pizzaburger labs. No one will bother her there, he leered, nor even lay an eye on her.

How start to thank you, Dr. Poncho? And Blue's eyes filled up with stern yet gentle tears.

Ho ho! *De rien*, as they say in Montparnasse. Make sure though, that she dons her hat, the Doctor goggled, for ofttimes the sun at midday can baste the brains of tender womenfolk. And, trousers curiously tented, he watched our Blue clunk off into the brutal glare.

« 27 »
Elegy for
Jacques-Paul Surreale

Yes, my friends, Surreale has passed from this mortal curl to a better world; Jacques-Paul Surreale! Is there one among you who does not remember him? Does his memory fade, flake, and founder, now that he has, as they say, cached his chops? Let me then, as the Mayor of Blatherville, refresh, if that is the word, and it is the word, refresh, I say, I insist, your collective memories. I have had this little talk mimeographed or something, and will pass it out to you when I have desisted.

What did the sight of this man, this dear Jacques-Paul, bring to mind? I mean, uh, what were his attributes? They were, and I mention just a few that the vox populi noticed in his forty-seven wondrous years here on this spinning glob. He had a bagful more, but and however: shoofly moron and peach toddy; migraine warbler, masocherian and ashcan baritone; nimbus cerulean and orangeade psalter; lockstep motherfucker and dangler asshole; serendipitous album, aztec microscope and wedge exposure; teterboro rapidoprint, eversharp daddy, verlaine camel and sawbuck marmalade; royal blank book; vegetal dundee; kilroy clean 'em up; rocky swingline and ballpoint anjou; bauschlomb petillance; bonsoir la lune; bistro crackerjack and submarine living room; blue disaster; epiphany lemon; zarruzzi; octagon kate; zippo enameloware; fudge skippie; moscow rose and ward eight; dutch mulligan; crayola rock; reproducing red ashtray; endpaper pastoral, systemic agfa and elmer scotch; cordon bleu royale; paideuma label; buckram austen; russo millefiore; cinzano south; mint alcool; close-order paper clip and fiction filed beginning.

And if you think that *that* is supreme hot stuff, do any of you citizens and chunky-faced neighbors remember what JP looked like? His zotzed and circumambient eyes? Moon zephyr white and russet hair? Alluvial nose just slightly quetzalcoatl? And don't neglect his maced and thund'rous eyebrows black as Christmas shoes, lashes long and caustic like a livid lunar lay, a brow broad as a pyk walwed in galauntyne, beige ears almost lemon waxy white, gladstone mouth with hint of eerie snowfall, and blank teeth alla vino paradiso bianco. Moving around and about, recall Surreale's lips the very pinks o' borders lavender, latex ice and minty barrel tongue, a chuckling agamemnon of a neck, two shoulders deep in kali stupor, a chest touched on in the azure billet doux of paloma miss, a foxed and am'rous bloomsday of a belly, libby krasdale biceps bloomingly del monte, slanged forearms glittering with bix, petite ebon and sappho darksome wrists, and his fingers cobalt, fingers coal, fingers cadmium, fingers cool, fingers ginger. Bejesus Christ! his nails all a loony luminous quintessence, haut monde crotch zinged into silence, a penis appleblossoom rabelaisian in hearts, a sighing maniac in twilight of a scrotum, hot santa ana crackling pubic hair, testes brave and reckless as apple pies, winnowed thighs done rayon lackawanna, petite yet ponko buttocks pot au feu, kneecaps redolent of jesuits at the dentist, calves whizzed around korean avocados, boxed taped tied and labeled wettling ankles, plus toes trendy, toes torrid, toes torroncino, toes tungsten, toes paprika. I sob, I sigh, recollecting this champ elite's smile parasol azul yet mansfield park, his dotting wizzering and boining glance, his spanked cerise that busts the garters laugh and frown to fulminate flann's flan and finnan haddie, a sigh riised out as leda swacked and feathered, warmy moist sub-nylon lace rich stretches, zit bellows wedgwood orangery, inhalations exhalations balderdashing brilliant, wildly stewed and mildly brunswick thrashings, his crazed maccool of a lordly gait, such jumps and leaps all blarney of a dew, kisses in the mode of sulpicia cum cerinthus, fists blamming gesticulent noirs sur la lune, hospitable gargantuas of shuffled shamble, his soles as out of date as all big doors and his jacked detonate erections quadriviis et angiportis.

I say: This was a man! And if his attributive stuffs and the way he struck, in his full bearing, the peeled and naked orb, ain't enough for you good appleknockers republicanos, entertain for a nonce or two, what he did in his life, his deeds heroic, deeds hierophantic. He gumballed and shenangoed endless crates of white labels in the north river bitter winds; waned at dirty desks and beamed out flyblown windows at baltics, smiths, and presidents; gazed at balding bookkeepers with the sing-sing heebie jeebies; furbelowed in four-in-hands and listened solemnly to fools with oatmeal haircuts; filed green for glum and boring, white for ho-hum, pink for wait a second, and red for cut the bastard off; stretched ten minutes to fifteen and twenty mumbling his toasted corn and joyless joe; crammed commodes with piles high of intelligence courtesy of Dun and Brad; spoke pompously of lilacs in the dooryards blooming to a pipe and high black shoes; ballooned and samboed not to mention glaumed the swell flatiron tall; waited patiently for views of strapping hose madisonly metropolitan and leafy life; whiled his tulips, swept his chimneys, and cosmodemonized the ranks of crippled couriers; lammed it on the jesse owens and bolted breezily with his final check; reinsured, complete with a thousand twangling errors, feeble fey and fecund sons of bitches far and fulsome; peered beneath the stalls for gentil-hommes with agued Al to put the latter's mind at rest but always failed; purloined for sophomoric laughs the amarillo mongols of one Walter King, a pure prince of a psychopath; retched and ratcheted at the snapper's panama, the snapper's stetson, and the snapper's bowlertrilby; wielded a red-ink bejayzus stamp but for what and whom was at a loss to know; laughed for Red, the Marxist carl, as he lobstered in from beachy weekends with his nubile novia; old golded smoke at his panama's hatty elder bro, a corpulent kraut if dair effer fuss fun; stood in amuse at the corrugated corseting of Miss Wexler, the iron spinster on terms su preme with warts and washcloths warm, but not with wantonness; boffed zok! and whammo! nervously at the promise of the white shirt wondrous diurnal, also starched; bowtied and polkadotted, schlepped loads of first-class mail for Mr. Jiminy C for Christmas Nelson; heard the plump and puerile pals from Jersey Nassau blither black and orange to each other; swayed awestruck, sat cock-eyed, stiff in his tented trousers, at the girdled yet gorgeous hips thighs and bottom of Miss Lewdy Lovelie, ravishing receptionist; crunched and powed into desks and other items in a cloud of musky attar from a dozen ordering broads, though middle-aged yet toothsome; sudsed and dove for pearls in apron blank and slammed down china thick and laceworked to raucous drunks till Sunny Sol limped in from the Atlantic for some ham and eggs; green-aproned, hoffed and skiddoed multitudes and myriads of poster paint all brown for third-rate art; queasied, bored as Jesus Aitch, over garbage parcels, trash, and Xmas xrap in the tattered costume of the red-white deuce; spat and ambuscadoed Freddy, the shame of Bensonhurst, outcast of the tribes of Schmaltz; bled flats and humped palettes for assemblies, reeled and staggered skids and sweated handtrucks (by Hernia), daunted dollies like any other asshole ace; drummed down the booming windows almost but not quite on the dirty digits of north river dasheroos; slambangoed diesel manifests blue-cold to the bone in a borrowed skullcap courtesy of toothless Jack from Hackensack; honest as the day is lone, cracked his gonads, spoining the silvuh of the roadwise horde; sockdolagered and often poozed the groaning new-pine shelving with paper products straight from redwood land; listened, bored and bilious, to busted swedish bullshit anent the bright lights of old Gotham and the absorption of a zillion cocktails; belly full of cheap baloney and cheaper seeded rolls, assisted people looking for some book about some Greek by some Homer-I-forget-his-other-name; wondered about what went on beneath the weighty Wanda Wasserman's woolen skirt and watched her languid limbs between her hugest hips and highest heels; dispatched old trucks to farthest Morristown, checked them in from stupid Newark, allatime accepting tacitly the foreman's wampum of hyperbole erotomania; did not get straight the zany lather and the casks of oil produced and sold by one Suds Stanley and his sluggard Sons; punched and pressed and washed and packed and pushed and poked at teflon (made by maniacal Maigne) and meantime heard his stomach fall apart; pushed diegos, hustled rastuses, and was pushed and hustled by abes and sys in turn, and all to transport tinny presents culled with coupons; bamboozled and was thus bamboozled by his lawless boss, king of sales, duke of copies, all made by heat and heartache; salammboed lamps and blew the inventory, popping at a gallon jug of manahattas all the while; observed amour ablossom twixt a grinning suit and a titless typist, right beneath the eye of hubby Harry Horns; wrote a billion letters to burgs and also suburgs 'neath the worried lamps of Madame Starr, owl-founder, brace buddy, harcourt helper, and a vestal in her heart of hearts; in a daze of mania, whizzed out reams of platitudes in re wordy waifs up for adoption under the direction of a woeful walker, lonely and latent in Cos Cob; and drank his sadness into foolishness as prelude to a demise of all his occupations as an average joe.

And if this, delightful denizens, still ain't enough to melt your moral hearts, cock an eardrum to old Jacques-Paul's legacy to you, yessiree bob! To you and to your children, and to your children's children, all this until it is plumb gone, all this, these, items: hillocks blue and mounds macabre of root beer barrels lissome and monsterious; candy eat-the-paper buttons aglitter in synthetic colors scintillant; shoeleather with the tart biaggio of apricots achuckle from Salerno's sun; thwell thuckers that lathteth all the day to pop the eyes and round la boca; lashings and larrupings of lucky stix to which the man in white affixeth corny syrup froid; Emperor Frank's, by the grace of God Almighty, nectar for each and every nonce; Dixie Shakes in umber domino; waxlips vermilion and sweet as Sydelle Seize's kisses that pluck up the very soul; potable punch in odd bottles inedible; les twistes marshmallow à la Alpine; the whips you wuv aw bwack and chewy; Van Amsterdam Hooten's hunks of crazed cacao; rubber ice cream in criminal cones; maryjanes created by the League of Dentists, U.S.A.; sombreros mejicanos con naranja y vanilla frio as a fontbonne freshman; splintery ice from the splattery bed of the sputtering truck of the iceman Baresian; stale scots mincecakes and buttergrease shortbread piled plumply in paper Queen Marys; lickerish lickrish tortured into button your lips; phials of phony beebees multihued although mighty mingy; eyeless nigger babies courtesy of Andros Kingfish, Nights of the Dark Peculiar; olympian egg creams avec ze secret tweest, to wit: ze lait mus' be frigid unto frizzing; bonomo bananacherrychoc from Turkey; tiny tired AWOL bags aburst with chewy chunks whipped up from sweat and sun and salty water; peppercorns the core of splendid suckerballs; apothecary branches in which sit anisette to suck; crooning fluted tins of petey barnum pie with slicy spoons to lacerate the lingua; charred and charming mickeys in the boining bowels of garbage conflagrations; the blistering delights of depression sangwiches brought to you by Heinz and Gulden; George Washington Saturday pies with the Swedish maiden's four-eyed touch to turn you spicy crazy; a jitney's worth o' luscious buns to make masticators mousy-grey and stupidly agape; Charlotte Anne Russe to cream all over mobs of maniacal admirers and their holy keds akudo; fish and chips that fuck up folios of funnies; those whiz delights, baloney cheese and potato slaw on seeded roll to nourish harps and donkeys; Honey "Jelly" Apple, the Brothers Caries' crude assistant; fullchock samiches of meins and chows hot from Canton-on-Cinq-et-Dix; a bag of whimperstale and vilerot wafers, two tons for a dime and dear at that; pinkglass pitchers every Wednesday nite, rotten with epco cereza, epco limón; the U.S.S. Navy Bean, foundered in Vinegar Sea; le pain New York avec la margarine avec pains and aches of Cuban gold atop; a glass the sister of our friend the pitcher luscious with bread and milk to her blushing bottom; last month's baking crunched and greased in last week's bacon blood; the fat face of friendly Jack O'Lantern all agrin just asking for a licking; Skippy's Sunday, white as weddings and as red as rouge; corn popped pink and wheedled white; carmine cutesy dollars that fire up the gums; a royal hook off a royal jab and zut! the mouth's all purple; and Jesus cream vanilla as a vestal to help you glide into a heaven sternly clean and protestant that don't mean maybe if you got the urge.

« 28 »

Pastourelle:
Dr. Poncho Tells
of His Afternoon of Ecstasy

Ah, there she was, scuffling through the hedges,
The glorious and thinning-haired Helene Gavotte,
And I, decked out in my Dr. Poncho garb,
Gazed hornily upon her in her trav'ling clothes;
Her tattered shmatte, peasant skirt, her blouse
All washed to airiness, her filthy "desert" boots
From Sears, and a disreputable torn fedora.

I caught up with her 'spite my stiff'ning rod.
"Helene, my dear," I said, "my lollipop,
My heart is cracked because you look so warm."
"Oh! Dr. Poncho," croaked this sweaty miz,
"Don't for a sec belabor your deep brains
With worry or concern about this greasy flush.
I'm perfectly O.K., and cool as splashing clam."

"Fudge," I said, "how sweet yet thick you are;
I ran like crazed opossum down the road
To walk with you and be your guard.
A luscious wife like you should never schlep
All lonely through these glades and bosks,
Without a staunch professor by your side.
These woods are full of sex-crazed academics."

"Oh, noble Ryan," blushed the blowsy broad,
"Do not think that I, the wife of simple Serge,
Would ever listen to the bullshit lines

128

That scholars use to lower ladies' drawers.
Nay," and the sweetie heaved her little bosom out,
"As a doting wife and mama of a darling brat,
I'd sooner let a freshman stroke my sacred corse."

"How lumb'ringly your words take flight," I smiled.
"It's clear as plastic wrap that you're the daughter
Of a college graduate, a well-read salesman
Who poked your half-crocked mother in far-flung motel.
I'm wacked out by your gorgeous charms
And would be even more entranced could I
But protect your bony albeit toothsome flesh."

"Academic cynosure," the lass then sighed,
Wringing out her sweat-bedrenchèd coif,
"You are a sport to think that I'm the product
Of a gay and casual boff ripped off by
An ace sales representative and a rustic slut.
But I must tell you that my parents coarse
Worked like slobs in a grungy candy store."

"The more amazing then your tempting looks,
That make the ravishing Medusa gawk!
It must be, then," I leered, "that a flitting fairy,
Thinking that you were a boy, gave you your beauty
At your birth. But when I fantasy
How much more beautiful you'd be
If I rode betwixt your thighs, I plotz!"

"I feel a quart or two of torrid blood
Crashing toward my secret parts," she squealed.
"It's hard to think that a distinguished prof
Like you, my Doc, with beaucoup degrees,
Would wish to hump the afternoon away
With such as I. I am sore tempted,
But enchained by wifely modesty, I reck."

"Your modesty," I drooled, "makes you
Even more a prize. If you do fear

129

That a passing student or a truckload
Of idiotic farmhands will spy us out
In our raptures wild of pump and thrust,
We'll saunter off the road and commit the act
'Neath that clump of sumac shingleberry there."

"My female yearnings," said the gasping piece,
"All command me to a wild unfettered fling
With you, scorching Doc, and urge me toward
That foliage, where we may do a lot of
Dirty stuff. But," she reddened, "I fear
That you will lose respect for me as a person,
If we play horsy-horsy in the shadowed weeds."

"Lose respect?" I laughed. "Miz Gavotte,
I'll cherish in my lonely memory, as the years
Limp by, each second of our wild, abandoned leaps.
Besides," I winked, "I would be honored
If you'd allow me, creamsicle, to commemorate this day
By permitting me to buy for you a new,
Drip-dry shmatte, and a previously owned chapeau."

"Your words send jabs and hooks into my soul,"
The trembling doxy breathed. "I'll treasure up
The bagatelles you'll buy with academic loot,
And treasure, too, the memory of your lust.
Now let us crunch into the nettles here,
Undo our garments, and in a trice or twain,
Jazz each other unto heights of craziness!"

"Oh pepsi, twinkie, milky way," I said,
"I'm in your thing and, oops, I've shot my wad!
A million thanks, and now, so long. I'm off!"

"Wh-what?" the whore cried. "I hardly knew
That you were on! Is this the type of hump
That scholars throw?" she keened through rustling leaves.

« 29 »

In Which
Poncho Takes a
Poudre and Bone Playes Dumbe

Blue is discovered on the road back to The College, his head filled, since we can, because of the Magic of Literature, see inside his head, with what he is pleased to call "notions of Mortality." He recites odd ends of the Nature Poets: Words-smith, Bligh, Froth, the Gocourt Brothers, Jem Casey, Slater, Mio Cid, Dixie Lowell, Zangwill Pendejo, T. Pallidum Stickney, Jeff Jeffers, Snod Snodgrass, and Gordon Gilbey Booth, "spicing up" his recital with critical snatches (old but still elastic) of Jerzy "City" Kosinski. As he is ripping through Booth's "Elegy on a Birch that Crushed My Lean-To," he spies, in the golden dusty haze of the typical Indiana road on which he wends, his . . . wife!

BLUE: What is shaking, spouse divine? I thought that you were off to yonder Shopping Mall to exercise your sacred right as a consumer?
HELENE: Doctor Poncho "bumped" into me upon this very road and made a coupla indecent advances on my person, like, "What think you of a casual zig-zag, my bobolink?"
BLUE: It boots no further madness thus to mouth such crippled jest, and yet, as faces oft do skid upon the welkin shattered o'er with blasts, I fear me that the starling's oath will carry 'round the globe like th' ungirdled seas!
HELENE: I blushed so that you could not tell my face from the arse of that ba-boon who hangs around the exits of deep Africa! He was as mad in his erotic craziness as that violent wop men call Hieronimo!
BLUE: I've always loathed the name, which, to my perusal, smacks and slaps of pizzas found upon the roads that zip through outlands like Nebraska! Oh, cursed am I to have a piece whose fletch from lechers' eyes not even tattered schmatte covers o'er! Then let's to campus where, as smold'ring butt confronts a funny ashtray that may say it hails from Lake Hopatcong, I'll throw into the very

orthodonture of his craggy face this charge so base and vile that only filthy frog-gos like Georges Bataille would even think to write of it!

HELENE: I traipse in the gaping holes your sneakers leave in this sad dust!

In a snap of the fingers they are on the campus of The College, running, running, as if their great revenge had stomach for anybody's hairs! And in their mad ca-reer, they bash smack dab into tweedy Bone, sucking placidly, as was, and is, his wont, upon the seasoned bowl of his old briar cob.

BLUE: A hasty ciao, sagacious herringboned professor. Is Doctor Poncho in his chamber, deep in applications? I must see him on a matter of most vile and op-portune purport.

BONE: As chuckling misfortune has it, secure within the purse he wears upon his belt, Dr. Poncho has flown from these, the hoary leaves and sunny lawns that burst the very bounds and bonds of sublunary vulgar concepts, to attend, all in a rush of feverish emergency, a conference somewhere in that quarter of this once-great Nation that lies toward the inky forests where the goop-hawk dips and bangs against the noble grizzly. He left with naught but umbrella and the AWOL bag he's treasured ever since his long-estrangèd wife did keep her soiled unmen-tionables in its depths.

BLUE: Oh wicked blight that foists in clay!

HELENE: He tried to make me do some naughty acts or else!

BONE: Wh-what? My colleague, Ryan? A WASP so deep and true that folk mis-take him for a game-show host or other breed of grinning simp? If true, this is, as the honest churl who delivers beer unto the "student" "lounge" might say, a fucking shame!

HELENE: Oh, 'tis true, wise fop! The man did clutch my female thing a nonce.

BONE: My heart, deep as it is in pain as though 'twere in the fiendish grip of the stoccado, whispers to me that you speak the plain and knobby truth. I've seen our Doctor in the stinking grip of mad erotica when in the presence of a female stoont, his homely cardigan athump with yearnings that dare not speak their monickers. But to make vile proposition to a guest . . . Such cafone-like acts are, so to speak, canaille. How I wish that he were here, so that I, pipe all askew and fuming, could confront him with you and so watch him squirm!

BLUE: The vast imbroglios that creep beneath the tincted closets of the stars do cry out in their wonted innocence for vengeance pitiless, aye, though the wom-anish side of my great raging heart doth tremble in the breach!

HELENE: Soft you, Serge. It comes!

BLUE: What sayest thou? "It" comes?

HELENE: Such limpid expletive but seemed a good idea, given us the context of this strange scene that we inhabit.

BONE: When the miscreant and malcontented Machiavel returns, I'll have a word with him, then take this case to the highest levels of our sternest officers! Ryan Poncho will never get, no! nor will he e'er present another plaque!

BLUE: For this belief, much thanks, kind Weede. And now, let us collect our Zim, my love, and pack the cart and start off for The University.

HELENE: I saw the babe this day this morn happily engaged in tearing ivy off the walls of the Hall of Eclectic Disciplines, named for its donor, the wondrous Mulligan.

BONE: He was still there, the chub, at the luncheon hour. Sweetest boy!

BLUE: Then let us go, or as the Spaniard says, vamoose!

They leave, plowing through weird leaves and mounds of football cheers, while Dr. Bone smiles knowingly right through his clouds of Granger.

« 30 »

The Gavottes Come
at Last to The University

Then through the bresh that heaves and gloams
    the fey Gavottes did trek;
Through baldrypress and crossleaf loams,
    up to their knees in dreck.

When, jeez! they came to Skillet Fork,
    where Blue pitched to the ground.
There did he sacrifice a pork,
    upon a pecan mound.

" 'Tis Illinois! or Illini!"
    his loathsome mouth did spew;
Meanwhile, Helene poked in her eye
    an elbow, soaked with dew.

And quick as half-assed leatherleaf
    toils in the Kankakee,
His dust-bespattered pangs of grief
    apace fled through the brie.

Then rested they 'mid sassafrass
    quenching away the noon;
Serge stretched full-length in whango grass,
    Zim and his Mom in broon.

What dreams then rose from Bonpas Creek
    only Great Pan can know;
(And mayhap Hera, queenly Greek,
    high in her bungalow.)

⟨ *Blue Pastoral* ⟩

Oiled with bananas (so Serge dreams),
    his glist'ring instrument
Sends forth its noise; thus loony beams
    crash on a tenement!

Bud Koussevitsky, Homer Welk,
    and ilks of others such,
Fix 'round his neck The Crooning Elk;
    hosannahs praise him much!

La douce Helene, in gronko's shade,
    slumbers (though vetch sore prick);
She dreams her Blue has made le grade,
    and found at last a shtick!

She dreams her Blue has found his Phrase;
    great Art will ne'er be same!
His phiz from T-shirts forth doth blaze,
    the Congress whoops his name!

From little Zim, among the chard,
    rivers of drool ooze forth;
His visions are of steaks and lard,
    of fried jacoons and broth.

So did these three rumbaceous clucks
    snooze in the torpid glatch;
Fantasies gave the grinning shmucks
    respite from bri'ry patch.

Till, with the clamb'ring of the moon
    (that looked just like a poil),
Up from his bed of macaroon
    great Blue burst like a boil.

"The throne of knowledge squats avaunt!"
    (the phlegm cracked in his throat);
"Let's heave and hump our corses gaunt
    unto its chancred moat!"

135

Then humped and heaved they through the elms,
    through ironwoods and gleets;
The thorns of ninebarks, binks of whelms
    tore at their hands and feets.

All night beneath the pearly lamp
    they sweltered toward their goal;
E'en Serge's bike clips were all damp;
    his face all doit like coal.

Still they clanked on, past Sangamon,
    through Charles Mound and DuPage;
Over the snowy Big Bon-Bon,
    skirted dark-sodomed Zage.

Then, as Big Sol leaped from his sack,
    and Wabash silver turn'd,
Our stooges glimpsed through bosky crack
    the U! Their numb legs churned!

They smashed through burningbush and gorse
    through mountain heath and rose;
Pity the moosewood, or the horse
    that stumbled 'neath their toes!

Noble Des Plaines, proud Apple Creek,
    saw but a frantic blur;
Kaskaskia, stern Calumet,
    heard an elated whir.

Then they were on those regal grounds;
    and stood with lips askew.
They sighed, "Great Fuck," "Oh Zut," and "Zounds";
    rooted like flies in glue.

"And now to search out sage Dubuque,"
    roared Blue, knee-deep in beech;
"I'll hear the Secret Phrase—or puke!"
    he vowed, and popped his breech.

〈 *Blue Pastoral* 〉

They gave brief thanks to Doctor Chick,
    to tweedy Bone, to all;
Then Serge, his ass in gear, all quick
    set off to pay his call.

« 31 »

Dr. Dubuque's Eglogue
Joyned with Miss Clarke
Grables: An Erotickal Interlude

Siddown, Mistress Grable, here is honeycomb fit for Emperors, and grapes, and the curious peachy peach and lettuces, and escarole so to speak or some other quaint legume consumèd by your swarthy Italiano. Siddown, muh dearest, and remove your shoes and let me kiss your toes right through the slipp'ry nylon that encaseth them and that encaseth all, yes, all your lovely albeit slightly heavy nether limbs up to that spot o' which I dare not think without groaning and waxing so enflamed I fear my homemade cardigan will burst, as it were, into belching fire.

Oh Dr. Dubuque—may I call you doc?—Oh Doc Dubuque, to find myself with you, alone, in this vast ringing plain surrounded by the rude and homely yet so vivacious hunks, chunks, orts, shards, sherds, and fragments of carrots, Swiss chards, cucumbers, and the repulsive tare, and God knows what all else, is mother to emotions so wild and tingling that, despite my face encarnadined, I'll toss my high-heeled slippers into the encroaching furze wound round with hollyhocks and stuff, woodbine clematis and the like, and thrust my dainty dogs all joyously into the caressing air! Note how my nylon stockings do enfold them and my legs as well like unto a second madd'ning skin. Oke?

How insanely wacked-out I am for you, my so-called secretary, or assistant, you'll soon know. Permit me a moment while I doff my trousers and fold them with some care along the creases, prior to laying them with gentle care, almost dovelike in its solicitude for this polyester pure, here upon this stringbean bush so that no man can guess we've gamed and joyed and tumbled all the afternoon by glauming on grass stains tincted green upon my trouser knees, or, failing that, by thinking on the fact that the magic cloth of which these trousers are enweaved achieved a rumpled state because I left them on while a-jousting in the lists of love. What they do not know will not, as Baba Rhum Mañana says, fucking bother them. Ah darling secretary, your twinkled orbs are as the blue sky and its stars that act as roof or maybe ceiling to Mount Rushmore and its granite phiz or phizzes, and your breath's as sweet as fields of jalapeño peppers in old Louisiana or wherever that rare spice grows nowadays, if you follow me. Or for that matter, where it used to grow, so to speak.

I do not follow you, dear Doc, because my simple woman's mind treks back and forth between subjects domestickal such as laundry, kitchen, shopping, cleaning gobs of dust off filthy surfaces, and the need to please and joy men such as you! Administrator! Leader! E'en, yes, gross capitano of le business, making money hand over hand. Yet somehow I do know what you are uttering for I feel it, yes, we weak creatures have that knack, I feel it deep deep fathoms down betwixt my ruddy thighs, the latter full now of mosquito, fly, and chigger bites, there where we all truly live, 'spite the wild and dang'rous talk of those jew anarchists who think that we too should make wee-wee in a urinal and study on the ways and means to shoot off bazookas and hit fungo triples and such stuff. Fie! But soft— come close to me beneath this lettuce here and gawk your dear and rheumy eye-bones out as I slip out of my skirt, my slip, my pantyhose, my panties, girdle, body shirt and bra and blouse and dicky, and my sweater and my vest, my necklace, scapulars, ID tags, and another item or two that have flown clear from my whirling fevered brain! Doc? You aren't fallen into Morphine's arms, my love? I'll be but another quarter-hour. Meanwhile, my snowy, pillowed bosom, white as cauliflower, is now more or less untrammeled. Here, I offer it to your burning gaze, my sad sweet guy.

Asleep? Har-har! You do insult my wanton carnal envelope! How can I drift into that sleeve of care while here, rapt in my BVD's, I lie amid the nettles and the shyly nodding clovers next you, my eyes, despite the fact I left my cheaters in the office, riveted upon your intoxicating décolletage, which reminds me, as it were, of a filthy story, one not fit for your chastely icy Luth'ran ears. But enough of chatting of my knowledge wide as Ocean's aqua swells and crunching breakers that even now are busting the bejesus out of some poor little tyke's half-assed castle made of sand, but where, only Jove hisself can tell. Here, here, my starling, let me pelt you with a mittful of these rosy razzberries! My heavens! How their pink and gorgeous juice does set off the arctic damask o' your cheeks! By the living word of ev'ry thund'rous preacher on the air o' boring Sunday morns, you're not half-bad! Half? Har-har! By twice the squared hypotenuse o' dread

Infinity! Perhaps a trifle overweight, now that I ogle you sans gripping corselette, but how like unto a field of oats is your compassed and circumferential belly! And your heaving thighs are like a clamorous battalion upon the chow line! And your breasts, now all free and proud and dedicated to philosophical idears and all such stuff, do stand upon your tented chest like two jeeps painted all immaculately white!

Forgive me, rapturous Doc, that I wrinkle up and squinch my azure orbs until the tears pop out as big as baseballs, the better, espouse I, to dig on your flabby, middle-aged, yet manly torso, but as you see, I too have left my specs upon that desk that I call Home, dizzy as I was but a scanty time ago with your sizzling and lewd proposal that we flop here in the lap of Nature, here to let that wise old goddess take her course. Yet! Yet I do affirm most potently that despite my cursed astigmatism, I see sharp enough to know that your small but willing engine of engend'ring is all swolled up with passion and the simmering humors of careening lust, so to speak, if I may clutch at one of your endearing mots. May I, coot?

Clutch at? Aye! And more than clutch, my seeded hollyhock! Clutch and keep unto yourself as your very own, to be employed all profligate in letters, conversations, aimless bullshit on the phone, and even inter-office memorandos! Great Priapus! That I should live to lie here with you, beneath these kohlrabi vines and blowing eggplant blooms, alone and far from the backbiting city and its mad farrago and charivari of cupiditous ambition and its asshole stars! That I should fasten these my gummy eyes upon your gen'rous flesh, your corse half-naked save for these silken hose from some Parisian nuthouse of a boîte, and a few other lacy odds and ends of undergarments that do but serve t' enhance your plumsweet flesh, that is, those parts of it that do gleam naked! It is enough to make me an amnesiac moon man, and for a jot and tittle place in some stinking closet of my brain the fact that I'm a family man as well as a crackerjack administrator of a fifth-rate yet upward crawling university! Take pity on me, Mistress Grable, and let me void my smarting seeds, I think the sentence goes.

Shall we then, doting Doc, shall we perform the act of shame, make with our yearning and besweated bodies that famous beast, it of the double deck? My golden head pressed close as cigarettes within their pack against your thinning white one? My secret parts commingling with yours like two hurried citizens bashing one into the other on the crowded thoroughfare? Or shall we simply scarf each other up with poor weak eyes, content to know that we are free from those conventions Life chucks over us like so much plastic wrap, to know that if we wish we may in a trice or two, blithely screw our asses off, as free as these minuscule and disgusting gnats that swarm about us?

Let scarfing be enough, wanton, brown, and nutty secretary. I am, I do confess it, so rusted in the arts o' love, that I am scared to death, aye, shitless scared, that I would cut the figure of a dribbling moron should I attempt to mount you, front, back, top, or side, although the latter cannot, by what I ken of the copulative act, be construed as "mounting" one's enamorata. And besides, a crazed and industrious bumblebee, zooming home with bags chocked full o' nectar saccharine from his last-suckèd aromatic flower, has tarried for a moment in this shadowed glade or glen in which we lurk in cool and wondrous deshabille, and driven his annoyed and choleric stinger into my ass all trouserless.

Then let me, agonizing Doc, dress myself in these careless crinolines and thick velours and little frou-frous as swiftly as I did but a moment since wrench and pluck and tear them from my quaking flesh all mad with equatorial and torrid hots! And then I'll lead you by your soft and sweaty duke down to the drowsy crick where we may discover cooling handfuls of rich and oozy mud to clap upon that angry welted blister that our friend, Sir Bee, has raised upon your slack and flagging bum. Some other still and humdrum afternoon, when the ennui of our wonted jobs is about to drive us ape and bonkers, we may loiter once again like two erotic vagrants here amid the brussels sprouts and pears and, who can tell? mayhap then we'll consummate the wild dark act that men call humping?

How wise you are, my fondest poggy! Lead away, sweet Clarke, and I'll stumble in your wake, my familiar trousers flung insouciantly o'er my arm, to where that rich mud and glop may lie and its secret alchemy of whatever the hell that promises full-voicèd to remove the pain that now spreads far and wide o'er all my ass's sore expanse.

I'll have this whaleboned and excruciating corset tightly laced up in a flash, as soon as I have brushed it free of tares and pits and petals and these pesky ants that seem to have a fixed idea that urges them to bite the hell out of my yielding and delicious flesh. Begone, you curious yet loathsome creatures! And see, here's one little bastard of a nipper who waits in ambush in my capacious bra! You little snot!

Mistress Grable, may I interrupt your jovial harangue? One thing irritates my college-educated brain to such a pitch of worriment that I must ask if you would deign to let slip from your swell and rosy lips a wise and womanly opinion concerning this small matter.

Of course, dear Doc! Hello! Here we are at last at the slippery and o'ergrown crick bank and there is, as I had prayed, tons and tons of black and gruesome mud! Now, your matter? I'll do my best to satisfy you while I slap and smear this salutary guck all over your weak yet totally enchanting butt. What reck I that it is mostly flab and fat?

What, my lissome mink, do our frolicsome bucolics have to do with the story, so to speak and as it were, of one Blue Serge, about whose musical and knotted head this whole work, if you will, is supposed to amble?

That man, my academic Jove, will soon, a little bird did cheep to me, enter the great University wherein you reign as sage administrator sans peer or peeress, there to get from you a lecture or a wise opinion or some other wondrous educative thing. So the bird did cheep into the very snaredrums of my ears.

Merci, ma tweedy femme. But soft you. Do you think it wise to shove me bodily into this mud as you are doubtless doing? It will be tough as nails to bullshit my wife anent the gross and filthy, aye, unspeakable state of my garments, despite the fact that her poor eyes will be red and bleared from countless hours of television dramas and whatever other crap she watches all in hussied rapture.

I'll join you in the muck, designer skoit and all, you silly bourgeoisie! And together we will roil and gambol in the slop! We'll say we fell into a hidden mudhole while investigating sites for a new cafeteria and student lounge. That should make the shrewish bitch bite on her coated tongue!

Your grimy eyes! Your pitch-black hands! Your gritty bra! I faint!

The dirt upon your sideburns! And your crusted shirt!

I fear that here, in this unlikely place and covered o'er with healthful mud, my manhood must be satisfied! Come, come, my blushing wren, undo your clothing once again and receive my impatient and importunate dread organ!

Oh, Doc! My Doc! My dreamy Doc! I chuck my garments 'mid those nodding sedges and accept your madd'ning peg! The very gods peep down all jealously upon us!

« 32 »
Doc Dubuque's
Idyll, or, Ah, Nature!

The excellent Doc, located beneath the glory of a giant breadfruit tree just now, as we look, bursting into a million chartreuse blooms, bends a rapt and sated gaze upon Blue Serge, and speaks.

I know why you have come, my boy, so to speak. Intelligence concerning your sedulous quest has reached my ears from The College, and I may, just may, mind you, as it were, be able to assist you. For the present nonce, allow me to point out to you some of the glories of Nature, here in Illini, a state where the boll weevil swoops in majestic grandeur down upon the great horned owl! And the catalpa sends forth its shy tendrils to feed upon the baby woodchuck in its subterranean home. It is love that makes the spring go round, young fellow, and even a toiler in the lamplit study, such as myself, feels the wild juices bust and flow as the great solstice flings its warming trends about. Sit, dear boy. Let me point out to you some of the glories that are often lost sight of in the hustle and bustle of the marketplace. I was remarking on these things just today to my right-hand assistant, Miss Grable, a woman of sensibility and appreciation.

Thank you, Doctor, Serge says. I have myself often remarked upon that potency that men call Nature, in all its warps and woofs.

April! Or maybe March! Love! With a peppery pinch of lust! The wild attack of your basic crabgrass and marigold weed, a choice patina of some oddball color against the sad skeleton of tenacious winter, is rather hysterically cheered and hallooed, like the fresh-faced girl next door whose role as a voracious nymphomaniac in the high school musical allows the local rubes to think of her as something more than their kid sister. Yes! And though she will ne'er again be thought of in later years in just this way—this lasciviously wanton way, may I add—at the present time, she is metamorphosing this paint-flaking and ungodly ugly auditorium into a shining whorehouse, as she whips her innocent pelvis around to the bursting strains of the tin-eared yet enthusiastic "band."

143

And while the lips of these debased yokels are still foaming with kudos of varying intensity and volume, May—or perhaps April!—zooms in like a cockroach surprised by homely incandescent light! And May is tremendous! An aura of dandelion seeds charging up the feckless nostril, an ambience of hairy caterpillars eating the trees, the shrubs, the candid stones, even the grey flapping wet wash on a million clotheslines. This socko month seems to be everywhere at once, scoffing up the earth and leaving a redolent spoor of happy springtime lavender shoots, each shyly hiding a glass-eyed lover adrift in fantasies of sweaty fornication! It is the sort of month that bashes simple folk right in the superego, silky and volatile as sinful lingerie what the Pope has urged us all to get shut of lest a fleeting lewdness seize our private parts with grip of white-hot steel!

It is like—a large picnic, or perhaps . . . a barbecue! It is too much, more ribs or wieners or deviled eggs than we can gorge on all at once, more beer and lemonade than we can handle, yes, even though we could make pee-pee from now until the ding-dong knell of doom—or even beyond! We hardly know, by God, what sangwich to snatch at first, what swelling bosom to diffidently prod as we pretend to search for a paper napkin to wipe the melted butter from shocks of bubbling corn from off of our greasy fingers, each one quivering with wild desire to grasp and wrest purest Beauty from the nodding accordion close-nestled by the hirsute apple glade, a-thrum with bees and lice!

And as we clutch at its insubstantial beauty, just as we clutch at the last soggy potato chip, it is . . . going, yes, just as that last chip is being borne away on the tiny shoulders of a busy ant, going, and changing into . . . June! or whatever the next month dares call itself. Let the fete commence, we urge. Let the gala step off smartly, we clamor. Bid the soldiers, so to speak, shoot, or anyway pick up their three-day passes.

Whereas May ran around like a crazy person unsure of the difference between his ass and his elbow, June is sane and sober, something like a mature yet handsome woman employed as, perhaps, a secretary-assistant to a crackerjack exec or administrator, svelte yet zaftig, as our Israeli friends are wont to say in their quaint tongue when they cease for a tittle or a jot from chasing Bedouins across the oases of the Sahara; June is peaceful and serene in a universe of juicy saps—many of whom, by the by, are still prostrate under the blowing lavender shoots that they now call . . . Home! And while the early months of sweet primavera were merely acting—and badly at that—the role of slut and tramp, June is your true ace whore, your superstar call-girl, with the savoir-faire and the sang-froid of those filles de joie who know the arcane secrets of the snapping snatch, the Chinese hanky trick, the aluminum-ball delight, the voyage to Cythera, the cross-stitch rubadub, the back-door two-step, the tumbling bongo-press, the eyeball popper, the Casanova crosslock, and other carnal ploys that boggle the steaming brain pan.

Yes, June! It is the finger on the machine gun, the slug in its chamber ready to fly down the barrel, the breathless moment before the bullet finds its unfortunate target. It is that split-second in an amorous relationship where all the blather and smirks that have eaten up the evening are forgotten in the vast symphony of popping buttons and the whine of yielding zippers. June! A new day! The beginning of the future, the end of the past, the middle of the present, for June . . . is *all* present, nothing but ecstatic sunlight reaching down with warm fingers into the height and depth of your being, sending you, in nameless joy, nose crammed with pollen, into fits of sneezing as you stumble, all snots and tears, into the newly dug sump! And always . . . always . . . stumbling in the everpresent present of . . . June.

In the heart, which is, as we all know and remember from our salad days, a lonely hunter, perhaps the one with his finger on the trigger what we have already mentioned, all the leprous lesions of Old Man Winter are fixed right up, just as they are all across the great yawning pride that men once dared call "the country." The cuts and gashes are stitched and clamped, the punctures, abrasions, incisions, and lacerations are doused with penicillin and dollops of iodine. We stand transfixed, sunk in idiocy like wrestling fans or mayors, our brains as idle as the pupae of the loathsome house fly, dreaming their deathless dreams of endless shit and rotting garbage heaped up to the vaulting skies! Spring, as the bard implied, is far behind once again, and summer, with its heat, humidity, sunstroke, lightning bolts, mosquitoes, chiggers, gnats, deer flies, stinking armpits . . . looms! Autumn, that season of mellow and misty-eyed fruits, and bare-assed winter, achock with slush and the memorable frenzy of gloom that attends its holidays, are both still far away, sleeping, so to speak, on the cusp of silent Time; or, perhaps, beneath its cusp.

Trite and banal crap, so to speak, as it may be, June *does* bust out all over, as Kenny Baker sang, surrounded by enchanted negros, in the film of the same name, so many many years ago. The roses, the spavinias, the brilliant gonococcae in off-fuchsia, dusty grey, amaryllis purple, in every cheerful color, slither, jump, and shuffle across the beaming green face of the countryside, inundating with a riot of shades, tones, and tints the filling stations, the hamburger joints, the bowling alleys, the supermarts, the beer distributors, even unto heaving recklessly through the grime-covered frosted-glass windows of the forever-locked rest rooms! June! How meet and swell it is that this word has the same root as the word "jewel"—for June *is* a jewel, far superior to the gaudy schlock of the sprawling colors that scream and whine April, for instance.

The crazed and neurotic mind wanders peacefully amid the endless soporific balm of all these soothing hints and bits and pieces of color, nodding and blinking in the vast oceans of verdure, in the slothful sargasso seas of putrid geraniums. It is better than a talk with your local pastor about unethical ejaculations, better than a hearty bowl of mulligan on a torrid afternoon in August, when one's thoughts ceaselessly return, as they will, to the dimpled knees of one's beloved, the odd insouciance they display as she falls, often heavily, into the cool depths of the mountain rill that bursts profusely through a breezy glade while the patient bot-fly waits to consume her head when it surfaces in the glorious sunlight.

The vetch quivers. The tares rip. The nettles yearn. Everything is ruthless light and deep poiple shadow on the house that one calls home. Time, space, seasons, the universe itself, are suspended like a pair of nylons from Mother Nature's flow'ry unmentionable. The elders shake. The birches break from the nature poet's weight. The bayberries, the sweetferns, aye, the wax-myrtles ache sweetly for release. And the great cycles of eternal change seem, for a moment, as the beer can groveling in effulgence by the side of the shining blacktop.

The days grow longer, or so it seems. Or is it that the nights grow . . . shorter? We will never know, just as we will never know why hornets like to eat each other. We think that nothing will ever end, that winter will remain locked up in jail somewhere in Argentina. Or Chile! The calm is alive! The silence . . . speaks! The grass grows so slowly that, stare as we may, we can never catch it popping up even a half an inch, nay, not even a quarter of an inch. Or a eighth! It is, surely . . . a miracle. There are no atheists in the brambles.

Roads run east and west, north and south. But where is the east? Where is the west? Where is the other two? Gone where the jest on the lips of the hobo has gone? Beyond the waffle shop? What is past the final liquor store huddled on the pale-golden horizon? Shuttered houses? Weedgrown hedgerows? Busted birdbaths? Fantasies? Dreams? Life, death? A bad summer cold? We know no more than does the tit-faced jackybox that gnaws the porch . . .

June . . . wasteful, lush, plangent, limpid, gross, overweight . . . the fool's paradise, the fool's gold that July pays us for May, only to be paid itself in turn to August by brooding October. These days of effete joy . . . these minutes and seconds of pied Beauty that stick us like plenty of myriads of needles sailing wildly from God's great pin cushion in the towering blue . . . an ancient, hoary knot deep within us loosens its crazed strings . . . a buried lump bursts free at last . . . it is passing strange . . . whither? . . . whence? . . . an unearthly orgasm occurs in the vast trousers of the world as the pulsing lump . . . explodes!

« 33 »
The Doc Makes
Blue What Men Yclep
a "Deal" (Or So It Seems)

Great tortured Jesu on his rood of rough-hewn pica sumac! Blue breathed in adoration. Doctor D, though I have humped and schlepped a thousand mile, yea! and seen mens in performance of a bevy wonders, yet nowhere have I heard mortal throat spew forth such fulsome sentiments! Nor, I dare say, has my wife, the sweet Helene, which whom, by the by, I wonder whither hence has fled, since I see her nowhere.

Be spritely as the double-taloned wickiup, my friend, Dubuque replied, and cease to fret your "brains" in re: the wife. It has been swift arranged that she and your gnashing son should take a powder and sail up and down the fabled Orinoco or the Ganges for a space or so, that faithful readers of this tale shall not get on a wonder anent their unexplainèd absence for a chapter or two or three and take it out upon the author of this History; like, he don't know what he's doing and cannot handle simple fictional techniques. For the woods are filled with critics, who, when they are not ripping off the gowns diaphanous of Dryads, busy their restless hands with the writing of "reviews." Thus, let us leave them to their swelt'ring voyage.

It is jake with me, monumental academic, Blue chuckled heartily. And now, may we chatter on about . . . the . . . Phrase?

A ha, ha, ha! the Doc joined in, and I ween, no less robustly, till the very sycamores stood all leafless and aghast. It is a possibility that what you search for, laughing varlet, is indeed here, and we will look for it before you see another week pass into insubstantial mulch! But meantime, the power of your voice pricks and also prompts me into asking of you one small favor. Huh?

Ask, renowned boss of the great tower that looms beyond the ivy-choked athletics building there! . . . on the lissome, flowered hill!

Sweet fellow! It is this: Each year upon St. Patrick's Day, which I feel it in my very bones is coming 'round in but a jot of time, a person from the U gives a talk upon this great Saint and the land from which he chased the lizards, snakes, worms, garbanzo monsters, and the like. The talk is delivered in the town square and is for the benefit of the rubes and yokels whose whole existence depends upon this puissant U; thus, as you will ken, these apple-knockers loathe and hate us to a seething flame of passionate despisement! To make them think we care a fig about them and that we spend long hours worrying lest their opinion of us take a turn into the worst, if such is possible, we drop a scrap or twain onto them once or twice a year—it is a great humanitarian tradition! In actuality, we do not give a turd for their opinion, but render, as I say, unto laughing Caesar, whatever *that* may mean in this bedraggled context. Thus, but, say I, will *you* give the talk, that great traditional crock of purest shit to calm the raging rubes, asweat in their quaint plastic shoes and strange white belts?

It will be my duty, sir! And an honor that I clutch all wildly to my thudding hairy breast!

How staunch you are! Like a veritable Ajax whacking sheeps! Come, we'll be off to what we, in crazèd jest, call "the English office," where I'll get the speech that you'll spurt forth mañana! And you will give this stirring talk as one "Blarney Spalpeen," a monicker all oozing forth with Celtic echoes. Thus, the restless hicks will be placated for another stretch of what proud Newton labeled "Time," and fall to chomping grisly hamburgers and odd pizzoid stuffs with quickened faith in the intelligentsia's deep care for them.

And after . . . ? Perhaps then . . . ? The Phrase . . . ?

Patience, potent chunk! From chinchy acorns monstrous oaks don't grow by dint of bitch and kvetch, nay! But by the patience of the rock that's been dissolving since some grungy caveman first thought to heave it at a wombat! And now, let's away!

« 34 »
"Blarney Spalpeen" Gives
a Speech on St. Patrick's Day

I have been asked, by the Sons of the Emerald Clout, to give an impromptu speech, whatever that may be, on the meaning, the *true* meaning of St. Patrick's Day, and, as my handle on this foine broit day, ha ha, is Blarney Spalpeen, who knows more about this devout religious than I? unless it be the Great Papa himself, whose presence, because he can only talk dago, would be, as I'm sure you'll all admit, even those of you who are the fabled wretched refuse, the bricklayers, the garbagemen, and the longshoremen, a hell of a half-assed trick to pull on a good American audience, well, more or less, here surrounded by nodding corn stands and blowing oaks!

Yes, the *true* meaning of St. Patrick's Day! What exactly is it, me darlin's? We all know the sad, the shadowy, the pathos-ridden disrepute into which this Holy Day of Obligation has pitched, yes, yes, don't shy away and edge carefully toward the modern parking lot that your cretinous Congressman has had carved out for you from the living granite and humble shale and Christ knows what other goddamned stones and rocks, courtesy Department of Defense! Your stupid crackerbarrel autos will wait for you, decaying the while in the rays of the harsh sun, the few moments it will take me, me blushin' gawms and bemuscled bawneens or something, to finish these impromptu words on the saint who has made your lives what they are here in what for today has been renamed Little Dublin, this typical small town sprawled stunned on the great rolling and fecund plains of Illinois! And environs!

I have said, I suspect, too much already, but let that be, and I implore you, each and every one of you in your hilariously priced "jogging" shoes, to forgive this drumbling, drumbling? bullshit, as Jesus and his mama, Mary, and her long-suffering and no doubt suspicious hubby, Old Joe, will forgive me, knowing, as of course they know, exactly what I am about to spell out in language at once clear and exact, language that gives no quarters nor asks none, language that neither

149

pulls nor pushes punches! Or what's a heaven for? For that is my way, and I'm not a shrewd and cunning cruiskeen for nothing, bedamn!

I have said, I seem to recall, that the true meaning of this glorious day that we will soon be celebrating but a week or two after the Feast of the Aspersion, that purple day on which we commemorate and remember, to our undying shame as good Catholics, if that is not a redundant term, the nasty cracks that were made by Judas O'Scariot about Jesus Christ, who happened at the time to be indisposed, and so could not defend himself against the malicious gossip and chit-chat of this depraved kike. And believe you me, it is no error that St. Patrick's Day falls in the liturgical calendar when it does, or where it does, depending on your view of the space-time hassle, for it was that Great Heart himself who, bumping into O'Scariot on the street, or in a nearby saloon soon after—soon after what? you ask, aha, but Time is jealous of its great secrets—said to him, "Yer a backbitin' bassoon an' a slitherin' maureen!"—and he was talking, me strappin' gossoons, directly into the shifty little mockie's face at the time. What do you think of that? Huh? There were giants on the turf in those days! Now, since he said this in that old-fashioned wop talk, with the amat, esse, illibus, and tubarum types of words, an odd tongue and Christ knows what to make of it, I have translated his sacred words loosely, but you get what I'm driving at. But, *but*, you can bet your little speckled wangeens and your cromlechs that he wasn't just passing the time of day with the rat-faced twerp! And then, bejesus, he hit him a blow on the side of his knotty little head with the great green shillelagh in his gnarled mitt so that a man could hear the bloody crack all the way over to hell and gone in Bronx County! That was a saint for you! None of your creepin' little ginzolas flinging stale bread crumbs to a gaggle of pigeons about *that* monumental chest!

But beating the piss out of this jew fink—is that all there is to commend St. Patrick to us? By God, I say no! What, then, is the *true* meaning of St. Patrick? And also the swell and glorious day we set aside for him, a day when the vomit from a million Irish throats threatens to drown the very world? Or at least parts of Yorkville? I'll tell you, and since our friends, the police, have cordoned off the area, making it impossible for your pitiful attempts to take a powder to succeed in any way, shape, or manner, making them absolutely academic, you'll be happy to listen! And if you're not happy, then may your daughters be married in a pigsty!

What, I ask, and have already asked, if these creased and crumpled notes in my hand are to be believed, is the true meaning of St. Patrick's Day? As legend, great Celtic roaring and stout-soaked legend has it, the Hero of Ireland is St. Patrick—not Finn MacCool, not Cuchulain, not King Sweeny, not Count O'Blather, not Blazes Boylan, no!—but St. Patrick! We all remember Ireland, do we not? That lime, that almost chartreuse-colored island nestling close off the coast of Chile or someplace close by, give or take a league or fathom or whatever they call it in nautical argot, what am I, a commodore? Yes! The Hero of Ireland! He is the man who hustled the snakes out of the country, chasing them until their poor little legs almost fell off as they ran like scared sheeps into the Kill of Fundy or Erie Basin, whatever majestic body of water is nearby that great Port of Eire, that port ever busy, ever bustling, with a merry song on its lips and its wharves crowded with spar and sail and a ready laugh and jest always about to drop or fall or some fucking thing or other.

Yes! We all know this old walnut of a story, and as walnuts go, a damn good one, and I'll not take no for an answer, now matter how you punks and bawds shake your sinful flesh and stand instantly déshabille! And that, as you all can imagine, even the stupidest donkey among you, is a French word for mother-naked, but we all know the lewd and lascivious French, drunk and disorderly and choppin' off the heads of kings and up to their blushing elbows in snails stinking of garlic and bedamn knows what all else and black garter belts! We know it! Yes! But still, 'tis a grand tale. Each and every varmint, critter, and reptile squeaking and moaning and hissing and trotting bejesus into the green ocean surrounding that pleasant land by God like so many crazed lemons! It is, matter of fact, from the juggernautish sight on that historic day, with the crowds of lizards and newts and everything else all cheek by jowl down on the beach that we get the name lemon squash. But be that here or there. We all know, I say, and say again, and *will* say until the last breath in my throat or larynx or wherever the last breath resides, struggles manfully on that ding-dong day called Doom, when the earth shall crack open and the dead rise from their graves, including all your miserable relatives and in-laws that you thought you'd never have to say hello to again, as well as deadbeats like Hitler and Stalin and so many, so many others, that . . . that, whatever, you get what I mean. For the laws of Doom are strange laws, and no man, least of all you ignorant fake harps, can hope to understand them! Or even one or two of the easier ones, for that matter!

Yes, we all know the old story, if story is not too weak a word, for truly it is more than story, it is what scholars call *legend*, as in "The Legend of Weeping Wimpy" or "The Legend of the Choke-Up Phillies." You're hip to what I'm pullin' your coat about? Cold, baby! But. And, but . . . *But* no one ever hears about the tiny little wee people, or as some researchers into the Celtic rites term them, the wee-wee people. Who are these wee-wee people? you ask. Perhaps not all of you, but a few of you, and I, for one, don't go in a big way for majorities, so those of you who don't ask can take a flying glasheen for yourselves for all I care—what am I? your father? Who, I ask again, in vaguely stentorian tones, are these wee-wee people? They are part of Ireland too, believe it or not! Yes, the great Port of Ireland is not solely composed, as most of you ignorant goddam gringos think, of great hulking colleens in cracked brogans and tweed caps. There are plenty of wee-wee people too, puh-len-ty! And they are part of Erin too, yes, a great part, for it is the wee people, which in the Irish tongue are called leprechauns, and which others call dwarfs, who helped—who? Right! Good St. Pat fight all the evil forces and win victory for the Irish!

But victory over whom? The door of Time has slammed on this knowledge and shoved its gasping sconce into the waters of Lethe, but we may guess that the wee-wee people assisted St. Patrick in booting the crawly varmints out of the green land—or why, for Christ's sake, use your head, why would I bring them up? But for sure, they didn't do a goddam thing about getting rid of the English and their kidney ragouts and kippered omelettes and all the other half-ass things they invented—top hats and oatmeal cookies and Bloomsbury and God knows what else. Polo! So though our hearts are full to the bursting point with tears of gratitude for the laughing wee-wees, we must in all fairness admit that they at least partially blew it—or, to use a gross patois that you two-bit yokels will understand, standing there agape in your white plastic slip-on shoes and your peach safari coats, they fucked up a little. A little?! Brothers and sisters, in all candor and to be honestly and sincerely blunt, they fucked up beyond all recognition, as the old army saw would have it, and, by God, does!

But everybody's entitled to a mistake, so let us forget as best we can, the—how shall I call it?—oversight, on the part of the carefree and go-happy plucky wee-wees that permitted the accursed limesuckers to use Ireland as a kind of vacation spot, like maybe the Catskills or Miami Beach, and fill its northern half up to the brim, yes, *mes amis*, to the very gunwales, with a gang of Protestant dudes, all carrying big goddam orange signs and what have you and driving their neighbors right around the well-known bend with their endless off-key hymns. Talk about your dissonance! Talk about your Bella Bostock! So, O.K. Taking all this into consideration, let's give, shall we? the little green dwarfs a break.

There are some, namely Americans all, though I throw no stones, but one feels a spade is always and forever a spade, so, yes, Americans all, I repeat—as we all are or wish to be, your Albanian, your Haitian, your sneaky Mex, your corrupt Vietnamese, your swarthy Sidge—in this fat land of lies and lechery, who still in their thudding bosoms clasp an atom, a tiniest smidgen of what I may term, if I may be forgiven such a glaring chunk of rodomontade, *pique*! And wherefore? Because a foul and degraded story has it that each little asp and cobra and rattler and newt and iguana and gila monster and bushman and python and copperhead who ran for his very life into the Bay of Blather, splashing, fear-crazed, like so many dobermans and pandas, managed—oh, not all of them, but only the hardiest, subscribing, as they did, and by the Precious Blood were glad to, to the great Darwinian Proof of every man for himself and to hell with the women and children!—managed, I repeat, these few, these happy few, to swim like billy be-damn to these States! or, as old whitebeard Walt wrote, "these States!" Here to subtly transmute themselves into policemen! But this is, as I'm sure all of you will agree, a base slander, and there is not a copper alive whose heart beats high and free who will stand still for it for a split second, including those peace officers there on the outskirts of the gathering, gently nudging, gently prodding, gently clubbing and maiming for life that mere handful of you who are attempting to slither off to the parking lot—for shame!—wherein your ludicrous cars are even now, as is their custom, conspiring to throw a piston or decimate their badly installed transmissions, carburetors, and, yes, though it pains me to say it, their rumble seats!

So let us, as I have quietly suggested, give the benefit of the doubt to the jolly wee-wees, those stout dwarfs, who assisted good St. Patrick in his hour of darkest need! And, touching on these funny little bastards, it gives furiously to think, that is, how could such little gombeens scare the living bejayzus out of a king cobra or giant newt? A cobra or newt, I beg you to consider, who, even hunkered down, or lying prone, was at eye level with the tallest and most strapping wee-wee? Despite the fact that the wee-wee people were, as the indelicate might phrase it, pisseyed drunk and filled to the rafters with false bravado, still, they were awful small, awful, *awful* small! Well! That's something to ponder on, is it not? And while you are taxing your headline-sodden brains with it, me glowing potheens, I'll give you the benefit of my own long musings on the matter. It was the very *look* of the little rascals! Speculation, educated speculation, has the wee-wee horde wearing the traditional green of Ireland with little pointed shoesies and little pointed caps, and with a pot of gold in their arms. All this was furnished them by the jovial saint we dub Patty, or Paddy, or Patsy, who allowed them to pick up all these items on time, a dollar down and a dollar when you catch me, as my dear mother used to say. But this is no time for personal reminiscence or self-indulgence, not when the very future of the gross, and I do mean *gross*, national product is at stake. What that product may be is not in question today, yet I may touch on it in another brief talk to you good-natured yankees, but at some future time. Sufficient unto the day, etc.

Now, put yourselves, your lithe bodies, your jogged-out brains, your ruined digestions, all, all the molecules and atoms of your firm flesh and red blood, in the place of these snakes and stuff, lolling around in the emerald grass and laughing triumphantly over the fact that every last Irishman and his sweetly blushing lass was confined to his and her apartment because of their natural fear and disgust of all these slimy sons of Lucifer. Suddenly, as you blow another, yet another smoke ring into the crystalline air of dear old Erin, you hear—as snakes have, as I'm sure you know, ears in every foot and, by God, numberless feet they have, or may God strike me dead! You hear, then, a noise in the brush and you glance up, aromatic cigarette all forgotten. Jesus H. Christ! There before you stands an ugly little gnome of a dwarf, dressed in these loathsome green clothes, I mean strictly plain pipe-rack stuff, brother. The little harp has a pointed hat on and these little emerald good-morning shoes, looks like a goddam elf! He's got a pot of gold in his arms, or stuffed under his oxter, and maybe you're not aware of it but snakes do not cotton to gold, a well-known fact of natural science, which has proven, beyond any shadow of a doubt, that when snakes are given gold to eat in lieu of eggs and little birdies and helpless old ladies, they refuse it and pine away. Consider then the sheer, the overpowering horror of this sight—this grinning wee-wee, with his black-stained teeth, peeking at *you*, Mr. Cobra, from behind a shamrock! And all the nauseating snakes and such dig that there are thousands of these little schmucks, maybe even millions of them, and all are being urged forward, ever and for always forward, by the great trumpeting voice of St. Patrick himself, who is yelling horrible war cries like "Erin Go Bragh!" and "A Shot and A Beer!" and bashing every serpent he can reach, male and female both, with an empty Jamieson bottle. The terror of it! It is mute testament, my buddies, yes, even those of you who are lying broken and bleeding out there by the police lines under the soft spring sun, to the truth of the old motto, "Clothes make the man."

And so, with the snakes and their compadres all swimming for dear life in the giant waves that crash insensate on the rocky shores all up and down that great coast that dares not tell its name, the wee-wees had nothing much to do but sit around under mushrooms and shamrocks and petunias and drink themselves insensible, while the good St. Pat marked the day, March seventeenth, on his calendar, with a huge strapping felt-tip marker, ah God, yes indeedy, the same kind that one may still buy in little out-of-the-way mavrones and machrees in the ancient Roman city of Dublin. St. Pat, a man who was not your usual run-of-the-mill saint, always loitering out on the desert somewhere waiting for a vision or a voice like so many of your greaser saints—shure, an' it's the difference in climate that does it—strove with might and main, sloshing gallons, by God, oceans! of black coffee down all those wee gullets, of both sexes, but by the time he'd sober up a million or two of the little spud-chompers, wouldn't you know that he'd find the first ones drunk and ossified to a fine powder again, associating with evil companions, falling into occasions of sin, leering after women, crawling around in the clover and peering up every skirt in the Emerald Isle, and puking bedamn veritable Amazons and Niles of worn-out ale, stout, and porter—not to mention Irish firewater which, some say, was invented by an eccentric wee-wee who was casting about in his laboratory for something to keep the point of his hat starched. But be that as it may and, as they say, it will be.

St. Patrick was, as you may well imagine, if you dim bastards can be thought to imagine anything, highly wroth and filled with a great sense of futility and despair. For what had happened? The wee-wee people, in their first foray out of their bogs and their mud-floored public houses had stampeded every varmint into the boiling drink, true. But now they were become foul and shiftless varmints themselves, with nothing to do and all day to do it in, if I may exert a little levity—and those of you who are being bashed into a show of manners back there by the split-log picnic tables have only brought it on yourselves, you rude louts, by giving my little unpretentious *mot* what is grossly called the horse laugh. See that the rest of you suckers pick up on those howls of pain, oke?

So what was the good St. Patrick to do? A year passed, maybe two, maybe two hundred, because it's a fact, by God Almighty, that the saint lived for five or six hundred years, long enough, as some of you know, to found the great Blarney Stone saloon chain in the City of New York. That was in the good old days before the Irish in that fair city learned to speak good American and still worshipped the lowly bathtub as a god, allowing nothing to touch it except maybe a quarter-ton of soft coal or so. They were, those early Irish settlers on the shores of lofty Gotham, absolutely wacky over coal, from which dates the curious term "black Irish," this unfortunate condition being a result of standing in slathers of coal smoke. But I digress.

What, I have asked, was this lovely man to do? No, my good friend over there with the denim pipe, not "take a walk," as you were about to say before that friendly flatfoot busted your face with a neat twirl of his blackjack. No, not "take a walk" atall, atall. He sat and thought and thought and then, on the anniversary—never mind which one—of the day that he and his mite-like pals shoved the snakes into the thundering thalassa, or thalatta, depending on which diner you favor for your yankee pot roast, string beans, and mashed, he roused himself, a light bulb having appeared in the air above his head as if by magic! He slung on his girds, slapped braces on his loins. He had an idea! And an idea so good, so true, so packed with felicity and pure old Irish know-how, that the harps to a man still marvel over it, having little enough else to marvel over. He decided to let the wee-wees work some magic over Ireland. That, by the by, is how the annals and the sagas and the eddas and the kells and the epics and even the histories put it: "It is the wee people who work the magic over Ireland." And what is this magic? They are the ones, yes, me red-faced dears, they are the ones who "spread the waves and the carpet turns a silky green." What these "waves" are, I haven't got idea fucking one, but *they* do it!

When the kindly old silver-haired St. Patsy broached this idea to the throngs of sodden wee-wees, barely able to keep their little pig-eyes open, and hopping about like Spanish flies committing adultery with trees and every other thing else, and coveting and copping everything that wasn't securely nailed down to the glorious green dirt, and blaspheming a mile a minute each time they quit sucking on a bottle of the devil's brew, they stood shamefaced and embarrassed before that good kind man who had, for the occasion, dressed himself in a Kelly tweed suit and a snowy vest made all of clay pipes, and bedamn, with his great honest policeman's brogans fashioned with fairy skill from the skins of the finest spuds. By God, he was Mister Ireland that day! The wee-wees, soused as they were, realized that this was their last chance to be almost human, and they jumped upon its back, or however you thick norteamericanos phrase it. Let's say they dug on the idea. Can you get behind that, Jim? The male wee-wees cleaned their green threads of barf stains as best they could, and the females searched diligently through the nodding tares for such articles of intimate apparel as they had chucked away, figuring, such was the action, that, who needed them? Then, straight and strong and sober, with but a trace of the shakes, the legions of little folk started in spreading the waves and bedad turning the carpet a silky green. And ever since that day, about 1936 or 1937, if memory serves, as indeed it does whenever it can get its tux out of hock, most of us fondly recall the legend of the wee-wees when we think, as oft we must with tears and banshee wails, of Ireland. *Don't we!?* How thrilling to hear the thunderous "ayes" gushing from your throats and zinging off the firmament, those of you, that is, still capable of emitting noise of any kind. There's nothing like a friendly crowd.

So that, my eager amigos, is the true meaning of St. Patrick and his merry day. He gave the snakes the heave-ho, he recruited the wee-wee people to assist him in his thankless task, his dirty task, the sort of task fit for jigs, wops, and greasers, yet not held, no, not even for a moment, in contempt by the noble St. Pat, and, last but certainly not least, if I may lapse for a moment into the banal, when the lousy little dwarfs got out of hand in the sin department, he straightened them out, he allowed them sole possession of the wave-spreading franchise, the green-carpet market, etc., etc. Between you me and the ashcan, buddies, this was strictly bush-league work, but the wee-wees have never been accused of being stars in the brains department, being more like your actor, your dancer, your state legislator, and so if they're not running off at the gob with a lot of annoying pissing and moaning about their rights like a passel of maladjusted and malcontent welfare clients—how I love that word "clients"—why should *we* take it upon ourselves to criticize the imbecile connemaras?

So. St. Patrick, for all the honor we do him each March the Seventeenth, drinking ourselves into a frenzy of unrequited lust, making ourselves half-mad with staring at the drum majorettes in their indecent costumes, watching and listening to, with rising nausea, the professional Irishmen in their green cardboard derbies describe the parade to us on television, and driving ourselves into a state of moral catatonia with the obscene sight of the half-assed, half-baked, semiliterate whores of politicians who would cheerfully kill their mothers, and their fathers too, for the privilege of standing like a bog-trotter of a gawm with a button as big as paddy's pig on the wizened and dried up chest of him that says to all the rotten world, "I'm Irish." Bejesus, it's enough to turn a decent man into a bloody Presbyterian! Still, and still, St. Patrick was real and the poor dear man cannot be held accountable for the disgusting antics of your mayor, your congressman, your local priest. The man walked! He talked! He sometimes hopped and trotted o'er the green face of Ireland many years ago, how many I don't know and I don't give a rat's ass anyway. The Irish love this gentle man and celebrate his day faithfully, beating each other into porridge and flinging themselves in desperate gambols on the green silky carpet that the wee-wees have worked like a bunch of niggers to prepare. 'Tis a grand day, when every mark in Christendom has the chance to delude himself into thinking he's important!

And I implore those of you who are still moving under your own sweet power to think on this day all through the year, and to help you remember, you dear lovely dyspeptic hamburger-eaters, you may empty your pockets of cash and other valuables, not forgetting watches, bracelets, earrings and the like, and turn them over to Sergeant O'Mara, who is standing there as big as life—the foine-looking lad with the riot baton, that's him—at the entrance to the parking lot. He'll be only too happy to assist you, the lovable brogue! Thank you for your attention, me hearty macushlas, and a good afternoon to all of you!

« 35 »

Miz Gavotte
Tells Her Mate
a Little White Lie

Our Blue, back from his Celtic stint, relaxed in his rooms, awaiting good Doctor Dubuque and further intelligence concerning the Phrase. His heart leaped up when Helene peered 'round the transom-jamb, her eyes still misty from the memory of the sunset on the rippling Amazon. Yet her jaw was firm as if to belie the sparkle in her peepers.

How nice to see you, wife, back at last from your trip up the thudding Orinoco! I've not been idle here, as I'll soon relate.

The Orinoco? So *that's* why the crocodiles spoke Spanish! Anyhow, my love, it was a pleasure not to be dismissed with a phrase like unto, "And while Blue conferred with Doc Dubuque, his wife busied herself with a tour of the campus and its leafy environs." The little river steamer we were on "huffed" and "creaked" by the way, and the smell of petrol was often overpowering in the heavy tropical heat. How the natives splashed!

I hope that the placid boredom of our little home away from home does not instill in you a vast ennui? Serge said, for he was worried by the rigid jaw-set of his pal.

It's not the fear of boredom that has firmed my jawbone, Helene quavered. It's that I've something I must tell you while I have the moxie. First, let me turn our Zim out to humming pasture. (Which she did without ado.)

Tell me? Serge began, his hands still . . . at last!

Yes, my sweetie. You'll recall that I told you but a space or twain ago a coupla days just past that Dr. Poncho at The College had accosted me upon the path and made a couple foul suggestions to me in reference to the act that dares not show itself in daylight on the street, or boulevard?

How could I forget? seethed Blue. Had I that perfidious caitiff here beneath my hamlike fists he'd soon feel the weight of vengeance bold that sugars up the dish of wild regret!

I fear, my cupid, that they were more than mere, how do they say? "advances?"

What? You mean . . . and it was as if proud Serge's body had slumped down in his chair. Slumped down in his chair, his body looked at her, in the eyes belonging to same a wordless questioning pain. You mean . . . ? But he could go no further.

I *do* mean, Helene nodded in a kind of stunned hysteria. You have been given the horns, or in this case, perhaps the antlers.

Great clattering palm fronds! Blue shuddered, his face buried in four fingers of his hand. H-how? Wh-why? B-but? Wh-where? His eyes were fixed upon the carpet in a bleak despair, probly searching for the face of Henry James

He, as they say, seducèd me, and I followed him into the rustling maple-stand all trembling with that well-advertised wild delight, with, I might say, a sophisticated adult-type joy. What a mature attitude we had about this basic male-female relationship; no false shame sullied our gentle caring; no hypocritical prudery debased our strong, proud nudity; what tender, patient foreplay heated up our sexual needs; how we acted out those fantasies that actual doctors say are good and healthy and also practiced by some of this great country's most respected and well-dressed honorable citizens; how we casted off our binding and restricting clothes, why, the good doctor's very tweeds took flight! 'Twas not just a quick boff, but a prolonged sashay into delights replete with those reckless positions he-men really like. We acted out a thesaurus of idears on the meeting of our fletch!

Groan, said Blue.

It was abandoned ecstasy, yes, and wild, free, unfettered joy! The beauty of healthy human-person bodies aglow in shackleless nakedity! The doctor's thrumming sex plumbed me to the basement of my core and my female id did tumblesault with a wacky grin upon its face; not even the thorny dogface-tares clutching at my tender bod annoyed me. The doc refused my pleas for mercy; I laughed at his. Gracious! my multiple orgasms scared the crap from a host of teeny cicadas and such other oddball creepers and creepy oddballs that hunkered in the bresh! He e'en bared my seat and greeked me afore blushing Nature, so that She stood up and said to all the world, "This is a can!" Ah, when I compare this neat perversion with the sleepy pops you've given me of late . . . the heart pines and drops a tear or such.

Woe, mumbled Blue.

Elegericals and reams of pedometers in the original Greek and Latin eased from his learnèd lips as he pegged me underwater in the sedge-choked pond, and the lenses of his pince-nez cracked, as did my reservations; I felt much like a lady psychiatrist speaking lightly yet with frozen face upon the TV screen of fetishes and fellatio, so filled with mad sophistication was my brain; like a gay puttana dressed up like a nun in a technicolor stag flick. By crocky! my homely dirndls and my serviceable burlap hose busted into flame! I was a Pasiphaë when the prize bull hopped on her in her weird cow suit; a Leda getting banged by that arrogant flamingo; a Danaë when the wild doubloons creeped up her skirts; a Helen when young Paris slipped it to her in the sheepfold; tall and free and laughing with, like, white even teeth, and with my so-so figure glowing like a majoun sassafrass! Poncho is no big-deal bargain, yet in his rage of passion seemed the very spirit of Apollo, or Dionysos drunk yet again at closing time, his bleary bloodshot eyes fixed upon the quivering bosom of the waitress counting up her crummy tips.

Whinge, whinged Blue.

I myself felt like Calypso when the sly Odysseus, know as "Red" to all his non-coms, bent her o'er a stalagmite or stalactite or heavy rock or sumpn; like Circe when that same wily Greek tore off her basic little black dress, simmering as he wert because of the möly he had dropped just prior to his entrance; like any liberated femme surrounded by a buncha creams and aids and fully illustrated books for sale to over-twenty-one. Yes! The spirit of great Eros fell from out the sky like sleet or freezing rain, shattering, in its mad career, not a few branches, the leaves of whom the panting Poncho gathered up and used to make our bower, somewhat like Varlayne's except we was short on sherbet.

Argh, gasped Blue.

I wert ga-ga like the fair Europa, another bull-freak lost in mad depravity; like Io, who was horny Jupiter's sweet veal scallopine; like Aphrodite, getting it on with Mars while the old man put in his time at the foundry; like the dissembling Penelope who did not tell her long-gone hubby when he made it home that she'd run through all the suitors like a dose of salts and was about to start in at the top again: she tore off more than warps and woofs at night, believe you me; like Clytemnestra, who plummeted into the sack with staunch Aegisthus when Agamemnon—

Cease! Serge blathered. I get the drift and e'en the tidal wave of your purport! But...why? Why, why?

Your attentions to my yearning fletch have fallen off until I feel as if you do not care for me, such, such are the tumbles lately. Quick and sans delight. Your obsession with The Phrase driv me to it with the horny Dr. Poncho.

Woe, woe, what can I do?

Seek assistance, and stop your dull behavior. Or sundering divorce will be our guerdon, fast-fuck!

I'll seek the counsel of the wise old Doc Dubuque. He'll know the sources whence flow remedy for these, my limping sacrifices to Amour—else comets shall crunch down upon the flagrant phlox that shiver in the marsh!

Do, my lumpish friend. A little candid talk on dirty lust will do you still a world of good, mayhap.

I'll seek the Doc eftsoones, roared Blue.

《36》
Father Donald
Debris, S.J., Gives a Talk on Sex

How wise and kind and good of Dr. Dubuque to send you over to see me for a little chat, Mr. Serge. Although the good doctor is a Protestant he has a kind and full heart, and fourteen-karat gold to boot. He tells me in this eensie-beensie note that I hold in my careworn hands, here in my Spartan study, my vow, as it were, of poverty, as it were, made physical—nice word, that—aha, ha, ha, that you have run into a raft of trouble, a jagged shoal of same, concerning what we call, in our secluded way, here in the bosom, ahem, of Mother Church, that is, we who labor in the sparse and ofttimes sour vineyards of the Great Ma, in, as it were, Peter's Backyard, heh, heh, sex. And not a rare or extraordinary problem at all these days, young fellow, with even men of the cloth falling beneath its flashing high heels, hot bellies, enormous breasts, heavy thighs, and, ahem! Huhf! Yes, where was I? Ah, yes. Sex!

Yes, sex, this sacred mystery that involves all humankind in its byways and dim alleys. I can see by a quick and somewhat furtive glance into the dark yearning pools of your eyes that this mystery is rendering you an ignoble and even loutish dolt. Lean closer then, and let me talk to you as best I can about the place of sex in our lives today—or even the win and show, if you will, the show being inextricably intertwined with checking out carelessly drawn blinds over at the nun's residence, and some of those young novices . . . The place of sex! In our lives, we, who are the fallen buds of the glowing tares, pitched about the cold floor of the Forest of Life—a forest, like as not, waiting to burst into the consuming flame! Only we may prevent these infernos, or, lacking that, at least we may use them to, so to speak, heat up a pot of coffee or singe a rustic burger or two.

Sex! Is there another word in our beloved mother tongue that raises such expectations, only to see them shivered into splinters and toothpicks, and small ones too, small as the mindless amoeba that has no sex at all, but is always swimming around glumly wondering what exactly went wrong. You'll pardon my

162

immoderate grin which verges, even now, on the edge of hysterical laughter, but that odd rictus is often the result of long and somewhat irrational fasting, since it is roast beef and the good red wine, to borrow a phrase from Bob Frost, that makes for your solemn padre—an old saying, surely, but one that rings and clatters to the very canopy and baldachin of heaven itself, if baldachin is the word. I knew a plethora of words when a cloddish youth in the seminary but as life, Great Life, has slouched by, they seem to have fallen by the wayside, right into the yellow wood, and some, if you'll forgive the sudden blast of glaring truth, in rather grotesque positions, like maybe on all fours, or abandonedly akimbo, free from all shame, face flushed, the glitter of sunlight on rosy flesh— Sometimes...

We Jesuits, holy men all and as celibate as good King Wenceslas, who, as the old hymn insists, *looked down* on the feast of Stephen, looked, yes, but did not feed his fat and greasy face, yes, we, holy and chaste yet with great understanding of the ills that afflict mere lay persons, and with A-number-one imaginations, the latter all astew when we are not engaged in our regular-guy roles of baseball fans and such and with being all things to all people, you know what I mean, sort of like whacked out on bourbon and with the fatherly arm draped around the shoulders of some pure blue-eyed lass at the annual faculty shindig to which selected graduate assistants are invited and so forth, I don't have to spell it out, do I, Mr. Serge? Of course not. We Jesuits, and I, Don Debris not least among them, are students of and watchers over sex as practiced among the faithful. And you would be surprised at some of the odd methods used to avoid the sinful use of contraceptives and yet, how shall I say? "get off." Let me tell you, Mr. Serge, let me speak directly to the rich dark sediment that swirls about in the deeps of your eyes, sex is not dead among Christians! It may not be in the proverbial pink—to borrow a word from Jerry Lewis—but there's nothing the matter with it that a good stiff dose of clean Catholic copulation won't fix up in a trice, good as new and jack-a-dandy! You cotton to what I mean? The pitch-black room, the muffled sighs so the kids won't hear, and Jesus hanging over the bed in his useless agony peering through the dark at the straining bodies sweating the bed up below.

Dr. Dubuque may or may not have told you—occasionally he can be small, very small—that I am the author of a new book to be published next fall by Plastic Missal Press in Scranton, P.A., leafy burg! to what already shows itself to be general acclaim by all good Catholics, and that will be available at the pre-publication price of eighteen ninety-five at every Las Vegas night the length and breadth of this country, discounts to educational groups, all proceeds to go to the Sodality of Chaste Wives. Interested? Of course you are! Even Jewish persons like yourself are curious about—to borrow a phrase from Carl Sandburg—piling into bodies on the grass—or anywhere else, for that matter! Sandburg had your basically provincial mind, as witness his legions of crew-cut fans. No matter. There is a line somewhere in my book—I love the careless modesty of that "somewhere"—that runs: "Sex is not dead, but has a heavy cold." My book, entitled, *Sex Unleashed Among Christians*, is intended to be, if you will, the Vicks Vapo-Rub, the Vitamin C, the soothing hand on the brow, that will *cure* that cold. I was never strong on the metaphor and tend to agree with Plato that all poets should be picked up on vagrancy charges and set to making fly-swatters. He was, as I'm sure your reading will show you, one smart Greek, and I have often argued the point that had he come to America instead of lazing around the dusty agoras he loved so well, he would have been in on the ground floor of the fast-food biz, probably whipping up instant dollops of Salisbury steak with side of mash, side of carrots and peas, and God knows what else. Marvelous things to help our economy along, keeping it pump-primed or something, though I'm not too astute on these Marxist terms, having done my doctoral thesis on "Masturbation Symbolism in Flannery O'Connor." I assure you, however, that I *did* vote for FDR, not wanting to shoot the horse in midstream of the great river of war in which he was wading—and at a smart gallop too! But I fear that I speak too much of my own interests. Anyhow—out of my years of research and thought, out of all the sweat and headaches and fantasies and peeking through jalousies and Venetian blinds, out of the experiences of numberless faculty blowouts—odd word, that—all of these things going to make the pith and the vinegar, to filch a phrase from Omar Khayyam, of my *Sex Unleashed*, allow me to pluck from same a few choice nuggets, some eloquent pistachios of deepest thought, to assist you in your desiccated and morose sex life. To wit:

Sex, as sexualityness, is the essential personal property, like a pair of galoshes, a fedora, a brassiere, with lace trim, semi-transparent so that one can make out the, uh, yes, it is the personal property of being masculine or feminine. It is held, and, if you will forgive my node of levity, close to the chest, too, to be identical with the unique personal manifestation of your average human being, morphodites excluded by popular demand. A man/woman attempts to achieve and identify himself/herself precisely as a correlative, a Pole Star, complementary to yet opposite from—what else?—the opposite sex! And therein therefore finds himself/herself alive and aglow with singing joy except, oddly enough, at the moment or so of orgasm, in which he/she finds himself/herself "dead." If we push, shove, and bully these swell and perfect limits outside their respective pales, and being a Jewish type, you know what that means, we find that bulging sweaty masculinity becomes the caricature called machismo; and the luscious curves and musky perfume of the feminine turns into that slovenly and degrading parody that we may term the pin-up, the sex symbol, the cheesecake model, the beaver shot, and so on and so forth. Disgusting to the mature mind, I grant you, and I have spent years up to the elbows in these horrifying representations of semi-clothed young women in divers grotesque poses, and I've come to the conclusion that the fantasy of the young wife in torn housedress, maybe with sneakers and black nylons . . . Uh. Uh, under this, or perhaps around this fundamental perception, this ABC of sex roles in our changing world, to borrow a phrase from Sara Teasdale—not a bad-looking lady, though a little lacking in the umm, what can I say? physical endowments that we associate with the female person. What was I saying? Yes, this perception, I say, under this percep tion, it is impossible not to realize that for a human person to be a human person that human person must first be a human masculine or a human feminine person. Which puts many a gay-type individual right out in the cold, or so I read it by my lights. In other words, my dear Mr. Serge, a human being cannot be a human person first, and then a male or a female person, nor can a human person be a male or a female person first, and then only a mere human person. "Mere" is, you understand, a figure of speech, of course. No! This odious dichotomy cannot be! God has intended us all to be jampacked together, human, male, female, cheeks by jowls, and not a bad position either as I can see you understand by the fiery glint in the raging cesspools of your eyes. And jampacked at work even as at play. In Nature, we see the same phenomenon at work among the flowers of the field, such as the striped anorexia and the bunched lochia, which are not anything *but* striped and bunched along with the irrefutable fact of their being also plant "persons," nodding and drooping and dropping their little seeds like mad, with the homely bee buzzing around in the hot sun like a maniac and so on and so forth. In the fields, there you will see sex as it was meant to be, with none of the corruptions of tight slacks and sensual perfumes and colognes and underclothing not meant to clothe but to make a poor man get crazy as he riffles through the pages of various catalogues that find their way to him with such regularity that his mailbox is crammed and stuffed with nothing but the occasion of sin and I for one don't think that I can stand it for another min— We are become a nation of saps and suckers, wonderfully vivid words if you'll but think on them for a moment. We sap ourselves and we also suck . . . uh, suck the vital moral juices from our spirits, anyway, you see what I'm driving at.

To many moderns, perhaps even you, my boy, sex is not a theme to study and perfect but a catalogue of lascivious description like the endless pages of Molly Bloom's aberrant musings as she performs the beastly acts so dear to her in the foxed copy that I own of *Ulysses*—and who else but a depraved Greek could have even *thought* of such shenanigans? The hallmark of this corporeal mystery used to be permanence, yet no one any longer needs or wants this permanence, am I right? Look at your own junkyard of a life! In the old days, things were different, it was not, as it is now, to lift a line from Jerome Kern, anything goes. Do we read, for instance, of shining Hector "ripping off a piece" in the back seat of a Chevy? Ha! Does Don Quixote "get some head" from a dark-eyed señorita in a ditch behind the high school athletic field? Pshaw! Ridiculous to entertain for the merest second such sacrilege! But *now*. Men and women, devoid of the old idea that they are persons as well as vessels of sexualityness, say "why play?" Play what? you ask, I'm sure, down there in the fundament of your whirling brain. *The Game!* I reply, with, and you will pardon me, a jot more than my usual heat. I speak, of course, of the game of permanence, that is, good sweaty fumbling Christian copulation in the privacy of your own little home, the children rattling the locked door with their sticky hands, hollering for some Frooty Loopies or Puffy Cokes, the aromatic coffee perking viciously away in the sunny breakfast nook, the heaped leaves smoldering behind the leaky garage, while you, as a human male person pound dutifully away at the holy body of your helpmeet, while she, ideally, although this is certainly not necessary, tells her beads. I recall that years ago, when I was a younger man, a priest at the parish of Our Lady of the Bleeding Eyes, there was a nun by the name of Sister Rose Zeppole, who would take her rosary and . . . well, let it be shrouded in silence.

Anyhow. Instead of the sedulously pounding husband and his wife, the, so to speak, poundee, what do we see before us? Some crazed and askew idea of *equality*. Or, if I may, let me say that we are at a far remove from as well as at odds with the idea of male person-female person, as I have already briefly outlined. Equality says, oh, not in so many words, but it's right there in front of you like a great shining blackhead, it says that your human person wife may, on a whim, when you come home exhausted from a long day at the water cooler or in the stock room hiding from the boss behind some cartons, she may, I insist, jump on you in nothing but a transparent apron and some thigh-high nylons, the kind that stay up by themselves have always, by the by, seemed to me most interestingly ingeni— ummm, yes! Jump on you, I say, and copulate *you* as if *you* were the poundee! Copulate and copulate until you are blue in the face and begging this boiling witch for a cold beer and a simple dish of home-made stew. What do these women, these "equal" women want, who think that they are female persons before they are human persons, or maybe vice-versa, what do I know of the thought processes of the lustful wife? They want, if you will forgive a smatter of the vulgar, they want to hump you cross-eyed and open up a can of Campbell's beans!

And of course our modern wife cleaves to herself her diaphragm, her intra-uterine device, her calendar, her pills, her vaginal-spermicidal foams in various flavors, and why? So that she may "enjoy" pounding and/or poundeeing without for a moment having to think of the joyous burden of having another child, another mouth to feed, body to clothe, dentist and doctor bills, plenty of victuals, and all the rest of the elation and the glorious worries that another child will bring to the ducky little family and its poppa's laughable paycheck. No wonder she can afford to spend her milk money and her stew money and her beer money on transparent house dresses and frilly aprons and insanely sheer hosiery, uh, and uh, tiny undergarments that, that, the names of which we Jesuits may not utter. For she is safe from pregnancy! But where, then, the sweet danger? There is no danger, and hence, there is no challenge, if the outcome of Christian sexual love is a sure thing, am I right, dear boy? There is no meaning in the eternal struggle on the bed if Danger is not in bed, so to speak, with the grunting pair, check? As the dewy anoxia is almost extinct because Boy Scouts—all of them, I hasten to add, attached to troops that meet in Protestant churches—pluck it with fierce abandon in the foolish belief that it can, as they say, zonk you out, so shall the traditionally flat-broke Christian family reach the razor's edge, to use a phrase from Whit Burnett, of extinction if "equality" allows female persons to jump their hubbies from behind the door before the poor fellows have had a chance even to slam down their old rusty lunch pails and holler, in voices made stentorian by years of bowling, "Hi, Honey! I don't smell nothing cooking!" But, Mr. Serge, we know what's "cooking," do we not, in this madhouse filled with lace and satin and naughty novels, a house sans Douay, or even a cheesy little religious pamphlet to help bore the couple to sleep and hence, innocence, and in that sleep of innocence, who knows, maybe the old man will do his duty, even all a-snore, before his crazy female partner has a chance to put her diaphragm in, or on, or under, or whatever they do with these Satanic accoutrements. What *do* they do, by the way? Don't tell me!

Christian love is indeed dead in such a climate, hot and steamy, and with an orgasm, so to speak, on demand and around every cozy little corner. We have so much sex—I use "we" rhetorically, of course—that we are bored to death by it, sort of. We are so bored that we are no longer interested in Good Healthy Sex, which may be your case in a peapod, Mr. Serge. Does my wild punch land on a sore spot? Recent reports in *Lights Out: The Marriage Manual for Catholics* state that there are indications of a great lessening of interest in the orgasm. And why is this the case? Because, beyond the obvious desirability of the wife person as a paradigm of sexualityness in her tangible and probably deliciously warm person, especially if she has just taken a hot bath and . . . Beyond the obvious, I say, what is there? The same old body! We must go beyond, far beyond the body in all its godly and remarkable swell curves and such, beyond it to the true meaning of copulation—another child to break, to coin a phrase of Le Moko's, the bank. It is not the *body* that the good Christian husband should care about, but the awesome organs of reproduction themselves, or itself! In other words, the dutiful husband should forever repeat to himself the old saw of The Tumbling Fungis, famed family of acrobats, "They're all the same upside down." The organs should be the Christian husband's only goal, and he should zero in, so to speak, on his spouse's uh, "forked" area, where her legs, uh, well, the *spot*, blinding himself to her overly familiar face and forgetting how she might look in oh, say, although I don't know too much about these items, a Merry Widow, if they still make them . . . would you happen to know if they . . . ? No matter.

We must learn to think of the orgasm, then, not as a pleasure—perish the thought!—but as a tool or device or thingamajig by means of which we keep foisting Christians on the world, not, surely, in your case, Mr. Serge, but one speaks ideally, or should I say, ideally speaking? Ha ha. What, after all, is an orgasm? Very little, very very little indeed. Recent research has shown that if a man is rigged up with oddball and sensitive equipment enabling him to have an orgasm every two or three minutes, he will adjust to this rather extraordinary behavior of his genito-urinary system within twenty-four hours and go about his wonted and homely tasks in the workaday world with not so much as a grimace, grunt, groan, or twitch, not much of a twitch anyway, and with a minimum amount of time lost from the job—in factory, office, or on the broad sunny fields of the echoing plains—and *that* simply to change his trousers every hour or two in order to avoid embarrassing accusations that he is a slob, a mess, disgusting, and so on and so forth. The human species can be cruel, cruel indeed, as I don't have to tell you, my son, for one can take one quick gander at your seamed and lined face and tell in a shot that you've had your share of heartache and adversity, your depressing sexual problems of the present being a case in point, if I may dare breathe your shame. Female persons? Ditto. Super ditto. Or as our Spanish friends might put it, clumped, as is their custom, around the colorful siesta, *dittito*. They are a warm and wonderful race who long merely to breathe free. Or at least cheap. But I was speaking of your average female housewife, pert and natty in a cotton housedress and bent fetchingly over the stove, let's imagine the good woman with trembling thighs slightly apart and with— Um. Yes, your average woman. A housewife in Mineola, Long Island, a town than which you can get no more average, was, ah, fitted, if you will, with an ingeniously designed—what shall I say—"stimulator," for want of a cruder term, its control switch cleverly designed to look exactly like a "Smile" button. She was told that any time she felt the need, or the desire—*there's* a really interesting word—she was to touch the switch and, as the young man who told me this story put it, Whammo! At first, she was compelled to "stimulate" herself while sitting down, else the surge of bodily wildness that swept her from head to foot would have knocked her flat— and hard, hard it would have been to explain this to her friends and neighbors, right? Yet after only a week or ten days she was having orgasms at the supermarket, the bake sale, the bank, the bowling alley, here, there, everywhere. And, apart from the fact that once or twice her eyes rolled back in her head, and, on one rare occasion an inadvertent flinging about of her legs knocked down a Mallomar pyramid in the above-cited supermarket, she went about her usual tasks with a placid face and a posture of absolute ladylike composure, sustaining, on one record day, four hundred and twelve orgasms before picking up the children at school. So you will see, my dear young fellow, that the orgasm is, in itself, nothing, perhaps even the existential *néant*. No wonder good Christians are bored with it.

But I fear that these tales, hurled into the body of my talk, may open me to a charge of digressing from the main text, so to speak, although as you can see, I speak extempore and a capella. Thus, let me press on swiftly with my analysis of sexual angst as it is known and suffered by the great majority of poor slobs in every hamlet and bursting metropolis in this great land we dare call Home. The sex dodge is often identified with copulation of one kind or another, the church preferring, if I may sink to a bout of levity, the one kind. In any event, it is mainly pretty physical stuff, the intellect being more or less parked outside while the parties go at it hammer and tongs, or thongs, if that's your pleasure. Speaking of thongs, it was Ovid who, somewhere in the *Ars amatoria*, first noted the amusing fillip called bondage. It is clearly defined in his tale of Aphrodite and Ares in which, I'm sure you'll recall, my dear Mr. Serge, Hephaestus, the wily crip, and a man crazy with secret lusts, bound the two with a gossamer yet steely strong net while they were in the very act of making the beast. And who can forget the lively scene when all the other gods and goddesses entered Aphrodite's boudoir and saw the two locked together like a couple of mongrels? There must have been a passel of Hellenic wisecracks flying through the Olympian air. I think of them all as no better than your modern voyeur, and though I am given to understand that the sedulous Peeping Tom occasionally glimpses a flash of swelling flesh, he is rarely lucky enough to see a ripe and luscious woman in the filthy act of . . . Lucky for them all that this happened before the birth of Christ or else they'd have more to gripe about than being bored into stupefaction in Limbo.

Hm. I find that I have digressed once again—whenever my mind calls up the Venus to me, I find that I . . . However: Ovid, yes. Ovid says that that dark act is

the physical representation of the old Latin motto, "I-in-you-me-us." And if
you don't know what the old dago is getting at, think deeply on precisely what
the wild and untamed flesh performs when it performs. I've seen an odd photo
or two and have some idea, enough anyway to permit me to speak to—odd
phrase—the proposition. Sister Zeppole once had the most engaging deck of
playing cards and when we turned a rubber or two of Old Maid we often fell to a
minute examination of the instructive photographs that . . . I recall especially the
Three of Diamonds, starring two nuns, a monsignor, and what seemed to be a
bellhop, although what a bellhop would be doing in the rectory— In all events,
to be in-you-me or me-in-you or us-in-us or me-around-it or it-up-you or however you want to slice it bespeaks, as any casual oaf can see, the demand for a
certain kind of *involvement.* You can't very well, as a Christian gentleman, be
mouthing snippets like "me-up-yours" or however one might put it after a dry
Martini or three, and not be what must be called, or I am not a nodding eremite,
involved. That is, you cannot "get it on" with your spouse if you are standing up
looking out the window at the pathetic joke that you call a "lawn" while the good
woman sits across the room buried under cookbooks and their domestic ilk,
mixing bowls, spatulae, whatever. Right? Perhaps that's your problem, young
fellow? Don't tell me and no names please. Even frontier wisdom, and by God
that was few and far between, else Great History lies, had it that love and marriage go together like a horse and carriage. Amusing couplet, no? and one based
on the metrical experiments of Gérard de Nerval—but don't let me tax your
manly brain with pedantry. That metaphor, if that's exactly what it is, although
it seems to me that it may well be a pantoum, seems to suggest that in wedlock it
is desirable for one partner to pull the other about the boudoir, or that one partner
ride atop the other—the latter of course clearly points to the husband as the person doing the riding, since a moment's reflection will serve to prove that the human female finds it difficult to be such a rider because of the encumbering effects
of a skirt, unless, of course, said wife hikes or lifts the above-named feminine
garment up to her, uh, the, well, what we call here in the silence of the life we live,
upper portion of the lower limbs. In that way, the male husband may well serve
as the horsey. Of course, proceedings may begin with the glowing wife skirtless,
in which case . . . Of course, this obscure couplet may simply be a reference to the
theory, held by some of the finest minds in academe, that steeds of the Old West
were wont to mount their carriages in an excess of affection. Those nags, it is
rumored, were game for anything.

In any case, the idea is one of involvement and inextricable partnership, nags
or carriages or skirts and such—human persons simply must be involved! But
what do we see all about us now? Is there a whole heck of a lot of pushing and

straining and heaving and shoving of human person bodies together nowadays, actions that should go on well into the years of dotage, often called "golden" years? Very little, very very little. Very little obeisance is made to the hoary "up-you-in-me-you-me" concept of conjugal love. Whence issues all neuroses and all the crude and brittle casting aside of the churnings and bubblings and even the slow drip of the dark secret blood hovering just beneath the surface of the glowing skin—to employ a phrase of McKuen's—of radiant spouses of whatever gender. Sometimes, given the weather, not too radiant, but why quibble? The modern boy-girl relationship is one of cool and loveless accommodation, with the kissing and the hugging and the petting and the necking, accompanied by furtive glances at the movie they are supposed to be "seeing." Ha ha ha! Don't make me laugh! The young organs of generation quake and tremble as they blush, so to speak, at being handled like so many cheeseburgers. Is this the way to treat a sacred vessel? Before this age of sexual permissiveness, it used to be that a boy would pursue a girl from dawn to dusk, trying every ruse in the book, "book" is a figure of speech, a fuchsia to be exact, every ruse, I say, to get her sweet little bottom into— Meanwhile, she fought him off with ritualistic phrases, excuses going down the corridors of Time all the way back to the days of the Greek gods. You'll recall the lame protestations of Daphne and Syrinx of course, to name but two. Meanwhile, the two smoldered away, occasionally bursting into a small tongue of flame. Finally, this chaste courtship was ended by marriage, and the steaming groom would have his bride's odds and ends down around her silken ankles almost before the smirking bellhop was out the door. Then was there a crashing of bodies and the slap of Christian flesh against, God willing, Christian flesh such as to make the welkin shiver! And the object? More Christians!

What do we have now to take the place of such sublime frustration, almost Provençal in its intensity, such dizzying release, enough, as I've said, to make the heavens themselves light up like with a clutch of Roman candles? We read in the paper of some baby being born in England in a laboratory, like some kind of disgusting germ or virus. Ugh. The old man is led into a sterile room, all white and tile and such, like in the movies, in some out-of-the-way clinic, handed a copy of *Playbox* or some other petit-bourgeois rag, and a Petrie dish, and the door is locked behind him. In five minutes the nurse opens the door, grinning obscenely at the savaged pages of that publication, which just last month had a photograph of the Chairperson of the Board of Amalgamated Film Critics in the buff, and not a bad-looking woman, although her . . . The lewd nurse takes the Petrie dish from the exhausted clod, chucks a couple eggs in there, eggs taken from his good wife's body, and the whole godawful mess is squirted back into the lady with, probably, a lot of doctor jokes, and by, no doubt, some atheist Jewish person, no offense. Is this "in-me-you-me"? Is this the lustful conflagration that adolescents used to douse in the deep end of the pool of marriage? It is to laugh. But that's the English for you, leave it to them to invent such a scam, or dodge. They'll do anything rather than take the risk of allowing English female persons the possibility of bumping into an Irish male person, a broth of a man who has never heard of a Petrie dish but places his whole faith in the homely spud and the jar of malt and likes nothing better than to involve himself with a female person of whatever nationality and may the pigs grunt so long as the springs of his homely straw pallet creak all night! And you wonder, young man, why no English unmarried person is allowed into Ireland, except for the Orange Counties, which don't count? Why, by my Maker, if a brawny glasheen of a lad ever saw a transparent apron he'd feed it to the hogs or, better, to the great-mawed polyphagia, that grows on diseased shamrocks. And there would be an end to *that* frivolity.

So What's That? becomes the name of the thing that emerges from the bemused mommy, courtesy of the Petrie dish. Is it boy, girl, or encrusted androgyne? And can you imagine the poor cluck of a specimen when he discovers the unnatural shame of his conception, guck and all? When he hears, as a tyke in school, the mocking voices of his chums as they bedevil him with such nicknames as "Artie Agar" and "Jarface," "Glass-head" and "Seaweed Sammy"? He'll realize, and with what cruel amaze, that he's nothing more than an experiment, like the golden bantam and elephant basophil that Luther Burbank whipped up of a winter's evening in his finished basement! However, my dear Mr. Serge, although *something* has happened to what you myriad carnal envelopes—a phrase made prominent by Vernon Royal—jokingly call your sex lives, you must see this difficulty as being essentially solvable. Sex is a Sacred Mystery, and the mysterious act does not cotton to lacy frillies and soft lights and overpowering and musky attars and the like, but is most happy when bursting forth, with red glare if needs be, in the open, under, when conditions are ideal, a bare 150-watt bulb, preferably dangling from the kitchen ceiling. In settings such as these, not quite sylvan yet as bluff and honest as a good spit, with the female person in an attitude of what Mother Church calls conjugal tolerance, her placid bottom among the crumbs and dirty dishes of the supper table, sex's great quivering sacrament asserts itself and soon flesh will call to flesh in the hollow stentorian tones, often plangent but always raucous, of the Christian Union. As St. Paul in one of his more cryptic phrases put it: "Husbands, love your wives, as Christ loved the Church." Now, as any Jesuit can tell you, St. Paul was a tricky little guy, and it's very hard to interpret his meaning here. I cannot credence the belief, held by a bunch of renegade priests and nuns, some of the latter having taken to wearing skirts which, though severe, are still short, so that their nether limbs, often as not encased in sheer nylons that, of needs, travel up the legs and— The belief, I say, uh, yes, that has it that Paul meant that Christ had a sort of liaison with the Church, or that He had a strange and off-kilter attraction for the building itself, now lost to us beneath the shifting sands of the Middle East, tromped on daily by wailing Jews and Arabs who happen to be very big on rank body odor. I suspect that He loved this Church as it was in the old days, that is, sans candles, flowers, pupils in the freezing courtyard, bums on the steps, loved it, that is to say, *naked*. And that is how Paul means for the hubby of Christian persuasion to love his little honey! Such that after the rack of lamb and the new potatoes and the mint sauce and the asparagus hollandaise and the flaky apple pie with aged cheddar and the aromatic coffee, the good housewife will divest herself of all her binding garments and, in the silence and darkness of the connubial bed, whack her ample belly against that of her husband's, unless she prefers to get on her hands and knees, in which case . . . And they will croon and gibber to the wheeze of the worn and sagging mattress—for if you eat like these two, young fellow, you won't have any money in the old sugar bowl for a new mattress, and you may take an old priest's word on that!

And as in primitive tribal rites, the orgasm that they achieve will be a utilitarian one, a workaday one, and worshipped as same. Perhaps, thinking on what I have just said, I should emphasize the orgasm that the husband achieves, since women have them only in sex clinics, hooked up to sophisticated machinery of all sorts and formidable wattage, chock full of high-speed attachments of phallic purport, and so on. Anyway, this orgasm is greeted with Christian humility, e.g., clenched teeth, blasé if not shatteringly bored air, glazed stare, sticky perspiration, and so forth. The couple's eyes may dart about involuntarily seeking out the felicities of the wallpaper design, and the like, pictures on the dresser, you name it. And if I may parenthesize, psychological depression and sickness unto death often occurs in the furtive affair because of the wallpaper designs in seedy motels. If I have to look, one more time, for instance, at a pink kitten tangled in a ball of twine, repeated over and over until . . . But forget the tribulations of a man of the cloth, I beg you, and let us return to our sated couple. After the culmination of God's will, the holy pair breathe soft orisons together that the old lady may have, once again, a bun in the oven. And when Mom grows big with child, and her other tykes say, "What's the matter with Ma? She's so fat!" the tenderly smiling couple can return to the sweet myths of a bygone and gentler time and tell the black-fisted brats one of the heartwarming tales of innocence that were our grand tradition until the advent of the condom and the Petrie dish and pleasure and such, as: the stork brought you all and is once again on the wing; we found you in the cabbage patch; we discovered you in a garbage can; we took you off the dumbwaiter; we bought you at the hospital; and so on and so forth. Stories to guarantee that healthy nervousness we call adolescent neurosis. And if one of the kiddies, wiser than his years, should ask how the stork got the baby into mommy's belly, the good couple, after a blush and stammer, can smack the clamoring rascal in his chops and send him to bed without any supper, as was done with George Washington, if memory serves.

For, my dear good Mr. Serge, mystery is sex and sex is mystery. Sex, laden down with this newfangled knowledge that proliferates, odd myths about things like the clitoris, which everyone knows simply does not exist, with sneaky whispers about multiple orgasms, an absolute impossibility and a canard that implies that a good and pure woman, free from attachment to some diabolical coitus machine, can come and come and come and just, my stars! keep*on* coming until your eyes are almost banjaxed out of your head and still she cries for you to *do it* and *do it*! . . . Well. Um. As I was saying, sex must be always and forever aswim in blissful ignorance, it must, to be worthy of sexualityness, be robustly boring. If you get yourself involved in odds and ends and trivia like positions and funny clothes and playing doctor-nurse or boss-secretary or priest-nun—and that strikes me as *particularly* crude—sex is nothing more than a worldly exercise in pleasure and not what God intended it to be: a job! As I contend in my new book, sex is all right when thought of as something akin to bowling and Barry Manilow and Merv Griffin and having a couple with the boys. When you mix it up with "fun" and excitement, it is nothing but the dry and soulless search for the orgasm—and we know what an orgasm is, do we not? Sort of like a sneeze. I say be done with the bric-a-brac and the bibelots and simplify, yes, much like our good sisters who wear, or so the laundress tells me, the lightest and most delicate things beneath their . . . Anyhow, my son, I trust that this talk has helped, and when you see the good Dr. Dubuque tell him that I've tried to steer you into the path of Duty, all right? And now I must to my frugal dinner.

« 37 »

In Which
Dr. Dubuque's
Insincerity Is Revealed

I've just come, Doctor, from a most enlightening and illuminating discussion with the good padre, Blue said. I see that it is now possible for me to have a life of unchained fleshly joy with my lawful spouse, rather than the mere existence of split-second boffs that have been my way of late. Now, and with all deference, it seems to me that the requirements of these episodes in my life of picaresque adventure have all been met. To wit, and id est, as well as videlicet: Happy greetings, short warm chats, speech on mysterious Celtic rites to assembled rubes, wife and son shipped off on all-expenses-paid junket for two on the mighty Zambezi, grovelling request to your most august person anent a small matter of personal genito-urinary difficulty, and rapt attendance on the wise yet worldly counsel of the resident sexologist, the good Father Debris, S.J. Thus, since the sun, as is its wonted habit, will not stand still, but careers acrost the azure as a madman hight doth suffocate the very breath of flowered innocence in fury most benign and idiotically fixed upon the Pole Star as stare of drunken Congressman, I feel we must all three be gone. But foist: Have you the Phrase? If you will lay it on me then may I return unto my dozing domicile in tawdry though belated triumph and cease my quest.

Ah Serge, my boy, continued Doc Dubuque, upon whose arm hung daintily in mutest adoration the female charms of Miz Clarke Grable, how glad I am you've brought this up! As is, I'm sure, Miz G, renowned assistant, queen of the buffet lunch, and memo-writer! (At which the hefty broad did blush.) Yes, and more than glad! You know, of course, that I, in my difficult position—but I do not complain!—my difficult position of profound responsibility as chief of paperwork and memoranda, holder of meetings, and giver of small, "working" lunches, must needs employ all the arcane arts and varied tricks that keep the groves of the academy, how shall I say? green! In thus wise, I use with might and main the steel stroke, the Chicago trap, and "shots" known to the happy, happy

175

few as the Jaques, the Brooklyn, and the Bailey. And all to keep the vasty population, and such pilgrims as thou art, happy and contented. It is not an easy job, I must insist.

The guy has flensed hisself unto his marrowbones, la Grable cooed.

Sweet child, Dubuque leered happily, his fingers straying naughtily. I have been a kind of warrior, yes, strong as Major Drummond of the Tillicoultry Guards, wily as the Old Fourteenth at Fianchetto, and aggressive as Flora Temple when she led the rustic Paisley Boys in Philidor's Defense at Waterloo.

But, said Blue.

As is written on small placards in libraries across the land: SILENCE, yawped Miz Grable.

A loudmouthed wop—and aren't they all?—name of Giuco Piano, came here all the way from sunny Alma, to stand as you now stand, the Doctor said, his straw hat in his trembling fist, asking for assistance. What was my answer? Tell him, luscious lass!

The Doctor gave him, 'spite his awesome everpresent tasks, gave the garlic-sodden dago a job helping out our faithful Denny Kelso, who cleans the terlets over there in Nailor Hall! And you stand there *demanding* things?

I only— Blue began.

Innocent naïf! Dubuque said sadly. To stand here in the pure, free sunlight, to stand in wing-tip shoes and plaid orlon suit, to feel upon my skull the soft and oddly shaped coiffure that proclaims me WASP . . . you have no idea what struggles I have waged for the right to listen to your pleas.

Plus also his old lady likes to bust his chops because of our innocent and rigorously professional relationship. She got some dumb idea we play laird and lady in deserted Whilter Hall o' nights. Prudish slut!

Now, now, my demoiselle, Doc smiled. No need to hurl invective like a raging dyke. As the poet Henry wrote in *Double-Corner Dynamo*: "Ere the centre holds in Boston Cross/The fife will shrill in Bristol." Words that ring with proud defiance!

When your voice clangs up like that, higher than the highest branch of diseasèd ginkgo, the cutesy Clarke sighed joyously, I feel like the Ayrshire lassie in Walter Scott's great *Edinburgh Pioneer*.

But I've digressed, Dubuque mused on. I was speaking of my struggles, am I right, dear Blue?

Uh? Blue nodded.

And struggles have as vile concomitants—an host of enemies!

I feel my bosom heaving with the memory of all them little bastards! Grable spat indignantly, straining to hold back her bra the while, which item yearned to hurl itself right through her shoit.

Soft, Clarkie dear, the Doc admonished. Let not poisonous contumely bite you on the tit. As I, good Blue, struggled up the ladder of success, a gang, a shoal of people, mad with envy, tried to kick me down, or anyway to stomp upon my hands. Such formidable adversaries as Ruy Lopez, that grinning spick, Mario Nimzovitch, hale and hearty denizen of men's rooms, Jennifer Switcher, "the Will o' the Wisp," whose famous Glasgow Address, "Humanitarian Roots of Genocide," won for her the Caro-Kann Brotherhood Award, and Albin Zugzwang, who proved that fetuses have invisible moustaches and thus are actually people—all these, and more, fought me every centimeter of the way up to the top! Life has not been, fond trekker, all reddish posies.

My Vince! Courageous sitter on committees! Mlle Grable offered.

I only— toadied Blue.

Furthermore, the sparkling Ph.D. speaked on, and furthermore, has anyone—except my right-hand arm, the indispensable C. Grable here—has *anyone* given me even a gill of credit for the way in which I sped graduates on their way each and every motherfucking June? In broiling sun, in roasting hotness, in paralyzing fountains of humidity, I monologued my way into their hearts: flashing-eyed boys and high-breasted girls, melting in the loathsome heat of early summer! I pulled out all the stops of lofty rhetoric in my sedulous endeavors, till, by J. K. Christ, I sounded like unto a chaplain of the now-deactivated Second Army, "Red Deuce" to those who served beneath its demented officers. I employed the Dundee hyperbaton, Bowen's Twin exergasia, scotchaeresis, the Sicilian picciuriddugoge, petroffasm, colleasmus, Souter's metaphor, morphymoron, and a dozen twain or twice times twelve or a score and four or twenty-four. Maybe even a few edds and onds tacked in!

While I sat upon the dais, tittered Clarke, while curious orgonic things occurred beneath my sturdy gown.

D-Doc? Blue keened in his wild lament.

Lots of problems, boy, lots. And all smashed through as does a gnarled fist whack its way through a sodden piece of cardboard. Oh, I will not deny that there have been rewards: the Benno Wagram Medal for "a senior scholar who wears his cardigan with flair"; the Bruce and Muffie Alekhine Plaque for "the use of the same class notes for twenty years" hand-running; and the Réti Tarrasch-Steinitz Scroll for "an administrator who cleans up his cardboard plate, including cole slaw, at faculty galas." I admit, yes, that there have been compensations for this long career of giving pretty girls their unearned C's.

Fearless figure of fatherly flab! drooled Miz G.

Doc! Blue yelped at last. I only want to hear that fabled Phrase you intimated you might have, buried in a drawer deep beneath an clutch of sex aids.

Ah, my boy, of course. How glad I am you've brought this up. I fear that we, meaning I, we possess no "Phrase," as you so robustly put it. We went along with you, caught up, as we were, in the madding music and the heady wine of Paddy's Day. I know you'll understand, my gadabout.

Understand? quoth Blue. Understand? Nay, if understanding holds its seat in dread of massy planet's scorching flight! I understandeth not!

Then shame upon you, shabby prick, the Doctor beamed. Pack up your family and your crap and scud away like water spider cast adrift upon a sea of Pepsi.

Or like a China-wagon bowled along by hurricane, you ungrateful shit, the svelte CG mocked bitterly.

You mean? stared Blue in vile and caitiff disappointment.

I mean, growled Doc Dubuque, that you will get your ass in gear else I'll set loose the starving Dobermans to fatten on it! Comprendy?

Vile load of syphilitic come, mused Clarke, lofting after the retreating figure of our hero a small stand of nestronia that she had lingered under oft.

<< 38 >>

*"La Musique
et les mauvaises
herbes," Continued*

IX THE VISIT

Friday last André is making a visit to his family. As he has a brother and a sister and varied comrades, he has much of things to recount to Émile when he has returned to the University Sunday night.

ÉMILE: You have the air of repose, my old parsnip. Did you make a good voyage? Did you have the "ashes" hauled away over the wick-end?

ANDRÉ: But yes. I am depart from here on the train of four hours twenty-five. I am arrive at the house of my parents at nine hours Friday night. At ten hours fifteen I am with Catherine, the maid, making the animal of two spines. She has some couple of biscuits!

ÉMILE: Suzanne might well be in choler with you should she discover this. Is it not so?

ANDRÉ: You may bet a boot on this! But what Suzanne shall not be knowing will not be of any ill effect to her. Do you agree, my old man?

ÉMILE: I do agree. And how are your family? Is the father still as all the time rooting amid the turnips?

ANDRÉ: But yes. And now he passes some time of an evening swinging on the birch trees of the forest.

ÉMILE: Ha! Ha! What a foolish old fuck-head your father appears to be!

ANDRÉ: In effect! It is what arrives of perusing on the Yankee verses. What garbage they are!

ÉMILE: And the rest of the family?

ANDRÉ: All the world goes well, thank you. They are all coming to search for me at the station. My little brother made the honor to carry my valise until the auto. Then he dropped it down on his club foot. My idiot sister Anne recounted to me all the news of the neighborhood.

179

ÉMILE: That there may have been some things of much interest in the place? Things of dirt and lowly gossip?

ANDRÉ: One thing of great amusement solely. It is that Mlle Lorpailleur, the schoolteacher, fell into love with her bicycle. Is it not wealthy?

ÉMILE: Very tasty! What a perverted lady she has to be!

ANDRÉ: In effect. It is whispered that she sleeps even atop the vehicle.

ÉMILE: Do you have other nice little tidbits of Catherine?

ANDRÉ: Mama prepared all the plates that I love: the hogface in cream, the broccoli with apple juice, the whipped-cream-and-onion-filled éclairs, the goose in Jell-O. And Saturday night, when I am returning with a little sack on, Catherine is even mounting up to my chamber for to carry up a cold goose flesh and a jug of whiskey. I made her to drink herself crazy and soon we made a number of fascinating tableaux in the looking-glass.

ÉMILE: You old debased weasel! You had then therefore gone out Saturday night?

ANDRÉ: Yes. I am going out to say good evening to some comrades what are left. The most of my ancient comrades are at the local colleges of applied agricultural arts. Some others are in wild flight on the morals charges. Yet others make their military service, many of whom which have make the bad in the blood from the Old Joe.

ÉMILE: It is as in our village. When one has said how does it go to the family, drunk oneself to craziness, and banged a chicken or two, there is nothing more to make.

ANDRÉ: You exaggerate a piece. But I admit that I am content to be returned. Suzanne may have had a blue while I was on my voyage.

ÉMILE: Do not have a worry there. I made a small and intimate fest for Suzanne and me Saturday night. We had a good enjoyment! Wow.

ANDRÉ: What? You rotting mouse!

André and Émile commence to exchange blows of a great sharpness and strength upon each the other's noses, lips, and teeth. Just then, Suzanne enters into the chamber and lounges about on the sofa in an indecent manner, so that the two old comrades forget the difference they have and stand still while the eyes of them almost tumble out. It seems as if Suzanne has forgotten to wear her dress.

X XMAS GIFTS

Alice Cuisse, though homely as a horse radish, is a serious young lady, who never waits on the last minute for to buy her Xmas gifts. Yesterday, she is going into town, and, having prepared her list in advance, she has made her purchases in one hour flats. What a whiz. On returning, she has called Suzanne for to show her the purchases.

ALICE: Come to see the pretty items that I have come to buy. It will knock you off your pin!

SUZANNE: I wish to well, my swell old doghead. I have need of distraction. That foul odor, André, has chanced to reveal that at the house of his parents he made much delight on the maid's private pieces.

ALICE: I knew always that he is a grand stool. But did not you with Émile make the warm sex all Saturday night?

SUZANNE: But yes—but what manner of thing else may a young lady do who has the mammoth blue? But a piss on top of it! Show me the gifts, if you please, my old stick.

ALICE: Well then, oke. Regard the vibrator who I have chosen for Sophie. I like much that he has the form and color of a carrot, but I hope that he is not too much petite.

SUZANNE: Oh no! He is well enough grand and also very jolly. Ha! Ha!

ALICE: Why do you chuckle in such hearty manners?

SUZANNE: It occurs that he looks like the organ of Mr. Aine, but for the color of orange he can possess.

ALICE: Mr. Aine! How is it that you know of his manly piece?

SUZANNE: Oh well. We made some dirty things one time on the broccoli garden. It was but a quick bong, on feet against the old cypress tree down there.

ALICE: O-ho. It is clear presently now why it has been that you received the A in Kazoo Studies, you wicked . . . bun, do you say?

SUZANNE: It is of no importance. What is it that you might have bought for Monique Gaine, that bowl of depravity?

ALICE: A pretty couple of white lace garters for the attractive thighs of her. I have a small hot for her, do you know.

SUZANNE: I had the thought that you are of the Sappo-type of women. Is this for because no man or boy desires much to hump on you?

ALICE: I have the greatest of disgust for men or boys! All they desire for to be doing always is to shoot off their filthy hoses in all times! Foh! How do you like those garters?

SUZANNE: They are very jolly. And then, you have reason of to select of the white. They make hot excitement with black sheer hose.

ALICE: Is it that you might want . . . ?

SUZANNE: You are as red as some beets, my close-knit pussy. What is it?

ALICE: . . . might want to try them on? You own the very jolly brace of thighs also, Suzanne. Monique has them scarcely more jolly than you.

SUZANNE: Yes, I want to well.

(*Suzanne adjusts the accessories upon the legs.*)

There! How do they appear on my gams? Extremely fatal, I think.

ALICE: It goes very, very nice. Now, if you neglect to lower the skirt I will be racked around with an ardent attack and lose the control on myself!

SUZANNE (*lowering her skirt*): Very well. It makes bad, I think, for ancient pals to be making dirty acts together. And I am not a Sappic, you know it good.

ALICE: In effect. I know almost too good how much you adore those hoses of men and boys. Well, Monique perhaps will permit a suggestive liberty of her flesh.

SUZANNE: She is such of a little twat that I would not have a surprise, my girl friend!

ALICE: I am in large hope. Now, regard the some thing that I have buy for Jacques Derrière. A packet of the rubber sacks! Is it not a fine jest?

SUZANNE: You can bet the buttocks on that! Ha! Ha! Ha! This is a sort of somewhat piquant remark on the hygiene of those girl bums of the School of Fertilizer Arts. Each ones of them have the claps, the dirt clumps!

ALICE: I have the thought to make the fine jest, yet they also have the air of the quite practical, is it not so?

SUZANNE: It is of a great pity that you did not think on a gift for the latest blaze of Jacques, that hobo of the long legs and large crocks.

ALICE: Ah, but I did make the thought on this. Regard!

SUZANNE: It has the appearance of . . . oh, ha! ha! How vicious you can be, you serious plugger!

ALICE: Yes—a huge cork! What a sharpened remark, eh? Maybe this will serve to blockade the long hose of Jacques!

SUZANNE: Anyhow, such gifts will act to let them to know that all the world is aware of the base acts they roll in, the foul items!

Alice commences to pack up the gifts while at the identical moments making the glances toward Suzanne, what is disrobing the garters of her thighs. How Alice is wishing that Suzanne is loathing men also. Well, that is those breaks. We cannot all be twisted persons.

XI A QUESTION OF TIME

André hurries himself from the morning until evening without making the half of the things that he feels inclined to make. Is it that swell young ladies is always on his

brains? Perhaps so. Yesterday evening he has discussed his problem with his old pal,
Suzanne.

ANDRÉ: This morning I am promising myself of making a whole series of things, and poofs! It is nearly the hour of couching myself and it resembles to me that I have made nothing.

SUZANNE: Me, I have the same problem. Mr. Aine has said to me that it is all simply a question of organization. Recount to me your day and then we will essay to see if we can find a solution. I have the sick and also the tired that you are too pooped up in the night to make with me a quick boff, you lazy weasel!

ANDRÉ: Eh, good. I regret having the exhaust each night, my cute skunk. Today, for an instance, I am raising myself up at seven hours this morning. I am washing the hands and the visage after I make the pee-pee. Then I am dress myself. I have take a cup of coffee and dwell in my brains upon Monique Gaine, which displayed her new garters when crazy drunk in the Xmas fest of last week. My gosh! I think, and suddenly I discover that I am engaged in a piece of abuse of myself. Then I am arrive at the University at eight hours twelve.

SUZANNE: The unclean practice you make without doubts consumes up ten minutes. O.K. Did you pass the morning at class?

ANDRÉ: But yes. I pass the morning in the History of Accordion class and after the Class of Bassoon of Mrs. Chaud. By a by, Mrs. Chaud loves for to perch up on the desk in order that one might peep up into her skirt. Holy cows!

SUZANNE: And then? I venture out on the guess that you made a brief chat with Mrs. Chaud after the class, eh, you sneaky lewd?

ANDRÉ: I confess to this. Her scent makes me a wild creature!

SUZANNE: Where did you have lunch?

ANDRÉ: In the cafeteria of the University faculties, ah, in the company of Mrs. Chaud. We have ate up the lunch of prune ragout and bologna en croute in twenty minutes. Pretty spiddy, eh?

SUZANNE: I admit this. So? And what then ensued?

ANDRÉ: Afterward, Mrs. Chaud and I are reposing ourselfs during a half of an hour in the lounge of the faculties.

SUZANNE: Reposing yourselfs? You are handing to me a grand laugh!

ANDRÉ: Eh, good. In truth, Mrs. Chaud and I made a small amount of intimate acts. I perhaps suppose that we made a fritter of forty minutes.

SUZANNE: Until the present now you can regard that you have lost many minutes, all of that because of the ravage of ardent thoughts and acts. You are a strolling "dick," truly, my old man.

ANDRÉ: This is a somewhat rude judgment, my little tramp.

SUZANNE: Oh, shut up the trap on you! Where have you passed the afternoon?

ANDRÉ: In the laboratory of botany.

SUZANNE: You are filled with shits!

ANDRÉ: O.K. I have passed one hour there, but I have not can find the solution of the problem that they gave to us on the snap dragon.

SUZANNE: And?

ANDRÉ: And so, I make the cut and take on a cinema around which Jacques Derrière informed me. An extremely poignant study of American customs.

SUZANNE: You soiled bug! I am of the precise knowledge that you saw a vile cinema called "Hellions in Hosiery."

ANDRÉ: Oh well. You have clutched me again!

SUZANNE: Did you look on this mucky cinema and make an abuse of yourself beneath the waterproof?

ANDRÉ: Only two times, my yam. And this because one of the starettes what was making an oral act resembled you, and so I lost the control on myself.

SUZANNE: Don't make a grovel to me, you hot goat! On my count, today solely you have shooted off your thing four times! It is no mystery now why you make nothing all the day or why you are too pooped up in the night to make me a quick boff. What a decay you are!

(*Suzanne begins to throw some items and her chamber robe falls open.*)

ANDRÉ: If you permit your chamber robe to descend to the rugs, my thrill, I will make on you a number of boffs to make the eyes cross!

Suzanne permits her chamber robe to descend to the rugs so as to display herself in the nudity but for her mules. André commences to make with her an enthusiastic boff. But on his brains is the image of the enthralling legs of Monique Gaine. He is truly a sexy fiend!

XII A SOAP STORY

When Suzanne is returning from her dynamic rendezvous with André yesterday evening, Alice is waiting. What the else? She has been regarding a soap story on the "tubes," and she wishes to recount it to Suzanne. Suzanne has sleepy and wishes to couch herself and have a tropical dream on André, but she has to listen to the recital of Alice. What putrid! It is a duty of a young lady to listen when her pal of the chamber has a wish to speak. That is how a ball springs, no?

ALICE: She was truly beautiful, this story. The action unfolds herself in a village of France in the seventeenth century.

SUZANNE (*suffocating the yawn*): How does she call itself, your story?

ALICE: She calls itself "The Root of Love." The heroine was a lovely young blonde who awaits for many years the return of her fiancé. I tell you, switty, she is some piece of the stuff. Va-va-voo!

SUZANNE: And where was he, this handsome rogue? Couching himself with some other gash?

ALICE: Oh no! In Canada or the Wyoming or else place, where he makes the war against the English people or the redfaces or some things. And he is not too handsome, but an usual manly excrement.

SUZANNE: That you have a queerness in sex things makes you a bad critic, my old repulsive sis.

ALICE: Perhaps so. Anyway, this blonde chicken is walking about the orchard of peaches wringing out the hands, and all, how do you call? phlegms and tears?

SUZANNE: I have an ignorance of the argot. Any hows, he is never returning?

ALICE: Oh, but yes! But he has lost a considerable shard of his manly root in the battle, and he no longer wished much to marry himself with the cutie.

SUZANNE: And why not? Is it that the mange loved her no more?

ALICE: But yes . . . more than ever he has! But he had a fear from the doctor that he can no longer haul up her ashes. He tells to her on a scene to crack down the heart: "I am presently solely half of a guy." And the sweet visage of the blonde baby takes on a blush of a rose, for that she had a cloudy thought on what he was referring of. She is as naive as a driving snowstorm, you see.

SUZANNE: What is it that is arriving then?

ALICE: Well, my darling pearbush, the young bit is falling gravely into a bad malady because she has such a hot for this fragment of damaged goods.

SUZANNE: And the soldier is making a powder? Or is it maybe that he goes away "half-cocked"? Ha! Ha!

ALICE (*making the scowl*): Why must you always make the gag? No! He paces down and up in the drawing-room at the estate of his father, with the face on him all drawed up and grey and once on a while he peers upon his crotch area and bites upon his lip.

SUZANNE: Is it then that the chicken is dead from this malady?

ALICE: Why no! What a silly slut you may be at some times! When the soldier has seen that she has truly a need on him, he marries himself with her. He says: "My hot breath of life herself, there are many routes to love." And she permits her eyes to descend for she has the ideas that he is talking around some kinky stuffs. Oh boy!

SUZANNE: You must have at that moment almost lost the control on yourself, no?

ALICE: You could bet your face on this, birdy! I had a hot bolt.

SUZANNE: And the young lady without doubts retrieves her health when she has seen that her fiancé loves her always.

ALICE: It is so, and they are to live happy the rest of their days together on the large estate of his father, a grizzly type of chap.

SUZANNE: It is a regret that his root does not grow to its standard measurement. Then the blonde twerp would *really* live in a happy life.

ALICE: That is an opinion of yours, Suzanne. As for myself, I can neglect for all times the masculine equipments! And if I was to have been making the household with that knocked-out blonde, she would never once think on the tool of a man, big or small, I can make a swear to that.

SUZANNE: I can believe on that, motor mouth.

Alice and Suzanne prepare themself for sleeping. Alice is wrapped into a reverie of the blonde dolly, and Suzanne into one of André and his recent pleasure on her. And so to couch.

<< 39 >>

The Couple
Somewhat Cheered

Croak on, exhausted Muse! Of the weary fambly and its ugly equipage, sorta
sauntering and meandering from out the lush land of Illini and the mighty vir-
gin forests ripe with the litotes tree and the endless madd'ning buzz of the industrious swarms of B-B-eyed tempura, O croak!

Yawp wildly, like the bearded bard of bygone Brooklyn o'er what would be
rooftops were here there domiciles to carry them! Holler in limping choliambics
of the creaking cart and the pianner now much the worse for wear! Lithp in awe
ofth the land that braver men than I have called—Mithouri!

And so, they at last rested in a patch of merciful shade about as big around as
the sunny center of the Cola daisy. And Blue, after weighty pause, began:

The natural shocks my fletch is heir to wast increased tenfold by the sneaky
con that V. Dubuque employed upon me. He never had the Phrase I sought for
and simply used me to blather Irish jive unto assorted bumpkins. And all this
followed by the windy shit of a doddering priest! And now we find ourselves still
wand'ring like a buncha clouds that hover o'er the tupelos! Like, where in bleeding Jesu's name are we? Belike it seems a land of mud and caverns. That's bad
enough, but whither? Oh perfidious scholar!

It was a rude surprise, Helene agreed hysterically. The more so since he
seemed so nice with his bulky cardigan and sincere and friendly feet. Oh, I have
not felt so abandoned and rejected since that horrid day in high school when they
clipped my lock.

Yet, sweets, our Zimmerman sleeps peacefully, his trusting soul given o'er into
our hands as 'twere a baseball gathered in by what is called, for reasons dark, a
sure glove. What means "sure glove" I cannot tell, unless it be what old Diogenes
Laertius dubbed metonymy; or was it that this said metonymy gathered in a "can
of corn"? No matter, so long as he snoozes on.

You've lost me, bulging carlo, the wife breathed quietly, but just to hear you
once again spout forth your dizzy horseshit perks my spirits up like seltzer. We'll
fare forth, no matter where we are, or where go we instead!

187

Strong girl! There is, indeed, behind each man of greatness, or of great dreams, like unto Don LaMancha, a reticent woman, who stands close-ready with his coat or jacket, ready to slip it on his aching shoulders when he gets the rock-jawed Call!

I do but do my duty, husband, Helene glaumed happily.

Then, since we don't have a fiddler's-fuck idea of where we are, except that we must go yet further onward, let's rest a smidgen here in purple shadow, while I rummage in our gear and read aloud a while so that we may begull the time that hangs as heavy as an old pirogi. What book shall I— Hello! a little album-like affair to which is fixed a letter! Do you recognize this item, poopsies?

I'm darned if I know what dick-all it is, she smiled.

The letter "says":

Dear Mr. and Mrs. Gavotte:

We are bitterly disappointed by the crude and cavalier treatment accorded you by Dr. Vincent Dubuque, the Administrative Dean of our beloved University. We discovered, too late, that he was giving you what the vulgar term the "brush-off," and had no intention of giving you the Phrase you are so nobly seeking, and no wonder; for he has *no knowledge* of such a Phrase! (There are some wags who maintain that he has no knowledge whatsoever, but since he has a Ph.D., he probably knows something, at least how to get on a bus.)

We hasten to dissociate ourselves from this blot on our escutcheon, this fly in our milk, this beam in our eye, and to wish you the very best of luck. Attached please find a small token of our warm feelings for you, a hand-crafted "album" of heartfelt messages to both of you.

Affectionately,
"The Gang"

The hot tears are crowding to my eyes like ants hustling over to a ort of abandoned cake, or pie, Blue stammered.

I too feel a rush of deep emotion. But read the messages, my love. The world has some kind people left, though they be disguised as slothful academics.

I'll read them then, asputter all with joy!

MY ALBUM'S OPEN, COME AND SEE. WHAT? WON'T YOU HAVE A LIME WITH ME?: K.Y. Geli.

WITH THE BIGGEST WISHES FORE LUCK AND PROSPERETTY TO THE FINAL BUZZER.: Milhous Hoover.

BEST VISHES! HA-HA.: Sepp Schutz-Staffel.

SIN-SEERLY YOARS.: Nathan Famoso.

SCREW MANY, LOVE FEW, DON'T GO DOWN, IN A CANOE.: George Stardust.

NEVER B♯. NEVER B♭. ALWAYS B♮.: Manuel Joie.

MY PEN IS POOR, MY INK IS PISSY, BUT MY CARE FOR YOU, SHALL NEVER MISSY.: Juan Simón.

4-GET-ME-KNOT.: Sol Mallow.

FORGIVE THIS BLOT, FORGET ME NOT, I CANNOT HELP, THAT I'M A TWOT.: Lillie Bullero.

IN THE DAISY CHAIN OF FRIENDSHIP, BE NOT FAR AWAY !: Jem Spaa.

AIM HIGH! SWING LOW!: Medusa Queynte.

DO THE REST IN SPARE TIME; EVERYONE EXPECTS MORE.: Lewis Fielding.

WHEN ON THIS PAGE YOU CHANCE TO GLANCE, JUST THINK OF ME AND DROP YOUR PANTS.: H. Poloie.

I WRITE THIS NOT FOR GLORY, I WRITE THIS NOT FOR LOOTS, I WRITE THIS TO BE REMEMBERED, YOU WONDERFUL GALOOTS.: Aaron Alwitz.

LOTS OF LUCK! YOU OL' FUCK!: Michael Schiller.

GET ON THE LOCAL, CHANGE TO THE EXPRESS, MAY YOUR FORTUNES RISE, LIKE A WHORE'S DRESS.: Olive d'Oyly.

I WISH YOU A SUCESFUL SUCESSION OF SUCCESFUL SUCESESS.: Laszlo Syntax.

ON THIS LEAF, IN MEM'RY PREST, MAY MY NAME SWELL LIKE A BREAST.: Aubrey Hawtree Creek.

ROSES ARE RED, VIOLETS ARE BLUE, REMEMBER ME, WHENEVER YOU SCREW.: Olga Warner.

LAST IN YOUR ALBUM, LAST OF THE LOT, FIRST TO BE REMEMBERED, LAST TO BE REMEMBERED.: Robert Fischholder.

That is the summed-up total of the lot, Serge said, placing the little booklet on the grass with such care as would snatch a sob from the chicken-neck of Heinrich Himmler, now deceased.

With folks like this, Helene spoke up, can Spring long cop a z while snow and sleet thrash down upon the groaning oith?

Though we know not what we may do, let us do it fetchingly, and by God, we'll aimless plunge ahead, wherever that may be!

My darling Blue! I hear a growling, like, that seems to come from the tiny lion lodging in your swollen heart! *Let* us aimless plunge!

But soft, the sun, that staggers in his wonted drunkenness across the depthless sky, has fallen to his scabby knees, and crawls toward his sequestered crib. Let us hurl ourselves like so much jetsam into this cavern here, that yawns as wide as doth a poor unfortunate compelled to lend an ear to Aaron Copland.

I follow, hurling, your own body, hurled, and hurl with me the chee-ild!

Then they penetrated the Cimmerian cave, its darkness like the glop oft-squirted on John Wayne by rubber octopi, or whatever it is called. Hardly had they settled down around the friendly blaze when a sound so harrowing came from out the shadows that, as is their wont in fiction, danced around the fire, so that sort of like chilly temblors jogged up and down two spines, yea, jogged, and sprinted now and then.

Forsooth, it was a spectre, all in clothes that smacked of times gone by, a ghost dolled up as one might term, a "cowboy."

Who, said Serge, be you, strange person, whose head I seem to be looking through so that the cave wall that is behind you seems to be your brain? Huh?

I am J. James's spirit, doomed for a certain term to stroll about, and, for the rest, constrained to sit around till the gross flesh that hangs upon my ass-bones is whittled clean away. But that you are a jerk I'd tell the secrets of this slimming trick, so that you'd thrust your yogurt and your kelp far up your fundament, therein to sleep. And your two eyes would pop out of their holes, your sweetie's hairs would sprout like crabgrass vile, and her two tiny knockers would implode like potholes swift-appearing in the street. But these Missouri secrets must not reach two idiots like you. Hist! Hist! Hey, hist! If you would go on with your endless quest, the way lies westward—toward the Land of Stars! Yes, Stars! And money! And decaying brains! A land where dumbness reigns as Emperor. Though thicker are you than a hmalted hmilk, I think you'll figger out the spot I mean. But, whoa! It's time for me to haul my ass and fling it in my magic easy-chair. So long! And take it easy! And—I'm gone!

Then, with the celerity of the turquoise-tufted blackhaw when it swoops out of the mist to rend and tear the tender flesh of baby armadillos, the spectre vanished. In the boring gloom of the cave, two mouths open in astonishment could be descried. Did I say . . . *two* mouths? Aye! And will stand with pike and bludgeon to defend my bold assertion, or great Achilles did not pass his beardless youth in drag!

This ghostly tip-off, coupled with the merry greetings of our unknown amici at The U, Blue said in measured tones, showers a somewhat sanguine attitude upon my thumping chest. The Land of Stars! In what direction westward this may be, I do not now surmise, yet it is clear as the mind of a senior Scientologist that it ain't not here! And so, we'll push on as did Roy Rogers and his unlikely partner, Ramsey Clark, when they set out to find The Great Divide!

My cherished love, Helene mouthed languidly, I too feel rumblings deep within, and each is edged with silv'ry hope. I know that we shall persevere at last.

They slept, they woke, they bashed ahead through old Mizzoo, noting as they went its plethora of caves, that, unfortunately, all look alike in the dark.

190

A strange note, though, I fear, has sounded here in this ringing saga of the Serge Gavottes. It is that in the cave, they left behind, we know not why, little Zimmerman. The "chronicler" of this "adventure" is reported to have said that the kid was "not pulling his own weight" as a character, and so he thought it best to "dump him." When it was pointed out to him that such rifts and tears in the motivational fabric of the careful plot were detrimental to the development of credibility in the well-made narrative, he laughed, and then, more serious, said: "Maybe I'll bring him back in a little later."

So little Zim slept on, all unawares that he had been abandoned like the swollen-footed motherfucker of antiquity.

« 40 »

Wonderland of
Opportunity, Where
the Apple Mocks and Blossoms

And suddenly, since Time is but a quibble in the Great World of the Novel, it (Time) passed, and with it, flying right alongside, cheek by jowl, hanging on, so to speak, as it were, to employ the great Dubuque's phrase as I enter the book, as is my privilege, hanging on, I say, to the wingèd chariot in which he (it) sits, Space as well passed. And our couple found themselves far beyond the borders of languorous Mizzoo, after which a battleship was once, for some inane reason named, and then shortened, to wit: "Big Mo," and whatever that may evince in the way of salty goblike attitudes, none dare whisper.

With what celery we have come into this land that Time will one day forget, Helene marveled from atop the gallant cart. One moment we were in that grisly cavern, replete with phantoms and odd pebbeles, and the next, here we press on in Apple-Blossom time.

Pebbeles? Blue laughed.

A mere typo that the author permitted to stand for a cheap laugh, its quaint orthography suggesting to him a Yiddish word for "rocks," so shot Helene.

Oh, replied Blue, looking about wildly. Then, calm at last, he continued: It is in the nature of fiction that its creators do whatever they wish, busting to tatters eternal verities and such things as the "unities," a word I seem to recall as having something to do with a true act in a brief time in a small spot or sumpn. But we have passed through the great state of Mizzoo in a sudden flash, the time it takes to turn a page.

I wondered why the so-called scenery zipped by so fast. It was something that made me very very noivous.

I suspect that the "text" is being "deconstructed" beneath our very feets! Blue muttered. And here, he raised his voice, here I thought that we were in a Novel of Ideas, one invested with a Desperate and Aching Significance and a Sadness filled with Smiles.

A . . . novel? Helene said, her tiny hand shooting rapidly to her breast.

Yes, my ruby flyhatch, Blue said. Figures in that great mirror held up to the side of the road by some crazy person running along down same. The fact that we are—poof!—in this new environ is a fact with a purpose, since all things must have a purpose in a fictions.

A . . . fictions? Helene said, her other hand furtively joining its companion.

We are but the creatures of a great master god, as are all men and women, shall I say, human persons? Yes, a god who sits aloofly in the sky remote and arrogant, sailing his pears to the clouds, allowing us to strut on this poor stage to the last syllable of something or other.

Oh! I thought for a moment that you meant that we were not . . . real!

Sweet swell nit! Blue smiled tenderly. Not real! I spoke in figures and conceited metaphors, making plain to you that we are in the same boats as are all persons, blown hither and thither by decaying winds, at the mercy of the deathless ones who amuse themselves with our scrabbling; in this, we are but folk in stories, and if we don't know what happened to Missouri, well, who does? What happened to the snow that fell on lovely Rome yesterday? Being alive is like being in a novel, which is why it don't make no sense, writhe as we may in the glades and copses of eternal spring.

At this, Helene felt better, but great Jesu knows why. For a brief sec, she thought that she was *not* real, was not a flesh-and-blood character, but a glob of *écriture*, although she did not know this word. Few do.

Let us pay to all this crap no, or little heed, Blue comforted, and keep plugging on.

So pluggged they on, past vast stands of apple blossoms and the huge herds of razorbacks that lowed their mighty ignorance to the distant azure. Birds cheepied, the pines stood pale and gaunt, and beyond the mountains a mighty thunderhead dropped snowy blizzards on the twinkling lights of cozy hamlets, all of which, had an invisible observer been able to see them, would have reminded him of home, as they dug out cheerily from the choking drifts in which were buried their cars and, more seriously, their stern fireplugs! Past fields of mud, past the laughing corn-faced girls whose eyes sparkled almost in a plethora of small-town goodness, past the belching stacks of somber factories turning out, who knows? luggage maybe. And more razorbacks, trampling the cotton and the pawpaw shrubs, pushing, straining, wild-eyed in their mad flight to better grazing fields, many of them ending up dazed in lamplit parlors, where Gramps sat nodding over the evening paper. It was a slice of America, this great land that has dreamed its great dream of democracy for ages and ages, or, in any event, for seventy-two years longer than CCNY. Yes! Or no! Never! Never did Blue feel more proud than that moment when the rains came, yet again! Those drench-ing, health-giving rains that turned the highway down which they slowly moved into a cataract, and on which, had an observer been looking at them from far above, they would have appeared to be very tiny people—such is the wonder of distance! Past the avid greasemonkeys and depraved soda jerks, the crippled bellhops and stout redcaps, the corseted schoolmarms and grimy conductors, the gardeners, shenangos, plumbers; past the ornamental-sheet-metal workers' ap-prentices, the junior assistant scoutmasters, the district supervisors in charge of sales and service, the bakers, and butchers, and always, always, the shouldering razorbacks, trampling the red dust into great red clouds of choking red dust! How many salesmen far from home, far from the little houses in which they loved nothing better than to have a friendly beer or two, how many, in imper-sonal hotel rooms, hands but lately freed from the Bibles tucked thoughtfully away in dresser drawers by people from the Gideon Company, Inc., how many in lonely lamplight, far into the stranger night, wiped the caked dust from their tasseled, plastic loafers? How many hung their plaid suits in the steamy bath-room, how many in their desperation got zonked at the hotel bar, the sound of the evening wind soughing in the bare birches that grew right up to the edge of the parking lot for guests and visitors? Past it all they inched, until Nature called, and they came huffing to a friendly service station, Smiley's Service, No Free Air, and his inviting Rest Room.

Into which they repaired to heed that call which even Great Augustus needs must have heeded, and the Emperor Napoleon, if they did not wish to make pee-pee in their toga and culottes, respectively that is.

(If he did not wish to make peepee in their . . . ?)

(If they did not wish to make peepee in his . . . ?)

(If either of them did not wish to make peepee in either of their . . . ?)

(If they did not wish to make peepee, the former in his toga, the latter in his culottes.)

« 41 »

The Graffiti
Set Up a Wild Twangling

If you like it dogwood-style, call "Wild Hydrangea" at GReenbrier 7–0001; I love to suck big fat elderberries; Up your albizzia!; For a hot cherry— try Rose of Sharon; Stop playing with your dutchman's-pipe; Fuck Virginia Creeper; Why are you looking up here, oilnuts?; My firethorn is all yours, yours!; Birch me! Beat me with a hickory stick! Roll me in nettles!; My love is like a red, red rose that to the sun doth reach, I like to kiss her on her nose before I kiss her peach; Boston Ivy eats it; If you like a good thyme, call Zenobia: REdbud 6– 3666; Daphne Hawthorn is a common privet; Confucius say: Old pimp is called box elder; Get your ashes hauled at the Tree of Heaven Motel; I like to jack my pine; Some come here to sit and gape, But I come here to peel my grape; Tits Willow does it down by the river; I like it up the old wisteria; False Jessamine gave me the horns; Rosemary Bog fucks like a hog; If it looks like a plum and is dripping with cum it's the hercules-club of your dreams; Matrimony vine makes vomen vild; The Rev. Basswood St. Peterswort wears Queen Anne's lace undies; In every pair of hot pants you'll find a burning bush; Heather Holly has a downy hudsonia; Sister Bumelia likes to suck the big ones; Those who write on toilet stalls bang their chestnuts on the walls; Socrates sucks Eastern hemlock; Pepper Vine is a hot hooer; Violet Gentian has an indigo bush; Play with my silkvine, comfort my black walnuts, for I am hot to trot; Asiatic Hydrangea's is horizontal; I want to stay out all night and come home with a trailing arbutus; Hazel the witch, the dirty bitch, gave me a dose of spirea; Here lives the crab that ate Little Rock; Red Ash, the S & M kid; Hal Glubit fucks Laurel Sheep; Robert Frost tossed off in the yellowwood; Stand closer! The next guy may have holes in his yews; Raggedy Ann has a buttonbush; I know a girl who in her spare thyme blows; The stiff ones are the kind I like: Sweet Buckeye Bruce from Pike; Magnolia Cash gives palm jobs; Mawmaw gives! Pawpaw; Draw the bit o' nightshade before you take a bath with a whore; Question: What do you call sperm in a lab? Answer: Cupseed; Honey Locust gave me acacia clap; Honey, suckle!; He married the lush with the strawberry bush; I like to goose berry much: Juan Pendejo; "Purple" Clemat is a pippin Tom; If leather would please you, call AZalea 3–1119, oak?; Single White Pine desires meet Dwarf Juniper on the heavy side. Object, bitter sweats; Tryon "Try" Foley, the pervert of Southern California, ate Orange County; Fuck oxeye Hera! Zeus; Current black digs white ash; Dear Lolly Pine: I love a large lob; Amelopsis without topsis panties were for Hazel Nut; Confucius say: Man who kiss prickly ash wake up with sour gums; Full-blooded Indian seeks spruce, elder white lady for marshmallow delights and moccasin; Rosebay Redbay Ucksfay; I love my sweet Alyssum much, because she is a whore; There was a young man from Persimmon, Who mistakenly thought men were women, In bed with a guy, With his cock risen high, He wondered just how to get in him; June Berry let Buck lay her; Coach "Bear" Berry buggers just for a larch; What are you doing with that mistletoe in your fly?; If you don't like my quaking aspen, baby, why are you squeezing my knee?; She married a man who had no balsam all; Don't screw on the beach unless you like dryas; Fuck Red Pine! H. Thoreau; De spirit gwine climb in you onymus; Lila C is a wild hump, dig it; A Dublin Protestant is a mock-orange; May the palm of Gilead fondle your chestnuts, ol' hoss; Senna's bladder wept here; Quoth Othello, "Suck a moor"; Counselor Siebold lost her briefs in the cottonwood swamp; Sade: Viburnum? by May Poule; I desire your sweet spire; Helen Hornbeam goes down on Fanny Fraser's fur; Would Alice Arrow suck Sy Sumac? Alice Arrow would; Andrachne has some pear!; Andrew St. Cross frigged the Flower twins in the raspberry patch; Cedar White kicks black ash; Macbeth sucks! Alder, Grass, and Hazel, Witches; Put that spindletree back in your pants!; They were only the farmer's daughters, but oh what apple-knockers; Barberry, Crossvine, Buckthorn, and Gorse: Bum-Bailiffs; Don't comb your teeth over the sink, sweet gums; Warm coffee-colored gent wants mutually thrilling afternoons with refined New Jersey lady in teagown; The girl stood in the bedroom door, her forestiera bare; Adam delved when Eve took her sweet leaf off; Chief Wintergreen eats it with a rusty spoon; Mme Dewberry was a lay, je dis; Smooth Allspice—the new shade coming hardon the heels of summer; If you like it the Greek Way, ring OSage 1–5657; Wayfaring stranger needs a hot pussy; Plant a diaphragm and grow your own corktree; Nora Wilde-Raisin is a dried-up old cunt; Stick it in a thimble, choke-up!; The Partridge Family needs a broom in their ass.

This is amazing "stuff," my blushing marmaduke, Blue said. It sort of makes me young again, filling my veins and other tube-like apparatus in my body with a reddish ichor that the medical profession dubbed—how many years ago!—blood.

To me it seems like dirty stuff and nothing but or eke a zillion daubs of bawd and vile obscenity, the belle replied in kind, her voice muffled from within the stall to which she had repaired in haste.

I know what you are saying, dearest doxy, yet I find my mind flying far, far beyond the grossness of the messages that slobber on these walls to the wild, how shall I say? *twangling* that the language sets up in this encoffined space. It has a kind of beat, a kind of rhythm, a secret time that owns but nowt except unto its own emblazoned right as doth the tawdry billet-pouch fix his great staring eye upon the dreaming perch among the weeds!

It seems but filth to me, Helene said, emerging much refreshed, as they say, much to one's chagrin.

Aye! Filth, yes, so it may be, I'm hip, said Blue, now sealed within the stall while honest H made vague stabs at her toilet 'fore the crusted looking-glass. Aye! Yet there is in it, as I have said, something so deeply musickal, so drenched in violent sublimity, that my soul in stunned amaze finds itself flying ass upon its heels through the infinite spaces of pure joy. It has its own weird time, and time, Great Time, is the nub and corazón of that gay art to which I pledge my life, my honor, and my lust for fame. As well you know, or should, since we are more than halfway through this questlike saga. I am but, when all is said and done, to Time but the caitiff slave and pleasant rouge.

I think betimes, my fierce-eyed lord, the word is "rogue."

Then "rogue" it be, and rogue and rogue again! By dazzling Jove, 'twere rogue all day and thrice o' Sundays when the heavens drop their sultry peace!

Merci, she wimped.

The hours passed, the sun went down, our pair traveled onward through the mudhens and the nodding aromatic vetch, and in the dark they stopped to pitch a camp, while Blue, silent now for minutes strung apace, mused on and on, then spoke.

When I spoke earlier of Time, my little chunk, I fear that I was somewhat murky. May I explain more clearly what I mean by it? Or does the Sandman, whom the Greeks dubbed Morphodite, claw fervently at your eyes? Or lids?

I am not ready yet for slumber, tweet. Expondiate.

Let's stretch out under the piano, far from the dew, then, and I'll lay this on you.

In the shadows Helene's smile flickered, flashed, and . . . disappeared. A loon croaked in the swamp, then all was still.

197

≪ 42 ≫

Blue's
Reflections on Time

Helene, sweet twitter, as we sit here beneath the great blinking comforter of the heavens, almost ready to embrace or be embraced by sleep in our colorful but not quite waterproof pushcart—I still dislike that term—our old piano sheltering us from the moonbeams that drive men mad, I think, though every fiber of my being cries out against such an act, of Time—great sacrosanct and bulging Time, that again, at this turn of the year, comes around once again; yes, as the old gives way once more to the new, it again forces its way into our consciousness with might and main and brawny shoulders that never say die.

As does, Helene transpired, the blinkered dysuria drop its mauve blossoms on the skittering rodentia of the forests.

It may not possess the reality we smugly ascribe to it, as some thinkers have suggested, whose hallowed names momentarily escape me—momentarily as awesome Time itself!—and also as clairvoyance has demonstrated, but it is a factor to be reckoned with, as reck we must or be damned to us!

Yet, grinned Helene, such recking is as difficult and as inscrutable as the "visage" proffered us by the humpbacked oliguria, whose scent in autumn once emptied out the comatose village of Los Cobardes.

Still, perhaps it is solely, or only, or lonely, a category which is resident in the mind by which we have to think, as one might say the ruptured cyanosis "thinks" in seed-time.

It's terrifically gratifying, Sergey, to hear you bring up, however bedecked with cavalier ignorance, the cyanosis and its shy pale-violet petals delicate as the autumn crocus, poisonous to les vaches, by the by.

As always, small-boned nuthatch, your B.A. in Ed permits you to shed new albeit brilliant light on our talks. Thank you. Nevertheless, the concept of Time must be considered by those who wish to live, and not even especially well. Nor can the individual extricate himself from the toils of the past, present, and future. To do so, in fact, would be as bootless as the desire of the spindly sapsucker beetle to haul his metallic frame from out the "jaws" of the gummy hypoplasia, churn though his tiny limbs may.

Or the dust-grey blattidae, Helene reflected, to slither through the bony spines of the rickettsia furiosa to freedom!

A point, if you will forgive me my little joke, well put. Those who ignore Time become its victim, struck down in the full flower of their years, pains much like arthritis nagging the psyche and other organs. For all practical purposes, one would do well to come to terms with this important factor in life. Perhaps in death as well, yet who can say? For in that undeveloped country no traveler is born.

What?

I say, no traveler is born.

No. Before that.

Perhaps in death as well? One would do well to come to terms with this important factor?

That. What an absolutely marvelous hypothesis, Sergey. Yet . . . don't you also feel that the above-average human person has the capacity to look back and review the happenings of yesterday?

Nor have I ever implied anything to the contrary, sweet hostess of golden daffodils. My point is that this, like other faculties, may be used so as to help or hurt.

Something then like the nauseating ichor of the slimed cochlea, which can drive one to the heights of erotic ecstasy, or, when applied too liberally, give one an awkward, not to say momentous rash?

Exactly! Your ceaseless rummaging through the giant volumes on wild flowers and other faunae, or fauny, that we have down on the floor of the pushcart, has sharpened your mind to marvelously and wonderfully unique acute sharpness. How wonderful to have more than just a wife! But, to press on, as Abe the tailor said—ha ha—one should learn from one's successes and failures, but one should not be deterred from further living by them. The plangent truths, values, and methods of the past can be helpful in the present, and even in the future, which is no more, according to Henri Berg, than the present of tomorrow, or maybe a few days or a week or so from now, but having learned what the past teaches, which, today, is yesterday, but which, tomorrow, will be today, or even right now—such is the mystery of ever-smoldering Time—having learned that, I insist, one should go on living in the present. Whenever that time may be in— or *upon*.

So does the ass-faced bobolink know, Helene stared, through potent Nature's inimitable instruction, to eat the berries of Jupiter's calcaneus today *and* tomorrow, sensing that tomorrow may be nothing more than yesterday if he hesitates in his greed but a single instant! How all of a piece everything is! It *must* be true that we are all gifted creators who, though knowing not—yet know!

That's lining the old bottom, perceptive minx! And to take your barely articulated suggestion a step further into the Platonic light, allow me to suggest that *the living present is the moment of existence.* It is in the now, so to speak, that one lives, no matter the cardboard shoeboxes filled with yellowing photographs. This is not to say, I insert, that the future, whatever that arcane organism may be, is to be ignored. No! I trumpet.

Who could possibly think such is implied, good bole? That would be analogous to suggesting that the waxy cerumen in its first "glimpse" of the April sunshine thinks that fall, with all its melons of misty fruitfulness, will never come. Yet we all know that "If Spring should come, is Labor Day not nigh?"

How I adore the way you use mighty poesie to put a point on an argument! It is the sign of a true statesman and surely that weird and useless art's most valuable raison d'être. No, as I have said, the future is not to be ignored although the true now is now. Unattained goals must be worked out, likewise methodologies. One must know where one is going, and how. Strangers offer monetary help toward middle of month. Travel looms and romance may blossom. But even all this focuses in the present thought, or battery of thoughts, and is implemented in present action. What one is *now* determines the goal that is to be worked out— and even seized!

I think, Helene coughed, of the way Cohen's maxilla seizes on the innocent dew that falls upon its pistils. No wonder the vulgar call the inobtrusive weed "Two-Gun Maxie."

Ha ha. I had forgotten that amusing patronymic. By God, a laugh comes in handy on a long journey toward the Ineffable, like this one, in which Time seems to be, if not precisely an enemy, then a summer soldier, whatever that means exactly. You know how I've always loathed the military.

I hate to see your penetrating brow all wrinkled up so ugly like that, honeyed clot. The Perfect Musical Phrase *is* waiting. I know it deep in my womanly torso. So do go on. I feel that you are nearing the synthesizing peroration of your analysis.

Thus, the now is the only time any one ever has. One is to so act in the present now that the future now will be richer and more meaningful for having known it than the past now—which seemed so important at the time. Fond fools that we be! This means: 1.) The thoughtful planning; 2.) the wise decision; 3.) the kind and helpful word; 4.) the skillful work of the moment. These are the steps by which one rises, as the long stamen of Browning's apnea rises toward the churning compost above its fuzzy head, rises toward the goal—often still to be worked out, and what joy and sugary fulfillment is in the working—the goal and the Ideal. One lives, if one lives at all, in the living present, the heart loving, the goal being worked out, or worked over, if we but falter for an instant of all-chomping Time, the hand always, even in sleep, creatively active.

As the Omaha purpura, Helene whispered, though an ugly brown in color, is yet always active, at least when the sirocco blows hard and hot against its woody stem.

Well put, bursting pod. And now, as the dew is beginning to soak playfully through my shirt and pants, and the Pleiades have set, I think we should crawl into, among, and under the odds and ends we call our gear, there in the damply glistening pushcart, and await the coming of incandescent day that lies, if my senses work all right, there behind that tree line, a Southern phrase.

You bet, Helene moped.

« 43 »

Land Where
Guitars Softly Creep

They, oh to be sure they, in a daze of intellectual delight, a *virtu* cerebral, because of the dazzle and flickering flash of the great argument that Blue had rendered or propositioned, or whatever, in regard to ever-changing Time, paid hardly heed or gave but even a tacit nod to the swiftly rolling-by (as well as along) landscape, such did the pure white light of thought burn in them.

Burn? Aye! Although they stopped in—or outside of, if one wishes to be a stickling accurate class of a reader—a number of oddball dumps deep awash in chili dawgs, bar-b-q, soft ice cream, and gouts of lambent catsup, catchup, and ketchup, and odds and ends of what some dreadful wag dubbed "sody pop." But take them all in all, you shall not see their like again of sich a pair, embafflement and quintessential joy scrawled large upon those two faces that we know by now so well! Yes, and seem to have known forever!

Indeed! and so they rolled ahead, crossing at last into that curious land shaped, by the Hand of the Great Creator in a moment of unfettered levity, like unto a license plate: the dozing quiet land of Big Sandy, the Great Smokies, and the Knight of the Corncob, Sir Popeye Cigarrillo.

Talk? Talk? 'Sblood! Had drunken barnswallow crashed through the attic window of deserted Penshurst rather than plunge into the cooling pond of the Lady Seraphina, such mad tumult had not stopped their seamless colloquy! Nay, not if the King himself, the wise Jacobus, bellowed in his cups o' Twelve Night.

When we were still trying to get to Little Rock, wherever that may be, or wert, stomping, so to speak, toward Tennessee, how swift, like a sudden torrent of jambalaya it came to me! What? you ask? Don't think twice, it's all right, I'll tell you, my special little orange blossom, my crazy heart, my pig, so to speak, in a pen. Let's turn back the years. Do you remember Ole Joe Clark, the famous Dancing Hemorrhoid, who did the hoedown with a Polynesian baby? Think, my treasure of love. Don't let the stars get in your eyes! Meanwhile, I'll wank out a couple pentatonic variants on "Take My Thing from Your Wringer," to fire up your house of memories.

E'en though time changes everything, how in the Sam Hill could I forget Joe C? Are you teasing me? He was the man who sent me the pillow that you dream on. Burning memories! Filled with bright wights, cunty music, golden guitars, rhythm and booze! What makes you trek down that lost highway to the hills of home, or, in any case, those lonely mounds of clay? Smite me with your stealin' feelin', like I was a sledded Polack on the ice.

I think of the sweet dreams of happier days, just a wedding ring ago, days of candy kisses, Spanish fandangos, and satin sheets! Days when I was but a small-time laboring man, the tender years, when you were my little Rosa, my proud Mary, my Filipino baby, my girl, so to speak, on the billboard. Every year, it seemed, was a good year for the roses. But, shoot! we can't get there from here, here on the long rocky road. Maybe little baby we should have stood there, 'stead of slippin' around? Satisfy my "mind."

True, I fall to pieces on these tumbleweed trails, walking after midnight, hearing the boids mocking, moanin' the blues, skipping in the Mississippi dew that drops on us thick as a vast wet deck of cards. But when you groaned, "Walk troo dis woild wit me, my li'l love bug," I threw, as you well dig, away, as well I might, the rose of home sweet home, and plotzed along in the wake of your male fireball. I'll follow you up to our cloud! or your cloud! sure as the Family Bible is unread. I admit that loving you could be better, it would be a gasser if you lit up my pin-ball machine once in a fucking while, but nothing, no, no, never nothing, can stop my love, my large and bearded snowbird! But again I ask, what makes you trek?

I'm thinking that maybe I'll find this Phrase when the grass, like, grows over me, and not a zit before. I am how they say "fill up" with the color of the blues. Yet I know, as I tear into my version of the Greater Cheyenne area hit, "Soggy Mount in Fake Down," its weird pitch jist out o' reach o' muh five little fingers, let alone ten, har har, that this waltz acrost Texas or wherever we are, this song of the wanderer that shouts and hollers from our distended throats, is a quiz. Or a test? A test then of my resolve, a peppery seasoning of my heart, a, psychiatrically speaking, river of no return. I am searching searching for the password to that One— which is a Lonely Number, no?—Great Truth, like a honky-tonk gal searches

searches for the hearty heart that is not coldy cold. For this I'm a-settin' the woods on fire, to boin a phrase. Thus, is but human, out here in Heartbreak, U.S.A., that I think off and on and with tears in my eyes of the old brush arbors, the old-fashioned singing, and the old footprints in the old snow of . . . home! Of . . . chay Blue! Kin yew blame me, my luscious flash o' white lightnin', my cielita linda?

Blame, Serge? Blame? Ha! What? Nay, not as long as the lovesick blues do turn a maiden's prayer unto base boot-heel rags, nor hot-rod Lincoln sails his "ship" alone! I'd sooner grasp an old pipeliner or the roses meant for Mama to my breast, or guerdon that great speckled bird who rides the train o' nights to Memphis with sixteen tons o' Wabash cannonballs 'spite its wild complaint!

My wondrous crazy person! I knew, or knowed, that this was to be the great judgement morning! Shot Jackson and Big Ben Dorsey the Third set it down years ago that a satisfied mind comes about solely when a king of the road like me has a mate in re who he kin say: "She's all woman," and also "She is my sunshine." Six white horses could not tear me from the foggy river of your brains, La Golondrina! Shore as Jesus Krise yanked little green apples off of the tree from which Judas cut short his faded love, cross my heart I love yew! If my heart had windows, you could peep in and prove it to yourself. Without your strength to carry us through the thorns of the dread kaw-liga bresh and the nettles of the jole-blon vines, I would have, long long ago, hollered: "Stop the world and let me off!" Though home is where the hurt is, still, it takes a long time to forget. The bottle let me down, the weed-choked willow garden let me down, but you, lively as the bubbles in my beer, said, "Let's build a world together." And I know we will, to the last mile of the way. Freckled fruit! Sexy slowpoke!

Ah, Blue, I don't care that 'tis my wonted fate to be but ol' Freight Train 45 to your crack red-ball, Phantom 309, if I may make how you call a metaphor. Though we are tangled in the coils of the wild side of life, with you, my gentle Mr. Jukebox, the blues stay away from me, and as every tumblin' tumbleweed under the blue moon of Kentucky knows—not to mention the proud rubes deep in the heart of Texas, or soused at the border, or stern-jawed in Cimarron, or asthmatic in dear old dusty Abilene—no blues is good news! Close together as you and me is, a veritable syzygy like unto the fabulous Georgia Molly and dear John Tenbrooks, the fornicating felons of the Tupelo County Jail, we're gonna, as long as this golden ring on my finger stains it a fetching emerald, hold on. Y por qué? 'Cause I cain't stop lovin' you! And you know how mountain girls kin love! Though after but six days on the road it 'peared to me that things had sorta gone to pieces, and I had half a mind to make the request that you release me before I suffered the fierce Baker's breakdown syndrome, the symptoms of which is: hillbilly fever at three A.M., walking the floor over you, the weird apparition who calls hisself "Little Benny," and the voice of Laydown Sally, the lewd and lonely rose of Méjico, a-whisperin' and a-whinin' "Take these chains from my heart one by one," still, I waited in the lobby of your heart. I walk the line, my stubborn and indomitable Serge, knowing that love, yes, love's gonna live here again!

You make me proud to shout unto the hills of Kentucky, which are probly near enough, "She's mine!" But may I subtly hint that somebody's puttin' somebody on? I mean: "mountain girls"? Shame on you! There, on the quarterdeck of the doughty cart, stands the glass. Take a peep. If that's the face of a mountain girl, then I am a Okie from Muskogee!

You win again! But honey, you don't know my mind. Oops! Is that I? I look like a blue muleskinner thornbush! Still . . . though I'm ragged, I'm right. If, for instance, I had a six-pack to go neatly tucked under my arm, I could pass maybe for, if not a mountain girl, then at least a Texas-two-steppin'-rosy-San-Antone-delta-dawned-honky-tonk-angel, by God!

Oi! It wasn't God who made honky-tonk angels. Don't you ever get tired of hurting me? Squinting at your more or less lissome self in those sad rags not fit for Beaumont even, which, by Christ's mercy, is a long long way from here, I feel . . . I think I . . . yes, I've got a new heartache. When I said I'd share my world with you I didn't mean you should, like, take the best room. I think maybe we must have been out of our minds, or is that spelled "minds"?

Whoa, sailor! Are we to be just another couple married by the bible, and divorcèd by the law? While we lived at 4033 Lee Highway, home in San Antone, with my mommy and my daddy, I was so lonesome I could cry. Accidentally on purpose, I heshed my mouf, as they say somewhere, maybe in the Blue Ridge Mountains . . .

They also say "y'all come" in that doomed purloo. So, as the idiom has it, what?

You thought I was dumb and didn't know about your cheating heart. But still water runs deepest. I'd shoot my orisons to heaven, accompanied by the neighbor's lonesome fiddle, praying, "Oh Blue, don't come home a-drinkin'. Take me! Lemme roll in my sweet baby's arms!" Pshaw! I might as well've been developing my pictures. You wallered in your back-street affair, you'd come home with the moon over your shoulder, new, old, full, whatever, it was a-divin' into the river. I'd beg you, beg you—could I help it if I was still in love with you?—"Kiss an angel good morning?" You'd make like a joke, e.g., "Hey, good-lookin'! Remember me?" I'd sob, *sob*: "I wanna be back in baby's arms!" You'd sneer: "After the fire is gone? Look, let's say goodbye like we said hello, O.K.? Milwaukee"—or some damn place—"here I come!" And all this for the love of a girl, that little slut Sally, with her bangs hanging down, a nasty pussy who can't make the two-backed beast with half as much, how shall I say? "esprit" as your lawful hump, I mean I!

Don't think for a moment, my faithful sugar tit, that I do not remember, and with what shame! I used to get the fever down there, the maleficent bluebonnet crotch-clutch, that'd come waltzing in on the southwestern breezes. Alas! Eheu! I'd seek out slimy Sally, do the old Fort Worth drag with her—e'en standing up!—and all the while I was missing you. My sparkling boich! If teardrops were pennies, I could right now buy a used car! Maybe even a little blue Folsom. I know they stopped making the thing but it'll come back! It had a sweetie chassis strong like a jailhouse, and . . . but I wander away, or around. What I mean to say is that I forgot more than you'll ever know about aches and pains of total heartbreak. At one point I figured that I'd never get out of this world alive, can you dig dat?

There he goes! With that boyish just-call-me-lonesome smile on his face. You are forgiven as you have forgiven this occasionally blooming person, your spouse, moi! You will, of course, recall the fiasco of the flesh I partook of a fortnight or so back. As that pasty academic ground his loins on mine, did I think things like: wait'll you see this, Serge? Or: I'll get along somehow? Or: long as you're creaming, try it again? Or, shame of all shames: let's get together one more time? I did not! I thought a think like: Why can't he be you? And bleeve it or not, that was the day I started loving you again.

Oh, Hermes, god of people who walk across fields, she thinks I still care, and she's right! You think: She's got you! and *you're* right, wing-foot! Let us, my more or less hairless Helene, let us never, never look at each other and wonder, in sotted voices, "whose heart are you breaking now?" And now, my pee-wee bark-sucker, let us move on, from here to the door of Success! The race, she is on! And it is time to be . . . moving on! So settle your aromatic self 'pon the motley swag we dub our precious belongings, and sing me . . . sing *us* . . . back home!

Home?

Why query thus my "home"? I was mum when you eked out a "pshaw" some vocables ago.

And so you were. Creak on, my felsty ox! Home it is, then. Or whatever.

« 44 »
A Southern Idyll

Ole Tesh growed that hawg on pure manure.

Corn growed so big chawed Luther's elbow off.

Shittin in tall cotton, boy . . .

Miz Jewel's swet-ass taters an pig dick . . .

Lordamighty! Billy's corn likker'll take the skin off a nigger . . .

Sole his cotton t' some New Yawk jee-yew made darky clo's outen it.

. . . fairy sets down in J. C. Tyrell's diner out to Bleedville an orders a whole fruit pie . . .

Still blowed up, driv ole Roy inta a big ole pine tree like a goddaym rivet!

. . . hippie down to the fairgrounds talkin bout peace an integration got hissef cornholed by R.C.'s two boys come in from the delta . . .

Loreena Pogue come home from honky-tonkin bare-ass nekkid cept her flowered brazzeer wrapped round her middle . . .

. . . ole boy from Ringworm Holler took a pull o' Jimmy Ty's white mule an I declare his daym drawers melted off . . .

. . . big ole bullhead come outen the pond an et the okra . . .

Whitfield pulled that ole gal's drawers down an she got appleblossoms stuck in her shameful hair.

Miz Lemon? Bakes them godawful bindweed tarts?

. . . say Judge Poon's fancy lady down to Atlanta makes him eat raw spinach with dago red on it, shoot!

Miz Monroe'd stanch up her monthlies with a big ole fistful o' collard greens stuffed all down in her drawers . . . dawgs like to chase her to the county line.

Caught ole Billy Lee Simpson with a daym sheep's hind legs poked down in his hip boots . . .

. . . say that Reverend Jimmy Boo Purty over to Coon Lynch spent all the love offerins on mail-order corsets from the Sears an Roebuck stead o' seeds for the church garden . . .

Damfool son of a bitch jee-yew professor from Chicaga asks the ole boys at the Blue Palm Cafe where he can find nigras can still dance the hoppin john!

Ko-rea? Shoot! Take a daym shit an the gooks'd put a mortar round up your daym asshole slick as a greased corncob.

. . . big bull gator et up half the sofa an old Ty-Dee jus kep drinkin his Blue Ribbon . . .

Miz Compton's youngest gal, Rubosa? Come in thout her underpants an say the swamp up an sucked em right offen her . . .

Ham Smellie et a bushel o' peaches down to the Grange fair an daym if he didn't shit hissef when they's playin "God Bless America."

. . . an when the daym rooster fin'ly got outta the still, the daym ole bird tried to mount Calvin Pugh's prize heifer, no lie . . . woulda done it too ony he was too daym drunk to stay in the air.

. . . ole boys down to the body shop bust in on Councilman Jeeter to surprise him on his birthday? There he stands in his wife's cocktail dress all over flowers an stars an bangles, an her high heels? Jeeter say "Come on in boys, just seein how the other half lives . . ."

Elroy Bimm got drunk an' done plug up the hole o' the dressin-room wall o' Miz Zenobia's House Plant an Longeree Emporium with his daym glass eye! Hear tell the Mayor's wife fainted dead away when she seed it starin at her.

. . . them new lady college teachers at the A and M buy their shoes at the Boot Village out on Route 16 . . . don't wear no underpants . . . Fitch Gorn say the daym salesmen work overtime for nothin!

Jim Bobby Gritt got hissef jacked off by a jee-yew gal in the Central Park in New Yawk . . . didn't even know her daym name!

. . . dead ole crow frozed in the watermelon ice cream . . .

Cousin Mack, fella used to get hissef blowed by a calf? Said 'twas better than a woman, more deddycated, he said.

Gleet West come back from Chicaga slobberin for some possum ass an redeye gravy way his brother PeePee used to fix it . . .

Schoolmarm down to Bugface, Miz Zee-Zee Harriet, clumb inta bed with a big ole cucumber an they hadda call the vet . . .

. . . then daym if ole Banjo Pox didn't drink a dozen bottles o' Haddycol an shoot the turnip patch with his shotgun. Say, "Thought it was fixin to steal my new separator."

Then Vern Roach stand up outen his chair an say, "Well, I 'low niggers is God's own, Reverend, but how come when you mention work you cain't find one in a burnt field with a bloodhound?"

Ole Miz Tupelo set in one place so long the rhubarb started growin out of her, no lie.

Zonnie Futt?—own the Whippee-Soft stand out on Interstate 40? Got born again one Sunday mornin when his grits started talkin to him . . .

Pap Bloat say he done seen a Bible in a Nashville hotel with a oil paintin o' Jesus smokin a cornsilk cigarette. Say it musta been a daym Cath'lic Bible.

Vanilla Chard waited on ole Slope Jonson at the church in the sun all day long with her weddin dress gummed to her with sweat an her eyes gettin hard as a fice dawg's.

Sheriff Gawk seed a man 'lectrocuted in Alabama onct an he jump up in the chair like a deer fly done bit him in the ass . . .

. . . Clench Sogg bumped thet gal's ass crost the fer timothy pasture like a daym bullfrog . . .

Ole Dudley say a nigger in New Yawk dressed up like a daym scarecrow once *talked* to him like he didn't notice he was a white man.

Miz Chaundolyne's pap turned loose with both barrels on thet young Snooz boy, an by God, even with his overalls round his shoes he cut through the daym melon patch like a turpentined dawg.

I'd really admire to see that show up to Weaselville where some ole boy washes down a raw chicken with a jug o' bull piss.

. . . sun just a-shinin like a di'mon in a billygoat's ass . . .

Fella with Illinois license plates a-settin in Vetch Crump's diner? P'ints to his grits, says to ole Vetch, "I didn't order no mashed taters."

Some NACP commonist niggers tell the court they seen Mizzoo Trace a-puttin on his Klan robes an by daym, quick as grease through a goose, Mizzoo say, "I was fixin to personate the Easter bunny, Jedge." Courthouse like to come down with the hootin an hollerin.

. . . forty-pound bullhead come outen the river where Mack Buncombe was a-fishin an took hissef a mouthful o' ole Mack's Red Man, then jest slud back in the water calm as you please . . .

Roy Puckle, one o' the jedges at the fair down to Fevertown? Say he'd as lief eat a rat's ass as have to sample Jella Galoot's skunk an sweet tater pie agin.

Colonel Humphreys put on his uny-form on Decoration Day an it was so green with age a yella dawg pissed on him—thought he was a walkin hedge.

Them boys down to Clarke's Sump so daym ignorant they played basketball with a cabbage an got on a wonder why it didn't bounce.

Cuv Forrest's house done blowed down in a storm an Leake Wills say he'll wager a bushel o' corn to spit thet's the fust time it ever got aired out.

Miz Kemper stood out in the corn field in her ole dress all rags an tatters a-wavin her arms an Lamar Nucks say thet a brace o' big crows grabbed holt on her an like to carry her almost to Bolivar's Swamp. Lamar swears them ole crows was a-laughin fit to bust.

... white man couldn't drink it, but I be dawg if Fonzo Clay didn't make whiskey outen turnip greens...

Miz Yazoo a-settin on her porch all day chunkin corncobs at a big ole tomcat an singing hymns...

Alphabet Calhoun done fell inter the bayou an the daym gators done swum fer their lives.

Fat Luster say his nigger hands done et fire ants las spring to keep warm.

Them Quitman boys is such white trash thet the fust time they seed a toilet—over to Leflore Pines—they done washed their feet in it.

They told Verge Rankin to go on home when he said at night school thet they git nylon from lectric caterpillars.

Budge Lowndes? Ain't he the ole boy say thet if God made the boll weevil then Satan made cotton?

Saw in the *Reader's Digest* at the barber shop thet dragon flies don't eat nothin an just fuck all day... sounds like Sharkey Quantrell when he goes up to them Memphis cathouses.

... so Miz Pike, when Warren come home drunk agin, puts on a sheet, comes out from the trees, an hollers, "I am the devil!" An ole Warren say, "Howdy! I done married yore sister."

When thet young Wilkinson gal puts on thet thin little dress the color o' ripe tomaters, whoo! Make a preacher lay his Bible down!

I ain't sayin' Aspen Tate is ignorant, but he took up books in the third grade till he was twenty-three.

The Persimmon Cafe, thet honky-tonk down to Perry Junction? They got a high-yella gal waitress in there looks better than Miss America's ass.

Miz Claiborne give Lute his supper o' crabgrass an dead brambles an he so daym mean he et it an said, "I swaney, Gemma, yore victuals are improvin."

... say they found a bluebelly soljer's corpse sound as a dollar, belly full o' grits an grease, when they done cleaned Miz Raedell Jasper's septic tank...

Damfool sissy lights from his air-cooled Caddy-lac in a pair o' pink short britches, tears up an armload o' poison oak, an say to Omar Lutch standin there bugeyed, "Kin ah make juleps with this here?"

Broom Scott, Miz Scott's eldest, over to Flyblow? Said in New Yawk they give him a baked tater all over cream done turned bad in the kitchen. When he tole the waiter he looked at him like he was funnin.

Cheater Holmes busted his still after he woke up one day an saw his false teeth a-settin at the table eatin peanuts...

... ole boys blowed up Diddy Carroll's privy with cherry bombs an it like to rained shit over two counties. Montgomery Siff still thinks it was an act o' God cause they done let the niggers set down at the five-an-dime fountain.

. . . an when they give Webster Liveoak thet itty-bitty knife an fork on the airyplane, he say, "I ain't got no chillun with me, ma'm."

. . . thass a biscuit-eatin, pea-stealin, gumbo dawg.

Come up on Jelly Hancock mounted on a shoat an he say he's takin its temp'rature.

Hear tell that Linc Marshall married his cousin, Gardenia Mae, an had a boy twa'nt able to do no more than grin like a possum eatin shit.

. . . fool in a silk shirt leans outen his little eyetalian car an asks Booger Wayne, the sheriff over to Collardville, iffen he kin tell him how to get to Florida, an ole Booger arrests him for askin questions of a Sunday.

Miz Prentiss went on one o' them fancy brown-rice diets an by God one day slud right down the privy hole . . .

. . . an the preacher lays hands on Cash Hinds an shouts, "Lawd! Take this toomer, Lawd! Take this hyar poison lump away!" An all the time he's a-feelin ole Cash's sack o' Bull Durham.

Give that idjit boy a Sears an Roebuck cattylog open to the longeree ads an he's happy as a pig in shit.

They done found Margarina Jackson an Reverend Poole's missus, Gloretta, in the corn crib sound asleep with their drawers down round their knees.

Widder Mulch took that daym billygoat inter the house an I be a mule if he didn't eat the TV.

Got so dry over to Banshee County las summer the daym gators attacked a Co-Coly truck.

Husk Benton is so daym peculiar 'bout that prize sow o' his he wants to put her in the kissin booth at the county fair this fall.

« 45 »

A Transition,
from A to Z

AS Blue and Helene staggered through the thick layers of dixie exotica, up to their knees in the aromatic, yet prickly clumps of *lorena houlka*, the noonday sun pressing through the feathery *bogue chitto* trees, Blue said

BABE, I think we are in one of them dead spots called, for want of a better nomenclature, a transition, like, we gotta get through it to get on to the next really vital and interesting part of our continuing saga; apropos from this, a odd-looking duck is peeping at us from behind that yonder *toccopola* tree. And so it wert, and thus discovered, a guy who introduced himself as

CHEECHEE Docque sauntered out from behint said tree and all in clearest view, amid the lice-infested stands of *acona* and *sarepta* weeds, doffed his hat, and smiling said

DON'T be alarmed! I am known to men of brawny will and heavy heart as Cheechee Docque, as you know already from the paragraph above; I have been sent down here to the land of violet *eudora* by a dude name o' Doctor Piscardi, a sort of colleague of Doc Chick, who wants to keep a eye on you vis-à-vis your mouth and all its attendant something or others.

EH? the two Gavottes chimed as swallows do in the limbs of sweetest *sylvarena*. Doc Chick is still aware, still cares about my

FATE? Blue grinned through trembling lips, a hot tear or two splashing in the dead *tunica* thorns that lay at, as well as upon, his feet.

GODDAMNED right! Cheechee opined. And as sure as wild *tuscola* fills the April air with loathsome seeds and stuff, your present fate, in this transition, is mine to mold and shape so that we don't get bogged down in a lotta talk and

HEMMING and hawing, can you dig that? Blue and H not only could, but did, dig it, and settled down with the hearty Cheech beneath an itty-bitty *itta bena* stand, there to chat and listen to the emissary's

IDEAS. First of all, the man plucked an armful of wild *bovina* plums plus a brace apiece of juicy *bobos*. Nothing like a surge of purest sugar! When they had et their fill and were lighting up their pipes around the old campfire, the lake a sheet of molten gold, the crickets thrashing in the nearby *wenesoga* fronds, Docque glanced from one to the other

JERK'S face, and sighed into his mess kit, or tin. I'd like, he began, nothing better than to set here toasting weenies and watching marshmellers burn up into blackish gloop, while the bass-mouthed sunnies and the pike-wallers frolic beneath yon *coila* lilies! But I have a job to do, you

KLUCKS, and I use that word with all due respect. First of all, was ever praying mantis, locked in the deathgrip of the dreaded *buckatunna* vetch, more desperate than youse, who have arranged this transparent alphabet structure for to alleviate the boredom of an obligatory transition? Huh?

LOOK, Blue started, this is not our idea! Right, Helene, my *lula* blossom?

MINCING prettily about the fire, blazing high now with the armload of *shubuta* fronds she'd flung upon hit, Miz G agreed:

NAW, she tittered gaily, her eyes snapping like *sabougla* vines caught in an early frost, or perhaps a late frost, or a vicious hailstorm, such as is known in Ole Miss to come when they, the folks therein that is, least expect it.

O.K., Cheech said, relaxing visibly into the sleeping bag he'd stuffed with *derma* leaves. That out the way, I got to inform you that this Southern talk that just a little while hence, or is it thence? No matter. That just a while ago, enchanted youse, is not what we like to call "representative" of the Deep South, but of a very very small minority, a red-necked few, a trashy clutch of churls, a bunch of

PECKERWOODS! In short, before you get on with your journey, I have the pleasant duty to straighten out your heads a mite concerning this vast, somnolent, yet rich-in-human-nature area, this South! This Dixieland! This oith of *lena*, *tyro*, and *wanilla* bresh, not to mention the majestic *tippo* tree, from which dangle strands of pure *pinola* nuts! Do you

QUITE get me? Thus Docque spake and turned his socks upon the glowing spit. There was the heavy soughing of the wind in the blue-shadowed *pheba* copse that limped down to the lake; the moon had turned to purest silver the *pelahatchie* leaves. Then Blue rejoined, in a soft

ROAR, We get you Cheech. What is it you must do to set us straight anent the deepest truth concerning this mysterious land? If the things we hoid do not represent—no more than the arctic *ofahoma* represents—the Real

SOUTH, what do? Cheechee Docque's heart leaped high as do the *kolola* spores spring when the brown bear tromps crazily through the silent glens upon the misty mountains. He knew, as though seeing it writ in jools upon a barn door,

THAT they were ready! That they would welcome, indeed, *did* welcome a, what you call, "balanced" presentation of this place that men have called, for many years, "the South." Now they would soon know that "the South" is more, much, much more than the rainbow-hued *chicora* daisy, nice as that is. He sat

UP. Down the road, my charges twain, past the wheezing stands of pied *pachuta* and the multifarious types and kinds of rarest *scooba* shrubs, lies Jean Toomer Tech, and though some ungrateful darkish brethren call it Jean's Tomb, 'tis the Southland's most prestigious hall of learning for the underprivileged, for which word read "colored folks." It is there that you'll discover a powerful and

VERY different South from the stuff you just heard about what you think is the McCoy, as different as is the *looxuhumu* blossom from the *bolatucha*!

WHERE is this? said Blue excitedly, filling his old corncob with a kind of fervid, almost passionate intensity. Down the road? Can we start now, or is it best, as I have read, to stay kind of put when the sun goes down in these hyar parts, lest the *rena lara* or the *nitta yuma* types of ivy louse you up with running sores?

XYLOPHONES can trill no sweeter than did Cheechee's laughter, as he saw that Blue, by this remark, was the soul of mature and manly probity. By gum, Gavotte, he chuckled, the firelight making his face as red as the leaves of the *osyka* oak on Labor Day, or sometimes earlier, depending on the rainfall during August, we'll sleep now, or, as you suggest, "stay put." And when the dawn climbs up above the yonder hillocks, I'll point you on your way. The place to go at ole JT Tech is the Auditorium, and there you'll have a scale or so lifted off from your eyes. Oke?

YOWZAH, Blue grinned. I'm gonna curl up here with the old lady on these fluffy *eastabuchie* leaves and less all now cop some

Z'S. And in less time than it takes for a *cascilla* stem inadvertently popped in the mouth to stop the heart with its deadly sap, they were asleep!

« 46 »

Big Black's
Lecture: Elegy on
the Theft of Black Flowers

Some jive-ass mutha-fucka sambo bump into me the other day cold in his tweed
vine like some dark-skin guinea on a humble, passin for pale, dig? his ugly garlic
face grinnin like some goddam grey ceLEBrity cause he bees talkin to the fuckin
Law, you dig, Jim? Thass zackly how this sad dinge look. He say, "Bro, what is
your story, my man? Why don't you lay back an cool it bout this nigger flower
shit fore you get the man mad? He gonna wear your black ass out you don't
lighten up." Shee-it! Mutha-fucka's lip was all poked out so he look like some
jive blue-hair jew lady can't breave with her hunner-dollar corset squeezin her
chicken-fat guts.

I say, "Look, nigger, lemme pull your coat. Don't be layin shit on me bout bein
cool with the fuckin honkies. Thass tom talk. Mutha-fuckas bees coppin our posies an heavy blossoms an shit for a thousan years, like they copped our music,
you dig? An don't be runnin no shit past me bout how they got they *own* flowers,
cause the white man ain't got shit that his own." This pee-da-bed jive mutha-
fucka give me a shitface grin like some mockie hab-dasher layin some shit
threads on a ignorant blood, you dig, two-fitty suit "mark down" the jew say,
yeh, to eighteen dollahs. No wonder the mutha-fucka call his crosseye daughter
Laurel April or Michelle Claudia or some such shit an park his El Dorado up in
Westchester or some other jive place while them dumb niggers payin his mort-
gage bees draggin round all day listnin to fat-ass ole white womans run they
mouths at the welfare. "You can't get this thirty-eight cent this week, Tyrone,
cause you mop a floor las week for a dollar an a pint a Gypsy Rose." You dig? So
my man, this trick woogie, he gone, Jim! Ain't nothin but a shufflin house nigger
anyways got his tongue up the man's ass a mutha-fuckin mile lookin out for
some ghett-to bread from the crackers down in D.C. who bees talkin dumb shit
bout negro aspirations out they mouths while they bees whippin willie's head
keep they jive-ass suburbs safe for Laurence mutha-fuckin Welk. One-a these

216

days the bloods gon' fuck up they shitty little lawns bad, bro, an waste all they files a *Time* an *Playboy* an all they books by they lib'ral honkies tell the brothers how to live. Shee-it! You remember what Malcolm an Stokeley an Rap an Huey say bout the ofays' faggot-ass books an shit, right? They say be tight an bad, don't look sad, don't git mad, whip haid! Them mutha-fuckin books an shit bees the runnin dawgs a the jew-guinea-square-ass mutha-fuckin zionist conspiracy, Jim, an if the bloods don't get down behin' some heavy nationalist shit they gonna spen they whole lives drinkin the man's sweet wine an pokin that mafia smack into they arms jus like the silk-vine mutha-fuckas want them to—dig? Blanks wanna keep the bloods dumb an stoned so they bees dreamin a bad shorts an hip vines an layin up somewheres with some yella hair pussy. Man may be a mutha-fuckin faggot like to get poked in his ass but he know how to suck out willie's heart, Jim, believe it.

This shit bees goin down everywhere! Kike faggot white man ain't never had nothin he made hissef—every mutha-fuckin thing he got he cop from the bloods. Them mutha-fuckin Greek assfuckers steal they philosophy from the brothers in Africa, Jim! The Phonishuns an Trojans an them dudes. Steal they mathematics an geometry an all that science shit from Arab bloods. Steal they mutha-fuckin art, man, from hip spades live in caves. Shit! They even steal they dramma from the mutha-fuckin goats! No jive! An they music? Man, them dudes like Mozart an Beethoven an Wagner, you dig, an them hooknose jew mu-tha-fuckas, Stravinsky an Kossakov, oh, man! All that tired shit, they need a mu-tha-fuckin army to get it on. An they snatch that shit from the cool dudes in Af-rica, man, that shit carried over by the slaves an the cracker, he say, "My goo'ness gracious! How marr-vell-ous our nigras soun!" An the next thing, bro, they snatch the bloods' rhythm an harmonics an his whole fuckin scale! You dig how Martha an the Vandella soun, right, brothers? An the Marvelettes an my man, James Brown, the Supremes fore Diana Ross got her mind all twist up with kike bread, ole Fats Domino, Sam Cook, Marvin Gaye, that hip ole dude, Louis Jor-dan? Well, shit, man, them bloods turn jive-ass Mozart an Kossakov *around*. They bees playin all this jive trash on flutes an hopsycords an mutha-fuckin axes nobody know the mutha-fuckin name of, Jim. An then you hip to this jew, Gershwin, dig? He write this trick sambo faggot opera, suppose to show you happy spooks singin an dancin. Shee-it! I see that mutha-fucka two years ago on the TV I thought I watchin science-fiction! Onct they bees puttin ole Sammy Davis in they bullshit play, man! You dig? This trick shuffler bees creepin after white pussy all his life, bees up tight with a buncha greaseball Lass Vegas faggots, bees puttin a shuck on people to buy sweet jew wine. Am I right, brothers? Right an bright! Ole one-eye Sammy spose to be a mutha-fuckin exAMPle, dig on it.

Man, you plant that mutha-fuckin nigger up on Lenox an twenny-eight the dudes bees fuckin him right thoo his designer pants, Jim.

An now the jive turkey blanks bees stealin our *flowers*. Snatch up the bloods' seeds an shrubs an all that kinda shit an some foureye mutha-fuckin scientist in his white coat in they cracker university, he call our heavy African plants—dig this—he call them flow-ra. You hip? Flow-ra! I like to flow-ra that jew faggot mutha-fuckin dentist upside his head! He bees talkin jive shit bout how this flow-ra for all mankind, shit like that, you know the kinda shit them shylock lib'ral mutha-fuckas talk. All mankind my black ass! Zionist Israeli faggot gen'rals snatch they piece off the top, then the dark-face dagos whose great-great-great granmommas got some African jelly-roll an that how come these wops be so dark, they stop they oil an garlic scoff for a minute an they spaghetti an shit they so hincty bout, shee-it. Act like they invent that shit steada the ole dudes live in China, man, black dudes, dig? You think them bad spooks who bees with Genghis Khan *white*, man? An they garlic an oil, bro, that shit ripped off ten thousand years ago from the cats built the Pyramids. Shee-it! These guineas with they mafia judges an commissioners an shit an they jews they shylock with, they cop some bread, too. Then the Irish drunk-ass mutha-fuckas send they red-face pigs round for they piece, then the resta the devils, them mutha-fuckas all the same anyways.

An las, oh yeh, las come the mutha-fuckin toms an all them sambos an trick *negros*, you dig, Jim? Buncha shines wear they Afro wigs on the weekend, man, you dig? They get the smell lef in the pot! An they shuffle they feets an kiss up over the man's ass, oh thank you, sir, thank you, sir, would you care to see me do a mutha-fuckin tap dance? Shee-it! They like to bust out in some white man gospel songs thankin Jesus for the man's kindness like the mutha-fuckin beast sing in Georgia after he pay some ole nigger five cent to shine they shoes. They snatches our flowers an seeds an turn em into some faggot-ass hybrids, is they name. An these trick sambos get a deuce or a trey an say, thank *you*, Mr. Man! I will surely go home now an pick up on Andy Williams, yassuh! I'm tellin you, Jim, these mutha-fuckas ain't wrapped too tight! The blank lays bullshit on em an they lays all *in* it. They Afro wigs they put over they conks on weekends must keep the air from they *minds*, brothers.

You know who I bees talkin about. These mutha-fuckas all week long they bees talkin jive shit like, "Why, certainly, sir, I will be delighted to assist the committee in this new project." You dig? Bees talkin thu they black noses an eatin all that fairy shit French blanks make—scoff ripped off from Arab bloods when they *wan't* no France, Jim. An then on the weekends these Amos an Andy turkeys put on they Afro wigs an they hip vine an they bad shoes, oh they straight, brother. They bees standin on a corner uptown, man, layin jive shit on the brothers bout how they bees raised right around the corner an how they was the baddest mutha-fuckas, mean as a hungry dog, an goin down on porduhrickans an wops an how they all miss fatback an greens, how they wanna wrap they chops roun some hoppin john an cornbread an drink some spodee-odee an shoot some mutha-fuckin nine-ball. God-daym! Mutha-fuckas stick out they ches'es an get blacker by the fuckin minute, make the homeboys look like a buncha dumb hippies! Well, fuck that shit! Ain't the time or place to lay hard shit on these niggers in they trick hip bag. I got heavy business to take care of here.

I bees talkin bout these slick jews snatchin the brothers' Black flowers an shit, Jim—the flow-ra, like them faggots call em. But you dig? The onliest flow-ra the greys know fuck-all about is bush, Jim, an the square-ass jive mutha-fuckas in they plastic shoes an they blue jeans an that long ugly shit call they hair even ripped that off the bloods! You think any white-eye fuckin pale got the brains to grow they own bush? Shee-it! They exproPRIated that heavy boo off the bad spooks in Algiers an Tangier an shit—only fuckin shit zionist-jew-faggots are hip to bees some damn lilacs an daffow-dills an jive plants like that, tomatuhs, dig, put all over that mutha-fuckin garlic trash them fat-ass bitches bees cookin all day long in they lectric kitchens in the suburbs in they pink lipstick an trick fingernails. But you dig these ugly-ass devils layin out cool smokin that heavy bush, Jim, an talkin shit like, "Oh man, thass heavy gold! Hey, baby, this fuckin red is boss shit!" Burn some ole funky oil rags an stick it up they nose an them faggots think they in heaven! Man, they bees corrupTED smellin they own self all they life, don't know righteous bush from turnip greens. An you dig, brothers, God don't like ugly, man.

Black flowers! Thass what I bees talkin bout. I bees talkin bout pure, brothers, like livonia icepick and saratoga lot-leafs, an the convent shrub an pinkeye st. nicholas. I mean like lenox lazuli an ellingtonia columbiana that the brothers call the satin doll. Shee-it! Can't even remember em all—honeydripper an k.c. mcshann an king bedford oliveri, brown st. james, supreme rossi, the mountain morris. Boss shit, Jim! Ayler bluebells an green dolphys, adidas jamaicas an fox skulls—big red littles! that bees the official flower a the Black Nation.

Brothers, yall dig what the honkies run past us, right? Them jew mutha-fuckas an they guinea lawyers an they Irish polis be stealin the niggers' flowers an fuckin em up in they white labratories, turnin them bad greens to they sugar-tit bookays sell to jive-ass white boys to give they bitches. All the *black* be whipped out the bloods' flowers, man. These jive marykones—thass porduhrickan language for faggot—suck out all the blood from our plants an quick as shit make em flow-ra. Willie's boss plants come out same as a mutha-fuckin

219

shufflin coon got his black balls cut off an his black ass shakin for the cracker pay him some little bitty coin at the welfare or let him have some ole funky vine not even a dumb-ass guinea off the boat wrap his greasy back in. An this ignorant nigger lay back cool, you dig? He bees suckin his jug a king kong and sayin "Thank you, boss, you sho bees a good white man jes like the Bible say you should. Praise the lawd!" Shee-it! Mutha-fucka be cool he put his foot in this cracker's *ass*! Make you cry see this dumb dinge grin like he *straight* cause he ain't got no job. Brothers, suckin the man's ass at the welfare bees a *job* you gets paid slave bread for!

Dig on it, you bloods, this bees an ole con to the pales. I bees in the liberry las week on a humble, dig, like some jive-ass weekend spade, runnin a number like I want to study up some white man's shit to *improve* myself, dig? This big-ass liberrian with her jugs fallin out her dress helpin me, dig? If she knowed I there to dodge the ole hawk snatchin my cheap jew-store coat offen me she a called some sambo pig to pop me for *creating*, dig? Or *loitering*. But she bees a ignorant white bitch think I want to get hip to blank bullshit so's I can bees a mutha-fuckin mailman, or mop up shit in a hospital. Well, bro, I read in this jive book a faggot poetry by some dude got a name like that turkey mutha-fucka, Captain Marvel, no shit. Anyways, I see some heavy shit. This cracker's pomes ain't shit, bees all about gardens an dumb-ass English dudes mowin the mutha-fuckin lawn, didn't have no woogies round to do it for them in they time, dig? But I read that when this long-hair blank write this shit, the greys were really behine too-lips, man, yeh, thass right, mutha-fuckin toolips! Bees payin heavy bread for some ole funky bulb, I mean, baby, you dig, *heavy* bread. Thousands! Jive book say them English dudes *buy* all this shit, dig? But you believe they *paid* the rag-gedy mutha-fuckas *growed* the toolips, well, blood, you ain't wrapped too tight atall. One-a these jive flowers, man, bees called the Marvel of Peru an the mutha-fucka bees growed in the West Indies. Now I a jew schoolteacher if it didn't be-long to some ignorant niggers lay it on these English honkies for some mutha-fuckin two-bit glass necklaces run up in some kike factry, you dig? I don't have to lay heavy shit on you, do I, make you pick up quick an slick on what I'm runnin down? Dig! Ofays in they trick bag way the fuck back in sixteen hundred some-thin, my man.

All this history an shit I bees talkin is to get you hip, brothers. I doan give a mutha-fuckin dime the man come roun like some jive scientist from a ofay flick bout some faggot vampire shit or some mutha-fuckin honkie monster bees creepin aroun like he got a stick up his jive ass, or the man come by in his pig suit all red in his face askin you why you bees sittin on your own mutha-fuckin *stoop*, Jim, or he slide up all nasty an funky in his bad vine talkin bout brothers an sisters an all that tired ole jew-lib'ral shit like some kinda nigger-machine. They *all* devils, blood, an they there to cop your righteous African flowers an your Black shrubs, man, an fuck em all aroun into flow-ra, sell em back to poor ignorant willies outen they kike flower stores, dig? Call the bloods' flowers jive faggot shit like phloxes an zinnas an holly mutha-fuckin hocks. Shee-it!

What I bees runnin past you? Blanks gon' take every mutha-fuckin thing you own, bro, you don't hold it tight an right! Take ole Erskine Hawkins' "Tuxedo Junction" an make it into some jive mutha-fuckin faggot song, snatch Bird's mean blues, "Now's the Time" an it pop up this goddam ugly "Hucklebuck," steal Lady Day's heavy sounds, bro, an Prez get fucked over you think some white mutha-fucka invent the ax ole Lester learn him how to blow. Shee it! Bad enough the honkies ain't got no music but they trick jew tunes—them ignorant pigs can't even play the shit they steal! They bees goin, you dig, toot-toot an shit like that, they bees goin oobie-doobie-shoobie so mutha-fuckin ugly make you thow up on your shoes, man. Dig! Pales snatch every fuckin thing ain't nailed down, bro. Bees snatchin the brothers' music and clo's, they talk an instruments an dances an even mutha-fuckin hair style. Now they bees rippin off the Black flowers an shit, next they bees coppin the bloods' veg'tables. Okra an blackeyed peas and collards an they be thowin them in with they mutha-fuckin garlic an frogs' asses an snails an funky ole cheese an shit like that an callin it quee-zeen, dig? So, brothers, be mean an lean, stay clean. Don't give the mutha-fuckin man flower one, dig? Wear his ass *out*. Mutha-fuckas on they las trip anyways. Black flower!

≪ 47 ≫

Dazed,
Our Friends
Reach Nawlins, Looziana

Louisiana, Louisiana,
Entre nous, entre nous.
Louisiana, Louisiana,
Je m'en fous, je m'en fous.
Louisiana, Louisiana,
Voulez-vous joujou?
Louisiana, Louisiana,
Ici Bleu!

Old Song

It is far from the raw power of my pen to detail the stroll that now ensued and on which the Gavottes found themself. In a hypnotic dump from the raw power of Mr. Black's speech or lecture to an admiring throng of pedants and folk crowding in from the rays of the hot sun and its fabled raw power, they pressed on toward the city long fabled as the raw and powerful "cradle of jazz" or "jazz" or "jas." Indeed, Nawlins! Brooding in its powerful rawness!

What a look crossed Helene's face as she occasionally rolled in the verdant fields of Spanish moss! And Blue was not far behind. There was what a look on his rugged phiz as well.

Adventures? Ha ha ha! You shouldn't make me laugh already! Their adventures were incredible, like those of Hercules when he ate Gorgeous Medusa, of Theseus atop the wooden horse on the plains of windy Troy, of the lisping Achilles knitting up afghans and doilies for Lady Omphale while dressed in a smart little black dress that could go right from office to dinner to a night on the town; and what those two did when they got home late and a little tight on the unmixed wine is not recorded even in the pages of Suetonius, and he recorded everything, as you know. Or maybe you don't know.

But it is not my intention to waste the reader's valuable time, since I know, better than most, that it's best to be up and doing, and off and out, and laughing hysterically into the teeth of adversity on the ski slopes, the dazzling beaches, under the hood of the old Chevy, into a plate of potato salad and hot dogs, the things that have made us, as a nation of persons equal under law, great. So I'll be quickly brief. Or let me say—how shall I say?—let me brief you quickly.

I have adumbrated the conception of adventures: like the howling sail they made across Lake Ponchartrain, and down its silent tributaries to the great brown sea of the Mizzipi! But you have heard this before, you are well aware of these boon adventures, whatever that means, you can go and read *Martin Chuzzlewit's Voyage*, as if you haven't! Remember the sail therein that Martin takes with his fag, Mark, on the lusty barkentine down the Ohio? The Gavottes' adventures were in no wise, or ways, at all like those of Martin and Mark, nor did they have a captain like the gruff Gumbo Pease to sail under, but they *might well have been*!

One morning, waking with the first tantalizing odors of simmering red beans and coffee with chicory and also with the laughter of the praline vendors plunging their wares—alive!—into great cheery vats of boiling water, Serge knew that he had been rocked to sleep the night before in the "cradle of jass."

Now to have a quick nosh of jambalaya à la king and then to set out in search of Frenchie L'Amour and Bunky Jimson. That's who it says to find here anyway, on this scrap of paper given me by a nameless stranger who passed us one night in his ship during one of our many adventures, as you will recall, sweet Helene.

I'm afraid that the stars had so entranced me that I've forgotten . . . everything but the good parts of our harrowing experiences while, as the French say, *en route*.

Thus wert ever it, Blue laughed consolingly as he shudderingly "took" her from the rear with sudden passion beneath the dewy bougainvillea shrubs that lent to the still morning air of the mysterious city a strange, what shall I say? mystery.

Nawlins has imbued a strange tropical verve to your shtupping, Helene blushed, clearing off the hand-carved rustic table that insolently crouched beneath the barely moving ceiling fan. I . . . like it, she screeched, chucking, with a robust clatter, the breakfast "things" into the quaint zinc sink.

Without further ado, Blue found himself before the door of a small club, his scrap of paper held tightly in his fist against the gales of the legendary sirocco!

It blew as if the dogs of hell had bayed, or—*were* baying!

It blew with a ferocity unequaled in his long experience of ferocious breezes.

As it ceased, a door appeared in the wall of the club.

A face peered out.

It . . . smiled, or did what Blue took to be a smile.

You 'ave come for ze Phrase? the face rejoined, while behind it another voice chuffed along.

They was Frenchie and Bunky.

That eez, if you please, Frenchy and Bunkie, the laughing frog maintained obstinately. And you 'ave come to a place where is possible maybe to fin' a *morceau* of azziztonce, no?

Come awn in, yew white mo'fo, the deeper voice boomed warily.

And so Serge did.

Meanwhile, Helene busied herself about their cheap room in the "Quarter" by taking in some washing and deftly sewing a small dresser in which her hubby could keep his bicycle clips.

I will wager a farthing to a ha'penny that you've forgotten about Blue's bicycle clips, though they may yet figger large in our story. Or not.

But let us listen to the conversation now taking place in the dim club in which we may stand as observers unseen by the three men who interest us. Or maybe interest us. Frenchy is spikking.

« 48 »
To Expand
upon the Subject

I reckon, mon ami, that you won't go too far wrong iffen yall listen to stuff and hot licks in which the hunk o' tune yall are lookin fer probly hides, n'est-ce pas? Le jazz hot like Clarinet Marmalade, Dippermouth Blues, Mahogany Hall Stomp, Muskrat Ramble, St. Louis Blues, Rockin' Chair, Tiger Rag, Black and Blue, Struttin' With Some Barbecue, Save It Pretty Mama, Chinatown My Chinatown . . .

Or, a deep voice clanged, dig, grey boy, mellow sounds known by the names ob Swing That Music, High Society, Heebie Jeebies, Baby Won't You Please Come Home, Back o' Town Blues, Storyville Blues, Panama, Royal Garden Blues, The Sheik of Araby, Nagasaki, Winin' Boy Blues . . .

I'm tuned in to your arcane jive, gents, Blue suddenly intruded, as intrusion was one of his few flaws. Also I Ain't Got Nobody, King Porter Stomp, Bucket Got a Hole in Its, Eh, Là Bas, Farewell to Storyville, Creole Bo Bo, Bill Bailey Won't You Please Come Home, Savoy Blues, Creole Song, Yaaka Hula Hickey Dula, Limehouse Blues?

Mais oui! An by such artistes extraordinaires comme St. Clair de Lune and his Jambalaya Jambos, Pops Ennui and the Crawdaddies, the Compote-Marmalade Band featuring Licks Mambeau, Jimbo Verlaine's Rainmakers, Mickey Butor and the Time Passers, Fats Gide with the Baton Rouge Boys, Valéry Conga, Zoot Roussel and the African Alligators, Booker Césaire, Cheech Mauriac with the Femmes Fatales, and Luigi Celino and the Noodle Band.

An' lemme pull your coat on Johnny Giono and the Blue Boys, Cocky Jack and the Astonishers, Sad Sam Zara with the Realists, The Inquisitors starring Bobi Pinget, Peanuts Prévert, "Mellow" Rooney Char and his Hypnotic Horn, Jenny Voleur, Big Julie Laforge, Ray Queneau and the Dogtooth Serenaders, Rambo Charlie and the Hell Raisers, an' "Bo" Delay with the Dawn-Light Stompers.

Hey! And I've loaned an ear myself via record to Izzy Ducasse, Red Renard and the Fourteen Carats, Al Robby Grillay with the Good Lookers, "Jaws" Hysman and the Git-Down Band, Clo Simon and the Grasscutters, Tony Arto with the Visionaries, Pat Jarry, Nathan Sarraute and his Golden Fruit Geechee Band, Go-Go "Blue" Bataille, Camoo with the African Stompers, and also Murph Malone and the Kilowatts!

Maintenant, is also musique of the Marmalade du Clarinet, Blue Dippermouth, Stomp Hall Mahogany!, Ramblin' Muskrat, Blues for St. Louis, Chair is Rockin', Ragged Tiger, Blue and Black, Some Barbecue Be Struttin', Mama Pretty, Save It!, Chinatown, Chinatown, My My! . . .

An', fay, dig on Music that Swings, Society's High, Jeebie Heebies, Please Come Home Won't You Baby?, Blue's Back o' Town, Blues in Storyville, Amanap, Blew in the Royal Garden, The Arab Sheik, Saki-Naga, Blue Boy Winin'. . .

Damn if *I* dint grow up on Ain't Got Nobody's Eye, Stomporter King, Got a Hole in Its Bucket, La Bàs, Eh?, Storyville, Farewell!, Bobo Creole, Won't You Bill to Please Bailey?, Blue Savoy, Song of the Creole, Hickeydula-Yaakahula, Blues for Lime House.

Et les musiciens who jouent the pieces! Jambo Jambalaya and the Clair de Lune Orchestra, "Crawdaddy" P. Ennui, Licks Compote and the Marmalade-Mambeau Band, The Rainmaker Six featuring "Valayne," Mickey Passertime and the Butter Band, Baton Rouge Fats and the Guide Boys, Congo Valerie, Al Afrique-Larousse Zut Trio, Césaire Bukka, the Fatal Femmes featuring Maury Cheech, et "Noodles" with the Celino-Luigi Band.

You done remin' me of de "Blue" Boy-Giono Jonny Band, the Astonishers with Special Guest Jacques Cocky, Sam Realist and the Sadzaras, the Inquisitors starring Bobbi Pangez, Trever P. Nuts, Hypnos Charhorn and the Mellowrooneys, V. Jenny, La Jules and the Big Forge Three, "Dogtooth" with Q. Ray's Serenade Seven, the Rayzelles with Charlie Rambo, an' the Dawnlight Stompin' Band with Delaybeau.

The renditions that have cloved to my memory are by the Ducassize Experience, Renard Red and the Four Teens, Goodlookin' Grillet featuring Robally's Golden Sax, the Git-Down Jaw Band and Hy Smann, Simon "Cutgrass" Clo, Art Tony and the Artovisions, Gerry Patt, Nate Geechee and his Golden Fruits, Bats Blue with the Go-Gos, the Africa Stomp Band featuring "Camu," and Kilowatt Malone and the Murphs.

Agreed! that they were hommes et femmes, dudes and foxes, gents and ladies, e'en though thcy hadda play in joints like Lafitte's Rump Dump, the Hot Red Bean Room, Jackson's Alley, Twisty King Oliver's, Fazola's Rest Room, the

DuBois Wood Womb, Hall of Berbin, the Red Light, Pelican Lounge, Cool D. Sack's, and the Chicory House.

Mon Dieu! Such large of l'esprit! In such smoky boites to hear the art like unto the Mama Laid Her Clarinet, Dip Ma Blue Mouf, Stompin' Ma Hawg in the Hall, My Muskrat, He Rumble, Blue Looie, Charokin, Tiger Rug in Rags, My Black Be Blue, Stutterin' Barbecue, Shove It Pretty, Mama! Shine it Down, Dingbat Music, Flyin' in Society, D.B.B.V.D.'s, Won't You Come Please, Baby?, De Blues Is Back on Down, Blue Story Blues, Pajama Shout, Royal Blue Garter, The Arab Bought a Sheik, A Nog o' Saki an' a Beer, Blue Wine Blues, Got no Body, Got no Head, Stomp-King Porter's Rag, Fuckit, Got a Hole in It!, Ayla Bas, Ayla Bu, Ayalors, Whoreville, Farewell, Bo-Bo Creole's Orco, D. D. Dailey's Flyin' Home, Savoy, Ça-Va, Sauvage?, The Old Cree (Ugh Ugh Ugh), Hula Dula's Hickey, et The House of Blue Limes.

And then 'twas settled that though these works were known and loved the whole globe o'er, they were especially adored in Bonnet Carré, Algiers, Chalmette, Marrero, Belle Chasse, Des Allemands, Boutte, Paradis, Lake Borgne, Terrebonne, and Plaquemines.

Lemme lay it on the record, gents, that the dee-finn-itt-iv versions of dem heavy sounds bees played by Jimbo Jumbo and his Loonies, Crawfunk Popshit, the Compote-Suckin' Bonelickers, V. D. Verlayne and the Smiling Syphs, Mickey Butt and the Pastimes, Guy Fatso and his Magic Stick, Congo Val with the Bad Vibes, Red Zoot and the Congolas, Caesar the Fucker, Cheechee and the Feminettes, Louis Noodles and his Electric Cello, The Blueball Band featuring Joanie Groan, Jack and the Astonishing Cocks, Tsad Tzara's Tsurreal Tsix, The Askers with Bobby Paris, The Perverts starring Pee-Pee Peenuts, Little Annie Rooney and the Horns, The Thieves featuring Jeanie the Weenie, Forge and the Family Jules, No-No Dog and the Tooth Fairies, Chuckie Inferno and the Rambelles, Bo Stompo and the Dawn Paroles, The Louse Band with Dizzy Izzy, Carrot Redd and the Four Foxes, Alan Robb and the Sex Thrills, The Jews starring Jaws Labasman, Sy Monclo and the Ass Rutters, The Artomatics featuring "Toutes" Tony, Jerry the Patsy and the Physics, Geechee Golden-Famous Nathan and the Five Fruits, Bo-Bo Blue with the Egg Whites, Angie Comique and the Afriques, an' Murph Watt and the Mugs from Malone.

And to keep up their strength? Intelligence has percolated down anent the victuals most desired by these folk to keep them cooking. The favorites were, hands down, beet gumbo, jambalaya à la okra, redbeans and schloque, rice-a-guini, shrimp mephisto, crawfish and crapmeat, black redfish, gin fizztula, pernod-persi, pralines au feu, and catfish chasseur.

Though numbed by your retailing of these grand old tunes by the grand old greats, Blue modestly opined, what of the new persons, the younger turks, the advanced guard, the, how you say? punkish-newish wave? I think of some heavy sounds as thus mayhap Red Club by Fat Stick, Royal Fuck by Seizer Blue, Heebie's Jeebies by Jaws Jews, Song of the Keyhole by Jon Voyeur, Congola by Kaymoo and the Stompers, In the Royal Garden by Trojan Paris, Panama Rag by the Feminappes, Creole Buboes by the Four Foxes, Zoot Loot by Tony Toutes, Blueballed by the Nutz, Eggwhite Blues by Batts Bataille, Beaucoup Paroles by Artvision, Git Down by "Licks" Coña, Farewell to Story by Bobbi Mahu, Tsorry, Tsar by the Nagasaki Nonet, Society High by Coky Jack, Astonish Me! by the Mellow Hypnotics, Shave It, Pretty Mama by Peanuts Pervert, Lousy Ditch by Ducks-Ass Sttrange, Bar-B-Q Slut by the Teen Fucks, Panama Hot by Big Mama Twot, So Long Shinetown by Blacki Blu, Winding Ploy by Malone Molloy, Savoix Bleues by Claude Flandres, Dogtooth Barks by Dan DeLion, Ray's Blues by the Flowerblowers, Hog Stomp by "Killer" Watt, Royal Pardon Shuffle by Roi Rex Renard, House of Blue Tights by Jean Velour, Clair de Nuttes by Mama Blewe, Eh, la Buck? by Dr. Huler, Makin' Rain by Louie Pluie, and Congageechee by Pajarry Rubu.

Though maybe weird and replete with noisy cacophones, the best of this music is lovely as the best of Nature, gawjus as Spanish moss, live oke, furious magnolia, jazzmin, alligator poppy, pelican pussy, swamp vetch, blue-eye ringtail, blackthorn water sprite, weeping tear, and the blooming elmwillow.

Non! We are not how you say, stuff-fee, Monsieur Bleu, mais . . . the mos' perfect examples of the pride of Nawlins is to be foun' in the discs classique. Right on, frog-bro! Soitin tunes bees played that show the heart o' the good sounds. Shall we enumerate, amee, for this lonesome yankee wanderer? Oui! Ze discography outstanding is this: Limehouse Blues by Murph Malone and the Kilowatts, Yaaka Hula Hickey Dula by Camoo with the African Stompers, Creole Song by Go-Go "Blue" Bataille, Savoy Blues by Nathan Sarraute and his Golden Fruit Geechee Band, Bill Bailey Won't You Please Come Home by Pat Jarry, Creole Bo Bo by Tony Arto with the Visionaries, Farewell to Storyville by Clo Simon and the Grasscutters, Eh, Là Bas by "Jaws" Hysman and the Git-Down Band, Bucket Got a Hole in It by Al Robby Grillay with the Good Lookers, King Porter Stomp by Red Renard and the Fourteen Carats, I Ain't Got Nobody by Izzy Ducasse, Winin' Boy Blues by "Bo" Delay with the Dawn-Light Stompers, Nagasaki by Rambo Charlie and the Hell Raisers, The Sheik of Araby by Ray Quencau and the Dogtooth Serenaders, Royal Garden Blues by Big Julie Laforge, Panama by Jenny Voleur, Storyville Blues by "Mellow" Rooney Char and his Hypnotic Horn, Back o' Town Blues by Peanuts Prévert, Baby Won't You

Please Come Home by The Inquisitors starring Bobi Pinget, Heebie Jeebies by Sad Sam Zara with the Realists, High Society by Cocky Jack and the Astonishers, Swing That Music by Johnny Giono and the Blue Boys, Chinatown My Chinatown by Luigi Celino and the Noodle Band, Save It Pretty Mama by Cheech Mauriac with the Femmes Fatales, Struttin' With Some Barbecue by Booker Césaire, Black and Blue by Zoot Roussel and the African Alligators, Tiger Rag by Valéry Conga, Rockin' Chair by Fats Gide with the Baton Rouge Boys, St. Louis Blues by Mickey Butor and the Time Passers, Muskrat Ramble by Jimbo Verlaine's Rainmakers, Mahogany Hall Stomp by the Compote-Marmalade Band featuring Licks Mambeau, Dippermouth Blues by Pops Ennui and the Crawdaddies, and Clarinet Marmalade by St. Clair de Lune and his Jambalaya Jambos.

« 49 »

Slightly
Crestfallen, They
Leave Nawlins, Slightly Crushed

Do you dig why my large and unassuming face is crestfallen? Serge spoke at last.

There was what seemed a nod of assent from his spouse acrost the haze of fatuous sunbeams.

I have toted up and calc'lated that the Magic Phrase I seek is probly buried in those songs just seriously discussed, but that to ferret—what a cute little word that is—to ferret it from out this mass of music would take a lifetime, even without taking into account the various mathematical combinations and permanations possible, what come to, as I reckon, something like a couple trillion. Thus do mortals ever slide from sundrenched peaks into a lake of liquid shit! Woe.

But stay your gushing eyes, my conifer! the good dame cried. Let us rest while ever wending on, and chunk upon the old pianner here, that gives you always and anon a surcease from your wonted bouts with snots and tears.

And so he did: and there, in poiple shade and to the shy and hidden audience of forest folk, our Blue composed this song, mysterious and haunting, to which the music is forever lost to us and all our as yet unborn descendants.

And yet, despite all, the welkin rang afar! And there was not an alligator in the sludgy bayou who slept that day!

Nor a cottonmouth moccasin.

Nor yet a garter belt waterback.

And to this day, Uncle Rebus tells of the tulip bulbs that leaped wildly from the omnipresent scum! And of those that leapt!

230

«50»

Blue Writes a
Mysterious and Haunting Song

I wandered lonely as a cloud,
O thou! whose fancies from afar are brought;
I was a Traveller then upon the moor,
I heard a thousand blended notes
Under yon orchard, in yon humble cot
With unrejoicing berries—ghostly Shapes
"And groans that rage of racking famine spoke!"

"Art thou a man of purple cheer?"
(The old Man still stood talking at my side);
"If from the public way you turn your steps
You live, Sir, in these dales, a quiet life."
Himself he propped, limbs, body, and pale face,
To gather leeches, being old and poor.
Grave thoughts ruled wide on that sweet day!

"High is our calling, Friend!—Creative Art!
Enough of sorrow, wreck and blight."
And now we reached the orchard-plot,
A gentle answer did the old man make:
"Why bleat so after me? Why pull so at thy chain?
Nay, Traveller! rest. This lonely Yew-tree stands!"
Here Michael ceased, and to the fields went forth.

Lost on the aerial heights of the Crusades,
A cart and horse beside the rivulet stood;
As I from Hawes to Richmond did repair,
Where silent zephyrs sported with the dust!

231

Jones! As from Calais southward you and I
Should to the breast of Nature have gone back;
A happier fortune than to wither here!

Whether the whistling Rustic tend his plough,
A white-robed Negro, like a lady gay
Remained imperishably interwoven
With heavy tufts of moss that strive.
(I was thy neighbor once, thou rugged Pile!)
When up the hills, as now, retreats the light
I'll think of the Leech-gatherer on the lonely moor!

Envoi
A white-robed Negro sported with the dust;
With unrejoicing berries reached the orchard plot
To gather leeches. And to the fields went forth!

≪ 51 ≫
Secrets of Tej-Mej

Then, loping, scudding, complemented by clouds of dust, they moseyed. Belike unto those critters men call dogies, hoided with a ready laugh and macho jest by swart vacqueros, they scuffed. Through live-oak stands adrape with Spanish moss, palmetto shrubs bedizened with the juicy berry Indians make into marmalade, past mesquite and loco weed, multicolored tumbleweed, the mescal and agave, the shrinking bluebell, cacti, nicotine, chilimac, and sawleaf sago bush, they plugged and sashayed on, deeper, ever deeper, into the heart of Téjas!

Helene allowed that she was plumb wore out, her voice like clouds of gingham in the dry-goods store.

Blue reckoned so but squinted through his sweat. Somewhere out there was laconic truth and he could almost hear it quivering with homely drawl!

Some few days later, they chatted by the old arroyo with their new-found friend, while tortillas and the hearty pinto bean refreshed them, yes, once again.

I declare, said Helene, I'd rather et them pintos then read up agin in *Herzog's Planet*! Sich is their holt on my affections. And with this she wolfed another hefty morsel down.

Por Dios! said their new-found friend, José Cizaña-Hueso, a swarthy chum who'd taken them beneath his "wing" one sultry day while our adventurers bewailed their lack of chuck. And again, Por Dios! uttered he, sopping up some bean juice with a crusty bit of habichuela. His face showed that it was powerful good.

I'm deeply obleeged to you, Mex friend, Blue grinned. It's mighty strange to meet a feller willing to share his spread and vittles out here in . . . God's Country! And his sweeping hand took in with mighty zest the purple sage that brooded just beyant the leaping firelight. And to think that folks call you hombres "greasers." Makes muh blood boil up like egg nog!

Caramba! said Cizaña-Hueso. The hands, they will be locked together in eternal friendship, sí? And with this his Meskin laugh like to bust the old serape that he wore. But you were, how you say in the inglés, hablando . . . ? Spikking!

233

Yes, old hoss, I *was* spikking till your calloused hands filled up muh mouth with beans and these funny little flapjacks.

Bueno! But, ahora, gringo buddy, let's lean back on the mesa here beneath the estrellitas so far away and muy mysterious, and smoke and have a talk. Your wife sleeps the deep sleep of the bean.

Podner, that is jake with me, said Blue, and with this he heaved his frame out flat like a tuckered-out paint. I was a-telling you about my long hard search, I recollect.

But yes! the plucky amigo said. My face is all ears to listen. Sombrero blanco! how I like much the good yarn, and with this he lit his faithful cigarrillo.

When Serge had once agin his tale of woeful quest retailed, the silence that collapsed upon the little camp amid the dappled firkey and the moccasin tobogan seemed to fill our compañeros with ineffable regret. But not for long! For brave hearts pounding leather on the trail the thorns of life are but mere bagatelles, if not mere varmints to be roped and crippled up for all eternity! Thus, in the midst of throbbing quiet cracked a chink by snapping faggots, the dark-hued Mex spoke through the flames.

Mi amigo, it is the fortune of your luck that we meet as we done this afternoon, while the sun turned cactus to potato chips, and the gila monster cooled off in his hole. Sí, Great Dios, my son, so arranged it that on the fateful day you humped through this vast land of mighty Téjas, I was on my way to J.C. Penney to buy a new pairs of huarache. It was a kind of fate, sí, brother to the sort that oft befell Jeff Chandler in the moving-films I used to watch in my little humble village out there where the sun sets each evening in a riot of the fetching colors.

Helene quivered once and then lay still, while a busy coon impaled some luckless critters on an appaloosa barb. What dreams were theirs? Or hers?

Yes, Mr. Cessnaywo, it was a flash of wildest luck we chanced upon you! In but a score of miles or so, we would have been within the vapid purlieus of Killeen, from which, I've heard, no traveler returns.

At mention of that dreaded name, the wind soughed choughingly, and luffed, the firelight burst up in embers amber . . . yet darkness flung its inky robe as well!

Ay chingada! rumbled Don Cizaña-Hueso. Pero . . . is no what I mean. My pleasure is it to share my lowly bins and gnarled tortillas with you and your familia. What I mean is that I think that I have the ancient Aztec power to give you the vison of your gale, bueno?

My . . . gale? Serge queried o'er his coffee can.

Sí, the gale, the how you say, the place you wish to end up with in?

My goal?

Harr, harr, harrñh! the great-hearted hacienda laughed. The Engliss, she is not so well, sí? But yes, I have the power, the secret known to but a few handfuls of the Meskin people. How you think, mi amigo, we got rid of this . . . Téjas? Hah? The magic powers makes us lose the Alamo! Sí! We fix the stupid gringos to think we lost! For many years the wise men of the Méjico think and pray, they make the Bean Dance, the Sacrifice of the Frito, the Margarita Ceremony, the goats, he is sacrifice to Mezcál, "He-Who-Makes-You-Fall-In-The-Dust." You goggle? But sí, I swear it on my father's bandolero! Still, the old ones cannot how you say? dope out how to make the blue-eyes take this place! We have been bad crazy with this, comprende? Houston, Dallas, Amarillo, imagine owning this basura! Waco! Caramba! Galveston! Ay chihuahua! Fort Worth! Madre de Dios! So the Aztec powers speak to us from the clouds one day, and say: "Why you no make the battle and . . . *lose?* The joy, amigo, spreads through the tierra like wild's fire, sí! We have the fiesta for nine years. Then we make the war and run away pronto. And now, the poor fucking gringos have this place. Is good trick, no?

As Two-Pairs Slim opened wide his dust-rimmed eyes when Marshal Judah Maim thrown hot lead into both his arns fore Slim could spit "Yew air a yeller-belly," so did Blue stare through the red-clay dust that fell upon the camp as thick as the drawl of the Mexicali Kid.

Yew mean, Blue faltered, yew kin tell me where I'll find . . . the Phrase?

Pero sí, hombre! And the great roar of laughter that tore from the caballero's throat was loud enough to flatten any billygoats or polecats that were foolish enough or reckless enough to be hiding in the shadowy pulque gulch.

El secreto of the Aztec power, caballo viejo, the lynx-eyed buddy said, is to the mankind give through the chili! Sí, the chili! I am on a level with you when I speak this. But it must be the true chili of the parched lands there, beyond the broody hills on which the sun creeps down.

B-but, chili, swell samaritan? I dang can't reckon sich!

Listen well, my good relleno. And with this, the campesino's voice dropped and quivered lower than the soles of his ole boots, what he called "Old Friends."

I am cottoning to your palaver, Serge spat—and how the campfire leaped into the air in a passel of sparks and glowing coals, sumpn like authors on a talk show if they wuz hopping like a branded dogie whilst waving sparklers on the Fourth of July like freckled boys in the streets of that hometown that will come no more since it already wuz.

The secret Aztec powers from the clouds come out to the hombre which the mind of whom is making the *visions.* And the visions arrive and stay there from the chili. Comprende? And the great secret is this: all Meskin cooseen *is* chili! Comprende? Even the beer he is chili! Even the horses, sí! Even the chickens is

235

made from the chili! You savvy up the country called the "Chile"? That is also made from the chili, yes, many suns ago the Aztec gods decide to see if is possible and they build up this place all from the chili.

Serge sat banjo-eyed, the blank look of a lawyer sifting acrost his tragic face, his lips chewing each other, or others, and he bit them together at the same time. Somewhere in the inky night, a critter howled. Or was it . . . a varmint?

But as I was have been telling, compadre, he must be the true chili, how the old abuelitas call this "chili verdadero," when she is banging and fisting up corn meals in the pueblos that time had a hunch to forget about. And on my old Tío Nacho's head, I give to you this present.

Blue frittered his old pencil thoughtfully, a scrap of foolscap smoothed flat on the worn denim that spoke volumes, at least two. I'm waiting on yuh, Mr. Cizznoosa. And wait he did, while lightning forked tuh hidden draws! How often it forks out here in the empty vastness! Or out *there*!

I give you the two recipes, as hand down from the time when Tenochtitlán is but a two-roads crossing with the filling station and the bar-b-q. Is many other ways of making of this, but this two is O.K. for the regular jobs. First is the carne asada con petróleo and goes: Whomp and mash severely the hands full each of the anchos, guajillos, serranos, and piquins. Slap in the small ladles full up of the oozing tostadas. Smash to bits and throw on top of steaming guacamole. Put every things in the clay pot. Put this under the collapsed adobe dust for ten days. The pot she is then pulled out and the peyote roots of Durango is added. The pot she is placed in a fire of dried frijóles and cooked. As the jugo boils off, maízes are entered in the sludgeness and when the stuff is too much of thick, a small goat goes in, completo. Then the quart of oil from the crankcase of the good padre is sloshed into everything and as she all starts to bubble up, she is ready for eating up with the maguey beans and chocolate rabbits. O.K.? The other instruction is this ones: is call marimbas verdes con gusano. In the clay pot fill up with simmering tequila, is throw a few old papá worms. Then goes in the chilies de árbol, the poblanos, the petines, the jalapeños. If is tomatoes, plomp in. If no these, plomp in a fish's face. When is all boiling merry and bueno, hands full of each these put in: bucktooth sage, persimmon thorns, eleemosynia, frito sacks. Pull off from the blaze, dot the top with pineapple hunks, marshmallitos, crumpled up cream cheese, and last a jug of maple syrup. Put in sun to give nice glazing, and eat with avocados marrónes and rock-salt kisses.

Quick and pronto as the star of a Western saga cashing his check in order to buy genuine oil paintings and Baudelaire's *Oeuvres Completes*, Blue sashayed into the surrounding bindlestiff, not caring a hoot for its cruel barbs. For what seemed like a long time there was nothing to be heard but the banshee wind roiling the pedernales clumps and the sound of a savage puerco's low chuckles. Then his gaunt frame loomed in the leaping firelight, his arms full up with all the goshdarn tarnation supplies that the dish required. Or maybe dishes. It was mighty hard to tell in the pekoolyar light that lit up the brooding land. And with the foolhardy help of his newfound pal, he soon had a pot just a-bubblin and a-steamin on the, so to speak, hob.

For what seemed an eternity, Blue pottered about the festering chili, worried as a schoolmarm whose shapely ankle has been glimpsed by a sweaty wrangler. And at last, as sure as the desk clerk in the Palace Hotel is a nance dressed up like a dude, the chili was ready!

And now, Cezaña-Hueso urged, is time for you, my son, to slop up this comestibles, to let your spirit be one with the spirits of the snake of the shaking feathers, Tomatlxusl, "The-One-Who-Puts-Grit-In-The-Eye," and hear his prophecy. And with this the humble spick gave Serge an abrazo like to bust his ribs.

Blue slopped chuck inter his tin plate and et, his eyes fixed on the moon that moved across the sky like a white cayuse. Then, jingo! iffen his eyeballs didn't up and roll back inter his head while his face took on the vacant, and powerful afeared look of a Nebraskan served a platter of scungilli. The voice boomed in his ears like the boom of bull buffalo fallin in the crick.

"Therefore are they counted the most pestilent, troublesome, and guileful spirits that are; for by the help of Alrynach, a spirit of the West, they will raise storms, cause earthquakes, whirlwinds, rain, hail, or snow in the clearest day that is; and if ever they appear to any man, they come in women's apparel. The spirits of the air will mix themselves with thunder and lightning, and so infect the clime where they raise any tempest, that suddenly great mortality shall ensue to the inhabitants from the infectious vapours which arise from their motions."

Then, fast as an outhouse falls down in a big blow, the voice vamoosed! And Blue returned from that land where time forgot to be itself and space was light in that eternal calm!

I am plumb puzzled up, Mr. Cissysono, he pleaded. And told the brooding breed the strange and shadowed words that fell upon him from the clouds . . . or what had *seemed to be* the clouds! I don't reckon I can calc'late or figger it, he bitched. It's too durned deep and sich. Whut do it have to say about a *place*? I reckon that I made the chili wrong, like a danged tenderfoot who jacks off in a batch of poison ivy.

Is not so, my Anglo bunkie, said the smiling bombazine. Is claro! Claro! The

237

Great One, the reptile with the chicken plumes, tell you the place, sí! And is so-lamente one place can it be! Mamacita! Think, hombre, think! What place is can be this?

I don't know! I d-don't know! Blue quavered, his manly face at last falling down toward his neckerchief. T-tell me?

Hña, hña, hña! rang the pistolero's mirth. Is . . . CALIFORNIA!

«52»
A New
Lease, or Is It Leash,
on Life for the Gavottes

How meet, Blue said, and hiply groovy that we bumped into this dusky vaquer-ito with his cutesy chaps and sagging bandoleros! A small lump packed with salty tears rises inter muh throat as I watch him ride away in a cloud of red Texas dust across the timeless llano beds and gurgling arroyos! How swell that now we know, beyond any shadow of a doubt, which way to go and maybe even how to get there. But straight, or maybe strait, will be the way! What say you, trembling sloven?

But Helene's emotions were so near the surface that, like Iago, she shut her yap, like unto the lonely bivalve on a wind-whipped strand.

Enough said! Blue yawped in virile splendor. I too know the sweet pain you feel, and will confess, although we are not getting along too well in the sexual-satisfaction department, that I am all empathy and a yard wide. Man does not live by head alone!

Like hairy, heavy-hearted, huge-hipped Hecuba, Helene crumpled in a heap.

Here, here, her mate said, enough of that! We must be strong and start right out for the Golden Land thus and such indicated by our greaser pal. Let me help you from this heap into which you've crumpled, for this is the type of heap found on the silent Téjas pampas that can give you a bad rash. And with this, he pulled her from the grasping nettles, nettles that had appeared as if alive by magic!

It is our task now to point the nose of this pushcart toward our goal, and now that we know what it is, the pushing will be as naught. So scramble up there 'neath the canopy and I will heave and grunt us forward.

She scrambled thus. And Blue began to roll the old scarred buddy of a cart toward what turned out sooner to be Oklahoma, thus adding a few miles to the journey but since it did not matter, it did not matter. Blue's itinerary, traced on a

239

map, would look like a diagram out of *Tristram Shandy*, but he did not know that, and thank God for small favors. Some things are not meant for everyone.

Fuck you! Blue said, and creaked to rest beneath a ginseng vine in flower just over the state line. It appears that he was addressing "me."

There they dozed after a coupla humble jujubes, for their provender was low. The violent sun sank slowly and the breeze rose faintly as a fairy's voice, in thus wise: whithk! whooth! Then with the rising of the moon rose Blue, and softly, quietly, yet passionately as St. Theresa in what one wag has called "her wild lament," he woke Helene, who was twitching away to beat the band, as always, a symptom of the vestigial unhappiness left over from four years of sensible shoes during her high school idyll.

She woke, her eyeballs bugged out her haid, as did once Guinevere one rosy morn as doughty Arthur nicked her queenly ass with great Excalibur!

Somewhere in the morning mist, the nettles sighed.

Somewhere, a hatchbald fell from out his eyrie with a thud.

Somewhere, an old prospector scratched and yawned as the coffee boiled; or boiled over.

As in a dream, like Chaucer knowed, Blue said, I saw the element that sits at the very center of our lives!

Whut? Helene said, scratching and yawning, then climbing down to watch the coffee boil.

The center! The core and matrix! The worm in the center of the apple! That thing what has been all things and the like to us, my yolk! It is not Doc Chick, the wise wop, nor the dazzling Glubits, giants of Georgetowr! Nor not Tom Piper, the shitfaced rustick lad, nor Big Boog Vinch and Doc Piscardi, rubes in spades, not the mournful numbers of the Dixie crooner, Blackie Bob Hunko! No! And don't mention the old snot, the rural repairer, nay! And as for those academic assholes, Bone, Poncho, and Dubuque, may Almighty God take away their office nameplates! Miz Grable, glassy-eyed with vile erotics? No help. The prurient priest, D. Debris, wuz a bum steer, no pun intended, he just raised me up a unrequited hard-on, and as for that cynosure of mystery, Cheechee Docque, he came and went like unto a fata morgana of the bresh. Big Black was an unfortunate mistake and a digressive episode, reet? And the Nawlins hipsters, Jimson and l'Amour gave little help, as well you know. And while I grant you that the grinning Mex, Cizaña-Hueso, has set us on the righteous path, no lie, still, what is it that without which we would not have been able to arrive at even this point, so to speak, in our quest that is not done but in which we doggedly entrain through heat and rain and elements of other climes? What?

Helene looked up from the bubbling chuck. So to speak. Make that "chuck."

The . . . cart! This! This faithful . . . cart! A great sob tore from out his bulging throat. And never have I paid thee, old clotted vehicle, the merest heed. And with that, he stood up to his full height, as against the various parcels and fragments, as well as figments, of height to which, or of which, or about which, he usually stood, and began to chant into the brightening air:

« 53 »

The Panegyric
on the Faithful Cart

Thou ain't, O humble cart, too much to see,
For many, thou art not their cup of tea,
Thy wood is wormy, splintered, and decayed
And also full of rot, I am afraid;
Keen shards of pine stick in thy riders' ass
And tear and puncture flesh of ev'ry class;
And some, of thee, have spake unkind, to wit:
That thou art but a rolling piece of shit.
Yet cart, from old New York you've schlepped along
With always (on thy lumber lips) a song;
A song, say I? By jeez, a symphony!
Chocked full of moves and tones and harmony,
Plus andante rondos and viola
And like other stuff in talk ginzola.
Thou stand'st, an Ancient Pile, there in the void,
Though vicious tongues dub thee Old Hemorrhoid;
To these dull wags my sacch'rine dame and me
Do murmur, ever and anon, "Fuck thee,"
Those two words thrumming like two drunken harps
Or like the noivous gills of fat old carps;
Yea, fat old carps that hang around in flocks
Like herds of gentle, ruminating lox.
But I digress (like early cherries hight,
Or later plums that shine all through the night).
Thou humble cart! thou'rt kind of like a fruit,
And plain and homely, like a Crawford suit;
As with that lowly garment, when folk see
Thee coming down the street they 'gin to flee.

As far as I'm concerned (as Mankind knows),
These churls can stick their ideas up their nose!
To me, O cart, thou art a big-faced pike
Of popping eyes; or else belike a shrike
Which is some kind of fucking bug, I ween;
Or thou'rt a poiple pheasant, with a sheen
That glisters like a worm, or woolly peach,
Or like a oily bather on the beach.
I thought to name you Cobra, like the king
Thou art or wert! or will be in the spring.
For spring, like ladies in the throes of lust,
Is coming! Why? Ha! Ha! Because it must!
Forswonk eftsoones do I speak of the time
When lads and lasses fall to hump? To rhyme.
Yet this does not besmirch my lofty praise
Of thee, my oddball wagon, and your ways.
Like coney shy you bump through lettuce groves
And fields of nodding carrots; all which proves
Thy skill and courage; for those crazy fruits
Will gladly savage trespassing galoots.
Do not the rural belfries sadly toll
Of hapless louts chomped up by escarole?
Do not the passing bells tell of the grief
That slav'ring carrots cause in ev'ry fief?
Yet, pushcart, though thou have no roof of gold,
Nor silver hubcaps, your great mind is bold;
And 'spite your brav'ry, thou art also kind.
How many nights thou shelter from the wind
(That fiercely blows from Santa's cold domain)
Helene's bald head, as well as her small brain;
You guard from frozen blast her teeny tits
And her bare ass; upon whose globes my mitts
Play manly music when we friendly screw:
At sunrise pink, you shield her from the dew.
Thou seem'st at times to me a shepherd's cake
Bedight with chawklit fudge; and that is jake
With me! And sometimes seem a stinking cheese
Like limburger, what brings men to their knees;
Sometimes a capon, sometimes a duckie,

Or nutty ale, or quince; or the plucky
Fig that weirdly smiles into the pumpkin
Patch like some fantastic eerie bumpkin.
And in the thin and loathsome light of dawn
Resemblest thou, at times, a shambling gawm;
But one with heart as big as all outdoors!
(And golden too, just like the hearts of whores.)
My eyes drop tears as fast as sailors fuck
When I do think upon the times I've stuck
My giant brogans roughly up your gool
To urge you from a noisome swamp, or pool;
Yet uncomplainingly, out of the slop
(With heaves and shudders, and a little pop!)
You've rolled onto the dry land and the grass.
Permit me, in my shame, to kick my ass!
Like slimy eels, you slither through the tares
As do the deadbeats who, t'avoid the fares
On New York's rotting subway system, leap
The turnstiles; or else underneath them creep.
The sun doth make thee glow like blushing bride
When from her horny husband she can hide
No longer; then falls he into a trance
Whose spell is broken when she rends his pants!
The ass-wise shape of thee that makes the gorge
To rise, O cart! is from black Vulcan's forge
(That jealous gimp who in his airy net
His wife and Mars trapped in their am'rous sweat).
The stinking mud and muck caked on thy frame
Are badges of thine ever-growing fame;
And rubes fall on their knobby knees to pray
As you go creaking on your honest way.
For all these things, O pushcart, stout and true,
I holler to the welkin praise of you;
Thou art, 'bove all, a modest heap, all pluck,
And name I all who quarrel with thee: Schmuck.

« 54 »

Captain Basura
Appears, Makes a Curious
Offer, Is Rejected, and Threatens

Sing and holler loud and crisp in military manner, O sacred Thalia, of the officer, the capitano, infantry, one Dirk Basura, who all the while that Blue did send his virile voice unto the scudding clouds, did lurk within the narrow confines of a copse of fatback peony, all eyes and ears! Sing of his valiant cunt cap and his wrinkled pinks! Sing of the .45 that slapped his thigh, of his mirrored sunglasses, sing especially of his Good Conduct Medal, glowing in the dappled shade and sunny motes that lunged and darted like the crested snatchhatcher zooming down upon the hedges and their unsuspecting worms and midges and their juicy ladybugs or errant cucarachas! Such is Nature ever wonted wert!

Sing of the Idea that showed itself within his piercing eyes, so that they danced like worn-out ballerinas! Sing of their plys and interchats and all the other goddam things they do upon their fairy feets! Sing of the sudden greed that shook his frame like that of potent grizzly ripping ope a camper's lunch! O sing! And sing and sing until Cimmerian night falls down around your ears as suddenly as twisters send mobile homes careering through the peaceful glades of lo! the rocky deeps and vasts of homely shopping malls! Yes, sing your brazen neck off! Sing out as counterman doth yell for a blt with mayo down!

Close-nipped within the bresh like unto the naked Greek who lusting watched a bunch of teen-age girls playing with a beach ball, the stern Basura felt his gaze drawn ever and anonce unto the pushcart, now dawdling in the shade. His manly whistle trembled on its chain, his powerful yet girlish hands squeezed the scarred and battered clipboard to which was fastened the secrets of the morning report, his feet plunked back and forth in the sifting dust, yet his shoes moved not!

Then as Blue's enormous gout of rhyming couplets died away as quietly as flavor from a stick of Juicy Fruit, the officer bestirred himself, and gripping close his courage, already all screwed up, crashed he through the trembling vetch and the clinging thorns of phony dickwort, and appeared within the clearing smartly, the kind of man this Nation sorely needs to fight and lead his troops in wild retreat!

The very wind stopped soughing or sloughing through the trees, and sloughed off into a nearby slough. There it scumbled with a brace of perch. Resplendent stood the proud son of the Point. Blue and the svelte Helene gaped though the sunny motes already mentioned, maybe more than once.

Art thou, Blue breathed, a sprite or satyr of the elfin boles and sappy limbs that dip and shake within this wild enchanted place? Or else a djinn from out a empty bottle that once housed a pint of Dixie Belle? Art thou wast but a phantasm hight beyant the very ignis fatuus that slumps past rotting stands of sorrel led by sorcerers like Morgana le Fay or oily Mandrake? Stand, holt, and speak in tongue belike unto a mortal man else avaunt my heart past these my popping eyes that start like gumballs from a sea of frigid sweat!

Me too! the agued wife ensued, for like her mate, she was all shitless scared.

Calm your fears, beloved yardbirds, said the officer. I am but Captain Dirk Basura, U.S. Army, Infantry, entrusted here for a certain time to walk this dusty land with clipboard, ballpoint pen, and low-slung automatic. I come—and with this he flung his weatherbeaten hand toward a beetling scarp—from trig Fort Swill that squats beyond that yonder scarp now beetling in the sun.

Then you are not a sprite or satyr, nor a djinn or phantasm of the ensorceled forest, but just a fucking soldier? Blue said, his cold sweat drying instanter.

But yes, sweet honcho, said the warrior. I beg you calm your fears, stand tall, get straight, shape up, fall in, and be at ease. I have been lurking there in distant bush, enchanted and quite pleased with the wondrous poem that you've just bawled out. And even more enchanted by its object, that little item so fulsomely apostrophized, your cart!

My . . . cart? said Blue. And why is that? What use is such a simple thing to the military might of the outfit what you serve, up to its ribbons in injuns of war?

We call them "engines," smiled the gentleman.

Whatever thus, said Blue. But what, brave captain, shakes?

As a military man, officer, and stupendous gent, whether in pinks, suntans, greens, or, as the French might put it, fatigués, as well as having been a purchasing agent in real life, I am prepared and authorized by the post commander of Fort Swill, to make you an offer for that remarkable cart, of which and to whom, and anent, you just wove a moving apostrophe—or is it comma? No matter. The Army has need for such a cart to serve as a prototype, a model, a paradigm, for a new kinda APC, which is, in the parley of citizens like youse, an armored personal cart. The Army has told me that I may offer the following items, most brand new, others slightly used by previous owners, every person jack of them a gentle soul awake only on Sundays and then but for a chitch of an hour or two.

I can offer you a fuckin' A, a red deuce, Patton's penis, Texas clover, the Chicago Five, a Jewish star, the stairway to Europe, a propellor specially chosen to be frozen, a black bullseye, an eagle and a griffin, a heavenly pentagon as well as a heavenly octagon, the big X, a triangular triangle, a true compass, the flying dragon, a tomahawk, the heart on the leave, the big natural, a Indian what got his ass handed to him at the pass, firmamental stripes, a big red one, wittle gween weaves, a diamond rouge et a rouge étoile, the smacked hourglass, duh flying 8, a patriotic posy, crossed swords, onze wit wings, the claw, miracle stars who don't know who they ares, a palm leaf or sumpn, unlucky lightning, dee why, the krimson keystone, yin with yang, a red dogie sconce all bones, Cathlick yout', the triangle D, a California sunburst, a Broadway rainbow, a moping maple leaf, the mailed fist, a Viking chapeau, a goldpanner, the raunchy rattler, seventy-one sergeants, a buncha all-Americans, the eagle what screams, a golden acorn, a hovering hatchet, lucky lightning, pine trees on parade, Injun Joe, a century, the big bear, the grounded griffin, hell's hatchet, a snarling panther and a brooding bison, a funny French hat, the lugubrious lion, a woodsplitter, a sword on fire, Miz Liberty, a free French cross, a weird critter, a yella bombsight, the puritanical Pilgrim with plunderpuss, a ticklish trident, old ironsides, hell on wheels, a spearhead, the Empire of Dust, Dixie volunteers, a pointy-headed grizzly, the Hondo Hurricane, lonely stars of Lubbock, bue jerseys, a busted black horse, a fleur-de-lis thass always ready, brave rifles, follow-me fools and fuckups, Sir Therwas: knight, an excited monstre, Dixie crackers, a thunderbird buck and wing, the floating sword, two lucifers, un cartridge rojo, special thunderbolts, twenty-nine mountains, a ghastly galleon, the Black diamond, Franklin's phiz, a chuting fall, Prez de deux, Senõr Conquistador Consombrero, a hollering cock, a tawch, the jumping dragon, a chickenshit bushmaster, Pershing's prick, some scarwafs, cadooses of all kinds, any truck with anything, lotsa logs, intimate support systems, divers commandos like, fighting blue star devils, sundry shapes, Kay Mags, rotten seas, MacVees with MonSoons, airborne ovals, and brassard bombs.

The mighty warrior ground to a sickening halt, his eyes clean misted o'er with tears as the full import of the divers items he had offered came, as they say, "home" to him. He glanced at Blue, a slow smile slowly spreading across his face, or, at any rate, the lower portion of it, as he smiled that smile that was wont to set the world's old weary heart on the bumpy road to coronary occlusion!

What do you say? Basura beamed. These goods can be delivered to you at any address you would wish and/or desire. F.O.B., packing list enclosed, all suitable for framing, designed to brighten up the little woman's kitchen, or function as conversation pieces when close friends dash over for a night of TV, book-chat, and smutty jokes. Where shall I send the shit? And, with this, the flower of the infantry followed his outthrust jaw toward the cart that dozed in the sunny motes—come back at last!

Odd corrugations furrowed Serge's brow as his thoughts sprang into turmoil. They trudged about behind the piercing eyes that had seen so much since that day, so many many years ago, or maybe months ago, that they, and the head and body that was host to them, left the office of Doctor Ciccarelli. The items pleased and tempted him like a glass of beer doth make the small *Drosophila* do loop the loops in mad abandon! Yet . . . yet . . .

No! he yelped. I cannot, sir, give o'er the cart to you or to the U.S. Army. It has been steadfast pal, kind mom, strong poppa, helpmeet, schlepper, hearth and home, repository of our hopes and dreams, and also waxes redolent of memories of Zimmerman, lost somewhere in the stalactites of red clay and petraceous shale slabs and the like.

Zimmerman? the hoplite mused.

My chee-ild! hawked Miz Gavotte, and fell where she sat like a stone. My chee-ild! what we abandoned by mistake somewhere back down the lonesome road amid the vast space of weird America's somber razorbacks or sumpn!

The captain's silver bars darkened for a moment and his sunglasses flashed fiery red in the glade's pitiless light. A fly buzzed, intensifying the silence as buzzing flies are wont to do. You mean, Basura said, his voice pitched soft with fury, you will *not* relinquish this cart, even though your country needs it to keep the barb'rous hordes away from the sacred profit motive and the flabby macho cunts who help to keep us great?

Although my heart is as heavy as that of the schmuck in yon old tale who never was allowed to put his foot on Coney's shores, or eat a plastic pizza in the nodding fields of Iowa's great shopping malls, I . . . I . . . must say no.

Then, subversive mockie, roared the legionnaire, you'd best, as swift as vague Rotarian or dumbo Elk doth swallow beers when unleashed upon the streets of unsuspecting cities sans the wife, pack up your shitty gear, attach and lash that faggot instrument, and make tracks for the state that lies due west of here; for you are not welcome in this here neighborhood.

Immejiately? quailed Gavotte, the firelight leaping on his face, then bounding off to run mad amid the bulfinches that lay sedulously clumped about.

If your ass is not from out this military reservation by the dawn, Basura snapped waspishly as Genghis Khan when served his egg foo yung luke warm, I'll call in on youse and all your tawdry, pitiful belongings an air strike machined to make of youse believers, dead or otherwise! And about the blowing up of pushcarts, the USAF admits no fucking peer! Indeed, I wisht youse had a ox or twain, for turning them to hamburger is the speciality of the vacant small-town lads who zoom and dip and roar around without surcease, to keep these skies forever strong and free, as well as ope and chockablock with boundless opportunity! And with that, the cap strode off into the sedge in clouds of perspiration and the twangling of creaking leather and tobacco!

The Gavottes, as you will have by now surmised, fled in fear and panic yet again. So continueth our adventure.

"Our"?

«55»

"La Musique
et les mauvaises
herbes," Continued

XIII A REALLY NICE CHAT

There is some days when everything seems dull. The professors are a thing to put one to sleep, the check of the parents is not arrived, the life is flat. At the end of one of these rotting days, André and Émile chat on the future. It seems to look too much flat as well.

ANDRÉ: In a fucked year, I will be parting for the Advanced Accordion School and you will enter in the School of Tubers. You love better the School of the Ocarina, is it not so?

ÉMILE: But yes. As to Tuber Studies, well, you can stuff it in the "giggy" so far as I go!

ANDRÉ: What pity! I like to knock out jivey bits with the accordion, at least, but I confess that I will have the blue not to have Suzanne about a place any more. She is some hot mommy—as you too good know, my old chump.

ÉMILE: Heys! I had believe we got this all straightened, no? I am sorry on my absence of discretion with Suzanne on that fatal wick-end, but it is a difficult labor to make the resistance with a beauty like she who makes on you the dry hump more quick as you can say Jacques Robertson!

ANDRÉ: Yes, well. O.K. Soon we will complete the studies here, and all this laughs and weeps will be ceased. We will have to work like some damn bastards!

ÉMILE: You squarely hit the head of the spike there, my gay comrade!

ANDRÉ: It is not the idea of to work that gives me an ennui. I have a worry of not meeting up with some swell cookies like Suzanne and Monique. I have a chagrin to say a toodle-oo on them. I wonder is it that they will think on me some time? I have the large hope.

ÉMILE: Are you fooling? Young ladies of these type at all times recall the lust of youths.

250

ANDRÉ: I pray this to be true, my old bud.

ÉMILE: You can often write to them the letter, you know. And stuff them up with all manners of the obscene, the salacious, the tintillating. This should force them to bust into a sweat!

ANDRÉ: And maybe it could be that they can come to make a visit on me at my solitary chamber? We could make a truly debased trio!

ÉMILE: Now you appear to be talking, oil-face!

ANDRÉ: I can make an entertainment on them, play some love bits on the accordion, ply on them some booze—even maybe suggest that we regard some blues cinema.

ÉMILE: It is it! Never speak die!

ANDRÉ: I almost feel a twinge of agony for you, Émile. Over there I will be, buried into depraved acts, while you—you will be having the nightly rendezvous with Marie Feest! Oh, ha, ha, ha!

ÉMILE: It may be so, my mean personal pal. But has it slipped from your brains that your school is three hundred kilometers distant, while mine is but ten from this ivy-soaked walls? Therefore, a ha, ha, ha on you!

ANDRÉ: Oh ball! It appears maybe that I myself will be saying good evening to Miss Feest, while you might be hauling up your ashes till the back breaks down. Craps!

ÉMILE: Only time will inform us. Meanwhile, how about a duet including us?

André and Émile are play the famous Parisian ditty, "Rosy Glasses." André is hugely pissed off on his pal for what he has been saying on this theme of the young ladies. He thinks to himself: "What a pain of the ass!"

XIV A QUESTION OF BUCKS

The last week, they had announce in the newspaper that Mr. Bas-Soie, Professor of Legumes and Forage Crops at the University, will participate at a contest on the television. It is a program what distributes vast sums of money to the people who know to respond correctly to a series of questions. Mr. Aine discusses this event with the Professor of the Hot Jazz, Mr. Fixe-Chaussettes.

MR. FIXE-CHAUSSETTES: What a luck for that maggots, Bas-Soie! He could well gain some thousands of grinbacks without getting himself fatigued.

MR. AINE: They are good in choosing their man, the rotting moron-brains! He does not recognize his ass from his shoulder, but he comprehends perfectly about the damn beans and stuff like this.

251

MR. FIXE-CHAUSSETTES: I demand myself how he will to spend his loots. What would *you* make if all of a suddenly one put on you a hundred thousand bucks among the hands?

MR. AINE: My words, I do not know. I probably will commence by to say, "So long, sucks!" on this putrid place. Then I might take a plane or a luxurious boat for to go live in the South Seas or Rio or some crazy place like this.

MR. FIXE-CHAUSSETTES: And this changing of place—you would make this alone? Just say a farewells and set the face to the far-off horizon? Or what?

MR. AINE: Well, I confess that it would be some nice fun to request of Suzanne Jarretière or Sophie Jupon or Monique Gaine to come along for a laughter with me. Do you know of these young lady students?

MR. FIXE-CHAUSSETTES: Do I! When they are in the attendance of the class of mine of Elementary Jive Bits, I get a wildness in looking on the bodies of them and the faces also. They are some fragments of ass!

MR. AINE: Ha! Ha! In effect! I made some minor amusement with Miss Jarretière once a time ago, but the other two I make the lewdness with in the fantasies solely. I would cast away many grinbacks to do the sexual orgy on all three of these switties at the once.

MR. FIXE-CHAUSSETTES: Whoo! A man might set his body on flames in such an adventure. But what would the wife of you say in reference on such a voyage?

MR. AINE: I will tell to her that I must make the voyage to do a research in the primitive tuba or the Brazil accordion or the African comb and paper or some damn shit like this, and buy her the minx. But what would *you* make with bucks like this, my old man?

MR. FIXE-CHAUSSETTES: I must admit also the insane dream. I have the ardent feel for some years on that juicy lady, Mrs. Chaud. Is she not some thing?

MR. AINE: Ah, Mrs. Chaud! I once made a fox trots on her at the Yearly Dance of the Faculties last year, and I vow to you that I was of the idea that she was going to grind off my crotch. That lady is one hot figure!

MR. FIXE-CHAUSSETTES: I just am thinking how content I am that these ladies do not have a thought on what we are chatting! They will have some scandal.

MR. AINE: I don't know on this. I saw a composition in a number of *Oui, Oui, Paris* soon ago what hold that the ladies have just as much hot ideas like the men.

MR. FIXE-CHAUSSETTES: Well, I wish that Mrs. Chaud will have the hot ideas on *me*.

MR. AINE: But yes! And also not bad if the Misses Jarretière, Jupon, and Gaine will have some, eh?

MR. FIXE-CHAUSSETTES: In effect! But, these are dreams from the pipes. We have got no bucks to speak on, so shit on this things!

MR. AINE: Yes. We are make ourselves banana!

Mr. Aine and Mr. Fixe-Chaussettes say a farewell and depart for the homes of them. Mr. Fixe-Chaussettes is a bachelor and when he is arrived he makes an abuse on himself. Mr. Aine rushes in and makes a sex act with his wife in the kitchen right when she is prepare dinner. She would not be content to know why is this.

XV AT THE BUREAU OF PLACEMENT

It will be soon the birthday of André, and Suzanne would like to gain a little grinbacks for to buy him a jolly gift. Yesterday she is present herself at the Bureau of Placement of the University, in order to see if she can find a position. It is no other lady but Mrs. Chaud, as a secretary of the Bureau, who poses to her the questions of rigor. What a sticky things!

MRS. CHAUD: Good day, miss. How could I be to you of some uses?

SUZANNE: I am search for a situation that will permit me of to work some ten hours for the week. I have no desire to raze the bottom in this job. To whom can I demand some piece of information on this, Mrs. Chaud?

MRS. CHAUD: To me, if you wish this. I labor at here for some hours of the week in order for to make some additional bucks and make my ends meet. The University—this is off my sleeve—is too much tightly wadded, I don't mind telling to you, my little jam pot.

SUZANNE: Ah, I see. By the bys, I have heard on you some few excellent tales of the teaching of you from a swell old bud of mine, André Lubrique?

MRS. CHAUD: Ah yes, Mr. Lubrique is a heck on a swit boy and a student of good talents, but a little too wacked out from his head by the young ladies. Well, that is a little cipher of the bagatelle, no? Let us commence by filling up this form. I have the idea that maybe you call yourself Suzanne?

SUZANNE: It is the fact, missus.

MRS. CHAUD: And how do you call your last name?

SUZANNE: I call me Jarretière, Suzanne Jarretière.

MRS. CHAUD: Very good. I am write it down here. Jarretière . . . what a foolish name that seems to be! Almost as crazy as mine. Ha! Ha! Well, enough on this joke. What age do you have, my honey buns?

SUZANNE: I have eighteen years, Mrs. Chaud.

MRS. CHAUD: O.K. on this. Eighteen. Now, which ones of your professors know you enough good for to give us some datas of you and say to us some things you have the talents on?

SUZANNE: Well . . . Mr. Aine will make this things, I believe. But . . . what it is you will have going to demand on him?

253

MRS. CHAUD: The jolly face of you is sporting up a blush, miss. Do not have a worry. I know how to take in what Mr. Aine tells on young lady students with the mite of salt. He made some licenses on you, I make a bet.

SUZANNE (*plunging the eyes to the floor*): I have the shame to say this thing, but yes. He make me do a sex act in order for to succeed in the Kazoo Studies class of his.

MRS. CHAUD: What a contorted creeps he is! Pardon my French, but this lousy shit fly each terms make a young lady student do a sex act with him—some time two or three young ladies! Among us, miss, I tell to you that I made a normal fox trots on him soon ago, and I think he will be shooting off the member into the trousers any moment, so crazy with a lust he was. Don't make a care, my apple tart, I have the number on Mr. Aine.

SUZANNE: Much thanks on you, Mrs. Chaud. I had no desire that the Bureau of Placement to think on me as a pushed-over.

MRS. CHAUD: Of nothing! Now, tell to me of what you like to make as a job.

SUZANNE: Hecks, I don't know, rilly. I know to tap at the machine a piece, and I have the habit of to assist students at the lessons.

MRS. CHAUD: Ah, it is well. We have much of demands for the assistance in the lessons by stupid people at the University, of what we have the vast mob. Is it that you have assist Mr. Lubrique at some times? I seem to have a recall he so told to me.

SUZANNE: Yes . . . now and then again I give him an assistance.

MRS. CHAUD: Ah, it is as I think. I have of the occasion give to him a quick lesson as well. He is a good student, no? It fills the teacher with a grand joy to work with him.

SUZANNE: In effect. He is a champion of the lessons.

MRS. CHAUD: It might be that if you get some jobs, Mr. Lubrique might wish me to assist him at a few extra moments, no? I will be much content to make this, Suzanne. After all, you have no wishes to poops the self out.

SUZANNE: It may be the fact. If I get some jobs, I will ask on André of this.

MRS. CHAUD: How swell this is! What an agreeable young thing you are. Now I tell a toodle-oo on you, and if we find some things, we will give to you the jangle on the telephone.

SUZANNE: Thanks in big heaps, Mrs. Chaud. A toodle-oo on you.

Mrs. Chaud leans in her chair back and makes a daydream of some thrills with André. She appears to be doing some short panting indeed! Suzanne is walking to her chamber, of the thoughts that she will no sooner inform André of the idea of Mrs. Chaud than she will make the jump into a cesspool. She mutters on herself, "Why don't this sexy vamp make some sex with the old gents?"

254

⟨ *Blue Pastoral* ⟩

XVI A LITERARY ARGUMENT

Mr. Coillon, Professor of Wild Flowers, never lets pass an occasion of vaunting the superiority of the English novels over that of the French. Evidently, that does not much please Mr. Aine, who loves with a deep the French culture things. This one responds always that the English novels is imitate of the French and that the imitation is not equal never to an original. Nevertheless, after reading on an English novel soon ago, Mr. Aine finds a nice things to speak about this.

MR. AINE: The novel by McCoy, *Sublime Porter*, is not too bads. McCoy would be content of to see that his book pleases a person of my nice tastes

MR. COILLON: McCoy is of a universal in this novel. It has pleased all men of culture who read on this, so I am content that it pleases *you*, my friend, or else one might have the thought that you have the brain made purely of the shit. On my other hand, I have read upon a novel by Latirail, *The Nail Seekers*, and what a pity! It is of clarity that it is a work that is absent of spine and the intelligence.

MR. AINE: Your ass sucks up the wind, my colleague. I am also of the opinion that *Sublime Porter* is of a universal state, but so is a "bull clap." Ha! Ha! McCoy is some times genial, especially in these description of young ladies in variant states of deshabille, but in an essence, he is a dull vomit of a writer. The brilliant of the glitter the *The Nail Seekers* makes reveal of the superior arts of Latirail.

MR. COILLON: Latirail is some how of a teensy interests if one has nothing else to be had to read on, as if one has been coasted up on the deserted island. But his novels, like *The Nail Seekers*, are of such a grand ennui that a person gets the jeebies on reading this things.

MR. AINE: The jeebies, eh? Any person who will get these jeebies is one too-thick bastard! McCoy is chuck filled up in blocks with the scenes of violence what he makes to give the psycho person the cheap thrills. But in Latirail we find no actions saving these who pass by in the brains of the characters.

MR. COILLON: And the brains of the characters, please do not neglect to speak, old dimmed wits, are such brains what makes a dwelling on thoughts of sexy perversions, on crazy fetish things as the matron ladies in the house dress and snikkers, and many creepish memoirs of sex acts in groupings of much people. *The Nail Seekers* has a great illness to it.

MR. AINE: Ah, you say to me an illness? You are speak as the man what has the asshole made out of paper! Latirail makes the picture of the illness in order for us to know how the world runs along daily in this age of dirts. *Sublime Porter*, however, has the scene of a grand nausea when the heroine does the sharp bite on the organ of the hero in the oral act what occurs in a garbage dump. If this is not of a too much disgust, I will eat up my hat!

255

MR. COILLON: I will say to you, my thick-skull one, that McCoy's scenes of potent acts in *Sublime Porter* are the symbol of a malaise who has done the relation among the two sexes so loused up. He is of the huge moral statures.

MR. AINE: I think on him as a blood-crazing nuts!

MR. COILLON: And I consider it that Latirail is of the type of a freaky gay fairy what rilly has the great hate on ladies, young and also old!

MR. AINE: You are an impossible shitnose! You and your lime-eating hacker!

MR. COILLON: And you! You and that twisted cracker of the frog toad are both of you wasted of a great sick!

MR. AINE: Stick it in your nose bones!

MR. COILLON: Place it roughly in the fundamental!

Mr. Coillon and Mr. Aine continue to do the shouting insults to each on the other until the bell rings out for classes. They rush away then, making some fists to each other. Mr. Aine then proceed to look up the skirt and down in the blouse of the young lady students of him and to make some smutty proposals to some. Mr. Coillon stands to observe with his eyes in a bulge the bottoms of the young lady students of him when they make it to bend away over to look in a microscopes. It might be that their talk of the moral in the novels is so much of the heated air and the horse shits.

≪ 56 ≫

The Land
of Enchantment

THE LAND OF ENCHANTMENT

You are probably wondering just what you are doing here, in the Land of Enchantment? Yes, this is the Land of True Enchantments! In its many wonderful ways it has, all the enchantments that you might think you can see in the Old Capitols of Europe and the Mystic East. But here, in "Your Own Backyard" you can be casted upon a spell of True Enchantments, to beat the band, for Vacation and Care free days and nights of Fun and Frolics! Famous persons of all stripes and sexes may be found here, "all year round" smiling and loaving away their troubles and cares. Why not you?

Perhaps you are thinking that this is a "hypo" about the Land of Enchantment and, if so we wish to please request you to read this colorful brochure about this land we are proud to be of and to which we welcome whom wants to come and throw away his troubles and as the famous song says, pack them in a kitty bag for a few days or weeks. What do we offer persons? Plenty.

Climate
Is dry and healthsome. The air is excellent for the consumption and asma, if upwind from the booming nucular plants that proudly work to bring the fruit of Progress to little sleepy villages. Yet also, experts for the Power Company have proved that studies show that even if you are downwind it is not without its boons, the slight touch of radiation in the air healthily killing all the dirt and filth garbage atoms as well as cockarocahes and scorpions as well as bobcats and wolfs and ciyots what like to eat campers and household pets. The mean temprature is 42 a low, and 65 a high, though once in a while it goes up to 145 degrees and down to − 55, so that wise natives find it a good idea to stay in the house then. Rain: Has been no rain in this sunny place since 1929, it is, as they say always, good golf weather. Once in a while we get here a small blizzard but with the crackling blazes in the quaint adobes the people live in, there is much family closeness at

257

these times, with card games, shooting craps, and other "together" pass-times. Water for healthful bathing and an occasional drink is trucked in from some-place. Because the heat is so dry it is never oppressive except if a person should stand around in the sun too long a time "loungeing about" in the colorful town squares when, the person could get a stroke in his or her head, that can be painful and cause a quiet death.

Minerals
There are many minerals lurking in the ground here in the Land of Enchant-ment. Many are precious to the working-day world of industry and others are to make into precious jewlry. Some of these minerals are, bingoite, marmalite, ni-cotine, zincox, crystalloid, birdlime, boxball, eggdrop, luddite, porsche, and the famous red clay that the prosthetics industry uses to make the feet.

Crops
Land of Enchantment is so rich in crops that can grow without the precious water that we have not had for a spell that one gives a pause to know where to begin on them all. Let us take a chance. Shall we? We grow in a great perfusion these diverse crops, in so far as the beans go: alachi, mastiachi, pinga, sancha, yenda, barragana, carajo, ganforra, chingada, cuco, ciscón, and caló. We allso raise in great perfusions these chilies: the bujarrón, mucló, pajera, quilé, zur-rona, coña, daifa, flete, jaño, magué, birlocha, cábula, balorri, and basto. We also grow the "dwarf" potatoes, the different types are the bombear, the tributo, the rudimé, and the cagar, also there is a small area devoted to the growth of the green tomatoes, which we have the bullarengue, chamberete, pendejo, and ñorga. Truly, this is called by many the Enchanted Garden of Eden!

Railroads
Many railroads serve this land and its wonderful inhabitants and makes the guests and tourists comfortable and able to arrive and depart from almost any spot they take it into their mind that they like to be. The major railroads are the Texas-Desert-Pacific, the Pacific-Texas, the Desert-Pacific, the Pacific-Okie, the Okie-Desert, the Desert-Mesa-Mojave, the Mojave-Okie, the Mojave-Mesa-Arroyo, and the Arroyo-Pacific. There is also an airport of the most up-to-date facilities that is open 24 hours a day all year round between sandstorms and the casual blizzard or two that passes by.

Famous Sons and Daughters
The Land of Enchantments has given to the world many famous people, many of whom have gone out into the world to "make their marks" and many of whom have stayed here to improve and make even more genteel the already much im-

proved and genteel way of life that we already live here in the "Aorta of the West" as a famous Heart Sergeon once "dubbed" it. Surely there are hundreds of them but permit us to note but a handful or two of the most illustreous ones. Juan Pecos, invented the Railroad sandwich; Juan de Cristo, said first prayer in English in the Valley; Juan Culebra, ate nine pounds of habichuelas at the White House Poetry Fest; Juan Cimarrón, got idea of putting the gusano (worm) in mezcal bottle; Juan Taos, first professional sunset describer in Tourist Board; Juan Santa Fé, made adobe house from flour and Pepsi-Cola; Maria Mora, opened bowling alley; Brick Las Vegas, introduced pancakes to Navajos; Juan Ratón, voted for Hubert Hoover; Juan Cerro-Blanco, forgot his name once; Maria Truchas, seduced Juan Taos; Maria Costilla, watched a horse all day Christmas; Juan Baldy, took a trip to Utah; Chet Lake, first Avon man in Los Cobardes; Juan Sandia, changed his name to Johnny Sandia; Juan Manzano, put ketchup on his beans; Juan Gallinas, first man in town to wear Windsor knot; Maria Jicarilla, disliked corn tortillas; Max Caballo, arrested for making pee-pee on turquoise display in market; Juan Oscuro, old friend of Maria Mora; Maria San Andrés, has no friends at all; Juan Orgán, changed his name to Juan Orgoné; Juan and Maria Animas, own Juan and Maria Animas' Roadside Cafe; Maria Hatchet, trying to get on game shows for 18 years; Juan Mogollón, once walked to the airport; Maria Pinos, throws lemons at priests; Maria Burro, first woman to wear net stockings in State Legislature; Juan Blanca, laughed at President Truman's shirt; Juan Capitán, sits on blanket; Maria Sacramento, went to movies with a bag of peaches; Maria Hueco, mistaken for Puerto Rican; Juan Guadalupe, mistaken for Italian; Juan Petaca, owns TV repair store; Juan Vallés, hangs around Petaca's TV repair store; Maria Nacimiento, drinks muscatel in front of Post Office; Juan Jemez, wrote a letter to *Popular Mechanix*; Juan San Mateo, washed his pick-up truck once; Juan Magdalena, suggested name change to Juan Orgoné; Maria Socorro, does not understand *I Love Lucy* show; Bill Black, makes wigs for Chet Lake; Juan Mimbres, does not wear sunglasses; Maria Florida, mistaken for Anglo man and elected to Congress; Maria Potrillo, lost her slip in a tornado; Juan Carrizo, makes Rosaries from ball-point pens; Juan Tunicha, ate a straw hat; Juan Choiska, is always sick and tired of everything; Chuck Pyramid, friend of Chet Lake and Bill Black; Maria Peloncillo, dropped a bowling ball in the Drive-In; Juan Zuñi, smokes a lot; Juan Datil, sent his wife to refrigerator school; Juan Diablo, does not like Coca-Cola; "Big" Hatcheta, discovered how to paint mountain pictures and moved to Palm Springs; Rod Tularosa, wears a denim tie.

Manufactures

Last but not least we must mention the manufactures of the Land of Enchantments! Although these are not destined to interest the frivolous folk who laugh and sing their ways through vacations and holidays here, it is of the first moment to business men, who come to look hard-headed at possible investments.

Many of these industries are important to the Nation's economy as well as to the local one, and some, though small, are always growing. A Sign of a Strong and Rosy America!

The area is rich in muscatel plants, mezcal plants, and tequila plants, as well as a brewery that makes the famous "Dos Pelotas" beer.

There is a growing pot industry, and along with the pots made for pinto beans, we are now "into" tea pots, laundry pots, stew pots, and large ceramic pots for cats. There is also a small shoppe in Old Santa Fe that makes one of a kind pots for eggs, which they call Huevo Pots.

We are putting much energy into the Groats Industry.

The herb tea industry grows apace.

There is an increasing demand from the thousands of Indian imitators in the large metropolises for polyethylene turquoise, and our three plants are on 24-hour shifts.

The Geiger Counter industry is also booming.

Finally, our Famous blankets are back-ordered for months and a merger is "in the air" to merge this industry with the pot industry to produce the first Blanket Pot.

So, it will be seen that we are On the Way to the American Way!

So, prospective visitor and guest, we say again, Welcome! Welcome to the
LAND OF ENCHANTMENT

Faced abruptly with this colorful brochure, or, perhaps more precisely, at one with it, since he held it gingerly in his quiet, bemused hands, Blue suddenly wanted to blurt! This strong and stalwart land, this land ... of (they were *right*) enchantment! seemed now, to Blue, as he reflected upon the horrifying waste and drang and such of his young life (and Helene's too), the place to rest for a couple of nonces, perhaps even a sennight or two, to recoup their strength, such as it was (and still is!), make a few repairs to the pushcart before they pushed out, or on, continue with his slow but steady progress on "Good Old Dolphin Boulevard," and cajole, urge, press, inveigle, threaten, wheedle, and plead for a return to work by his wifey. Why, there was really nothing that the chick couldn't do to scrape up a few shekels to keep them in beans.

Was there? he mused.

The answer came to him as it must to all men, in the slow soughing of the wind, the glimmer of the old moon on the melting snow, the shadows of the stately pines on the rumbling mountainside.

There were a . . . few things. He laughed, a delicate *frisson* riffling his hirsute wrists, at the end of which hung the large hands, and their even larger fingers, that would one day startle the civilized world with their musical power!

But a few other things, *that* she could do.

For a moment, her curled lip seemed to verge toward the negative. She had no way of knowing whether or not she could enter the labor market, it had been many years since she'd earned her bread in the hurly-burly of the job world and other popular songs. But just at that moment, as her lip began to curl as it, perhaps, had never curled before, just then, Serge gestured toward the West, where the sun was sinking in a mad explosion of what they call a riot of colors, with a few subtle tints and shades at the edges, and she was swept away by a sense of her destiny, her destiny as the wife who would stand behind, as she was standing now, her husband in the future, just as she had stood behind him in the past, often getting up on tiptoes to see over his shoulders, as she was perhaps doing now, and as she would in the future, as she would always, that is, whenever he stood directly in front of her, as he now stood, and as he had so often stood, strong and straight and unafraid, in the past.

So she went to work selling things in the market of a small city nestled at the foot of a jagged sierra.

First, she sold some small pamphlets pertaining to Arts and Crafts, and Doing for Oneself as Did Our Forefathers.

How to Open a Bottle of Muscatel
A bottle of Muscatel should be purchased with care and an eye toward personal needs. Muscatel, a bright, brittle, singing little wine, goes perfectly with Fritos, Twinkies, and unfiltered cigarettes, but is most often taken alone at room temperatures direct from its unmistakable bottle. Its unearthly sweetness may be slightly "cut" by alternate sips of a cheap blended whiskey or hunks of eyetalian-type bread. This sprightly little gentleman of a wine should be procured only at those times when you are in touch with your feelings.

After purchasing, step outside the place of purchase, walk directly to a doorway, an alley, a stoop, a curb, or a side street, and briskly twist off the metal cap. It is part and parcel of drinking Muscatel to enhance the sense of personal freedom it conveys by throwing this cap away.

How to Make Laundry
Throw soiled clothing on the floor, until it makes a pile, or piles, preferably in the corner of the living room. When it has reached the old mellow *vigas* of the ceiling, you will see that it has attained its own organic structure, and it is possible to relate to it in a constructive way. This soiled clothing has become laundry.

Carry the piles with care to the swift-running stream beyond the ditch where you burn the garbage and discard your empty Muscatel bottles, and throw the laundry into the water.

You have successfully, and quite simply, made laundry!

If you are concerned about your needs as a newcomer to our region this, it should be noted, is an excellent craft-discipline for beginners, since it produces excellent results with a minimum of effort, and permits the neophyte to immediately feel at one with his surroundings.

How to Drink Herb Tea

Put on a hand-made and ill-fitting woolen, or woollen shawl. Heap the fireplace high with piñon logs or faggots and set ablaze. Staring at the colorful *ojos de Dios* that are on the rough adobe walls above, below, and in between the oil paintings that you've made of the mountains at sunset, take a moment to get in touch with yourself and your feelings.

Meanwhile, the herb tea is brewing in the battered copper pot that is on the hob. A splash of Muscatel in the pot can be a special treat!

Soon, sip your herb tea from a hand-thrown mug that has the organic structure of the ancient clay from which it was thrown. (If you can find a mug that will not sit on the table without falling over, all the better.) Watch the dirty station wagons and pick-up trucks clatter by your house toward the art gallery. Call a few friends and, as you watch the sunset on the mountains, tell them how it looks. As the flickering firelight dances on the rough adobe walls, mention how great it is to be out of the noisy city where it is impossible to get in touch with your feelings and paint pictures of splendid mountains.

How to Eat Pinto Beans

Plunge a gloved hand into a bubbling *olla* (pot) of clay that is filled with pinto beans. Keep the fingers stiff, and when you feel that your hand is at one with the reality of the "life of the bean," withdraw it and eat the pinto beans that adhere to the glove. (It is perfectly permissible to suck the bean juices out of the glove as the Indians do.)

When the glove is soaked through and through with bean juices (three or four immersions should do the trick), remove it, throw it into the *olla* and lick your bare hand.

Indians have eaten beans this way for centuries. It is highly economical—a pot of beans once fed the Arikara Apache hordes for three weeks—and allows the bean-eater to relate to cooking in a natural way. Also, the gloves so prized by our red brothers for the buffalo hunt are those used in the bean ceremony; the juices make them tough, resilient, and almost impervious to the savage attacks of the maddened bison. Muscatel is excellent with this dish.

How to Start the Old Station Wagon

Put on your sunglasses and walk out of the house to the old station wagon. Dig it out from under the tumbleweeds and sand that have buried it during the night. This sort of honest labor will usually allow a person to relate to the harsh, stringent beauty of the region.

Remark aloud on the brightness of the day and the way the sun, that makes the snowclad mountain peaks so dazzling, is blinding you. Stop your work now and again to feel the personal freedom that is yours as you realize that you are in a large, peaceful sink, like.

Light a cigarette and take a pull from a bottle of Muscatel. About now, it will "hit the spot."

Start the old station wagon, and sit in it for ten to fifteen minutes. Turn off the ignition, and return to the house. Oil your floor, as you tell guests about the old, original *vigas* above the dining area. Remark on how you plan to cut some piñon the following day, how you have been meaning to get to the lumber mill for some cheap kindling, and how you think it wise to begin buying your Muscatel by the case.

How to Make an Egg

Get a fresh yolk from a sleeping chicken, preferably one that has been born in the region. (They are the stringy, sand-colored ones.) Placing the yolk carefully on a clean, flat surface (the hood of an old station wagon is ideal), surround it with the precious albumen that you've collected over the winter. Be careful when lifting the yolk to slide the precious albumen beneath that you don't break it (the yolk); yolks are surprisingly sturdy, but do not respond well to rough handling.

When the yolk is "blurry" and its yellow color seems subdued, you will know that it is completely wrapped in the precious albumen. Any leftover precious albumen may be discarded, or used to mix colors with which to paint pictures of the mountains at sunset. *Do not use too much precious albumen* as a "wrapper" for your yolk, as this will result in an egg useful only for throwing at galas and fetes.

Now, carefully suck the slop and slime out of an eggshell through a small hole punched into its smaller end with a twig. (The crossbar of a small *ojo de Dios* will do nicely.) When the "glop" is sucked out and the eggshell completely empty, spit this matter out and take a pull on a bottle of Muscatel. Allow the interior of the eggshell to dry.

Holding the dry, empty eggshell in one hand, carefully spoon the "wrapped" yolk into it through the same hole used to drain it of its slop and slime. When the shell is full (and if you've been careful there will be no "wrapped" yolk left over), seal the hole in it with a piece of white chalk, a pebble, a grain of rice, or a simple paste made of flour or corn starch and water.

You have made one of Nature's most complete foods, using nothing but natural ingredients!

With the courage and optimism deeply rooted in her blood what she got from her huddled forebears as they yearned and breathed for nothing in the rollicking steerages of so many crack vessels speeding them to the joyous streets of New York's own Lower East Side (already, at this time, filled with some three or four thousand future politicians and stand-up comics), Helene stood, for hours and days on end, the abuse heaped on her by the locals, the store-owners, and the stern-jawed *turistas*, all of whom, as the poet said, "threatened her with insult," as did the lousy *sansculottes* la belle France's Chief Whore in her golden heyday before, wild with stolen vintages and the vicious idea that the *ancien régime* was out to, how can one say? fuck them over, perhaps, they decided to chop her sconce off of her.

So, breathing quietly in the perfumed and enchanted air one balmy evening, she thought aloud to Serge, deep off in the bracken that was making an unearthly music, that she thought she'd try her hands at selling odds and ends, disguised like a old Injun squaw.

An' so that you sell whate'er you list, Serge roared from a rippling rio, may the Lord of Music cast, as gamesters throw the bones, his poiple mantle of protection on your weary head! Then swam he about a-laving with much splashing while popeyed fish gazed on apace.

Some days later, an absolutely authentic-looking squaw hunkered down before a—what else?—art gallery, her homely yet mysterious wares spread out before her. A closer look proved what the reader may have suspected: it was Helene, her creamy skin tinted a swarthy shade by berry juice or some kinda fruits.

You like-um babushka? Helene said. Real Navajo. Funny signs and stuff straight from the Toltecs and Aztecs. Or this blue, pretty stuff we Injuns twistum silver around? Cheap and look good on your pretty wife, Meester.

John! Just look at that bald Jew-lady pretending to be an Indian squaw.

Let's get back in the station wagon, Miriam.

Plenty nice leaves, too, you cook-um up in old man's barley soup and he'll have a little lead in his pencil once again. Names like poetry. Smutwillow, piggesbush, crutmallow, purple pout, wanlip, cockeyes Nellie, crazysquaw, blackstocking, happysnatch, bigstiff, titsucker, Queen Bruce, two-in-her, griefbitcher, weeping Willie, all guaranteed to cause a hard-on that'll raise the old WASP right off the floor.

John? Do you think that . . .

The car, dear, the *car.*

Real *silver* babushka? Tasteful gouaches of maize nodding in the sirocco? Map of ancient walled city showing where Loew's Teotihuacan used to be? Piece of Coronado's fingernail? Snapshots in color of Indian mating rituals? My God, folks! Indians are persons too!

John, that spray of bigstiff might be just the thing for the motel windowsill . . . ?

Miriam!

Palooza blossoms? Midnight blusher? Chicano fly? Can I help it if I'm bald? I made these phony braids myself! That should count for sumpn!

The happysnatch goes with my new black lace peignoir, John. John?

Let's drive down to the waving grasses by the river and eat our hard-boiled eggs, dear.

That's the Rio sin Nombre and it's coised, you Lutheran bastard!

The woman is coising at us, John! I've heard that an Indian coise can follow you all your life long, and if particularly bad, can wind up with the most terrible results, things like maybe the children not getting accepted by the college of their choice! Oh, John! Please! The bouquet of titsucker would perfectly match my new wardrobe of magically sheer pantyhose in exciting fall colors!

Miriam, these ravolitos or whatever these greasers call them are getting cold.

Coronado's fingernail-cutting guaranteed to turn him into heap big fucker? Helene said. Two bits. I give to my brave and he make the old mission bells ring again, yes sir!

Hear the old redskin, honey? Wouldn't it be fun to do it on the kitchen table, just like the Hollywood stars?

Miriam, dear, the spick at the grocery store said that if we didn't drink this polekay in an hour it would turn into dynamite. Now, are we going to sit in the peaceful fields of sumptuously flowering local blooms and watch the sunlight glittering on the river, or are we going to hang around and get taken by this old kike woman?

John? Look! The purple pout has a little label on it that says, "PUT A PIECE OF ME IN YOUR PANTIES AND . . . WATCH OUT!"

Cheap Baptist motherfucker, Helene said into a pot. May all his white bread be dipped in olive oil!

John, I'm going to use my *own* money and buy just a little spike or two of this funny, sweet little smutwillow, *then* we'll go down to the river. Just *thinking* of these little leaves makes me want to unhook my figure-flattering all-in-one!

I'll wait in the purring station wagon, dear.

You make wise choice, white lady, Helene said. I guarantee that one sniff of this magical plant and the old cluck will have his fly open before you reach the edge of town.

Oh, I hope so, Miriam said, blushing. My latest issue of *Ladies' Life* says that there's nothing wrong with a gently acting aphrodisiac, or a touch of fantasy-sharing, or a half-hour of sixty-nine—as long as these things don't take the place of the normal, healthy marital relationship!

Ugh. You stick-um plant in his schnozz and give him hand-job while he drive and maybe that new carpeting you want-um be yours when you get back to Indianapolis.

How on earth did you know that we're from Indianapolis? Miriam marveled and, if truth be told, blenched a little.

Miriam! Miriam! These burrotis are beginning to leak!

Coming, darling, Miriam trilled, swinging her hips wildly as she ran to her husband.

Hope the Methodist putz comes in his pants, Helene said to the dry, hot winds of the Santa Anita, that, as usual, said nothing in reply.

So the days passed in a haze of heat, sun, and sandy winds, and Helene sold whatever she could to the jabbering tourists, set upon occasionally by real Indians, or fake Indians of long standing, or others who also bravely sold. And their pennies added up, and Blue worked on the cart and practiced his . . . well . . . let's say his "scales."

And always in the foreground of his mind, on, as it were, the front porch, even out at the little strip of grass by the curb where you put the garbage cans, one word: CALIFORNIA. Why had he never thought of this? he often mused to Helene over the crackling fire of an evening, sometimes, of a number of evenings. She mused back and the java then, aye! 'twould flow merrily, as if there were no tomorrow! Or, perhaps, as if tomorrow would never come! Even better. Or even, as if, when tomorrow came, as come it must, and would, that it would be the tomorrow of their dreams, a bright tomorrow, despite the fact that it might be gloomy or grey or raining, the idea, Blue patiently explained, that the phrase "bright tomorrow" was what they call a "figure of speech." Did Helene, sweet, hard-working Helene, understand? Did she? Hah? Huh? Whaddayasay, kid? Hey!

266

But Helene's eyes had closed on who knows what sweet dreams, and her husband, smiling gently, tenderly bent to kiss her and then softly, oh so softly, took her blanket. Did not Othello do the same on Desdemona? Or what?

The sun stared, hard, like the eyes of a cop, an American cop, a state trooper, perhaps.

Helene sat in said sun, shaking and shimmying, squawlike, sort of. A voice issued forth from the beads and feathers that adorned her head and face, the weird rat's-eyes and the buffalo-hump grease, the bone bells and pussy fangs.

You like-um Mayan dung shovel? Pure stone, direct from Gallup dig. Guaranteed that it killed two nosy missionaries.

Seeds for garden? Benny One-Ball tomaters invented by Xochitl as strawberry substitute. Fruit gettum big as medicine balls, good love-potion make young girl crazy to take drawers off in public place. Hot stuff!

Zankoid, wheedle, rompf, syzygy plants? Put in stew, make "gay" guests straight?

Silver babushka? Last one, going fast, made of old Nazi pipe-bowl covers? Brought to States by Hans Dieter Pogrom, the famous German who saved a Jew.

Dead petunia grackle?

Turquoise suspenders?

Imitation oilcloth made of plastic from World's Fair Indian Building?

TV-camera lens left at Wounded Knee by genuine Protestant assistant producer? Drop in ginger ale, keep-um cold for two weeks.

Gah?

Wooj!

Um-um?

You take zitzerella?

Ugh-um.

And as the sun fell rather heavily into the gloaming far beyond the formidable range past the sinuous Cobardes, that river wherein the legendary Big Cal was wont to bathe his chaps to the music of ethereal banjos an' mouth organs, Helene decided that she'd go into a new line of work.

Jist a few more passels o' days, mebbe a week er two, an' we'uns is like to hev sufficient ter push on out with a spankin' new sorta cart, on our last push ter Californy. Thus Serge, one night, between gouts of cascading arpeggios. How the moon slathered lambently! The Golden West is more than just a word! It is . . . a reality! How soon they'd know this, although Blue, in a sense, were we a fly on the wall, invisibly, almost, observing, knew it already.

I have figured a new dodge to grab up some green these last few days, his wife said in her oddly sturdy way. Motes of dandruff and other scalpish matter danced in the dancing firelight! Such is the mighty yelp of Nature!

Good, honey, mighty good, the courageous voice whispered to the grunting mesquite and occasional coyote that abounded here.

Oh, Serge! she breathed, and went to him, swiftly.

And, as Viña Delmar once wrote, in a prose that echoes and re-echoes down the corridors of time as long as prose shall live, he took her into his arms. The moon suddenly darted behind a cloud and there was nothing to be heard but the sound of the snapping fire and the gentle clatter of Helene's falling hair.

And what was Helene's "new dodge?" 'Twere to vend and push, door-to-door, to the sunblinded natives of this balmy clime, a trig, terse, and easily readable pamphlet on a heavy gloss stock what no home should lack, this:

The Booklet on Winter Gardening

Oftentimes, the harsh winter months spell an end very often to outdoor exercising and the beginning outset of the battle of the midriff bulge.

Winter gardening fun may not be the answer. However, oftentimes it may be the answer instead. It is an exciting way to beat those winter blues, but the best part is that one needn't have to be a Luther Burbank or a Chet Burpee to master this growing winter sport indoors. We can start with a getting in shape program.

Winter gardening programs were oftentimes thought, at one time, to be a European sport like jai-alai, but that has changed. It's popularity spells an end to all that, and it's popularity has increased tremendously in our United States recently due to several reasons, of which the fact that it is fairly inexpensive may be the answer. A $100.00 will usually spell the answer to providing all necessary equipment; it is relatively safe; and it can be mastered in a very short time in an exciting way, which is not the case with jai-alai, which also takes more room than we usually have to offer.

Due to several reasons, one can stop in the middle of the plot of land at any time for refreshments to help beat the battle of these winter blues. Exciting wine and a favorite wedge of cheese seems to be of tremendous popularity among gardeners.

Before attempting winter gardening, oftentimes a conditioning program providing all relatively safe and fairly inexpensive equipment should be followed. The following exciting program was heartily recommended by Cuddie Doron, gardening pro at Penshurst, and may be the answer to mastering the sport.

1. Slowly, do ten ¾ knee bends very slowly and relatively safely. Never do ¾ of a full knee bend, although, this is tremendously popular among European sports, like jai-alai.

2. While standing, do forward splits halfway with the necessary equipment. A favorite item among gardeners seems to be wine and cheese wedges, a fairly exciting way to stretch the groin and thighs, and an inexpensive way to beat those midriff blues. Alternate each leg ten times before attempting to alternate each other leg.

3. While sitting in a chair in an exciting way, rotate your ankles clockwise, due to several reasons, and then oftentimes counter-clockwise, alternating each leg and ankle to spell an end to it's blues. Repeat ten times, ¾ of an hour, until one can stop due to an increased popularity of tremendous European refreshments.

4. While standing at any time, with all relatively safe equipment, to stretch the groin and ankles, alternate, in a very short time, your arms ¾ of the way from your knees to your sides and then to waist level, while rotating your thighs to shoulder level. Never do a full arm alternation while rotating your thighs, although, this is an exciting way to beat those jai-alai programs.

5. Lastly, practice balancing on one foot while spelling an end to ten full knee bends, and rotating your ankles in an exciting way. Alternate each foot and stretch your groin; at one time this was thought to be a European favorite, like wedges of cheese. Although not required, it is advisable to have at least one relatively safe and very short lesson with the club pro before "hitting the soil." This is to insure spelling an end to those winter blues and to covering any different aspect one might encounter with a fairly inexpensive though exciting European.

Now had our two rolling scones heaped up a pittance. Each night, when Helene trooped "home" from her schlepping, Blue added her shekels to the steady-growing pile beneath the mattress, if they had a mattress. Our narrator, so to speak, cannot remember if he gave them a mattress, and, true to his craft, refuses to check the manuscript, tattered, dog-eared, and stained, of course. Well, fuck *him*! *Now* they have a mattress!

Note this steadily growing pile of coins, plus some tired looking Federal Reserve Notes which the guvmint backs up with mighty ships, planes, and missiles! Blue laughed. We have got enough.

Thank the Lord of Hosts, Helene breathed at last.

Pero, Blue cautioned, we should have but a bit more to take care of odds and shards of thises and thats as we make our final push through howling sands and awesome vistas! Just a few more bucks, and we will have done. Besides, I need but a day or two more to perfect the harmonic subtleties of that grand old tune, "Green Is the Street for Godolphin."

Once more into the breech? Helene said, all perky above her secretly cascading heart.

If you want to talk dirty, it's jake with me, but yes! We need another few hours of simple, pleasant work from you. And I have just the thing, given me this morning by a genuine *vaquero* waiting for a baloney on roll, heavy on the mustard, and a malt liquor. How the sun glanced off his buckle straps and straining lanyards! It is a surefire item, big with tourists, shading toward the informational and historical like a serious TV show. Here it is! If I was you I'd start first thing in the morn, for tourists rise up at the first sure sign of crowded dawn in these here parts!

And so they did! And Helene, Helene was there to meet them as they poured forth from Howard Johnson's, in colorful camera straps and plastic shoes!

CORONADO'S FINGERNAIL
An Relick of the Mysterious West

Lost in the obscure haze of history for many hundreds of years, this relic was found in a stolen hotel towel under mysterious circumstances by James "Jimbo" or "Jizz" Zoltan, a humble drummer who had settled in the sterile splendors of the valley just west of the Pecos with his small but rapidly growing family. Professor Bracken Tarnish, Director of the Archaelogy and Human Life-Interests Department at Central Pecos University, wrote: "There is no doubt in my mind or in the minds of my colleague, Miss Wanita Hips, that this is indeed the index fingernail of Coronado, or as my colleagues in the History and Life-Enhancing Studies Department insist on calling him, de Coronado." A new method of dating and placing items from digs was used to confirm the Professor's suspicions, the method known as "egg-90," which consists of comparing the composition of an eggshell whose age is known to within a century or so, with the item unearthed from the dig. "When I saw that the eggshell looked just like this paring I knew we were home free," Professor Tarnish smiled. "Then it was just a matter of proving that the fingernail was, indeed, Coronado's, and not that of his trusted lietenant, Bruce de Vásquez y Chinche. It was fairly easy to do this, but for the present we'd—Miss Hips and I—prefer to keep our testing methods private."

Mr. Zoltan, who has since moved to a small development in the area known as East Pecos, has said that the fingernail was found—"fell out of," he claimed—in a towel that he dug up from the flooring of his home one Saturday when he was tearing up his floor. The towel, according to Mr. Zoltan, crumbled at the touch of the family mattock, and in the moldering debris there was seen a small, glowing object in the shape of a crescent moon. About to smash it to powder with an ax-handle provided him by his wife, Ceniza, he has said, on national television, that "something" stopped him. He had, he maintains, a feeling that the fingernail was somehow trying to communicate with him, and that, in his words, it was "not the fingernail of your everyday spick or greaseball, but one of which was from some big-shot honcho." "Honcho," Mr. Zoltan, a veteran of the Korean War explained, is a Korean argot type word for "Chief" or "Sport" or "Champ."

Packing the item in an insulated chest filled with ice cubes, Mr. Zoltan drove to Zuñi Agricultural and Technical College, where, he insists, a group of Science-Faculty members "had a high old time funnin' with me." He has noted that the Chairman of the Department of Legumes and Cosmetics, the Regius Professor of Market Refrigeration, and the Visiting Assistant Professor of Calculator Maintenance "made wise remarks," among which were: "You're full of s——!" "Tell me another one, hunkie." "What have *you* been smoking?" "Take a f—— walk, you dumb Polack." The members of the faculty deny that this incident ever occurred, and say that they were under the impression that Mr. Zoltan was trying to sell them some frozen paprika, as he had done many times in the past. The College Dean of Administration, Wally Coat, wrote, "Don't know what to employ with papreeka and don't want none, now or ever."

Professor Tarnish feels a touch of sorrow when he considers the *faux pas* made by the members of Zuñi A&T, but says that such things are all luck. "Had my distinguished colleagues over to Zuñi not been writing grant proposals they would have known what to look for," he insists.

The fingernail, which is on permanent public display in the lobby of the Buenos Dias Brewery offices in central Encantada, is said to have mysterious powers, one of them being that it somehow plays tunes. It also turns into a turquoise bracelet once a month, and shoots of maize occasionally spring out of it. A guard at the vault where the nail was kept during scientific testing, says that one night he heard it playing "Cielito Lindo," and that it sounded something like a kazoo. What is fascinating about this story is that in Coronado's "Ay, Mi Vida!" written during his last quiet years in Mexico City, he writes that "el instrumento de boca que me gusta más está el quazoo."

Tourists have been flocking to the small city of Encantada to see the fingernail, and tickets, nominally priced at $5.00, have been virtually unavailable for weeks.

Such is another Mystery of this Enchanted Land!

But stand in the sun as she would, e'en garbed in a "tailored suit," so to speak, with her gossamer hair tied in a neat bun and her flat-heeled shoes sternly planted in the dust, Helene could not push this shit on the ever-shifting crowds of gawkers. They even insulted her, to, like they say, the tunes of:

Fuck off, weedface!
Don't touch her, you don't know where her hands have been!
That "bun" of hers looks like Alan King's "face."

271

That's just a tabloid-newspaper clipping, you fake bitch!

And sundry other vile insults the like of which it is our fervent wish that you won't hear them, or your loved ones either, in a month of Sundays, despite the fact that the voice of the people, loud in the land like unto as always, is the voice of the sovereign will of Great Mankind! So the uncaring beetles stumbled against her as the sand whirled in crazy motes as it has whirled and will forever whirl, so long as the sun shall clamber wearily into the sky far above the lambent plang of the beautiful yet harsh plains where—was it only yesterday?—the Bison sang and galloped to the lilting tune of the wind in the harsh cactus-peat and dropping figwort.

She returned to Blue in tears, her bun undone, her "suit" in disarry, her tiny shoes a-scuff and caked with the harsh mud of the plains on which the Great Shaggy Bison once sang their haunting song in violent bellows to the echoing rocks that sometimes suddenly fall off the scarps and craggy brows of yawning chasms, there to (or here to) plunge into a well-deserved . . . oblivion! Yes, Nature was and shall be cruel, despite our petty attempts at taming her inscrutable ways. The Marquis de Sade oft whispered this in the moonlight to his companions. Now *Helene* was aware of this! But perhaps it was . . . too late!

It is not too late! Serge cried, never, *never* say that it is too late, oh my darling! My puffball dandelion! Dry your eyes and warm your dukes around a cup of jamoke, fresh made, with funny little tasteless cookies huddled together on the saucer that it would be wise to place on your knees or lap since with both of your mitts cupped around the life-giving joe, it will be impossible, or nearly so—and here he gave his wild, rending laugh!—to hold the saucer!

No, it is not too late, Helene said, for she was not averse to going along with her hub for a laugh or so, since it had become obvious to her lately that he often talked funny, funny . . . *crazy* things! But I can't flog these fingernail items. And I'm tired . . . so tired . . . I want to go to Californy.

And so we shall! But don't cry. Why, why are you crying?

A man said that I . . . a man said that . . . he called me "weedface." Another said other dirty things, like "gashface" and "shit-hair." Yet another, in a strange sorta cap with some green plastic over his eyes said that I looked like a plate of grits and greens. I don't think I can go on feeling this way about my essential value as a person and with many self-doubts that grow and grow and finally reduce me to inertial cessation.

My beloved! Such woids as these, but, are pet names to turn aside the dazzle of your beauty. How long has it been since I enumberated your charms?

Many a windswept moon!

Then let me rectify all this while I sauté a fillip of reviving hash. And he did, thus:

« 57 »

Le Blason Médaillon

Upon your face your nose sits, like a jewel;
And shines, white milkweed, with its glist'ring grease.
Its bursting blackheads make a man a fool;
For jet are they, like Eros's valise!
Your bulbous eyes are cherries, both cerise,
And over them hulk brows, like dark toadshade;
They meet, like elves who couple in a glade.
Your mouth's a splash of dead rugosa rose,
Whose nether lip descends as mad cascade;
And in that mouth your tooth like pigweed glows.

Below that witching cavern shakes your chin;
The purest tint of bloodroot that I know,
All speckled o'er with fire pink like sin.
Your neck's a ringer for a mound of snow
On city streets, and sports a hue like crow.
That vast, wise brow as pale as buttonbush
Seels close your thoughts, as dense as thickest mush;
And Hermes' flying feet envy your ears.
But best of all, your scalp rains down, my thrush,
A scurf that hides these charms that I hold dear.

« 58 »

In Which
the Desert Sands
Become a Colorful Riot

Once more emboldened with sturdy wherewithal and other necessities of provisioning, and with the chink of silver chinking in their chunky purses, they started on what we now know will be the last push toward that ever-elusive goal. After some days and nights of traveling, they entered a land rich in strangeness and saw sands, plain desert sands, of which they had seen aplenty in the past fortnight or so, even a month! But this sand was somehow . . . different, and with quickened pulses, they stood and looked at it all as if they had not seen it before, or as if they were seeing it for the first time, or as it must have looked, or seemed, to those first plucky Esquimaux who walked down over the ice and snow of what is now the great city of pulsing Sacramento! How fresh it must have looked, or *seemed* to look to those hardy aborigines. And so it was to Blue and Helene, who pulsed as all men must when e'er they pull up short in awe!

Here—were there but something to drink and bathe in, something to wash their garments in, clean of dirt and grime, not to say the grit that is part and parcel of such climes, and notwithstanding their nicety of attention to personal grooming such dirt is an unavoidable problem, one that even General Custer faced (and no greater cleanliness buff ever lived and sported in these parts)—here, they thought as one—such was the beauty of the "spot"—they might live forever, far from the tumult and corruption of the city, live in peace and tranquillity, even going so far as to postpone, and indefinitely, if need be, Serge's search for the goal of all this his long quest, the fruition of these hard travails, the Phrase to make all chime as one in Beauty! Yes.

For they had indeed come to a strange, a bewitched and shimmering land of profligate colors, shifting, blending, shining in the bright limpid sunshine all the way to the horizon, and perhaps—beyond! Who can tell? Not the ardent chigger nor the blear-eyed philosopher prone beneath his midnight oils and watercolors. No living thing stirred in all that vast expanse of tints, shades, and tones, save

274

perhaps for the quick scuttling Gila monster dragging a placid cow into his lair, or upsetting a faded Dixie cup in his abrupt panic, a Dixie cup dropped generations ago from the beak of a bluejay or chickadee who, though long dust, lives on in the songs that weave their way into the sky of nights around many a long-decayed bunkhouse. All was still, yet all was a riot of color.

Blue and Helene stood in the midst of these breathtaking colors, silent and awed, still . . . still as an unravished bride in a silent, perhaps Theda Bara or Lillian Gish or even the most silent of them all, Garbo. This they somehow knew without speaking, without uttering a sound.

There, before their astonished eyes, their worshipful glances, the colors seemed to shift and blend, yet curiously stand out clearly as crystal too, yes, shift and blend and meld and mix and slide together in a veritable riot. Some, yes, some clashed and exploded! Some slided mysteriously, almost imperceptibly into other colors—and all, all in riotous profusion!

It's what I've always dreamed of, yearned for, cared deeply about, Serge whispered, almost as if speaking for the first time. To stand here, alone, or with another person or two, or even a small group as long as they didn't chatter and yak it up—and here he squeezed her negligible hand in his manly one—lost, dreaming, rapt almost in that opulent, that majestic, that unearthly *riot* of colors! I could almost stand here forever, with but a few short breaks for meals, of course.

Yes, Serge, she beamed, with a small look of concern. You must eat regularly, but lightly.

Darling!

But you have promises that you must keep on going for, she said. Like the man who must let go of the appletree limb so that he can fly wildly through the air and into his neighbor's garden to hoe it like he said he would.

How well he knew! For hadn't he, as a boy, often propelled himself through the summery air on one of his many boyish errands? The truth of his wife's simple statement struck him in his deep heart's core. Yes, he must buckle! And, buckling, the great fire that would gush forth then would match, in its wild and almost incredible riot of colorful flames, this color, or colors, lavishly promiscuous before, behind, and everywhere! Yet it *had* been a wonderful dream. And somehow, the lushness seemed a kind of omen of success, the colors seemed to portend a certain victory, the innate beauty of the place seemed to assure a happy conclusion. But why? Who can know the secrets of the earth's wordless messages, especially when they cannot be heard? Yet they were somehow *there*, as is the pickerel in late July.

Look! Blue said, his voice become a veritable chocking block of awe. Like the spotless and chaste lingerie of a benevolent dictator's faithful wife and political confidante, some of the sands are a desert, whisper, winter white, a marshmallow, like star chickweed, oconee bells, swamp lily, or whitewash snowberry; some, akin to the pure thoughts of a Methodist minister, shine a sort of crystal, reminding one of grass of Parnassus, floating hearts, and goldthread; still others fill the misty eyes like the snow in a Christmas TV commercial and glitter as antique linen and pyxie, mountain sandwort, wood anemone, false violet, or the chuckling thimbleweed! Then there are the dunes that shine like the teeth of a fascist movie star, all chinchilla, rapt in tones of arrowhead, vervain, devil's bit, foamflower, and lizard's tail. And what about those that look like the socks of a Jewish tennis player? They are not sweet cream for nothing, lambent as fly poison, turkey beard, yucca, feather-bells, and pokeweed, not to mention shepherd's purse and enchanter's nightshade. The knolls white as the contract ceding public lands to oil companies? Sure! Look, they pulse bone white, similar to boneset, catnip, titi, dodder, and jimsonweed. And shimmering like a heaven devoid of the stinking poor, champagne white of course, those hills all goldenseal, nodding ladies' tresses, silverrod, pennywort, Queen Anne's lace, pearly everlasting, showy orchis, and the Venus flytrap; and now my eye falls upon a vision of purity like the clouds over luxurious Palm Springs, home of vague moronic moguls—a kind of white smoke and ocean spray inheres therein, bringing to mind the aura of bloodroot, colicroot, and death camas. And next to that sprawled luxury, yet another, peach white as a pimp's Cadillac, all over goatsbeard, bouncing Bet, sweet Cicely, and oxeye Daisy, not to forget painted Trillium, Carolina Anemone, and Daisy Fleabane. Some of the smaller mounds are as blank as the sound of Aaron Copland and the taste of American pizza, warm white in the sun, and undefiled as smaller pussytoes. And there, far off, so dim that one can hardly see that it is candid white as the mushroom cloud of a nuclear bomb, a hill all antique and cameo, sad as hobblebush, rue, and nightshade, still as one-flowered cancer root.

And at the edge of that gorgeous hill, blending into it, a small range of mesas, Blue, Helene gasped. See? All green as Kelly, shamrocks, seafrost, and the sea; as crème de menthe, lime fizz, sage, moss, and doublemint. Green as a goddess! And that luscious green of money, that stuff that politicians are not in it for, that isn't everything, that is not all that important, that the poor don't really deserve, that the rich work so hard to get, that bestows wisdom and moral superiority, that there are certain things people won't do for, that people are not ashamed of taking, that it's good to know the value of, that doesn't grow on trees, that congressmen vote themselves regretfully, that has no conscience. Just look at that rich glow! 'Tis the same shade as carrion flower, marijuana, stinging nettle, rattlesnake master, and false, very false hellebore, and also looks a little like the color of the bluebeard lily. It is a vivid panorama of the world! Purity and pelf playing at old sixty-nine!

Perception, as they say here and there, is thine, adorable doxy, Blue said. And as you were finishing your idyllic bout of nomenclature, it chanced that the odd desert light, waxing and prospering, as it will do at this hour of the day, has revealed, see? right up close, sands and such that seemed but ordinary in the shade, but can now be seen as reddish pink, or pinkish red, this sprawl of turfish stuff at our feet the color of the beans of the happy, happy poor, or perhaps the delicate flush of radiation lesions, a species of rosetone, ginger, fire dance, fiesta, one might say peachy creamy red! Looks sort of like eyebright or rough blazing star, crazyweed or goat's rue. And to the right, fantastic ridges, the lambent tones of the polluted Passaic or the blood used to dye the Soviet flag, adazzle like unto tomato, lobster, sleepy pink, and russet, flying the cracking banner of the locoweed, the obedient plant, the crab's-eye, the curly dock, and the wild bleeding heart. To the left, pristine and pregnant as the discarded sanitary napkin in the executive secretary's washroom and the Carlisle dressings scattered about on Heartbreak Ridge, radiant as tile, paprika, and shrimp, small whorls that bring to mind Sheep Sorrel, Cardinal Flower, Coral Bean, Moss Campion, Herb Robert, Rose Pogonia, Bull Thistle, Rose Vervain, Wild Basil, Virginia Rose, and the ravishing Rhodora, the queen of the prairie, as well as many other bloody folk. And out there by the dry arroyo, a narrow strip as crimson as the opium poppy and as pink as the nipples of the incestuous father's little girl—note the mélange of bricks, maroons, cherries, and burgundies, like nothing so much as wild coffee, ragged Robin, and the misnamed live-forever. Beyond the same arroyo, candy red as the blush that ne'er suffuses the book reviewer's face and April pink as the stain at the bottom of a sputum cup, another strip all spreading dogbane, New York ironweed, and Deptford pink, stirred in with Jack-in-the-pulpit and pinesap. And last, almost impossible to see, but throbbing crimson as the lights of classy Vegas, and persimmon as numberless necks in Dixie, are a clutch of majestical mounds of blooming clay that splash the weary earth with a bright thrum of bee balm, salvia, corn cockle, teasel, rabbit-foot clover, swamp smartweed, wild garlic, and steeplebush. How it all broods and beats like the foolish heart that has, as it is said, its reasons for doing so!

I see and am justifiably astonished, Helene said, trembling in the Beauty extravagant before her. But it seems e'en as we look that the reddish-pinkish stuff is metamorphosing into that happy color, orange! It sprawls delightfully like as that famous herbicide that helped achieve an honorable peace, like orange ice and scarlet pimpernel; like the millions of California oranges bulldozed and buried so the spicks and niggers cannot have 'em, like candelero orange and spotted touch-me-not; or as gay party lanterns by the dead and festering Potomac, as bandeau velour and flame azalea; or the sound of screams from magic Ulster, bittersweet, oh bittersweet, oh climbing bittersweet; it also has the gorgeous touch of napalm killing terrorists, of which there is a passel, like flame, like trumpet creepers; as well as the formidable flash from the sportsman's rifle, tiger orange, butterfly weed; some of it seems to wondrously implode, like the rocket falling softly on a hospital, all cinnabar and Carolina mallow; or else it seems the sultry glow o'er burning Southern California, coral beach and orange hawkweek in its subtlety; there's a tiny dune as bright as fire from pre-emptive strikes, as hot as orange jazz, as dense as hoary puccoon; and huddled next that mix, another staggeringly similar to the rash of secondary syphilis, kind of apricot or turk's-cap Lily; the huge area blending into the horizon far is the spit and image of hearty and nutritious ravioli in a can, amber, pumpkin, orange milkwort; and the wall of mesas to the right shine like the hair of has-been actresses, harsh as tigerlilies, frizzy as the yellow fringed orchid. And now, see, it is changing back again!

And as always, Blue continued, as certain as cheek is by jowl, and foot is in mouth, and elbow is an ass, the magisterial yellow plotzes languidly next its orange buddy. Dig on that alchemically transmuting mix and stew and huge ragout quiv'ring in—what else?—the yellow sun! At times it variously seems the color of the healthful smog breathed by the wondrous folk who live in Beverly Hills, the lemon peel in the drunken editor's fourth Martini, the wide and bone-deep streak down the anchorman's back, the tons and tons of butter rotting in cold storage, the pus from soldiers' wounds, the lovely color of orphanage sheets, the urine puddles in tenement hallways, the discreet stain in the fashion model's underpants, the dainty callous on the First Lady's dainty foot, the tortillas of the chiseler welfare Mex, the hard-hitting editorial against the injured and insulted, and that strange creamy goo that is called "mustard" in the Heartland! It's all we love, and seems to be together and apart, eggnog, lemon, harvest gold, sunshine, primrose, peach parfait, curry, forsythia, and too, a sky of buttermilk, a sunbeam, a mandarin, maytime, chiffon pie, the crazy carrousel, and buxom blondes in sunlight! All those things made to resemble stuff in Nature's woods and brakes and dales and glades and bosks—yellow thistle, yellow flag, golden club, yellow lady's slipper, showy rattlebox, golden alexanders, smooth false foxglove, evening primrose, common tansy, broom snakeweed, spicebush, pussy willow, celandine, frostweed, the giant sunflower, and the humble, hoary, hairy, and historical hedge mustard. Thus yellow, like a tidal wave of piss, doth engulf the world!

But, my darling boon companion, Helene wavered spousily, there is another couple hectares out there that must needs be enumerated; I mean those that celebrate your name: Blue! You got a fleet blue, a blue lake, a bluebell, a surf blue, a little boy blue, a chalk blue, a blue sky, a blue mist, a crystal blue, all mushed together in a kind of haze and cloud like so much starlight! How it all brings back to me the humble flowers that I used to grow in windowboxes, and gather in my yearning arms like so many . . . humble flowers! The bluet, the common blue violet, the blue curl and the chicory, the blue flag and the cutesy monkey-flower, the blue toadflax, indigobush, leadplant, blue salvia, Texas bluebonnet, wild blue phlox, and the wild blue Mary, what a broad! And how can I neglect to give honorable mention to the bluebeard lily and the silly little pokeweed? I can't. All of it together brings to mind certain emblems of our proud and firm-jawed civilization, blue as blue can be, like the minds of black men, the blood-lines of moronic families, the bruises on a neglected child, the vile stories that rot the moral fiber of our doughboys just before they get their limbs blown off, the lacy garter on the homely bride's scrawny thigh, the clear eyes of our most ad-mired killers, cheap gin in bad light, the circles under the beggar's eyes, the per-fumed exhaust from the Rolls-Royce, King James's Jesus' eyes, a bad Monday for the small investor, and the ruffled shirts worn beneath pink dinner jackets by sparkling celebrities. One might think the whole world this suffusing color, just like Alice did her gown when she primped in every shop window.

Whoever said, Serge shone, that you are but a nit was talking through his bowl-er! And if you'll notice, that blue on occasion shifts in the spanking sunshine to its bro, the pulsing purple and vivacious violet! Do you feast your eyes, my sister! There's the royal purple, like sea lavender, that the dumbest people are invaria-bly born to; the purple wine like the eyes of a mugger's victim, bright as sea lav-ender; the blushing violet of the battered wife's back and buttocks, something like the sea lavender; the wild orchid of the corona of the slum arsonist's match flame, burning cold as sea lavender; the deep purple of the plums given political ass-nuzzlers, dark and noble as the sea lavender; the lavender mood—sort of like the . . . sea lavender!—of Presidential proclamations; the puky purple of the old office clerk's black suit, the sheen of sea lavender; the purple haze in which the House of Representatives is wrapped, dim as the dumb sea lavender; the pale violet of the blues by whites, thin as the sea lavender; the lavender mood of a tux that Hugh Hefner might wear, loud as sea lavender; the orchid burst of high-priced suede, the lushness of sea lavender, worn by whores with hearts of purest shit; and the lilac brook, close-grown with scintillant sea lavender, that tints and tones the tooth marks on the lady lobbyist's inner thighs.

And now as the shades are falling, sternest schlepper, Helene peeped, and cimmerian night creeps up and around the shifting dunes beyant, I seem to see the furthest acres of these sands plunging into brown. Yes, I am correct! Color most germane to this great industro-technocracy! if you will pardon the coinage for a nonce. We see mocha, mahogany, nutmeg, rawhide, chocolate, cocoa, java, seal, coffee, tobacco, manila, caramel, potter's clay, and the ducal dusty sage! How it brings to mind the poison sumac! The prairie smoke! The giant reeds! How one is forced to think of barnyard grass and skunk cabbage and the spotted coalroot! These things rhyme and chime and clang in a poetic orgy of cognates with the things that are still not perfect with the world, although, by God, our leaders never cease from trying to perfect it all for us, the folk! I think of the mud of glorious battlefields and the tons of shit forever roaring 'neath our cities, towns, and hamlets to the rivers and the seas. Of the color of our world leaders' anuses, a common touch, and the cockroaches in the walls of the White House. Of the deep interior of a TV-producer's head and the color of the Broadway theater's soul. Of the lowly turd—by whom forgot?—in a toilet bowl in the Plaza and the once cream-colored paint of an unemployment office. Of the cigar-stained teeth of a corporation lawyer and the ultimate color of a best-seller's pulpy leaves. And of the sky that gleams o'er Pittsburgh and the smell of an Army base. So is the whole world, it seems, in a brown study.

You've hit the old bolt squarely on its hexagonal noggin, my love, said Blue, and as you talked, the sun slid further down so everything is now that greyness or that blackness that makes one think of sterner stuff, like smoke and steel and battleships! Like charcoal, famished gulls, and slate! Like putty! Like aluminum! Like the Wehrmacht's uniforms! What is this dimness but that of the call-girl's stockings, the ghostly air of Ellis Island, the mood of the welfare office? What but the tuxedo of the self-made man, the reform politician's limousine, the corporation president's hard stool? What but the motives of the Pentagon, the migrant worker's future, the rats of Harlem? What but Miss America's pubic hair, the interior of presidents' graves, and spunky Harry Truman's spot in Hell? And all held up, my dear, on that great, grim, nameless plant on which the universe does sway and disappear in mammoth chunks into the godless void.

The night fell suddenly.

« 59 »

"La Musique
et les mauvaises
herbes," Concluded

XVII AN ATTACK OF MALADY

When a student has some annoyances with the health, he takes himself to the clinic of the University. There he finds some doctors who make all to him possible for the cure. The day before some exams, there is a crowd of golden bricks who wish to find asylum at the clinic, because habitually the life there is enough calm. Last Thursday, André is going to consult the doctor about a small malady. When he is return to the old boarding house, Émile wishes to learn all the details of his visit because he is a nosing type.

ÉMILE: Hey then, my old man! How goes the bad?

ANDRÉ: Not too much bad, thanks. They have given on me a medicine what has already aided me.

ÉMILE: But what is that what you have? Is it that they have found something serious bad, like a "bull clap" or an old Joe?

ANDRÉ: My goodness, no! What are you trying to make me have the air of—a downed-out jijolo?

ÉMILE: No, my bosoms bud. I have a care on you is what.

ANDRÉ: It is but a little strain in the groinal region what is not very grave. It endures no more than forty-eight hours. But the doctor wants that I pay it attention and rest in the bed.

ÉMILE: Holy cripes! How does one achieve this strain? Is it from making the exercise or the imbecile jog or some things like this?

ANDRÉ: Ha! Ha! Ha! It is an exercise what calls itself "too much of crazy sex acts."

ÉMILE: Ah, now I see this. And Suzanne? Does she have the bad in the similar region? Pardon my rude quiz, if you please, but I know how you like to make with her the bizarre stunts.

281

ANDRÉ: Well . . . I must confess that the lady in these case is not *solely* Suzanne.

ÉMILE: Aha! It is also Catherine, the maid of your house, the young patootie of formidable biscuits?

ANDRÉ: No. That young lady is innocent of this case. It is—you will keep the mouth mummed?—my Professor of Bassoon, Mrs. Chaud.

ÉMILE: Whoom! Mrs. Chaud! If I could make a sex act on this gorgeous lady for five moments, I will permit my groinal region to have a bad for a week! She is some tootsie!

ANDRÉ: In effect! You should regard her when she has disrobed off her garments. I thought that I would go a piece deranged!

ÉMILE: I don't think I have the desire to chats with you on this topic. It makes me to stimulate too much.

ANDRÉ: I have a horror to speak on this to Suzanne. And I have also a horror to terminate off these connections with Mrs. Chaud. I am too dipsy on this lady.

ÉMILE: Do you wish that I might become a pal with Suzanne? I perhaps can make it easy to you to tell a "see you later" on her.

ANDRÉ: Boys! I have the fear that I can see in you like you are a cellophane. I have the aware, my raunchy mate, that you have the huge hot on Suzanne. And now it appears to you that you can do sex on her by the hours without having a care that I will make a harsh pummel on your face.

ÉMILE: Do you tell to me then that you have the plan to make sex acts on both Suzanne and Mrs. Chaud? What a greedy cupid things you are!

ANDRÉ: Yes, I have this plan, you sly popsqueak! And if I can, I make also a sex with Monique Gaine, Sophie Jupon, Marie Mamelle, and by damn it, I even make a sex on Alice Cuisse without a care that she is a levee!

ÉMILE: She is what calls itself a dike, you dumbo thing!

ANDRÉ: I don't care a piss jar how it calls itself! You are not to make the free on Suzanne!

ÉMILE: I don't believe in the ears I have. I think maybe that you would also do a soiled act with the men, maybe even with the wolfs and the zebras and the damn walruses. Whew!

ANDRÉ: It is only on ladies what I enjoy to make dirty things. But I don't care of your stupid ideas on me what ring like the usual shits from the homo-types of persons. Leave me alone and go play on yourself, eh?

Émile makes a storm out of the chamber. He is having a furious rage because he cannot bear up that André has such a fortunate career with ladies of all age and shapes. André rests in the bed reading on Suck My Whip, *an indecent novel. All the ladies of this narrative have the image to his brains of Suzanne, Monique, and Mrs. Chaud. He is a satyr type of bozo in every direction!*

XVIII A BIRTHDAY TREAT

In the leavy burg where André and Suzanne make their studies, there is a somewhat nice Chinks restaurant where they go for to fete the birthdays or on other important events, such as when Suzanne find out she has not got a bun in her oven. Evidently, this place costs much dear, but they do not regret for a long time the bucks who they dispense for a masterpiece of Chinks chow.

SUZANNE: Oh boys! We owe to command a dinner à la Chinks from a start until the end. Do you have enough of the mazuma, my potato-face?
ANDRÉ: I have ought to make of the economies during three months for to pay for this chow. My gosh sake, your chummy pal, Jacques Derrière, tell to me that I am squiz an eagle until he make a shits—I don't know what he mean of this, but I think it means of being too much cheap.
SUZANNE: Do not bring that wormhead up on me, eh? I do not have any taste for him for some times. Fuck on him!
ANDRÉ: Very good. I have want that this dinner of my birthday it will be perfect. I believe I have all the mazuma of which we will be having the needs. What a oddbell word is this "mazuma," no? It give me to chuckle.
SUZANNE: I believe that it is the name the ancient Aztec chieftain call himself, for that he was so flushed. But who gives a care? Let us go ahead and command a real Chinks dinner. Anyhow, I have some mazuma what I can give to you if you will have a need on this.
ANDRÉ: In what fashion have you gained mazuma, my casabas?
SUZANNE: I am having some jobs from the Bureau of Placement over here and down there.
ANDRÉ: Not bad, swits! I hear on you. Now, what is it that you wish for to commence on?
SUZANNE: I ought to think on my lovely shape, for I would not be too content to have too grand a buttock, and finish up with the looks of . . . Mrs. Chaud, for an instance. But I have too much of a famish tonight, and I want to take a soup made from the bird-eye and loco weeds.
ANDRÉ: Hey, syrups, do not have a worry on to get the looks of the buttock of Mrs. Chaud! She has this for the reason of laying down on these always. Ha! Ha!

But a damn hell on these professors tonight, eh? This soup, it is that cold one in what they place the small beetles? Me too, I wish to essay the son of a guns! Now, tell me of what tempts you as a meat plate.

SUZANNE: I want to have a goose balls in the chocolate and green peppers and onions gravy, what calls itself the swit and bitter . . . Say, you seem to have a large idea on the sex lifes of Mrs. Chaud—do you still continue to make the occasion of an intimate act on her, you two-timely rodent?

ANDRÉ: But no! What type of a chap do you take me? I was having to make the joke what makes around in the School of Music. Be a nice young lady, eh, and permit us for a single time not to look for a henshit quarrel!

SUZANNE: All right, sugars. It is just that I have the venetian blind on this lady professor.

ANDRÉ: You have the what on her?

SUZANNE: Oh craps! How does it call itself? I have lost this words. Ah! I have the *jealousy* on her!

ANDRÉ: Jesus in the heaven, you are some time a silly pussy. Venetian blind! Ha! Ha! Ha!

SUZANNE (*weeping of hot tears*): You are some vile oafs.

(*Suzanne honks off her nose onto the foulard.*)

ANDRÉ: Oh, my wild tickle, I beg a clemency. Let us go ahead on the chow, if you please?

SUZANNE: Yes, but have a care of your loosed mouth, eh?

ANDRÉ: In effect. I am going to command the rotted eggs poached up in sour milk. And I see that the ritzy cookies are served on this plate. Whum, what a thrill on the jade palate!

SUZANNE: Me, I would like some chicken grease with the smashed-up garlic. Is it that this will go with the goose balls?

ANDRÉ: These ought to go exceedingly strong as an ensemble. And what salad will you make a choose on?

SUZANNE: What I choose will be the Three Onions Special—the red onion, the white onion, and the Bermudas onion what has on this the dressing of scallions and shallots in the oil.

ANDRÉ: My goodness! Ha! Ha! Ha!

SUZANNE: Why is it that you make this big laugh on me? I do not believe rilly that I am content to be a pal this evening, birthday or not. You appear as too crude and nasty on me.

ANDRÉ: You are making a big big vex to me, softy, with this petty sulks. I am making the laugh for that with the onions and garlics and scallions and shallots—and who in a blaze could know what is it you will command for the dessert!—I am having the image that I must look over my shoulders when I make some sex on you later, or else I might have a swoon. Ha! Ha! Ha!

SUZANNE: Then make a sex until your hose falls off on this fat sluts, Mrs. Chaud, you decay of a smut!

Suzanne has great fury and commences to throw on André the china of the Chinks as well also as the knifes and forks and spoons, the glasses, the pitcher full up of water, the napkin, and the vase of faked flowers of the table. Then she whoomps on his head with a chair and a small moment after makes the thrust with her dainty feets upon his bottoms and soon after into a groin. It appears like a curtain for this romance, eh?

XIX THE END OF THE DAY

For the students, one of the best moment of the day comes in the evening when all the studies are terminated. The buddies of the old boarding house reunite in some chambers for the gossip in ensemble before couching themselfs. These reunions are never organized: they arrive spontaneously without premeditation.

Eleven hours are coming to ring. One hears the clonks of the books what shut themselfs, and two moments later, Charles Ordurier and Émile Fesses are seating down in a chamber of André Lubrique and Jacques Derrière.

CHARLES: I am much content of to have terminated that stinking paper of the beet-sugars industry! But I have a feat that it will be less fine than the other ones, even although Sophie Jupon made me a good assistance on it. She has the big brains, this young lady, no?

ANDRÉ: The big brains? Sophie Jupon? Ha! Ha! Ha!

CHARLES: These laughs has the sound of much dirt in them, you snail. To which are you driving?

ÉMILE: Pay out no mind on him, my old hump. André is a large amount of feces! Go forward on the story of Sophie, if you please.

CHARLES: It is not too much of the story, Émile. Sophie makes to work with me yesterday night in the library until they cast us outside. She did the good demonstration to me how to make the paper organize itself. But creepy Jesus! I have such a disgust on this boring beets I get an ennui just to speak this word.

JACQUES: If she gives an assistance on you in the manner of the young ladies of the School of Fertilizer Arts, kiddoo, you will be making the walk on the knees, eh André?

ANDRÉ: You can bet some long greens on this, bebby. Sophie Jupon has the big brains! Ha! Ha! Ha!

CHARLES (*his collar rising quick*): Listen, you . . . *beet*. I demand to know the reason for you to make this comical sounds!

ÉMILE: "Beet" is greatly piquant! Ha! Ha! One is at the lose to think on a fruit what is more to loathe like these beet. André the Beet. Ha! Ha!

ANDRÉ: Émile is pissed out on me for that I am the close friend with Suzanne Jarretière, what he has always some big hot on.

ÉMILE: Oh, yes? But I can hear no sound of your loose lip what describes how you want to make a sex act with any thing which draws up the breath. You liberty!

JACQUES: Aha! You have the desire to be the big Don Casanova, eh? You snikky shoe! I give a thank that I neglected to make a meeting of you and my young floozie. You would without a doubts probably put her down on the back in a flashes, no?

ANDRÉ: In effect! Or maybe on the knees. Ha! Ha! Ha!

CHARLES: Hey! I still desire to have a light shedded to this rotting laugh of André. Speak on me, you clap!

ANDRÉ: I have the impression it will give you a bad in the head, old socks.

CHARLES: Just speak on me!

ANDRÉ: All right, grease-nose! It is not that Sophie Jupon has the big brains what make her the honors of the class. Sophie is the sot in the head, rilly.

JACQUES: Sophie? I consider that you have been taking in the pipe, old man.

ÉMILE: It is not to marvel at. He has jazzed out the brains of him to a frizzle!

CHARLES: The sot in the head? Sophie? She has the list of A's like an arm.

ANDRÉ: Don't believe nothing on that, my poop-eyed friend. Do you know of the Dean of Womens, Berthe Fouet?

CHARLES: But yes. She is a lady of much charm and the exciting fatal shapes.

JACQUES: The rumor bruits it that she wears no undergarments beneath the clothes. Robert Caleçons had spoke on me that he had a fine peer on her one time when she made to bend over a file and a knocker emerged from her dress.

ÉMILE: Robert Caleçons is a fruity goon! He could never identify a knocker from the hole of the ground.

CHARLES: What is all of this have to make on Sophie Jupon, eh?

ANDRÉ: Hold on to the water, comrade, and I will speak on this.

CHARLES: Let the old porno-brains speak.

ANDRÉ: Sophie Jupon and Dean Fouet have make together—how does it call itself?—the "item"? Or to place this in a rude expression, they adore to make the unnatural smut acts together while Mr. Fouet regards them. Pretty twisted up, eh? So it is that Sophie, who has the brains of a slabs of Camembert, get the A for every things.

CHARLES: Is these a facts? Or some large fragment of the shit?

ANDRÉ: Who knows this as the facts? I have not regarded this in my person. I hear on this by Suzanne to which it was whisper by Alice Cuisse, who is, as all the world knows, a lady homu.

JACQUES: It calls itself a "homo," you crazy some things!

ANDRÉ: What it the fuck call itself I don't give a hail of beans!

ÉMILE: What a wised-up acre you are, André. How do you make an explaining why the professors of Sophie fail to make a clamor on this stuffs, eh?

ANDRÉ: Because Dean Fouet, you frig-face, has the Polaroid shoots, the recording tapes, the whole shooting-work of these crowd of professors and how they do the smutty acts and speech to the students of them.

JACQUES: Holy cat! This can of the worms would make some scandal!

CHARLES: Oh ball! So my paper of the beet-sugar industry is a damn F!

ANDRÉ: I think that this is the bad fact, my old saps.

Charles continues to make a large complaint on lack of the justice. Jacques and André speak to him that it appears sure that he is up shit river lacking the oar. Émile, who has the great odious on André, then makes the defense of Sophie Jupon and Dean Berthe Fouet, telling that they are as chaste like some old nuns. But whatever he makes to shout, no other buddies give him a tumbler, for that they are now chatting dirty things indeed on those two ladies. Émile discreetly wishes he should be Mr. Fouet, this vile hog!

XX THE TWO AUTOS

Each person knows that the modern lifes turns about of the auto. When the auto is running good, all goes good; but when one is deprive of this useful machine, one have the impression of having lost a member of the body, perhaps like even a hose or a nukie.

Yesterday morning, Mr. Aine is to go at eight hours less a quarter for to take him to the University at eight hours. A little before, he is come in the house for to announce a sad news on his wife.

MR. AINE: My cherry lips, it makes that I take your auto today. That of mine have the bursted tire, and I don't have a time of changing this. I have to be on the hour for a meeting with a student of mine, Miss Jarretière.

MRS. AINE: But you cannot take my auto, handsome poopsie. I have a need of it this morning in order for to make a rendezvous what is very important.

MR. AINE: My angel, I don't love much to derange you, but the appointment is of the first rank. Mrs. Chaud, Miss Jarretière, and I will be working in an ensemble all a morning longs. I must make an assistance in order that Miss Jarretière make the pass grades in Musical Appreciating. If I do not race to make to arrive on the hour, that wizzel, Fixe-Chaussettes, will steal my thunders out!

MRS. AINE: How is it that you make such an upset on this? You had always the huge loathe of remedy craps. Eh?

MR. AINE (*making the shuffle on his feets*): Well . . . Miss Jarretière has the good promises of great honors, and she is also of a young lady like a daughter what I don't got. And also, Mrs. Chaud has made a beggar on herself that I will assist on this matter. But how is it that *you* must keep such an early rendezvous?

MRS. AINE (*making the giggles from the nerves*): Berthe Fouet and her husband have made to invite me do a chats about being a chair peoples of a rubbish sales next month.

MR. AINE: It makes to find the solution then as quick as any things, for the time he is ticky-tocking away from us, no? Ah! Lend to me your auto; I will make the phone jingle on the garage man. He will come to repair the bursted tire of my auto, what you then can take. How does this sound on your ears, my idol-foot?

MRS. AINE: What a brains you have, my turkey! As smart as the whipping! I have the idea that every things will be jakes.

MR. AINE: Hot stiff!

(*Mr. Aine goes to make the jingle on the garage man.*)

MRS. AINE: Listen on me, my Grik god, if you please. Make the request on the garage man to send here Tisonnier to make a repair.

MR. AINE: Tisonnier? Is these the old gizzer what whittles up the logs all the days in the sunlight?

MRS. AINE: Ha! Ha! Ha! No, no, my tossed salad! Tissonier is the young and smart and bright and tall and strong and have the jolly face; the one what always make to smile and joke on us when we make to fill in the auto with petrol.

MR. AINE: Oh yes.

(*He makes the jingle through. At last!*)

MRS. AINE: It makes I think that you should leave. It is nearly eight hours. Here is the key on my auto.

MR. AINE: If I had no knowledge of who it is you are, I would be thinking that you are saying on me, "Here is the hat, why are you in a rush?" Ha! Ha! Ha!

MRS. AINE: Ha! Ha! Ha!

MR. AINE: By a ways, you appear of a great loveliness this morning, my hot fudge. The mascara, the eyelash, the black silk stockings, the stiletto heels? All this for a rubbish-sales rendezvous?

MRS. AINE (*she does a stutters*): Th-these ancient s-s-some things? They are as o-old as a h-h-hill. Ha! H-h-ha!

MR. AINE: Any ways, I speak to you, my sexy bombs, if I had some moments, I would do a sex act on you right here on the swill container. Whams!

MRS. AINE (*batting high and low the eyes on her*): Perhaps this evening, my bin-bag?

MR. AINE: In effect! And now I must run like the brizz!

Mr. Aine goes away in the auto of his wife for a very fruity meeting with Suzanne and Mrs. Chaud. They are taking from eight hours of the morning until near one hour of the afternoon. Mrs. Aine regards Tisonnier to fix the bursted tire and then makes on him some refreshment. How happy he is! Then she goes away in the auto of Mr. Aine to make the rendezvous with Berthe Fouet and her husband. How amazed she feels to find Sophie Jupon is present! They all make a very interesting morning. That evening, Mr. and Mrs. Aine fall into a sleep with the faces on them in the plates of dinner. It appears that they are too flagged out to make a sex act, or perhaps they have the bad in the head as an ensemble.

FIN

« 60 »

The Gavottes
Are Petrified by Awe

The sun is up and they are in an area to the south of the area they were in. The ground is arid and has been so for a long time and is stood upon by them. They are in a kind of large place that is one of six large places; that is, there are, and were, and will be six large places, one of which is the one that they are in. The light is bright and the sun is warm.

All around them in this place and all around them should they be in any of the other five places are pieces of what is, to them, stone. Or it may be rock. Some of this is to their front and some of it is to their rear, while some of it is to their right and some of it is to their left. Or it can be said by them, or others, or just one other, that some of these are to their front, rear, right, and left.

Some of it or some of these is, or are, on slopes so that these pieces are seen by them to be situated on an ascending plane if they are at the base of the plane; some of these are seen by them to be situated on a descending plane if they are at the crest of the plane; and some are not on slopes but are on flat ground; or some of it is on flat ground, or upward or downward slopes, as seen by them, that is.

Some of these pieces of what is to them stone or rock are trunks of trees that are very old. Some of these pieces of stone or rock (to them) are bits. Or pieces. Or bits and pieces and chips and shards and chunks. All the trunks are prostrate. Most of the trunks are broken and have been so for a long time. A few of the trunks are not broken and have of course never been broken. They have been not-broken for a long time too. Those that are broken will be broken for a long time, and those that are not broken will be not-broken for a long time unless they are broken soon or in a little while or in a long while. If they are broken they will never be not-broken.

The chips or bits or pieces or shards or chunks, or the chips and bits and pieces

290

and shards and chunks are from the trunks, or were from the trunks. None of them will be from the trunks for they are. Those of them that will be from the trunks are not yet and will not be unless the trunks are to be broken.

The bits and pieces and chunks and chips and shards are scattered. Most are scattered around and about the trunks, both those that are broken and those that are not broken. Some are not scattered around and about the trunks but are scattered around and about each other. Some are on flat ground and some are on ascending and descending planes; in this way they are like the logs that some of them are from. It is also possible that some of these bits, shards, chips, chunks, and pieces are not and were not from trunks, but are or were what once were trunks and are no longer.

Some of the trunks are large in diameter and length. They were large in diameter and length, and they will be large in diameter and length. These are both the unbroken and prostrate trunks and the broken and prostrate trunks. They are of the same shape that they were when they were not stone or rock. That is, they are of the shape of tree trunks; those that are unbroken are very much the same in shape; those that are broken are very much the same in shape as well, except that they are broken, as they were not when they were tree trunks and not rock or stone.

Some of the trunks are small and were small. Both the broken trunks and the unbroken trunks are and were small. Their shapes, as are and were the shapes of the large trunks, are and were the same shapes as they were when they were tree trunks, except for the broken trunks, which were not broken when they were not stone or rock, but tree trunks.

They are all cylindrical in shape and were cylindrical in shape. These cylindrical shapes are the shapes that they were when they were tree trunks and not trunks of stone or rock. The large trunks, all of which are cylindrical, and the small trunks, all of which are cylindrical, both broken and unbroken (all are prostrate), will be cylindrical. The broken trunks are not large or long unbroken cylinders, but are of smaller cylindrical pieces, all of which pieces are close to each other insofar as they are pieces of what is and was and will be the same trunk that once was not stone or rock.

The scattered pieces and chips and chunks and shards and bits are of different shapes. Some are round and some are square and some are rectangular and some are pentagonal and some are hexagonal and some are heptagonal and some are octagonal and some are nonagonal and some are decagonal and some are of other shapes, some of which are possessed of names and some of which are not.

Some of these pieces are large and some of them are small, yet the largest of them are not so large as the smallest of the cylindrical pieces of the broken trunks and the smallest of them are not so small as a grain of something. Some of them are sharp and some of them are not sharp. They have been large and larger and small and smaller for a long time and will be. The largest and smallest of the chunks are somewhere but no one has been known to know where and it is probable that no one will ever be known to know where. It is also possible that the chunk which is largest and the chunk which is smallest may somewhere have exact counterparts, so that they cannot be the largest, or the smallest, but must be part of a category of, for instance, the two largest or the three largest chunks, and the two smallest or the three smallest chunks, and so on. This is possible but not probable, the probable being that there is indeed a largest and a smallest chunk. These largest and smallest chunks will be the largest and smallest chunks, or, it is probable that this will be the case.

It is probable also that some, small, smaller, and smallest, and large, larger, and largest, were once of different shapes than they now are, and that they will be of different shapes than they now are and have been. If not probable in all cases or in any cases at least this is possible, was possible, and will be possible.

The trunks, broken and unbroken, and the chips and pieces and such are of jasper and agate. There is some iron in them. The trunks and chips of jasper and agate with some iron are those trunks that are and were large and small and those chips of varied shapes which are possessed of names as well as of varied shapes that are nameless.

Some are brown. Some are yellow. Some are red. Some are of a brown tint. Some are of a yellow tint. Some are of a red tint. Some are all brown, some all yellow, some all red; some all of a brown tint, some all of a yellow tint, some all of a red tint. Some were of one category, some were of another category, some will be of one or the other. Some are, were, and will be of mixtures of brown, yellow, and red; or are, were, and will be of mixtures of brown tints, yellow tints, and red tints.

Some are or seem to be, or were, or seem to have been, or will be, though this is possible and not probable, black. Or of a black tint. Or of black in mixture with yellow, brown, or red, or tints of one or two or all or combinations of the colors that are and were. Yet some are green! Or blue! Or lavender! Or fuchsia! Or cerise! Or beige! And tints of same. And some are of other colors or tints of other colors.

Some may have been orange. Some may be purple. Some that were orange may be purple and some that may have been purple may be orange. And some not. None may have been these colors and none may be. Some that are yellow, brown, red, black, green, blue, lavender, fuchsia, cerise, or beige, may have been orange or purple or may be although they are not now. And some that are tints of these colors may have been tints of other colors or they may be although they are not now.

Some may have been or may be, although they are not now, rustic brown and whinny brown; or sweet yellow and juicy yellow; or ranch red and suburban red; or wild black and pirate black. And some may have been or may be, although they are not now, swing orange and winter orange and surprise green and terrace green and cadet blue and mulligan blue and trumpet and quadrille and blossom and coquette and yo-yo and love mist and shutter. This was or will be, or was and will be possible but it is not probable.

None are white. Some may have been white. Some may be white. Nor are any grey or silver. It is possible that some may have been and that some may be. Everything in the six places is still. It does not move. It has not moved for a very long time. It will not move for a very long time. This is probable.

<< 61 >>

The
Great Ditch
of the Great
Southwest Greatly
and Grandly Appears
to Blue as the Grand
Symbol of the Profundity,
Nobility, and Gravity of
His Hopes, Now Almost Realized

Torn from the weird and witchlike shifting of colors and the unearthly inertia of
the timeless stone jungle as a pig that falls into the bracken and the spine-leaf
clover is torn from out it by the calloused yet how kind hands and fingers of the
cheerful swineherd with rough jest and merry song upon his split and calloused
lips, thus were Blue and Helene so torn from out the weird and witchlike shifting
of colors and the unearthly inertia of the timeless stone jungle.

Before them loomed, if one may use so insouciant a word, a ditch, a huge, long,
vast, and deep ditch that stretched farther than the eye could see without aid of
excellent and quite expensive binoculars. A great and grand ditch. Blue and Helene approached its vertiginous edge and peered into its depths, now soft in the
approaching twilight.

He saw within crowded campions and celandines of coconino cheers, and
heard them too!

He spied yelling yaks and yawping yanquis yodeling of yucca yakis!

Then too there were orisons and orotund oaths, all officious, of oxeye daisy,
orchis, orchid, and osier oyster plant o'neills!

Yes! And kudos, kicks, and knightly nods of cornflower, cattail, cohosh, coral
bean, and common milkweed, cannily catalogued as "kaibabs"!

Thin thrills and trills and toots and trembling tremors and temblors all over touch-me-nots and teaberries on a tray for tontos' tastes!

And there were those ingenious instruments that indicate that the inner gorge is intrinsically inviolate ivy!

And at the very bottom, or maybe not, but somewhere surely, the swell, subtle, stupendous sumners, scintillant and summery with smartweed, salvia, striped coralroot, storksbill, and the shiny, singing sweetness of the seaside gentian!

Blue sat at the piano and pounded it with those mighty hands that men have loved so well, and to a wild tune instanteously hauled from out his bowels, sang to Helene:

> The great ditch
> of the great Southwest
> appears to us! A symbol
> of the Profundity,
>
> the Nobility, and
> the Gravity of my
> hopes, my grand hopes,
> almost realized!
>
> Profundity!
> Nobility!
> Gravity!
> Hopes almost realized!

They excused, as the old saw has it, their dust! And the dust, as is its wont, excused them too.

And by dawn or thereabouts, maybe, say, eight, eight-fifteen, they crossed into Nevada, wherein strange things occurred, as will be seen.

« 62 »
Perhaps It
May Happen by Chance

Blue will find a copy of *Oui, Oui, Paris* that features a color layout of Miss Clarke Grable, in the nude, reading *La Musique et les mauvaises herbes*.

A toy piano will fall or be thrown out of the window of SAL'S BILLIARD ACADEMY.

A carhop at the BAR-B-Q DE-LITE will tell Helene that *her* name is Helene Gavotte and punch the former in the head causing the rest of her hair to fall out.

On the day that Blue and Helene arrive in Nevada, the top record throughout the state will be "Speak Nothin' But Good O' The Dead!"

Blue will glimpse Dr. Weede Bone wearing Dr. Ryan Poncho's clothes.

An old drunkard will sell Helene a white prune in which is carved what he claims is Tom Sawyer's face.

Zimmerman, now, oddly enough, nineteen or twenty years old, will find Blue and Helene.

In the Blue Palm Cafe, the chef's specialty will be Snow Peas in Orange Rinds with Chilies and Lemon Juice.

Helene will notice Dr. Ryan Poncho putting on a mask that looks exactly like the face of Dr. Ciccarelli.

Horace Rosette will be seen in a bookstore window autographing copies of *American Lake Poetry*.

Helene will find what seems to be her fedora in a ladies'-room stall.

Lesbia Glubit will buy Blue's bicycle clips for her private art-crafts collection.

The Rev. Tyrell Bloat will deliver a radio sermon on the important role of dental caries in the Search for God.

Rep. Harold "Hal" Glubit will officially open The Shearling Shoppe, assisted by Pops Ennui and the Crawdaddies, who will play their latest hit, "Green Old Dolphin."

Blue will suspect that the Mexican beggar on Zoshi Street is José Cizaña-Hueso, although he wears what appears to be Dr. Ryan Poncho's "palm-tree" tie.

Zimmerman will introduce his mother and father to his fiancée, a Miss Vincenza Grable.

Helene will begin receiving obscene letters on blue stationery, signed "Henry Flower."

The new, hard-hitting film, *Death in Dubuque*, starring Mariette Cliffe and Cheechee Docque, will open at the Sandstorm Twin.

Tom Piper will win $212,510 playing blackjack at the Red Swan Hotel Casino.

Joanne Bungalow will attend a publication party for her new book, *Rita's Agony*, wearing a pair of Blue's old bicycle clips, or copies of same.

Helene will eat a package of persimmon-flavored Oro-Sux lozenges and her hair will start growing in.

The Rev. Dr. Piscardi will return what seems to be Helene's fedora.

Helene's fedora will be copied by the new boutique, The Gumdrop Tree, owned by Clarke and Vincenza Dubuque.

Someone will mail Blue a copy of the long-out-of-print *Martin Chucklehead*.

Zimmerman will insist that he remembers nothing of any "cave."

A Blarney Spalpeen will threaten to sue Blue for libel and defamation of character.

Blue will notice Dr. Weede Bone picking up a package for Dr. Ryan Poncho at the Post Office.

Joanne Bungalow, on a talk show from Elko, will reveal that she is the author of *La Musique et les mauvaises herbes*, and will contend that it has never been translated.

Blue will find a beautifully-colored meerschaum inside his piano.

Helene will eat a package of witch-hazel-flavored Oro-Sux lozenges and her hair will start falling out again.

On awakening one morning, Blue and Helene will find their beloved pushcart newly painted.

Helene will receive a letter, on blue stationery, from Mlle Fifi Galleon, warning her to leave Henry Flower alone.

The sun will collapse in a panoply of horribly depressing colors as it used to do in Illinois.

Blue will see Dr. Ryan Poncho enter a house; a half-hour later, he will see Cheechee Docque leave the house in Dr. Poncho's clothes with Miss Clarke Grable on his arm.

A Bucol Suck will threaten to sue Blue for plagiarism.

The society column of the *Tonopah Trumpet* will announce the engagement of Dr. Vincent Dubuque and Miss Helene Gavotte.

What seems to be Helene's fedora will fall or be thrown out of the window of SAL'S BILLIARD ACADEMY.

José Cizaña-Hueso will be arrested for wearing the stolen undergarments of Miss Clarke Grable.

The *Reno Ratchet* will publish "Ah, Nature," by Fifi Galleon.

Father Donald Debris, S.J., will send Blue and Helene an invitation to his imminent marriage to Sister Rose Zeppole.

Blue will meet a man in The Shearling Shoppe who introduces himself as Henry Flower.

Zimmerman will break his engagement to Miss Vincenza Grable because of his passion for Miss Olga Warner, recently hired as a waitress by the Red Swan Hotel Casino.

Dr. Weede Bone will buy a completely new wardrobe and two days later Blue will see Dr. Ryan Poncho on the street in a suit from that wardrobe.

Mr. Jeeter Smiley will sell his rest-room wall to the Museum of Modern Art and move to Ely, where he will open Smiley's Symposium: Live Sex Acts.

Miss Olga Warner will fall in love with Miss Daphne Hawthorne, recently employed by station KYVD as a Production Assistant on the Rev. Dr. Piscardi's "Mouth of God Hour" and Zimmerman will disappear, taking Helene's fedora and the family copy of *La Musique et les mauvaises herbes*.

What seems to be Helene's fedora will be returned by Counselor Charlotte Siebold, who will discover it in her bunk at Camp Cottonwood, "Nevada's newest nirvana."

Mme Fifi Flower will perform in the first Smiley's Symposium stage show, assisted by two men wearing masks that look exactly like the face of Dr. Weede Bone.

Ole Joe Clark will make an indecent proposal to Miss Helene Gavotte, and, later in the day, an even more indecent proposal to Miss Daphne Hawthorne.

Horace Rosette will claim to have discovered evidence that *La Musique et les mauvaises herbes* is a French version of the eighteenth-century Spanish classic, *La golondrina*.

Freight Train 45 will derail in front of the BAR-B-Q DE-LITE.

Dr. Ryan Poncho will legally change his name to Dr. José Poncho.

Georgia Molly and John Tenbrooks will steal Helene's white prune and send it to Mme Fifi Flower wrapped in a sheet of blue stationery.

Judge Poon will close down Smiley's Symposium after it is denounced on the "Mouth of God Hour."

Miss Helene Gavotte will break her engagement to Dr. Vincent Dubuque after he is discovered in a state of partial undress with Miss Rubosa Pogue in some bushes off Interstate 95.

What seems to be Helene's fedora will be among the sex aids being auctioned off subsequent to the closing of Smiley's Symposium.

Rep. Harold "Hal" Glubit will buy a white pull-on girdle from the Rev. Jimmy Boo Purty and wear it in order to "brighten up" his flagging marriage, but will be chagrined when his wife identifies it as hers.

Zimmerman will return with his new bride, the former Margarina Jackson.

Joanne Bungalow will be arrested for assaulting Horace Rosette, but he will refuse to press charges against what he will later term "a distraught hack."

Big Black will create a stir in Elko when he claims that Marcus Garvey invented licorice.

Dr. Ciccarelli will denounce the Rev. Tyrell Bloat as "an oral upstart" and will be supported in letters to the *Tonopah Trumpet* by the Rev. Dr. Piscardi, Dr. Weede Bone, Dr. José Poncho, José Clzaña-Hueso, and C. Ducque.

Margarina Jackson Gavotte, singing with Mickey Butor and the Time Passers, assists in the gala opening of Ely's first Boot Village.

Blue will be publicly reviled by Jambo Jambalaya and the entire Clair de Lune Orchestra as "an enemy of modern music."

Accidentally meeting Blue, Dr. José Poncho will deny vehemently that he is the Dr. Ryan Poncho of The College's faculty.

Someone, as a cruel joke, will send Helene a blow-dryer and a size 40, D-cup brassiere.

Captain Dirk Basura (Ret.), will meet Catherine Thigh, his childhood sweetheart, at a Purity in Sex Seminar in Carson City, and they will register at the Torrid Time Motel as the Rev. and Mrs. Jimmy Boo Purty.

Margarina Jackson Gavotte will divorce Zimmerman and move in with the Misses Daphne Hawthorne and Olga Warner.

Juan Pecos will buy the Blue Palm Cafe and turn it into the Speedwich Stop.

Zimmerman will blame his problems with women on the fact that his mother and father abandoned him in a cave, but they will insist that they remember nothing of any "cave."

Sister Rose Zeppole will move in with Margarina Jackson Gavotte, Olga Warner, and Daphne Hawthorne to research an article, for *The Healthy Mind*, that will be entitled "Another Part of the Forest: The Holes in the Dyke."

"Big" Hatcheta will offer Helene fifty dollars for her fedora.

Zimmerman will conduct a brief but explicitly erotic correspondence with Catherine Thigh and finally discover his sexual métier.

Sister Rose Zeppole, after joining the staff of *The Healthy Mind*, will alter her habit so that it falls to mid-thigh, and there ensues a welcome revival of interest in the Roman Catholic faith throughout Southern Nevada.

Tom Piper will buy Hatcheta's "Fedora with Mountains" for $110,000.

Blue will discover, by means of a note sent by Miss Clarke Grable, that all of Dr. Weede Bone's clothes are in Dr. José Poncho's house.

Lesbia and Harold "Hal" Glubit's white pull-on girdle will fall or be thrown out of the window of SAL'S BILLIARD ACADEMY.

Blue will write Joanne Bungalow how much he admires her "Supper at the Kind Brown Mill: A Country Drama," and she will ask him over for "a good time."

Blue, Helene, and Zimmerman will leave for California as all Nevada watches the Sanitation and Buildings Department board up the window of SAL'S BILLIARD ACADEMY.

« 63 »
California!
The End of the Quest

Together again as do the Fates or Graces or Muses or Furies all link together hands, all three of them, or all six, whatever you like or remember or feel like looking up in your well-worn copy of that beloved Reference Guide that sits patiently and covered o'er with dust, they were on the way to that shining bay across which that Golden bridge magisterially chucks itself! How wonderful it was that Zim was big and strong now, perhaps not too strong, but strong enough to help with the schlepping. And what schlepping it was!

Across the standardly blooming desert, all arid in its severe beauty, the cart rolled and the piano bumped. The sands blew as did the muck and dustballs from out that Aegean stable that the mighty Atlas had to sweep out and on straight time, no extra bread to sweeten his mighty task. And what stern desert was this? Well might you ask, and yet, ask and desperately ask as you will, the hollowly ringing silence that greets the shyly whispered or muttered question will be your only answer as it was the answer given to unhappy Oedipus by the oracle at Delphi, stony-eyed over her pot, when he wanted to know how to rid the great city of Thebes and its suburban localities as well from what scholars have variously translated as "the pest," "the horror," or "the itch." Yes, silence.

Blue asked not only the land around at large but asked also Zim, figuring that the strong-thewed lad had been places since they misplaced him in that cave—good Lord!—how many months ago? Or was it years? To Blue's eyes it seemed years since Zim seemed, how shall I say? grown to a kind of manliness that portends maturity. He seemed old enough to serve with Jason had Jason been about, and who of you out there, wise and "sophisticated," dares prove that he is not? Or old enough to bend his shoulder to the wheel, or in this case, the cart, or the rope attached to it. Or is what attached to it? Whatever you like is all right here for semiotics prove that you have not the chance of a snowman in the wake of Dante down among the hollering cardinals and bishops!

But Zimmerman did not know. Know what? Somehow the tenuous and silken thread of discourse had been broken, and broken by Proud Nature with a wild sirocco of hot blasts. But is it, in the last analysis, important? I think not—suffice it to contend, but moderately and considerately like a boring editorial, that whatever the name of these forever slumb'ring sands, they were indeed sands. And nothing more.

And then they came to cities, oh, not cities like, say, windy Troy, although some of them were windy enough, windy insofar as they lifted Helene's simple dirndl or gingham or homespun or patchwork or denim skirt and gave a clutch of geezers on the fly-specked corners an eyeful. There they took refreshment in the guise of Cokes and hot dogs, and they were good. How the stories flowed around the board that they had balanced on two shifting stacks of books and clothes and other appurtenances—in short, gear. Zim told of many things—men in suits made out of plastic, strange tribes that heaved and flowed through brightly lighted shopping malls, whole basketball teams in wheelchairs! They settled back, enjoying their newfound son, or so it seemed. It almost seemed to Blue that he was not their son. It seemed that way to Helene also. And, if one could peer inside that head that sat so nobly on the wide shoulders and thick-veined neck of Zimmerman, it perhaps seemed to him that they, Helene and Blue, were not his parents! Yet, he reasoned, they were not black folks, nor was he, and so it must have been the fact that they were. Also their names and their often unmistakable visages were things to be thrown into the great pot of truth and simmered like a good stew. At night, when the stars shone down, Zim would often walk about their encampment, so to speak, and look wonderingly up at Calpurnia and Blitho, the Spear of Paraclete, and the wild Ostrich of the Plains of Hippolyte, but they were silent, like the desert! And once in a while, when out of the circle of the firelight, he would bump into maybe Blue, maybe Helene, maybe Blue and Helene together, he, or she, or they, looking too at those wheeling stars which give no answers to humble and foolish man.

Still, they pressed on, following the route of Rogers and his Rangers and the old Chisholm Trail, that almost effaced rut or pair of ruts that still show, in the mysterious sands, the route taken by our forefathers, or to be more specific, some of our forefathers, to that promised golden territory toward which Jane Darwell and Hank Fonda set their faces! If they closed their eyes they could almost hear the whoops of Chief Joseph and Weird Ben, Geronimo and Mighty Paco on the still air, still, that is, when the violent foehn was not tearing the belaying pins off their gear and trying to ruin the hair-fine tuning of the piano, those chilling whoops as they barbecued settlers and ripped the frocks from young gals before chaining them to the ubiquitous anthills that abounded. Then, not now. Such was the face of history in this ruthless land that man had not yet tamed! They were filled with a kind of awe, a religious dread, a sense of the true greatness of the rocks! On the wagon creaked, making perhaps the noise made by the famous wooden horse when a few privates on shit detail had to hump it into the city of Troy. So the creaks of wheels are forever different, yet—forever the same!

How ashamed and small Helene felt now, thinking on her vile and monetary Indian disguise, her knickknacks, doodads, bibelots, and souvenirs, as well as the other crap she had sold to those innocent and open-hearted tourists who had passed through the Land of Enchantment, desiring only to snap photos of the Red Man in his blankets. Better had she simply dug her toes into the living sand and let the soul of the land flow into her feet first. It was too late now. Yet it was not too late to breathe a prayer of reconciliation and confession, a humble yet womanly request for forgiveness, yes! Forgiveness for her forebears who had savaged this land, the sweating coolies who had put the railroads through, who had put up the Greyhound depots, the lunch counters, those exploited masses who had baked the Danish and the Mae Wests, the bowties and the crullers—the jelly doughnuts! And from her perch atop the swaying cart she would look out on the endless wastes and the cities that sprang up suddenly from behind buttes and hills and arroyos and such, cactus, for instance, of which there was a plethora, and think of bison! Yes, bison, which she had always thought were buffalo. Now, sadder and wiser, as must all men and women be, or strive to be, she knew that never had a buffalo clumped about these twisting streets or the highways linking them.

And Blue, sweating underneath his yoke, so to speak, his sweat-drowned eyes bent toward that Bay which was his goal, what did he think? Ha! It more behooves grave Ixion behind his large boulder, or Tantalus strapped to a wheel on that gaunt cliff to which the magpies had almost total access, to think. And their thoughts, when one or two flitted by, were long, long thoughts, as Emerson said, his face grave and sad in the shifting firelight of that house in Brockton from which there blew that trumpet blast that woke the world at Lexington!

Beneath the expressionless skies, the caravan moved slowly, deeper and deeper into the magical state, the scent of oranges rotting on the ground filling the air like the odor of souvlaki that hovered o'er the tents of brave Achilles the night he brooded over lost Christina. So the past and the future, or in this case, since the future of that past is our present, the past and the present—are seamless and unshakeable. Was it true what Sutter had said from behind the closed shutters of his mill: that California will be to you whatever it is *you* are, dependent on of course, race, creed, and amount of money and possessions that you have? Perhaps. Perhaps. For now, the Gavottes were content with the million joys of honest work well done. So they pushed and pulled, heading north-west into the smell of salt and decaying fish! These scents were as a kudo or two that soothed them with its, or their, balm. For even the most goal-oriented person among us, even Menalaos bending all his will toward snatching Helen back from the luxurious hands of perfidious Paris and his enormous family, yes, even he accepted, with dignity, indeed, and humbly but not cravenly, whatever kudos were passed his way: as Homer says: "Then kudos bright did Menalaos joyful greet."

There is a spot in California called the Center Valley, where fruits grow in a wild abandon, as do vegetables. How the pickers sing! Occasionally the showers are hot.[3] It is essentially because they don't wish to attend school, preferring instead to work, side by side, with their parents, brothers, and sisters, in among the joys of the lettuce, celery, parsnips, muscats, and peaches. The Gavottes found themselves here, and the cart sped swiftly now among these Armenians and Italians.[7] It was a kind of sign that the desert was behind them, this dearth of sand, and although they were delighted by the whole idea of abundance and cheap wine in glistening gallon jugs, they felt that nameless loss that one feels when one has left—perhaps forever—the desert behind. Certainly, the redwoods towered! That very sense of awful rolling majesty made them think of Vasco da Gama and Cortez, Ponce de Leon, and Pizarro, all the martial conquistadors who had first planted the hardy grape of Valencia and Bernalillo in this rich black loam. And how the nobility puffed greedily on that rich leaf that the Aztecs called "terbaxitl."[36]

But there had been trouble, or as Sheridan put it after the "Wheat War," a "considerable of bad blood."[40] Somehow, the Gavottes felt the old animosities as they lurched forward through the seemingly endless vineyards, arbors, orchards, and avocadoes, felt them rather than saw them, for there was, indeed, nothing to be seen but the sunny, profligate fields, orchards, and etc., etc. The stubbed toe, however, halted the determined caravan only for a moment: a bathe in crystal spring water,[44] a quick buss on the boo-boo by Helene, and a firmly anchored Band-Aid, and the trio was off again. But where they got the buttons to suck is anyone's guess. It was a trick that Blue had learned from some book.

And soon Fresno was far behind, although "far" is, perhaps, an instance of hyperbole. Let us say, rather, that it was but a hazy configuration of buildings in

---

3. The Indians called one of them "the-guava-that-blooms-in-motley."
5. This has been ascribed to the designs of certain pot patterns.
7. As early as 1665.
21. This celery "ragout" was used in mystery ceremonies by the Potlatch tribe.
30. A. Harley describes this basin as an "archetypal sink."
36. Kohlrabi was considered a noxious weed of magical properties.
37. Pinget notes: "Truth means binoculars, precision . . ."
40. The Germanic Legion of Quintilius Fabricanus lived for months on orange ice.
43. I.e., the *malocchio*, or "evil eye."

the distance. But gold was to supersede the sacred grape for many years as the motivating force that drove desperate men to these rich lands—the true riches of which lay at their feet, but which they, in their greed and madness, could not see.[51]

Not that they didn't stop occasionally, although each stop seemed actually to pain Blue now; he was so close, the whispering of the Sequoias in and around Oakland were borne to his ears on the faint zephyrs that carried the perfume of the Pacific in their little hands. As the migrants well knew, singing outside the bunkhouses of cool evenings, the lettuces in huge mounds blotting out the very sky! It was a new song that Blue played that night on the piano, which, quite mysteriously, had, somewhere in the vicinity of Madera, taken on a richer, a more ringing tone and timbre.[60]

It had been "Rock" Wagram who put all these little towns on the map, and Blue was quick to pay homage to his memory. Others hid in their tarpaper shacks when the Santa Ana veered north, admittedly a rare occurrence. Yet never had the cart rolled so effortlessly![67] And one balmy evening after supper, Zimmerman decided to tell the whole incredible tale of his years-long search for his mother and father, and of the directions given him by an old crone that led him finally to Nevada.[70] It had started in terror when he woke in that echoing Missouri cave. And, finally, he told Blue and Helene, Miss Catherine Thigh and he had promised to correspond faithfully with each other.

Somehow, they seemed to be always "just outside" Madera, and for more than a day could make no progress. Serge blamed, alternately, Dr. Bone and Dr. Poncho, claiming that they wanted him to fail.[75] Though small, Merced was a lovely town. The apple orchards grew in lavish profusion right down to the banks of the river, a river teeming with trout, muskelonge, pike, bass, sturgeon, lobster, and carp. The travelers were sorely tempted to stay for a few days, even Blue felt the pull, the wonder of the place.[81] The next evening they, too, were prevailed upon to join in the singing at the camp meeting, and they did, raising their voices in the beloved old hymns that have helped make our beloved land great—"Ring My Doorbell, Jesus," "I'll Cross the Jordan in a Speedboat, Lord," "That Heavenly Light Gives Me a Migraine," and many other favorites. The Mayor insisted when he heard Blue play: and so he accepted the Key to Merced!

They were, in a word, celebrities! He had kept that last letter from Catherine

---

51. Antony Lamont discusses this phenomenon in his unpublished novel, "Crocodile Tears," which the present author has been privileged to read in manuscript.
59. But the concept of knight-errantry was not known, of course, to the Arikara.
67. Professor Richard Blister suggests that this was an infestation.
71. These petticoats are described in James's *The Golden Bowl*.
75. Dr. Vincent Dubuque contends that these are imagined "bogeymen."
83. D. Basura denies this inference.

buttoned into his shirt, close to his heart.[84] Yet and yet the open road called to Blue and he would wake at night with a start, the salt odor of the Bay in his nostrils and his ears straining for the incredible Phrase. That *was* a paella! To the traditional spare ribs, pork butt, eels, elbow macaroni, crumbled fish sticks, and tomato juice, the ladies of the church auxiliary added midget marshmallows to bring out the other flavors. But now the repair of the wheel was but a matter of a half-hour or so, since Blue felt compelled to hurry to make up for the week he had lost in lovely Merced.[87] And, it should be said, Zim had got into the habit of making marginal notations on Miss Thigh's letters.

However impossible it seemed, the hand of Coronado had reached this far north! Here were Fingernail Road, Fingernail Lane, Fingernail Bridge, Fingernail Farms, Fingernail Bar & Grill. It was, of course, in Spanish, but they weren't daunted. It might have been the sun, but somehow Helene's hair had never seemed so rich, so full, so lustrous, so lovely![92] One of the things he lovingly jotted in the margin was: "What you like to do I like to do more." And now it was almost impossible for Blue to sleep, the fever of anxiety and expectation burning through and through him. Still, Fresno was a charming memory that they would all—especially Helene—cherish forever.[96]

Despite the wonderful feeling that they still carried with them when they remembered Blue's impetuous act of generosity, they all missed, more than they could say, the beloved copy of *La Musique et les mauvaises herbes*.[99] Yet despite the dust and the torrential rains, the sight alone of the proud and lofty spires of Modesto filled their hearts with a strange joy. Oh no! There had never been in any of their lives such apricots as those that greeted them as they finally waded ashore. He decided, a few days later, to write a long and lovingly detailed letter to Catherine, filled with minutely worked-out descriptions. It had been ages since Blue and Helene stood together like this, arm in arm in the velvety night, the fireflies lazily bumping into their rapt faces.[107]

What had seemed to be spires were now seen to be, as they got closer, the signs of hamburger stands, orange-juice stands, taco stands, and other stands. Another accident! What an enormous pleasure it was for Zimmerman to bathe with the local farmhands![112] There was nothing to do but wait for the glue to set, and

---

84. See *Wanton Flyer*, Vol. XXXIV, No. 11 (1975).
86. Tables were often set in the rigid patterns prescribed by John Calvin.
87. Not seen in the area prior to 1907.
92. Akin to Berenice's when the latter's was set afire.
100. Early settlers thought that carrots were gold.
110. Dr. Laszlo Syntax argues that the Merced River is dry at the time of year that apricot trees are bearing fruit.
111. This might have been what is known in the East as "Russian dressing."
112. As Laurence Sterne writes: "That's another story."
125. Carrousels were outlawed in this area from 1931 to 1949 by the Legion of Christian Wives and Mothers.

so they busied themselves with identifying wild flowers. It was quite a sunburn, but Helene remembered a good bit of first aid and a simple country lass brought a copy of *Buddy and His Boys and the Mystery of the Can of Beans*. And one morning, just before dawn, Blue heard the awesome thunder of the distant surf crashing against the antique shops of Sausalito![118]

The delicate sky exhaled, or seemed to exhale, the limpid purity of the blue that suffuses the spiked lobelia, the passionflower, and the manwort pyrexia, or what botanists for years thought the manwort pyrexia was, or appeared to be: thus they took their ease beneath it for a spell, that is, a spell as men reckon a spell in these parts. For even Blue had to rest! So near was he, but his inseparable companion, Helene, prevailed upon him to recoup his powers for what he liked to call, nowadays, "his final thrust." Zim, well, Zim was more than delighted, for he had met the fair daughters of a local clam-fryer, long employed by Howard Johnson's, a man of enormous zest and even gusto.

Oh, he still wrote letters to Miss Thigh, but now they were filled with what might be termed "cute" references to his gambols with these lasses of the aching fields and ditches, one such remark being that he had, one tender evening, with a damsel on either side of his essentially yearning, yet always manly body, "with one hand on the younger one's********************************, *******-************, and with just a little urging, the older maiden, pulling at her ********************* so that her skirts were in such a state that we three collapsed into a ****************** whose hands were a blur!"

Yes, he was having what the sagest of philosophers call [fun?] . . . while of the two young ladies it can be [said that they] gave their all as their mother had suggested in ********************* and afternoon and evening as well, taking turns! ****************************** of a torn petticoat? Of course! [What Catherine Thigh] . . . is not our purpose to record. And, knowing what we do about Miss Thigh, which is that she liked her ****** as well as her ***, we like to think that she would have not only understood, but even applauded! For though Diderot put it well when he wrote, "loin des yeux, loin du coeur," Miss Thigh had what some have termed an "inner vision" and could "see" the events in Zim's letters; indeed, so well, that it was, at times, almost as if she were there herself, making a joyous foursome. And at such times . . . with all her heart! What did she care if the neighbor's boy, a shambling yet kind bank teller, spied on her from his window, *************************, and *************-*******, and sometimes **************: once she even saw him and then she opened wide her **************, so that the poor lad's eyes almost *****-********! Once, yes, he even collapsed in blissful exhaustion. What a letter she wrote to Zim that night, and while she wrote it, the [frisson?] as she ********** made her usually neat characters almost illegible! She *could* be naughty.

So the time passed pleasantly enough for Zim while Blue and Helene made final plans for the "run to the sea," as Blue nowadays liked to call it, in addition to calling it "his final thrust." What these plans were we do not pretend to know, for even the most minutely examined life must have its small secrets. And Blue had more than a few and some were not so small as all that! [There are subtle references to . . .] *****************as well as the curiously peripatetic fedora. And the odd erudition concerning sheep? *********[a mistake that?] ************ with Harold "Hal" Glubit? So often, things that seem to have little or nothing to do with each other, prove to be . . . quite . . . surprising [correspondent?] **********, bicycle-clip collection but a manifestation of fetishism, much like that of Abraham Lincoln's for silk hosiery? **********that "every great man has his ******** in private."

. . . busied themselves with cheery decorations woven of the tough Canada thistle and the swamp pink, both, strangely enough, never before seen in these parts—while Modesto loomed and beckoned and Blue, one night, made it clear that it was time to be off. ******** knows, they searched for him, although discreetly, and finally heard the sound of groaning and laughter from amid the thick clumps of wild bergamot that grew in profusion from the compost heap. They called and **************, not precisely "indecent," but what might be termed deshabille, out they came, all five . . . which occasioned great [surprise?] and not a little laughter so that even the bunchberries seemed to beam happily!

[*Large portion of mss. missing*] ******* and with all the old and by now well-loved bumps and jounces, her dandruff flew about the sunny countryside, and Zim lay as if stupefied, a smile on his stalwart, so to speak, face or that [strange?] that men call . . . ["face"?] . . . but did his part wonderfully well. And why not? cynics and crips [*sic*] might sey [*sic*]? For just that morning he had received a long letter from Catherine Thigh, in which she described, at great length, a small party with some *******, who had come from *****, and were delighted at the idea of ******* and ******** the bank teller! It was . . . [newsy] . . . her bright and cheerful and sunny self: what a **** she had! And with it some color photos that . . . hard to make . . . without careful scrutiny. [It?] ******** a domino encrusted with pearls and ***** in the foreground, with his ******* in ********'s ******** Father [Dabree?] *******, it be an apron?

So they passed the time and were soon in Modesto, which proved to be a congenital [*sic*] burg, or what might be called a village or even a small town. *****-*** FREE CONCERT! And so he did!

. . . what is usually thought of as a fiasco, but it *was* a mistake. It should be said, in Blue's defense, if defense he need be said to be need [?], that his "mind" was not on it, his nose filled with the scent of the briny beauty of . . . just beyond the

*********, so it was really a matter of his thinking what some phrase *******, or, as he put it . . . go **** themselves! It was the one jarring note in these otherwise placid, although obsessive last days of the journey, and they ********, too. Helene's ****** and her ***** did not a little to calm him as they rolled by day toward the skyscrapers of Oakland! Oakland and her famed wild petunias! Zimmerman worked like a mule all day and at night was *********** off. Any way he could ******! was his moto [*sic*].

But how, now that they were in Oakville [*sic*] . . . the glittering bridge? Helene remembered *********** by Anton Harley in an anthology that had ******* ******** Rosette, she thought. So, in a way, she was delighted, even though the problem of **********, who was not delighted at all, his eyes on the hills across **************. Rolling *****************[fedora?], ********, and ***, and ***, and ***, and ***, he ***************** damn [Miss Thigh?], ************** swash and swish and heave that Homer ********, one street and up another, until ********** [careening?]***************:

[*Here the Ur-manuscript breaks off. The following fragment, arguably a variant version of an earlier, apocryphal manuscript, is in the Piscardi Library of The University.*]***** but nothing do but Zeem have dolly or he say he eat kitten's head. Blue hit him and say ******* in fucking cave, little bastard! ******** in piano, Helene laugh, and then don't nobody see him or hear him, you think that an good idea? ********* in [goddam?] cave, little son of the bitch! ********** and rolled toward Goldgate Bridge? Is not . . . You don't say? ******** pretty janty [*sic*] up there *********, slouching fedora! Tomorrow we roll right down and right ******** and up the Quoit Hill, highest point ********* majestic Cascades ranges? ********* just like Doc Chick in **********! ********* and them stahz [*sic*] pipped [*sic*] down like in movie you see *************, snore ********** fucking much!

Oakland the. Fair! Was it after all possible, that they? Were finally, here in: This booming! City? Blue got down! On his hands. And knees. And groveled in, the; dust. Not, exactly, dust, but, something like the dark vermilion. Clay! It was not, as. Zimmerman, knew. Dust. Or. Clay? But; it was the how do you? Say, "powder," from, The millions and millions of crimson moronia, that. Are the "Pride." Of, Oakland, along with of, course; gorgeous Lake. Merritt Linda, and Vista Park! But what. Ever it was, Serge, groveled? In thanks, his eyes, his great. *Staring eyes*! Fixed, on, the hazy Contra Costa. Hills! And the Hills! Of Berkeley, flung, far! Far, away across the: famed Skyline. Boulevard!

Say powder, then? Okay? Crimson, moron, millions of skylines and the Lake with, what? Duckies? Certainly, vistas! How to get from? Skyline Vista Boulevard to the Bay Bridge and thence! Ah, thence. Thence, past whatever? To the heart of the "Queen" of the Bay, strange. Bubbly. Gay San Francisco! A place where men are men and earthquakes fall to nothing in the blaze of comet's fire! Just like in the famous pome of Joaquin Miller, or Cincinnati Miller like what his friends? Well, okay, "friends," called him. So did Blue plant his knees thus wise. He got down! (In thus wise—in wise, thus—in such wise, thusly!) They would have to. Pass? Pass! Pass the towering pissweeds of Old Sequoia Park, the one of which whom a poet like Miller wrote his pome about the earthquake that did little or naught to dampen the spirits of them. Them? Well may you ask! Them! Yes, the grizzled parkies of that early and more innocent time, when the immoral zipper fly was but the figment of the depraved imagination. Of many people, yet in the main that of: who else? "Blowjob" Piedmont, a man for whom that hoary motto was sheer Reality! Long did he reign in those here parts.

But enough of gerrymandering and its boon pal, lollygagging! Did ever Piedmont stay his hand? Ha. Ha. It boots not well nor yet behooves to ask! Yet. Ask men must, and will, as long as Jove strides o'er this world with boots so *cracked and grimed that mortals dare not peer* into the welkin lest they see that curious rainbow formed from vapors like the blast of naked Boreas' bright glance, whizzing through the enamor'd firmament like the cruel shaft from mighty bowman's bow in shape unto belike the rainbow formed from vapors that shine and glint all over as do the eyes of that famous pig what once was a pet of Paddy. Or strike the numbèd oith with vile catastrophe!

It was: A problem! Albany, where the Governors served time? Sure! And sure again, and yet, maybe one wast expected to go through the suburbs? Of! Stern San Leandro, where *that fabled monk* once lived who all in solitude: Invented Zinfandel! What a robust sort of thing: yet all in modesty. Or; maybe? Hayward! That seemed to be like: It? Creakèd sure the cart where none had ever trod. Helene. Up? High! Serge and: Zimmerman, heaving toward that glimmer arching cross the Bay like the crooked index finger. Of a god! Or of God! Hart Crane knew this stuff and though Zimmerman, thought, it. All, malarkey? Yet did he bend the back and creak the knee as sure as cart creaked, for he'd as lief bust his father's, heart? His heart! As he would eat the pen that penned *those missives vile* to Catherine! Oft bringing a smile to the toughest heart: which, is. Nice work! If you could get it, like: thus always the tyrant is brung low? Or: Most, often.

What "stuff" they rolled by, Serge, hearing now the singing low of the piles and stanchions with hawsers out there well past the Vista Linda Prison, the Costa del Contra Beach (*what was filled with cuties!*), and the Starfish Motel, surrounded: By God, though the whole earth deny it and book reviewers hunker down amid the Well-Made Plot, surrounded by the softly blowing dill-fish and the starburst yearn-all. So this were which gave its bouquet to a place? Appar-

ently. All the signs were like, right! Whoo! Christ, they: rolled! And rolled! It
might of took the breath away from thems. What? Was REALLY WEIRD was
that they ROLLED as the Seaver fastball oft did in its glory times: Uphill.

Newton could've told them who in his long dark nights and smelling of the
lamp—*whatever that may mean*—baked those cookies which the tribe of man
will always for them him thank, which, when Milton received, than whom,
Cromwell except, none wiser sat, he et them up: out of what come: that opera,
L'Allegro Sforzando. (What Blue could not loin cuz of the "black-key" notes
which he wrote, Milton, that is.) What could he've told those brave folk, the
spawn of concrete, steel, long shadows, and crooked Mayors? Dat wot goze upp
muz cum dauwn? No! And yet, sorta? What comes up must go down! While
chomping: On a Granny Smith out in the Garden, the same which Andy Marvell
was in and up to his old tricks, viz., stumbling over those Melons, digging on li'l
T.C., checking out the Golden Lamps, and trotting after slow-worms, he, Newton, hit on this idear after thinking on the Sunne: He. Say. "This sunne, ofte coming up in robes of glory red, and even more than ofte, but every daye, this sunne,
I say, as oft, or every daye, must needs go down!" And thus: The Lore of Gravity
was bumped into: And ever since, all men who jump up out they chairs must fall
back into them, or maybe: on the floor.

So they rolled also: DOWNHILL! And what a thrill it wert! For they rolled
directly down splendid Chimborazo Boulevard, which, be it known—or ne'er
thought on even oncet!—to reckless men, was yet that highway that . . . Let's say,
ere we be accused by pointing digit of that willful obscurity and lack of duh gift
of turning a nice phrase or of neglecting to write well, for writing well, and
planting periods in trig and serried ranks, as any scribe can tell you thus, and
often will o' nights when the winds howl banshee like beyant the booming shutters and the gibbous moon doth hover o'er the soggy graveyards, yes! That the
world calls cemeteries, dis sorta writing bringeth many jobs and warm and wondrous houses out in vile Connecticut the cute, indeed! Those houses built by
hand-rubbed farmers of the age of Washington, whose sparkling winders look
out upon those graveyards what got them old stones filled up with many a sentimental Protestant cliché: Therefore? Let's say, ere this may hap, that this highway led toward that brightly shining bridge that creeped toward the wild urbs of
the Bay, City of Cupcakes! Thus: toward which they wended way, with woe and
lack of weal and with also wheels whingeing and whining as they wolled westward, wacing now to weach the wovely willage! Though: and here the question
deep will oft forever ring in sempiternal bongs: Was it a willage? Who; Can say?
'Twas enough to brave emote, as men will do when brains do fail their stated
purpose: It was there!

And even fair Helene, who high upon her "gear" (as well as all the other:

311

Gear!) beamed down upon *the caps of cream that flecked* and pittered? On the laughing soiface of the Bay beneath: Thus did she fix her piercing eye!

They'd. Come, far, far: And had they? Come far; enough! The still, small voice did ever whisper. What? Not yet, not yet, the pattern clear, 'bout which thou may ask Jesus Christ: Whut, jes whut is these patterns for? I say:—or wast it Blue who said?—No Matter! Some unheard voice, like melodies the same, sweeter than that one who is listened to, had asked the "Pattern Question," what a wag has dubbed: A quiz! (But a turd in that fuck's teeth!) And still, despite this odd shenanigan, I fear, like Blue, my comely hero, plus his wife, and plus his bursting son, the somewhat perverse Zim, that I may have lost my way, and cannot find nor thread nor rhyme nor reason in this subtly lavender display of schlock! So? I got Blue on the manly span and cannot get him o'er? Shall I write, thus: Beginning once agin and still anew? Like thus:

Oakland the fair! Was it, after all, possible that they were finally here, in this booming city? Blue got down on his hands and knees and groveled in the dust. Not exactly . . . dust, but something like the dark vermilion clay. Huh? Would Rabelais be content to read such stuff?

RABELAIS: Foutez-moi la paix!

Or so and thus I thought. So, what e'er the cost in human sweat and lack of interested readership, intelligent, knowledgeable, prone to rattling yarns and stately graces in a limpid prose, and snide remarks anent the Vast Body of a Lit'-rachoor Devoid of Self-Indulgence, I'll get: him: off: the: fucking: Bridge! (In my own sweet way and in my own sweet time—or Theseus ne'er did sail on leaky rubber raft from windy Troy to found Salerno!)

But these, jou say, ees hombres made of straw? These, jou say, is gouty blasts of sheerest kidding an tomfoolery? You don't shut uppa you mout I make a fuckin list go on three hundred pages! Ess mah breedge! I get heem offen her! Hokay!

And suddenly they rolled off the other end and found themselves, the cart's wheels humming gorgeously, in the streets (or one of them, at least) of twinkling San Francisco! Up they went. To a hill. To the top. And there beneath, the Bay. And Blue, slick with sweat, felt, thrumming in the very marrow of his bones, the almost tangible, and yet not quite, plangent plunking of the Phrase. Next him stood his family true. They leaned then all the cart against. It the hill rolled down in mighty speed. With in the lead brave Blue, chased they it down. Blue's face was smiling all for thought he deep that even this the cart toward the Bay headed was as if it knowed too that it there would find its Destiny. And lest it be forgot! Behind, on hawser taut and singing the piano bumped and rolled as well! And in the lead, Blue of the trip within his brains had Meaningful Mem'ries in bright

flashes called clear up to him. So as ran he thought he these things all wondrous
of the lonely road that hath wended they for such a space of time:

This madhouse with lace and satin and naughty novels filled . . . Profundity! . . .
Let us aimless plunge . . . Sophie Jupon? Is that her whorish handle? . . . Clouds
of aromatic dust surrounded by enchanted Negroes in the film of the same name
. . . Dutch Mulligan! A monicker all oozing forth with Celtic echoes . . . Sweeter
than cakes and custard sharper than crying mustard . . . Not to forget the loathsome ginkgo or tiny stinking monkeys! . . . I am the doughty vehicle 'twert
meant for you, the engine of your fate and Karmic destiny, also very big in terms
vitamins and enzyme juice . . . Nobility! . . . A quick nosh of jambalaya à la king
at SAL'S BILLIARD ACADEMY . . . Marie Mamelle? Is that her whorish handle? . . . La Musique et les mauvaises herbes, it is like a kind of a joke . . . We'll
strain our best, an' we gawp at last, firk as sunspot-blue clostridium . . . I may
lighten up the fardels and valises of regret on the smelted plains of legendary
Boise! . . . Dutch Mulligan? Is that her whorish handle? . . . Surrounded by enchanted films with Negroes of the same name . . . Tiny monkeys stinking in the
mauvaises herbes . . . The stewed Comanche gazes on a ginger ale, or the husky
terrene dregs of same . . . Silk-buttocked garter-strapped Suzanne Jarretière,
thou art a babe as simple as a cackarooch . . . Gawp at last, firk! . . . Aimless let us
plunge, else I'll set loose the starving Dobermans! . . . It was something that
made me very very noivous . . . What a cute little word that is, eh, Sophie? . . .
Harr, harr, harrñh! . . . André Lubrique! That violent wop men call Hieronimo! . . . Deadbeats like Hitler and Stalin caused by a hump tossed off in wild
abandon . . . Mr. Coillon, my good friend over there with the denim pipe . . .
Gravity! . . . Like coney shy you bump through lettuce groves: thus Dubuque
spake and turned his socks upon the glowing spit . . . They eat, ringed by adoring
ducks . . . Monique Gaine, is that her whorish handle? sitting in a chair in an
exciting way . . . A white-robed Negro sported with the dust, not to forget the
loathsome ginkgo . . . Marimbas Verdes con Gusanos, a wonderful woman! . . .
Took to fellin' trees and tearin' stone fences up by the roots, finger-painting
coasters for the USO . . . Thine eyes flash blacker than my dirtie nails, like a kind
of a joke . . . Sparkling and curvaceous thunder! Love! With a peppery pinch of
lust! . . . Girdled yet gorgeous hips thighs and bottom, sweeter than cakes and
custard . . . Silk-buttocked and all oozing forth with Celtic echoes, Mrs. Chaud,
let us aimless plunge: maybe a little shtup without you humming "The Trolley
Song," or "A Weedy Music" . . . Surrounded by enchanted Negroes, my great
gnarled hands lie lifeless on the piano keys . . . Claude Cul? A double pink starlike fairy . . . The gimlet-brained Dr. Dubuque will knock you off your lilting

little cadenza, chief! He twists the bangling changs! . . . Or so to speke . . . Sans
crotch, I base, and cronk the knee in volitude to Alice Cruisse, as in a dream, like
Chaucer knowed . . . At which the hefty broad did blush as in a naughty novel
. . . Hamstrung visions of the crass unspeakable? In the fucker goes! . . . Art thou
a sprite or satyr of the elfin boles and sappy limbs, or General Westinghouse,
known as the mutter of invention? . . . Monique Gaine? But who the hell are you
to come in here, all akimbo? . . . Your sweetie's hairs would sprout like crabgrass
vile as long as this golden ring on my finger stains it a fetching emerald . . . Cortez
silent in his pique in old Connecticut, yet I also serve who only blandly prate . . .
This madhouse filled with naughty novels has a wooden porch of agonized
memory . . . Gaston Gaine, Robert Caleçons, Émile Fesses, and Jacques Derrière: the courageous lowbrows of the muddy peaks and swampy valleys . . . The
entire ballyard that nestles just above my forehead, my blazing maple leaf, it is
like a kind of a joke . . . Aimless! Plunge! . . . The road has reft me of my merriment! *That's* why the crocodiles spoke Spanish . . . Again, you've whomped the
brassy tacks, my chef . . . Sparkling thunder? I speak still of the old and crippled
hen . . . Your soft sobbing as we watch the snap beans and the impeccable white
of the knee hose, hips thighs and bottom of Suzanne Jarretière, and then sort of
start another artistic career based on songs of the black keys . . . A sporty Negro
in the whitish dust said: "Now the jive turkey blanks bees stealin our flowers!"
. . . The teeth of a fascist movie star whose mouth's a splash of dead rugosa rose . . .
Let us aimless plunge from out this lace and satin madhouse . . . Current black
digs white ash, the former in his toga, the latter in his culottes . . . Concerning M.
Charles Ordurier and Mlle Mamelle one might say that travel looms and romance may blossom . . . Of my merriment the road has reft me . . . I'll hear the
Secret Phrase—or puke! . . . A red deuce! And so I *do* see as I ope my blinks . . .
At SAL'S BILLIARD ACADEMY the herb tea industry grows apace: that's why
the crocodiles spoke Spanish! . . . Save It Pretty Mama by Cheech Mauriac and
the Femmes Fatales, the former in culottes, the latter in silk-buttocked marimbas verdes . . . Forgive me, my darling snap bean, forgive me! though I'm very
big in terms enzyme juice . . . Femmes fatales of the black keys and red deuce . . .
Tiny monkeys double pink stinking . . . Marie oozing forth hips and thighs . . .
Aimless plunge us, let us . . . Marie Jarretière avec red deuce, *that's* her whorish
film . . . A robed white Negro bees stealin la musique . . . Porch of wooden memory, let us aimless agonize . . . Thine eyes flash blacker than curvaceous thighs . . .
Greta Girdle and her sister, Gertie, stars of the crass unspeakable . . . Or so to
speke . . . Speke or prate all blandly in the crabgrass vile . . . The bangling
changs! The changling bangs! Monique Gaine's her whorish handle? . . . Jambalaya nosh à quick . . . Toga, former Mustard, seeks Blazing Leaf of doughty
vehicle . . . Plunge aimless let us . . . A joke kind of, like a little shtup . . .

Harrñh! . . . Spotted in the dust: One white-robed Negro all enchanted . . . Bees gimlet-brained, chef! . . . Garter-strapped snap beans . . . Plunge! . . . Reft the black keys from jive turkeys . . . Suzanne, Marie, and M. Fixe-Chaussettes: little cute words are they . . . Con gusanos in the satin madhouse . . . Impeccable knee hose white as deuce is red . . . Muddy peaks! Aimless plunge! . . . The road . . . Piques . . . Valleys with bottoms gorgeous . . . Con profundity let's plunge! . . . Travel blossoms plungingly while femmes made me very very noivous . . . And the piano . . . The piano . . . Black keys . . . White keys . . . Aimless plunging, plunging aimless . . . The piano . . . Fate and Karmic destiny . . . Plunge . . . Plunges . . . Doughty vehicle con keys of black and . . .

Into the bay. The cart. The rope. The piano.

Thus: Cart---------------Rope---------------Piano.

Then the Phrase climbed to Blue Serge's trembling ears:

S   p   l   a   s   h

9 March 1978–22 December 1981

315

DALKEY ARCHIVE PAPERBACKS

CAROLE MASO, *AVA.*

HARRY MATHEWS, *Cigarettes.*

   The Conversions.

   The Journalist.

   Singular Pleasures.

   The Sinking of the Odradek

     Stadium.

   Tlooth.

   20 Lines a Day.

JOSEPH MCELROY, *Women and Men.*

ROBERT L. MCLAUGHLIN, ED.,

   Innovations: An Anthology of

     Modern & Contemporary Fiction.

JAMES MERRILL,

   The (Diblos) Notebook.

STEVEN MILLHAUSER,

   The Barnum Museum.

   In the Penny Arcade.

OLIVE MOORE, *Spleen.*

STEVEN MOORE, *Ronald Firbank: An*

   Annotated Bibliography of

   Secondary Materials.

NICHOLAS MOSLEY, *Accident.*

   Assassins.

   Children of Darkness and Light.

   Hopeful Monsters.

   Imago Bird.

   Impossible Object.

   Judith.

   Natalie Natalia.

   Serpent.

WARREN F. MOTTE, JR., *Oulipo: A*

   Primer of Potential Literature

YVES NAVARRE, *Our Share of Time.*

WILFRIDO D. NOLLEDO,

   But for the Lovers.

FLANN O'BRIEN, *At Swim-Two-Birds.*

   The Best of Myles.

   The Dalkey Archive.

   Further Cuttings.

   The Hard Life.

   The Poor Mouth.

   The Third Policeman.

CLAUDE OLLIER, *The Mise-en-Scène.*

FERNANDO DEL PASO,

   Palinuro of Mexico.

RAYMOND QUENEAU, *The Last Days.*

   Odile.

   Pierrot Mon Ami.

   Saint Glinglin.

ISHMAEL REED,

   The Free-Lance Pallbearers.

   The Last Days of Louisiana Red.

   Reckless Eyeballing.

   The Terrible Threes.

   The Terrible Twos.

   Yellow Back Radio Broke-Down.

JULIÁN RÍOS, *Poundemonium.*

JACQUES ROUBAUD,

   The Great Fire of London.

Visit our website: www.dalkeyarchive.com

DALKEY ARCHIVE PAPERBACKS

Hortense in Exile.

Hortense Is Abducted.

The Plurality of Worlds of Lewis.

The Princess Hoppy.

Some Thing Black.

LEON S. ROUDIEZ,

French Fiction Revisited.

LUIS RAFAEL SÁNCHEZ,

Macho Camacho's Beat.

SEVERO SARDUY, Cobra & Maitreya.

ARNO SCHMIDT, Collected Stories.

Nobodaddy's Children.

CHRISTINE SCHUTT, Nightwork.

JUNE AKERS SEESE, Is This What
Other Women Feel, Too?

What Waiting Really Means.

VIKTOR SHKLOVSKY, Theory of Prose.

JOSEF SKVORECKY,

The Engineer of Human Souls.

CLAUDE SIMON, The Invitation.

GILBERT SORRENTINO,

Aberration of Starlight.

Blue Pastoral.

Crystal Vision.

Imaginative Qualities of Actual
Things.

Mulligan Stew.

Pack of Lies.

The Sky Changes.

Splendide-Hôtel.

Steelwork.

Under the Shadow.

W. M. SPACKMAN,

The Complete Fiction.

GERTRUDE STEIN, Lucy Church
Amiably.

The Making of Americans.

A Novel of Thank You.

PIOTR SZEWC, Annihilation.

ALEXANDER THEROUX,

The Lollipop Trollops.

ESTHER TUSQUETS, Stranded.

LUISA VALENZUELA, He Who Searches.

PAUL WEST, Words for a Deaf
Daughter and Gala.

CURTIS WHITE, Memories of My
Father
Watching TV.

Monstrous Possibility.

DIANE WILLIAMS,

Excitability: Selected Stories.

DOUGLAS WOOLF, Wall to Wall.

PHILIP WYLIE, Generation of Vipers.

MARGUERITE YOUNG,

Angel in the Forest.

Miss MacIntosh, My Darling.

REYOUNG, Unbabbling.

LOUIS ZUKOFSKY, Collected Fiction.

SCOTT ZWIREN, God Head.

Visit our website: www.dalkeyarchive.com

DALKEY ARCHIVE PAPERBACKS

The Dick Gibson Show.

The MacGuffin.

The Magic Kingdom.

ANNIE ERNAUX, Cleaned Out.

LAUREN FAIRBANKS, Muzzle Thyself.

Sister Carrie.

LESLIE A. FIEDLER, Love and Death in
the American Novel.

RONALD FIRBANK,

Complete Short Stories.

FORD MADOX FORD,

The March of Literature.

JANICE GALLOWAY, Foreign Parts.

The Trick Is to Keep Breathing.

WILLIAM H. GASS, The Tunnel.

Willie Masters' Lonesome Wife.

ETIENNE GILSON,

The Arts of the Beautiful.

C. S. GISCOMBE, Giscome Road.

Here.

KAREN ELIZABETH GORDON,

The Red Shoes.

PATRICK GRAINVILLE,

The Cave of Heaven.

GEOFFREY GREEN, ET AL.,

The Vineland Papers.

HENRY GREEN, Concluding.

Nothing.

JIŘÍ GRUŠA, The Questionnaire.

JOHN HAWKES, Whistlejacket.

ALDOUS HUXLEY, Antic Hay.

Point Counter Point.

Those Barren Leaves.

Time Must Have a Stop.

GERT JONKE,

Geometric Regional Novel.

TADEUSZ KONWICKI,

A Minor Apocalypse.

The Polish Complex.

ELAINE KRAF,

The Princess of 72nd Street.

EWA KURYLUK, Century 21.

DEBORAH LEVY, Billy and Girl.

JOSÉ LEZAMA LIMA, Paradiso.

OSMAN LINS,

The Queen of the Prisons of Greece.

ALF MAC LOCHLAINN,

The Corpus in the Library.

Out of Focus.

D. KEITH MANO, Take Five.

BEN MARCUS,

The Age of Wire and String.

WALLACE MARKFIELD,

Teitlebaum's Window.

To an Early Grave.

DAVID MARKSON, Collected Poems.

Reader's Block.

Springer's Progress.

Wittgenstein's Mistress.

CARL R. MARTIN, Genii Over Salzburg.

Visit our website: www.dalkeyarchive.com

DALKEY ARCHIVE PAPERBACKS

PIERRE ALBERT-BIROT, *Grabinoulor.*

YUZ ALESHKOVSKY, *Kangaroo.*

FELIPE ALFAU, *Chromos.*

 Locos.

 Sentimental Songs.

ALAN ANSEN,

 Contact Highs: Selected Poems
 1957-1987.

DJUNA BARNES, *Ladies Almanack.*

 Ryder.

JOHN BARTH, *LETTERS.*

 Sabbatical.

AUGUSTO ROA BASTOS, *I the Supreme.*

ANDREI BITOV, *Pushkin House.*

ROGER BOYLAN, *Killoyle.*

CHRISTINE BROOKE-ROSE,

 Amalgamemnon.

GERALD BURNS, *Shorter Poems.*

GABRIELLE BURTON, *Heartbreak Hotel.*

MICHEL BUTOR, *Portrait of the Artist*
 as a Young Ape.

JULIETA CAMPOS,

 The Fear of Losing Eurydice.

ANNE CARSON, *Eros the Bittersweet.*

LOUIS-FERDINAND CÉLINE,

 Castle to Castle.

 London Bridge.

 North.

 Rigadoon.

HUGO CHARTERIS, *The Tide Is Right.*

JEROME CHARYN, *The Tar Baby.*

MARC CHOLODENKO,

 Mordechai Schamz.

EMILY HOLMES COLEMAN,

 The Shutter of Snow.

ROBERT COOVER,

 A Night at the Movies.

STANLEY CRAWFORD,

 Some Instructions to My Wife.

RENÉ CREVEL, *Putting My Foot in It.*

RALPH CUSACK, *Cadenza.*

SUSAN DAITCH, *Storytown.*

PETER DIMOCK, *A Short Rhetoric for*
 Leaving the Family.

COLEMAN DOWELL,

 The Houses of Children.

 Island People.

 Too Much Flesh and Jabez.

RIKKI DUCORNET,

 The Complete Butcher's Tales.

 The Fountains of Neptune.

 The Jade Cabinet.

 Phosphor in Dreamland.

 The Stain.

WILLIAM EASTLAKE, *Castle Keep.*

 Lyric of the Circle Heart.

STANLEY ELKIN,

 Boswell: A Modern Comedy.

 Criers and Kibitzers, Kibitzers
 and Criers.

Visit our website: www.dalkeyarchive.com

LANNAN SELECTIONS

The Lannan Foundation, located in Santa Fe, New Mexico, is a family foundation whose funding is focused on special cultural projects and ideas which promote and protect cultural freedom, diversity, and creativity.

The literary aspect of Lannan's cultural program supports the creation and presentation of exceptional English language literature and develops a wider audience for poetry, fiction, and nonfiction.

Since 1990, the Lannan Foundation has supported Dalkey Archive Press projects in a variety of ways, including monetary support for authors, audience development programs, and direct funding for the publication of the Press's books.

In 2000, Lannan Selections was established to promote both organizations' commitment to the highest expressions of literary creativity. The foundation supports the publication of this series of books each year, and works closely with the Press to ensure that these books will reach as many readers as possible and achieve a permanent place in literature.